THE LONG CON™

ONI PRESS

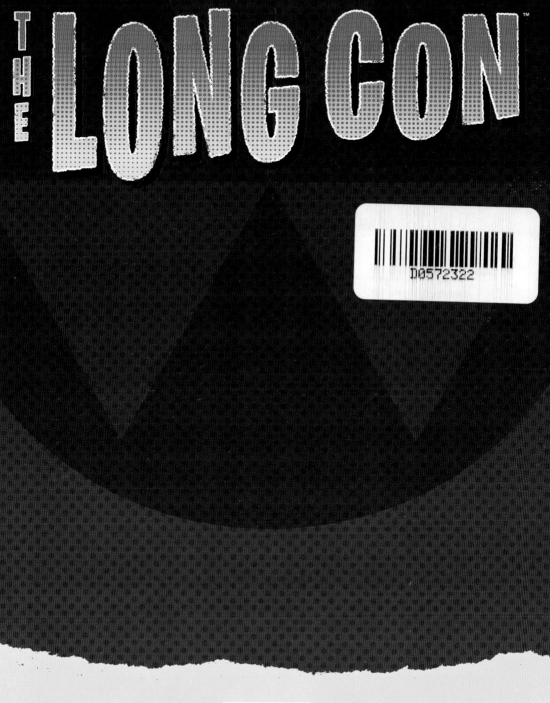

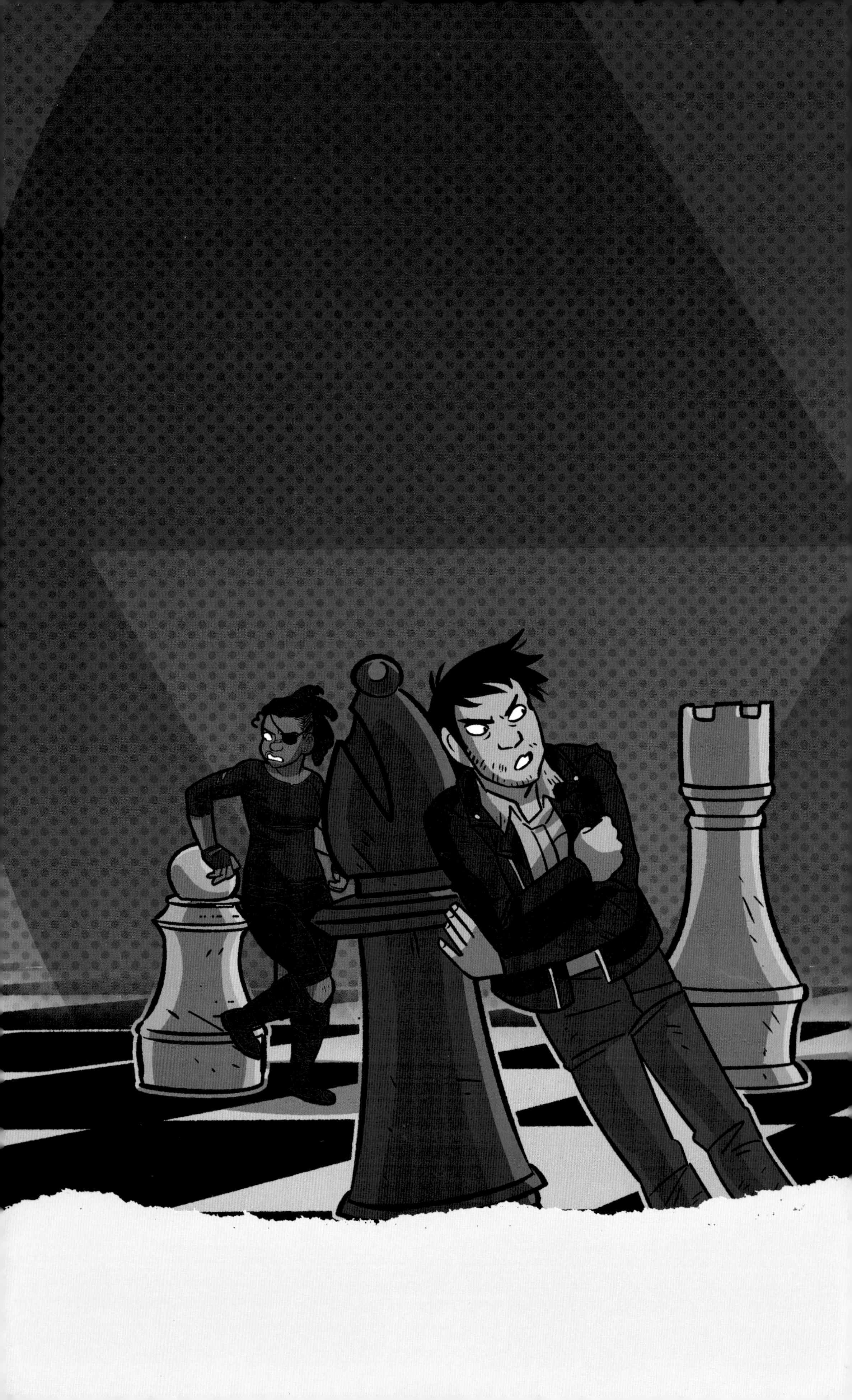

THE LONG CON

WRITTEN BY

DYLAN MECONIS & BEN COLEMAN

ILLUSTRATED BY

EA DENICH

COLORED BY

FRED C. STRESING

LETTERED BY

ADITYA BIDIKAR

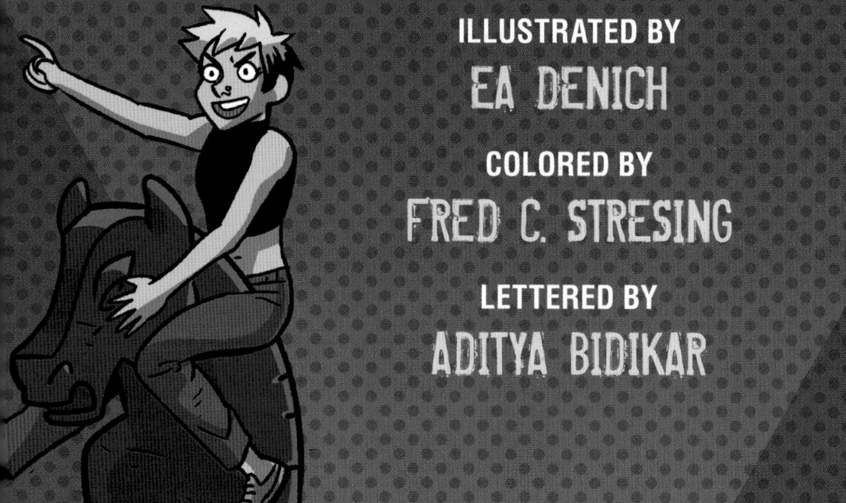

ONI PRESS

DESIGNED BY

KEITH WOOD & ANGIE KNOWLES

EDITED BY

ROBIN HERRERA & ARI YARWOOD

Published by Oni Press, Inc.

Joe Nozemack, founder & chief financial officer

James Lucas Jones, publisher

Sarah Gaydos, editor in chief

Charlie Chu, v.p. of creative & business development

Brad Rooks, director of operations

Margot Wood, director of sales

Amber O'Neill, special projects manager

Troy Look, director of design & production

Kate Z. Stone, senior graphic designer

Sonja Synak, graphic designer

Angie Knowles, digital prepress lead

Ari Yarwood, senior editor

Robin Herrera, senior editor

Michelle Nguyen, executive assistant

Jung Lee, logistics coordinator

1319 SE Martin Luther King, Jr. Blvd.
Suite 240
Portland, OR 97214

onipress.com
facebook.com/onipress
twitter.com/onipress
onipress.tumblr.com
instagram.com/onipress

@dmeconis · dylanmeconis.com
@OhColeman · about.me/OhColeman
@ghostgreeen · ghostgreen.tumblr.com
@FredCStresing / artofstresing.com
@adityab · adityab.net/lettering

First Edition: October 2019
ISBN: 978-1-62010-671-6
eISBN: 978-1-62010-672-3

1 2 3 4 5 6 7 8 9 10

Library of Congress Control Number: 2019934121

Printed in China.

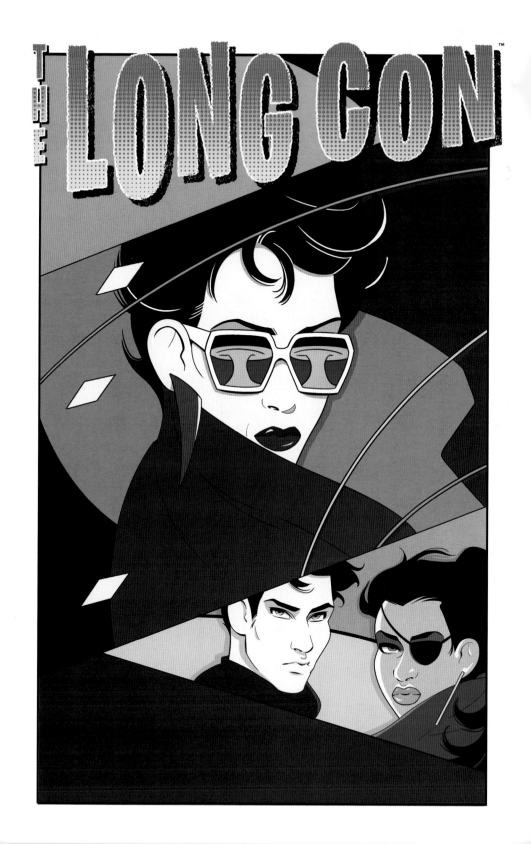

CHAPTER 6: FIVE YEARS AND ONE APOCALYPSE AGO (AGAIN)

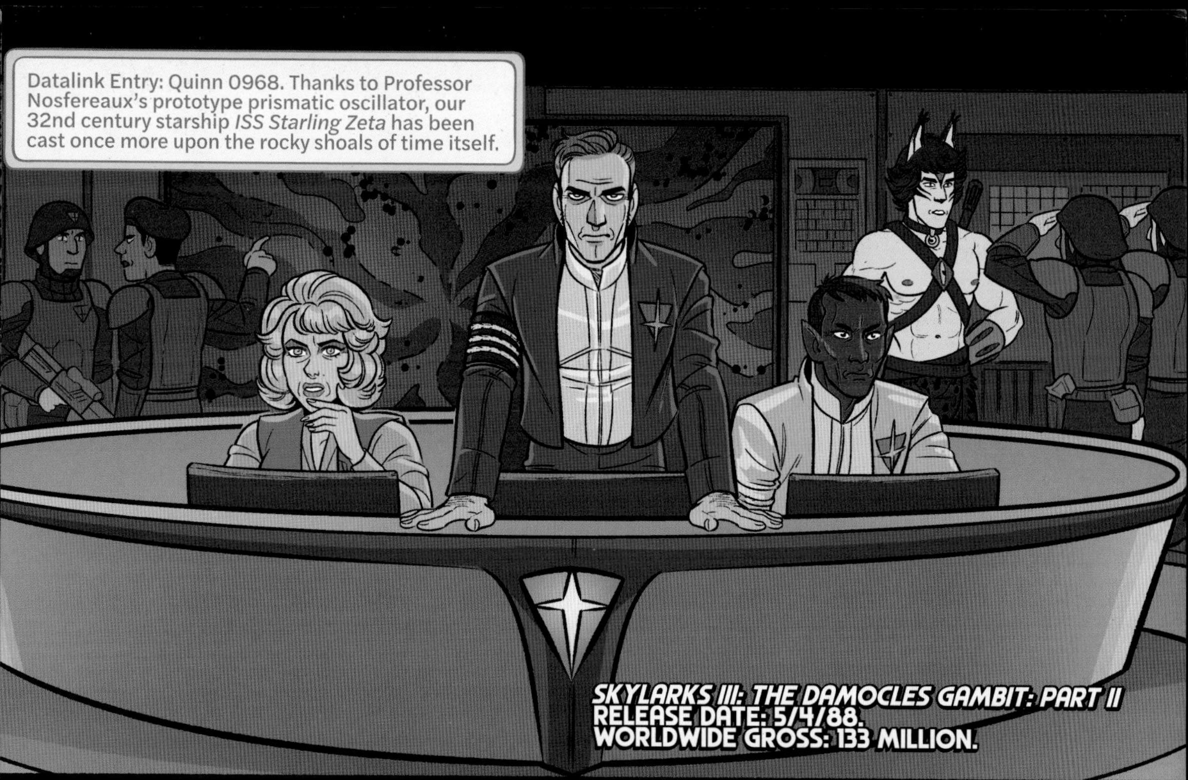
Datalink Entry: Quinn 0968. Thanks to Professor Nosfereaux's prototype prismatic oscillator, our 32nd century starship *ISS Starling Zeta* has been cast once more upon the rocky shoals of time itself.
SKYLARKS III: THE DAMOCLES GAMBIT: PART II
RELEASE DATE: 5/4/88.
WORLDWIDE GROSS: 133 MILLION.

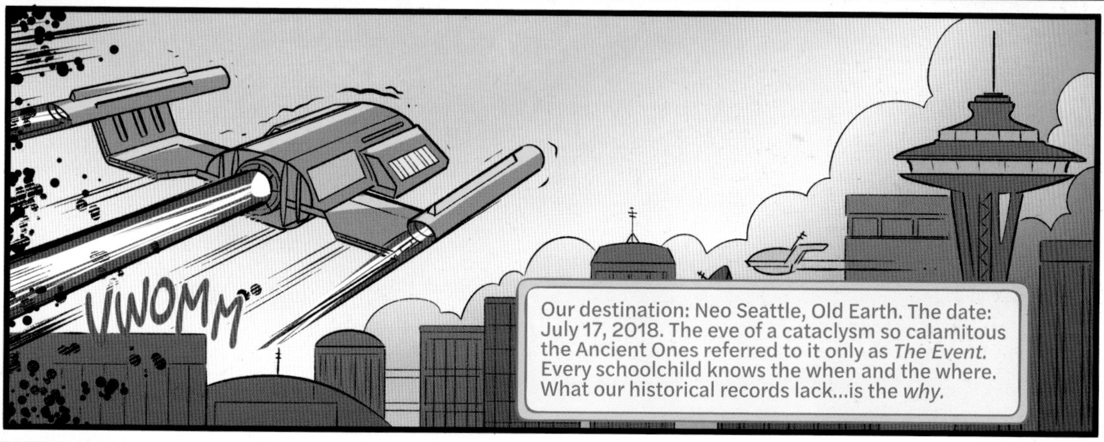
VINOMM
Our destination: Neo Seattle, Old Earth. The date: July 17, 2018. The eve of a cataclysm so calamitous the Ancient Ones referred to it only as *The Event.* Every schoolchild knows the when and the where. What our historical records lack...is the *why.*

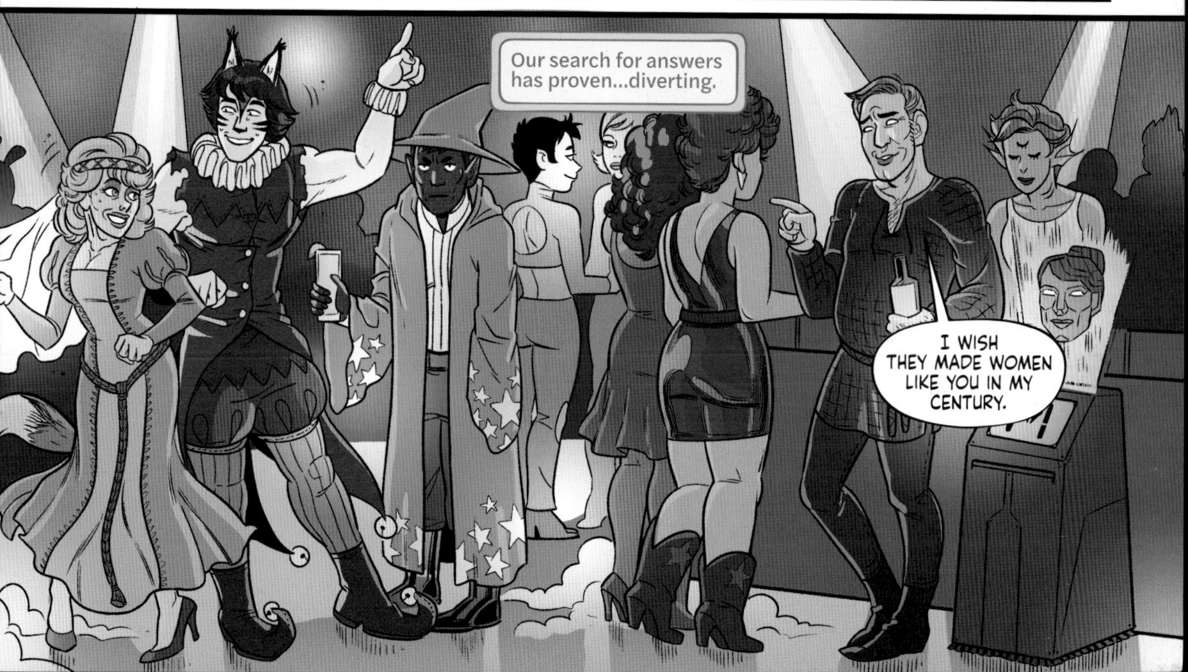
Our search for answers has proven...diverting.
I WISH THEY MADE WOMEN LIKE YOU IN MY CENTURY.

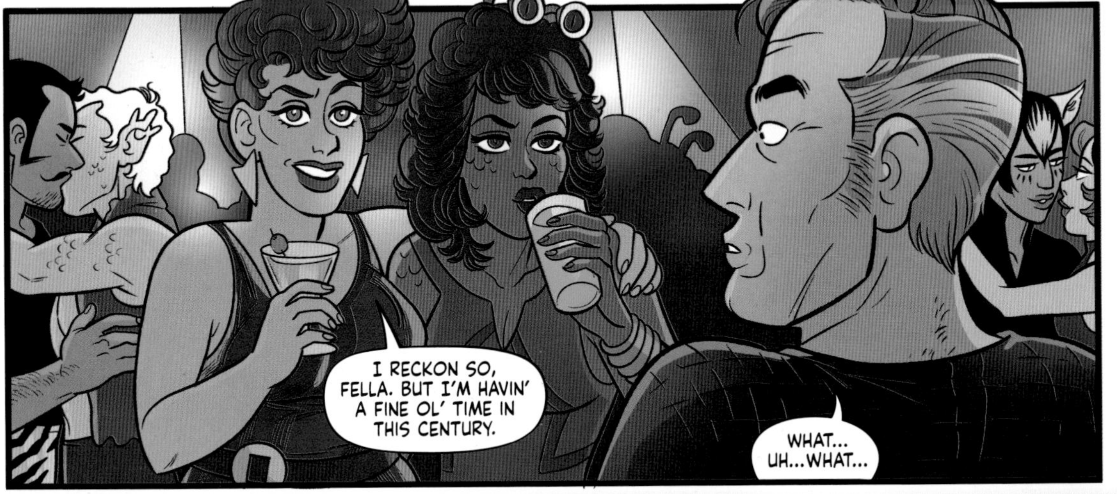
I RECKON SO, FELLA. BUT I'M HAVIN' A FINE OL' TIME IN THIS CENTURY.
WHAT... UH...WHAT...

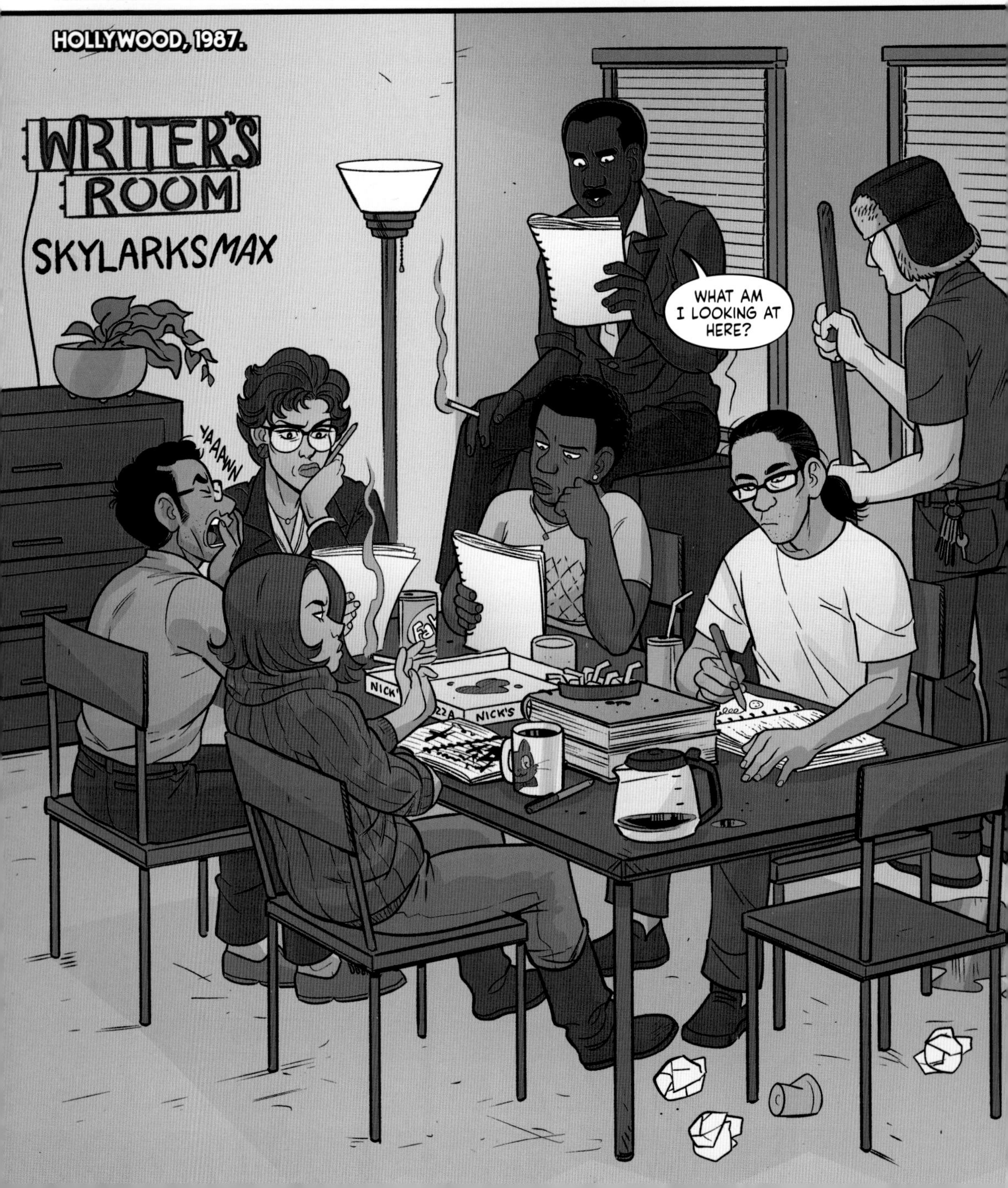
HOLLYWOOD, 1987.
WRITER'S ROOM
SKYLARKSMAX
WHAT AM I LOOKING AT HERE?
YAAAWN
NICK'S

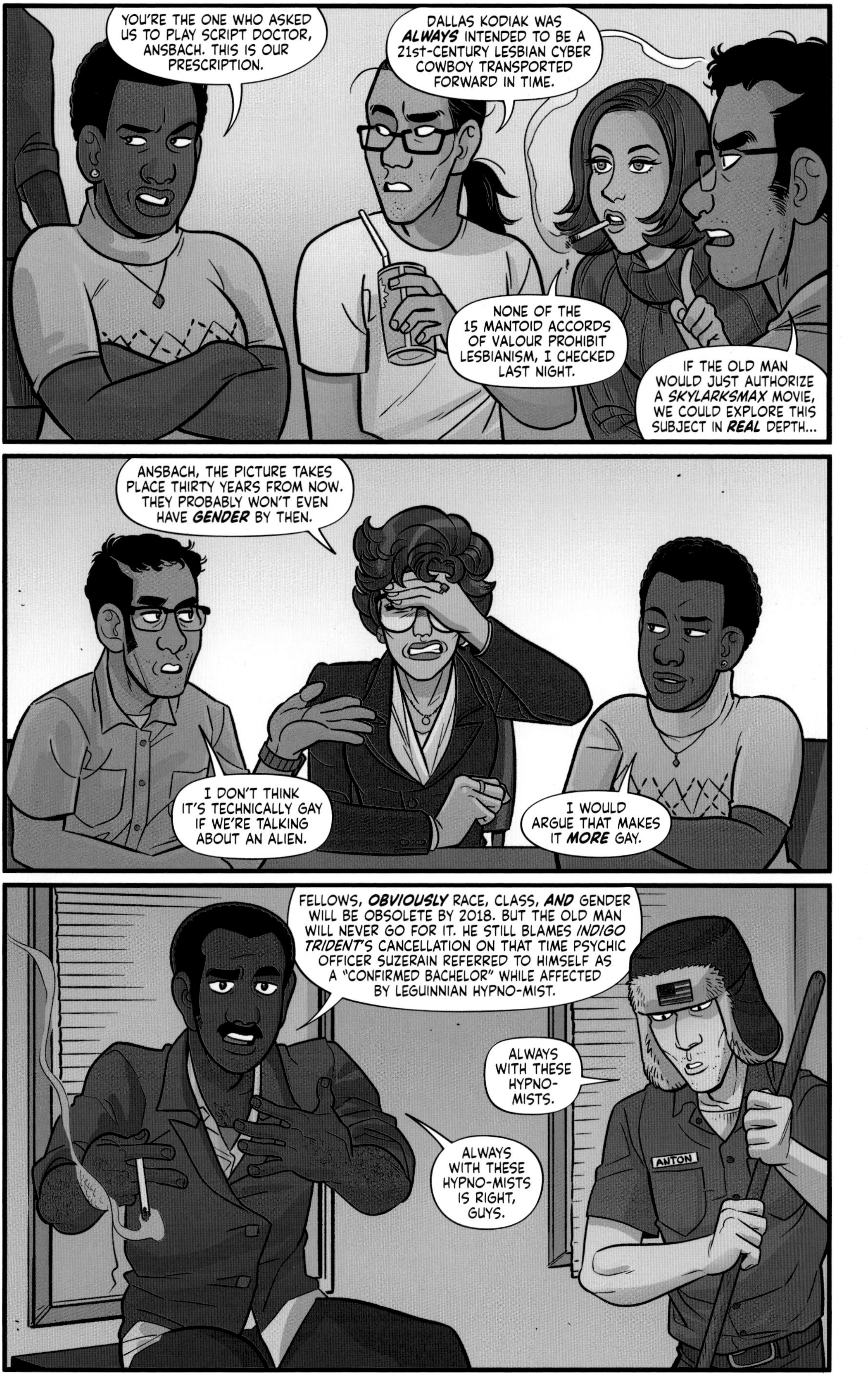
YOU'RE THE ONE WHO ASKED US TO PLAY SCRIPT DOCTOR, ANSBACH. THIS IS OUR PRESCRIPTION.
DALLAS KODIAK WAS ALWAYS INTENDED TO BE A 21st-CENTURY LESBIAN CYBER COWBOY TRANSPORTED FORWARD IN TIME.
NONE OF THE 15 MANTOID ACCORDS OF VALOUR PROHIBIT LESBIANISM, I CHECKED LAST NIGHT.
IF THE OLD MAN WOULD JUST AUTHORIZE A SKYLARKSMAX MOVIE, WE COULD EXPLORE THIS SUBJECT IN REAL DEPTH...
ANSBACH, THE PICTURE TAKES PLACE THIRTY YEARS FROM NOW. THEY PROBABLY WON'T EVEN HAVE GENDER BY THEN.
I DON'T THINK IT'S TECHNICALLY GAY IF WE'RE TALKING ABOUT AN ALIEN.
I WOULD ARGUE THAT MAKES IT MORE GAY.
FELLOWS, OBVIOUSLY RACE, CLASS, AND GENDER WILL BE OBSOLETE BY 2018. BUT THE OLD MAN WILL NEVER GO FOR IT. HE STILL BLAMES INDIGO TRIDENT'S CANCELLATION ON THAT TIME PSYCHIC OFFICER SUZERAIN REFERRED TO HIMSELF AS A "CONFIRMED BACHELOR" WHILE AFFECTED BY LEGUINNIAN HYPNO-MIST.
ALWAYS WITH THESE HYPNO-MISTS.
ALWAYS WITH THESE HYPNO-MISTS IS RIGHT, GUYS.
ANTON

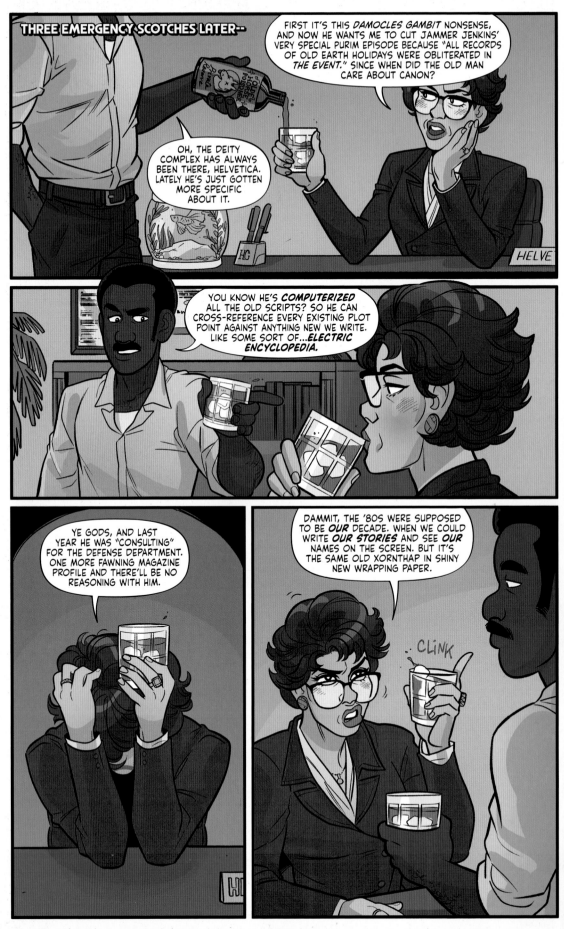

THREE EMERGENCY SCOTCHES LATER--

FIRST IT'S THIS *DAMOCLES GAMBIT* NONSENSE, AND NOW HE WANTS ME TO CUT JAMMER JENKINS' VERY SPECIAL PURIM EPISODE BECAUSE "ALL RECORDS OF OLD EARTH HOLIDAYS WERE OBLITERATED IN *THE EVENT.*" SINCE WHEN DID THE OLD MAN CARE ABOUT CANON?

OH, THE DEITY COMPLEX HAS ALWAYS BEEN THERE, HELVETICA. LATELY HE'S JUST GOTTEN MORE SPECIFIC ABOUT IT.

HELVE

YOU KNOW HE'S *COMPUTERIZED* ALL THE OLD SCRIPTS? SO HE CAN CROSS-REFERENCE EVERY EXISTING PLOT POINT AGAINST ANYTHING NEW WE WRITE. LIKE SOME SORT OF...*ELECTRIC ENCYCLOPEDIA.*

YE GODS, AND LAST YEAR HE WAS "CONSULTING" FOR THE DEFENSE DEPARTMENT. ONE MORE FAWNING MAGAZINE PROFILE AND THERE'LL BE NO REASONING WITH HIM.

DAMMIT, THE '80S WERE SUPPOSED TO BE *OUR* DECADE. WHEN WE COULD WRITE *OUR STORIES* AND SEE *OUR* NAMES ON THE SCREEN. BUT IT'S THE SAME OLD XORNTHAP IN SHINY NEW WRAPPING PAPER.

CLINK

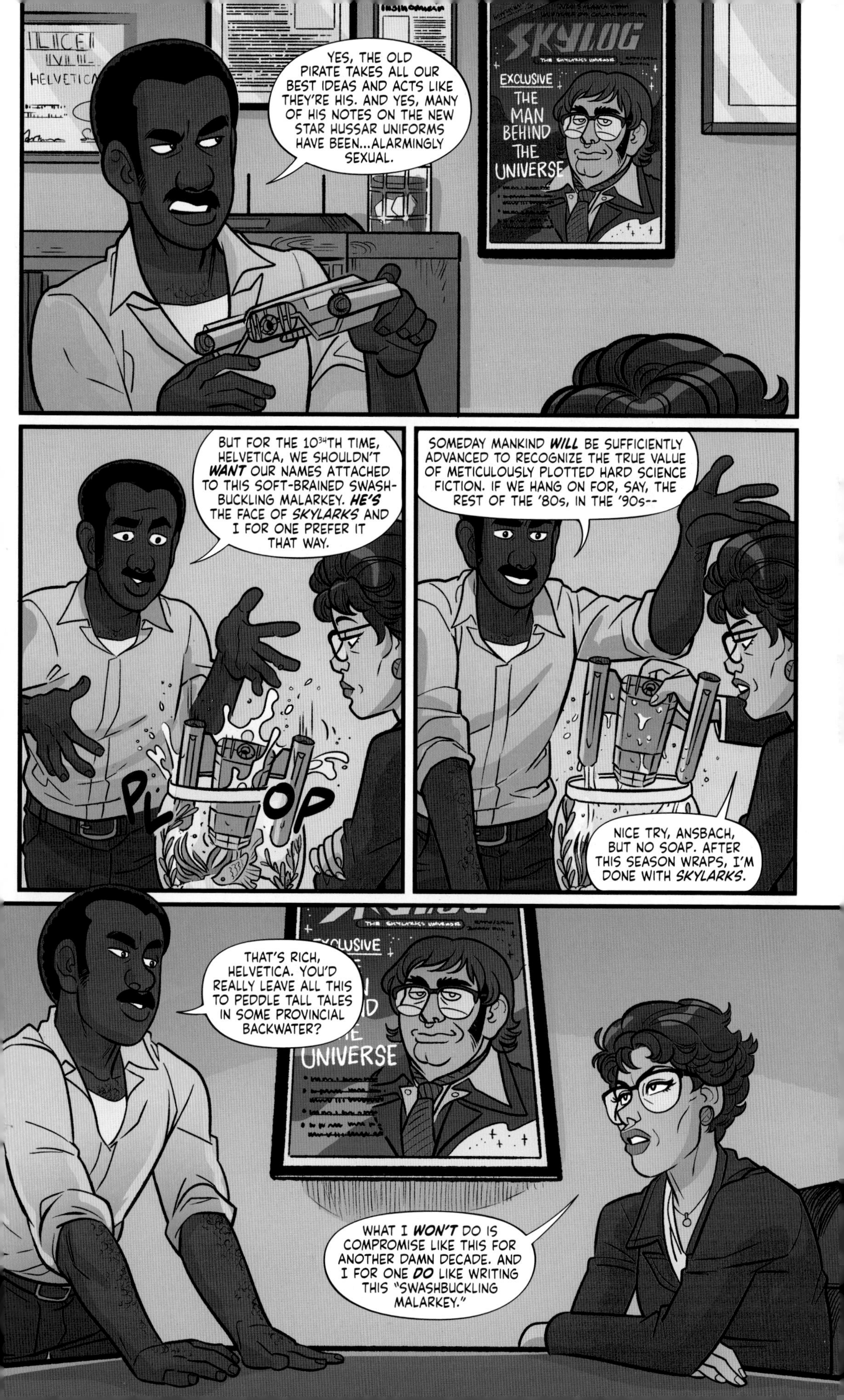

HELVETICA
SKYLOG
THE SKYLARKS UNIVERSE
EXCLUSIVE THE MAN BEHIND THE UNIVERSE
YES, THE OLD PIRATE TAKES ALL OUR BEST IDEAS AND ACTS LIKE THEY'RE HIS. AND YES, MANY OF HIS NOTES ON THE NEW STAR HUSSAR UNIFORMS HAVE BEEN...ALARMINGLY SEXUAL.
BUT FOR THE 10^{34}TH TIME, HELVETICA, WE SHOULDN'T ***WANT*** OUR NAMES ATTACHED TO THIS SOFT-BRAINED SWASH-BUCKLING MALARKEY. ***HE'S*** THE FACE OF *SKYLARKS* AND I FOR ONE PREFER IT THAT WAY.
PLOP
SOMEDAY MANKIND ***WILL*** BE SUFFICIENTLY ADVANCED TO RECOGNIZE THE TRUE VALUE OF METICULOUSLY PLOTTED HARD SCIENCE FICTION. IF WE HANG ON FOR, SAY, THE REST OF THE '80s, IN THE '90s--
NICE TRY, ANSBACH, BUT NO SOAP. AFTER THIS SEASON WRAPS, I'M DONE WITH *SKYLARKS*.
THE SKYLARKS UNIVERSE
EXCLUSIVE
UNIVERSE
THAT'S RICH, HELVETICA. YOU'D REALLY LEAVE ALL THIS TO PEDDLE TALL TALES IN SOME PROVINCIAL BACKWATER?
WHAT I ***WON'T*** DO IS COMPROMISE LIKE THIS FOR ANOTHER DAMN DECADE. AND I FOR ONE ***DO*** LIKE WRITING THIS "SWASHBUCKLING MALARKEY."

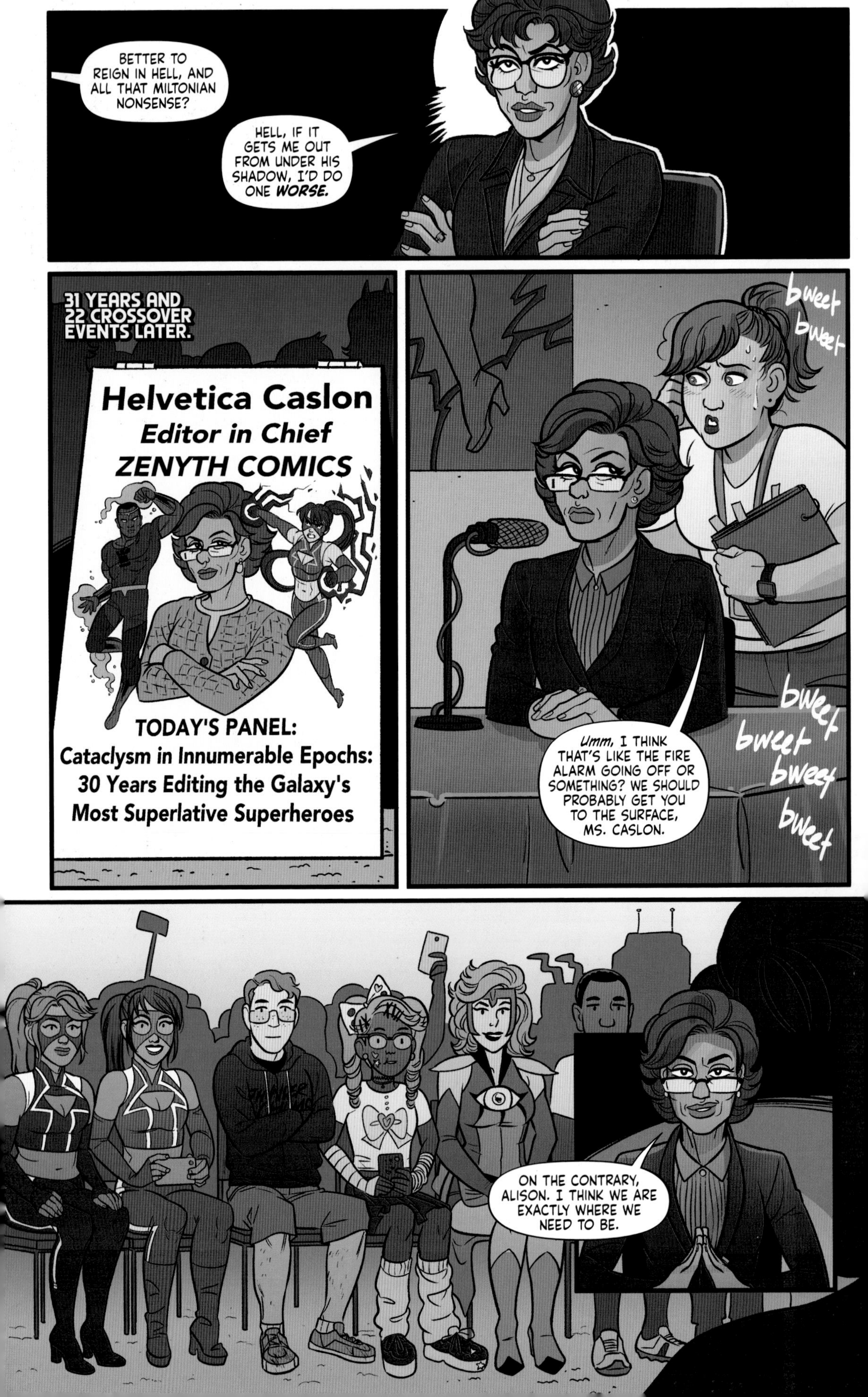
BETTER TO REIGN IN HELL, AND ALL THAT MILTONIAN NONSENSE?
HELL, IF IT GETS ME OUT FROM UNDER HIS SHADOW, I'D DO ONE *WORSE.*
31 YEARS AND 22 CROSSOVER EVENTS LATER.
Helvetica Caslon
Editor in Chief
ZENYTH COMICS
TODAY'S PANEL:
Cataclysm in Innumerable Epochs:
30 Years Editing the Galaxy's
Most Superlative Superheroes
bweet bweet
bweet bweet bweet bweet
Umm, I THINK THAT'S LIKE THE FIRE ALARM GOING OFF OR SOMETHING? WE SHOULD PROBABLY GET YOU TO THE SURFACE, MS. CASLON.
ON THE CONTRARY, ALISON. I THINK WE ARE EXACTLY WHERE WE NEED TO BE.

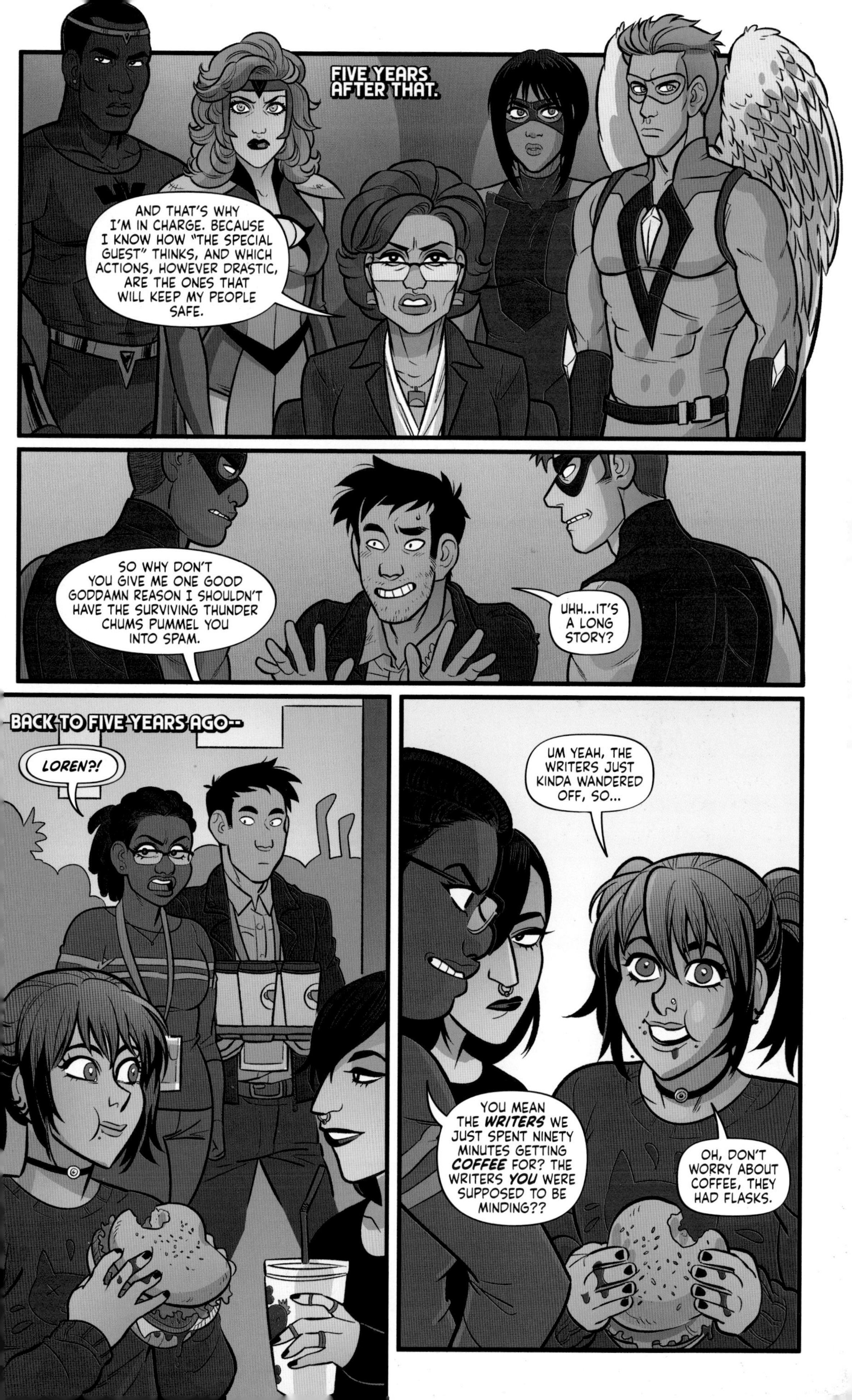
FIVE YEARS AFTER THAT.
AND THAT'S WHY I'M IN CHARGE. BECAUSE I KNOW HOW "THE SPECIAL GUEST" THINKS, AND WHICH ACTIONS, HOWEVER DRASTIC, ARE THE ONES THAT WILL KEEP MY PEOPLE SAFE.
SO WHY DON'T YOU GIVE ME ONE GOOD GODDAMN REASON I SHOULDN'T HAVE THE SURVIVING THUNDER CHUMS PUMMEL YOU INTO SPAM.
UHH...IT'S A LONG STORY?
-BACK TO FIVE YEARS AGO--
LOREN?!
UM YEAH, THE WRITERS JUST KINDA WANDERED OFF, SO...
YOU MEAN THE WRITERS WE JUST SPENT NINETY MINUTES GETTING COFFEE FOR? THE WRITERS YOU WERE SUPPOSED TO BE MINDING??
OH, DON'T WORRY ABOUT COFFEE, THEY HAD FLASKS.

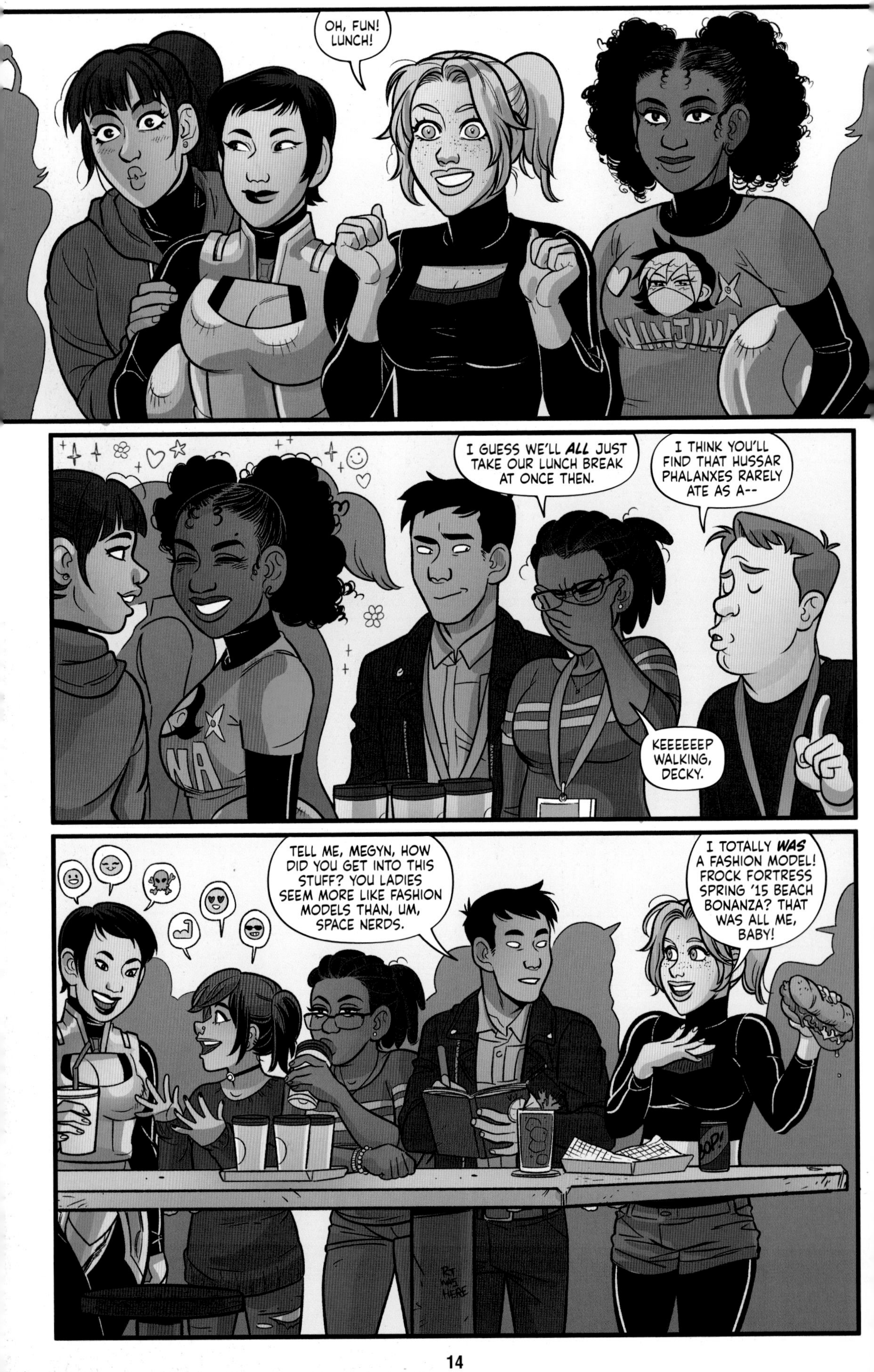
OH, FUN! LUNCH!
I GUESS WE'LL ALL JUST TAKE OUR LUNCH BREAK AT ONCE THEN.
I THINK YOU'LL FIND THAT HUSSAR PHALANXES RARELY ATE AS A--
KEEEEEEP WALKING, DECKY.
TELL ME, MEGYN, HOW DID YOU GET INTO THIS STUFF? YOU LADIES SEEM MORE LIKE FASHION MODELS THAN, UM, SPACE NERDS.
I TOTALLY WAS A FASHION MODEL! FROCK FORTRESS SPRING '15 BEACH BONANZA? THAT WAS ALL ME, BABY!

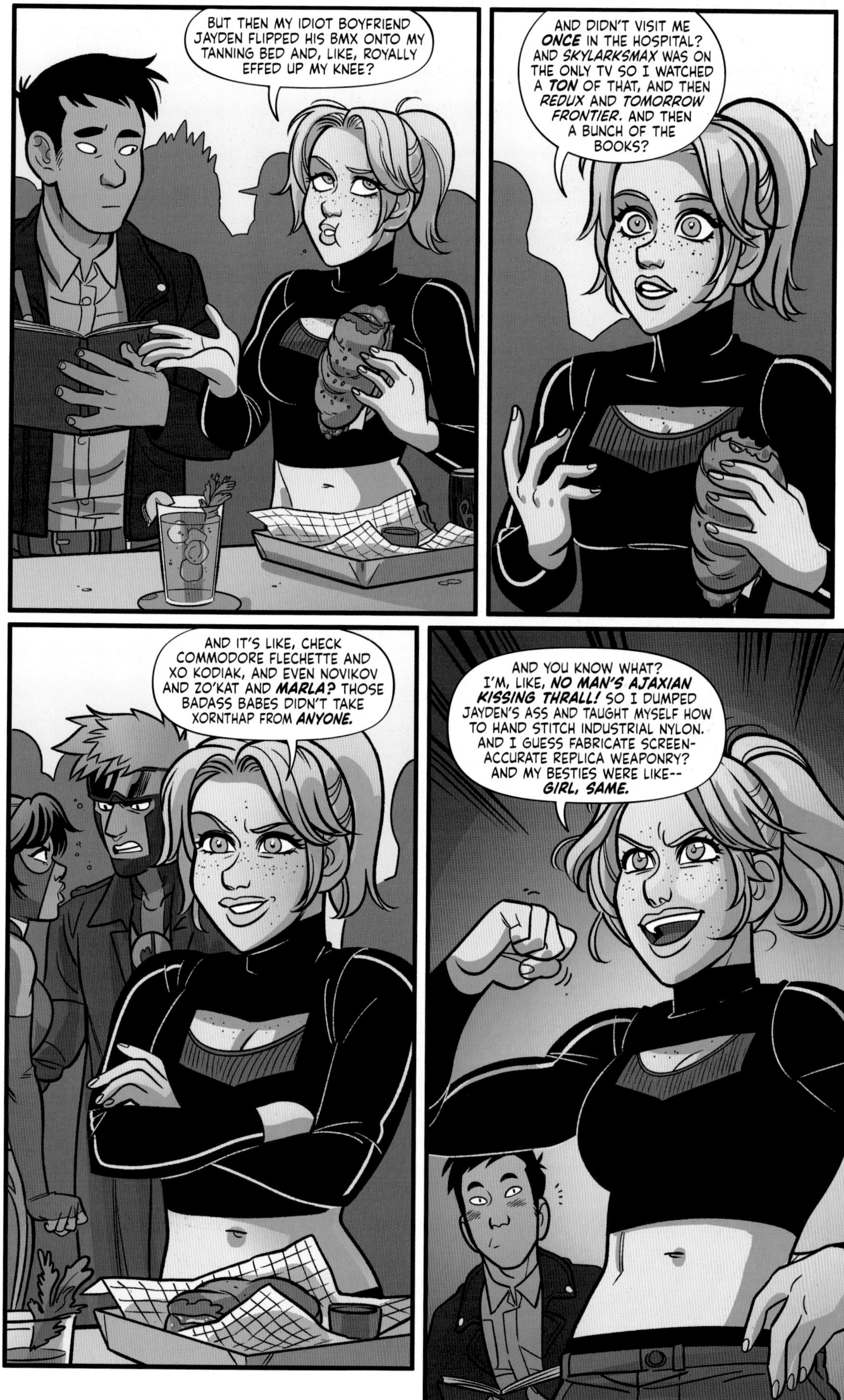
BUT THEN MY IDIOT BOYFRIEND JAYDEN FLIPPED HIS BMX ONTO MY TANNING BED AND, LIKE, ROYALLY EFFED UP MY KNEE?
AND DIDN'T VISIT ME **ONCE** IN THE HOSPITAL? AND ***SKYLARKSMAX*** WAS ON THE ONLY TV SO I WATCHED A **TON** OF THAT, AND THEN ***REDUX*** AND ***TOMORROW FRONTIER***. AND THEN A BUNCH OF THE BOOKS?
AND IT'S LIKE, CHECK COMMODORE FLECHETTE AND XO KODIAK, AND EVEN NOVIKOV AND ZO'KAT AND **MARLA?** THOSE BADASS BABES DIDN'T TAKE XORNTHAP FROM **ANYONE.**
AND YOU KNOW WHAT? I'M, LIKE, **NO MAN'S AJAXIAN KISSING THRALL!** SO I DUMPED JAYDEN'S ASS AND TAUGHT MYSELF HOW TO HAND STITCH INDUSTRIAL NYLON. AND I GUESS FABRICATE SCREEN-ACCURATE REPLICA WEAPONRY? AND MY BESTIES WERE LIKE-- **GIRL, SAME.**

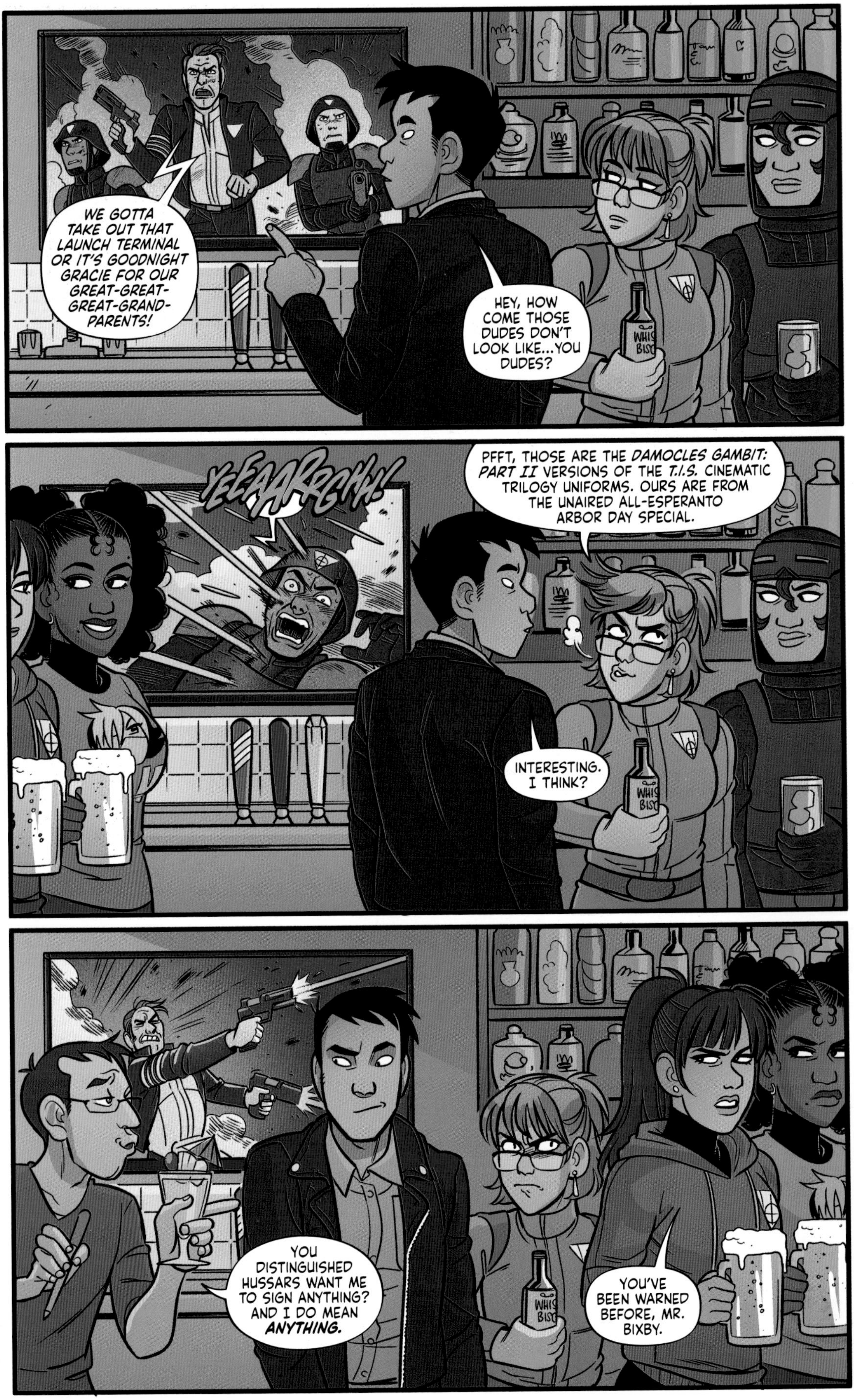

WE GOTTA TAKE OUT THAT LAUNCH TERMINAL OR IT'S GOODNIGHT GRACIE FOR OUR GREAT-GREAT-GREAT-GRAND-PARENTS!
HEY, HOW COME THOSE DUDES DON'T LOOK LIKE...YOU DUDES?
YEEAARRGHH!
PFFT, THOSE ARE THE DAMOCLES GAMBIT: PART II VERSIONS OF THE T.I.S. CINEMATIC TRILOGY UNIFORMS. OURS ARE FROM THE UNAIRED ALL-ESPERANTO ARBOR DAY SPECIAL.
INTERESTING. I THINK?
YOU DISTINGUISHED HUSSARS WANT ME TO SIGN ANYTHING? AND I DO MEAN ANYTHING.
YOU'VE BEEN WARNED BEFORE, MR. BIXBY.

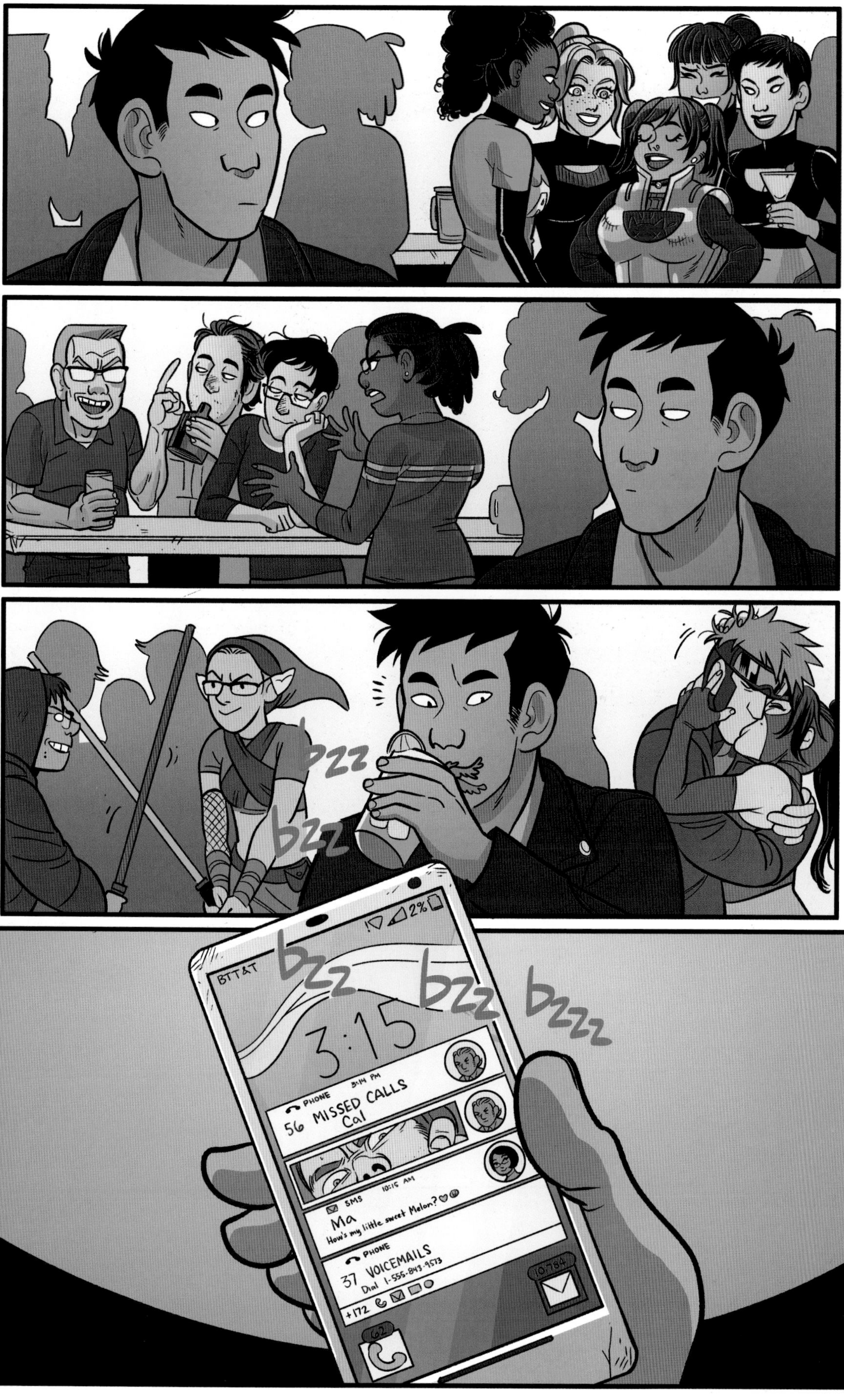
bzz
bzz
2%
BTT&T
bzz
bzz
bzzz
3:15
3:14 PM
PHONE
56 MISSED CALLS
Cal
10:15 AM
SMS
Ma
How's my little sweet Melon?
PHONE
37 VOICEMAILS
Dial 1-555-843-9573
+172
10,784
62

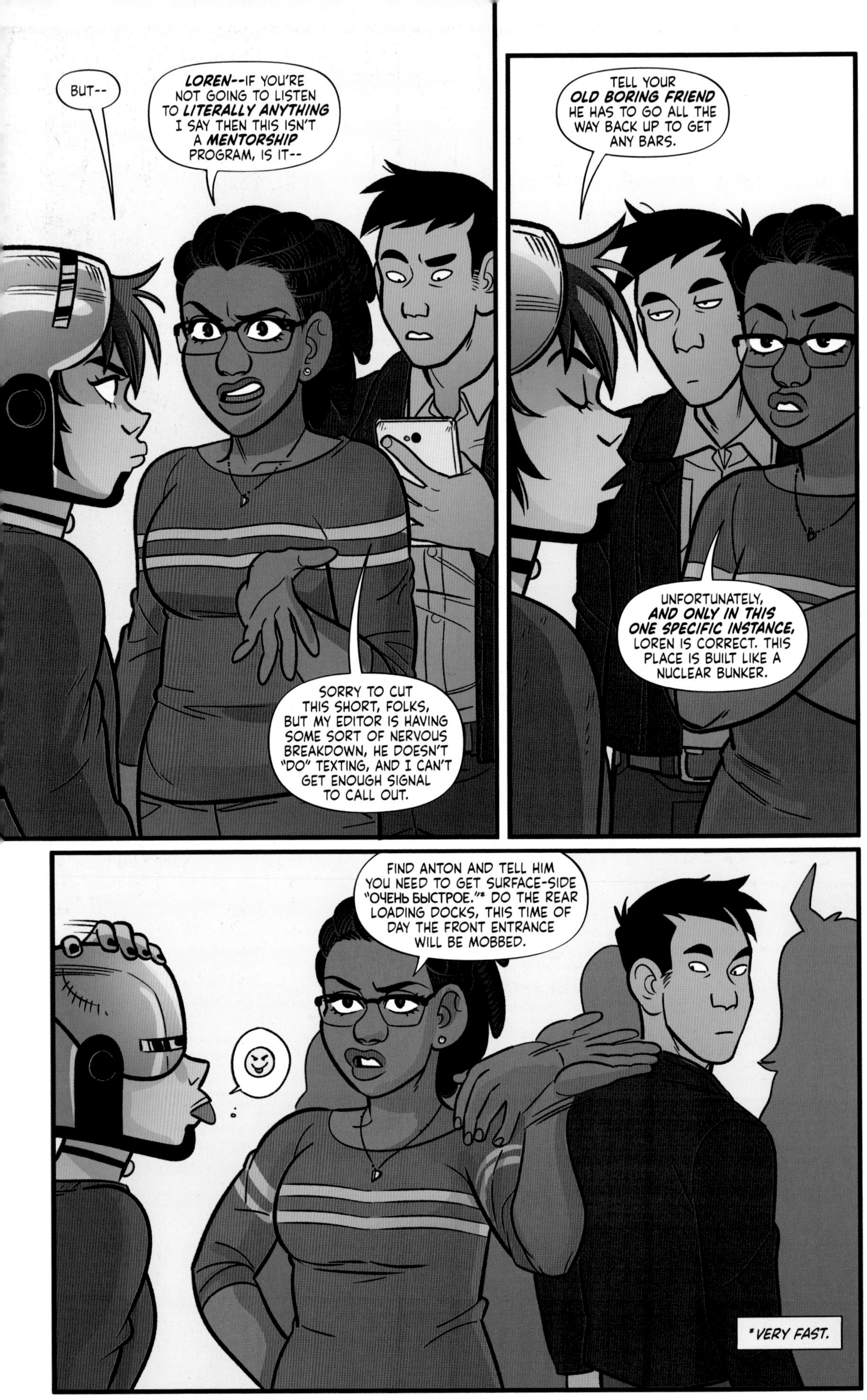
BUT--
LOREN--IF YOU'RE NOT GOING TO LISTEN TO LITERALLY ANYTHING I SAY THEN THIS ISN'T A MENTORSHIP PROGRAM, IS IT--
SORRY TO CUT THIS SHORT, FOLKS, BUT MY EDITOR IS HAVING SOME SORT OF NERVOUS BREAKDOWN, HE DOESN'T "DO" TEXTING, AND I CAN'T GET ENOUGH SIGNAL TO CALL OUT.
TELL YOUR OLD BORING FRIEND HE HAS TO GO ALL THE WAY BACK UP TO GET ANY BARS.
UNFORTUNATELY, AND ONLY IN THIS ONE SPECIFIC INSTANCE, LOREN IS CORRECT. THIS PLACE IS BUILT LIKE A NUCLEAR BUNKER.
FIND ANTON AND TELL HIM YOU NEED TO GET SURFACE-SIDE "ОЧЕНЬ БЫСТРОЕ."* DO THE REAR LOADING DOCKS, THIS TIME OF DAY THE FRONT ENTRANCE WILL BE MOBBED.
*VERY FAST.

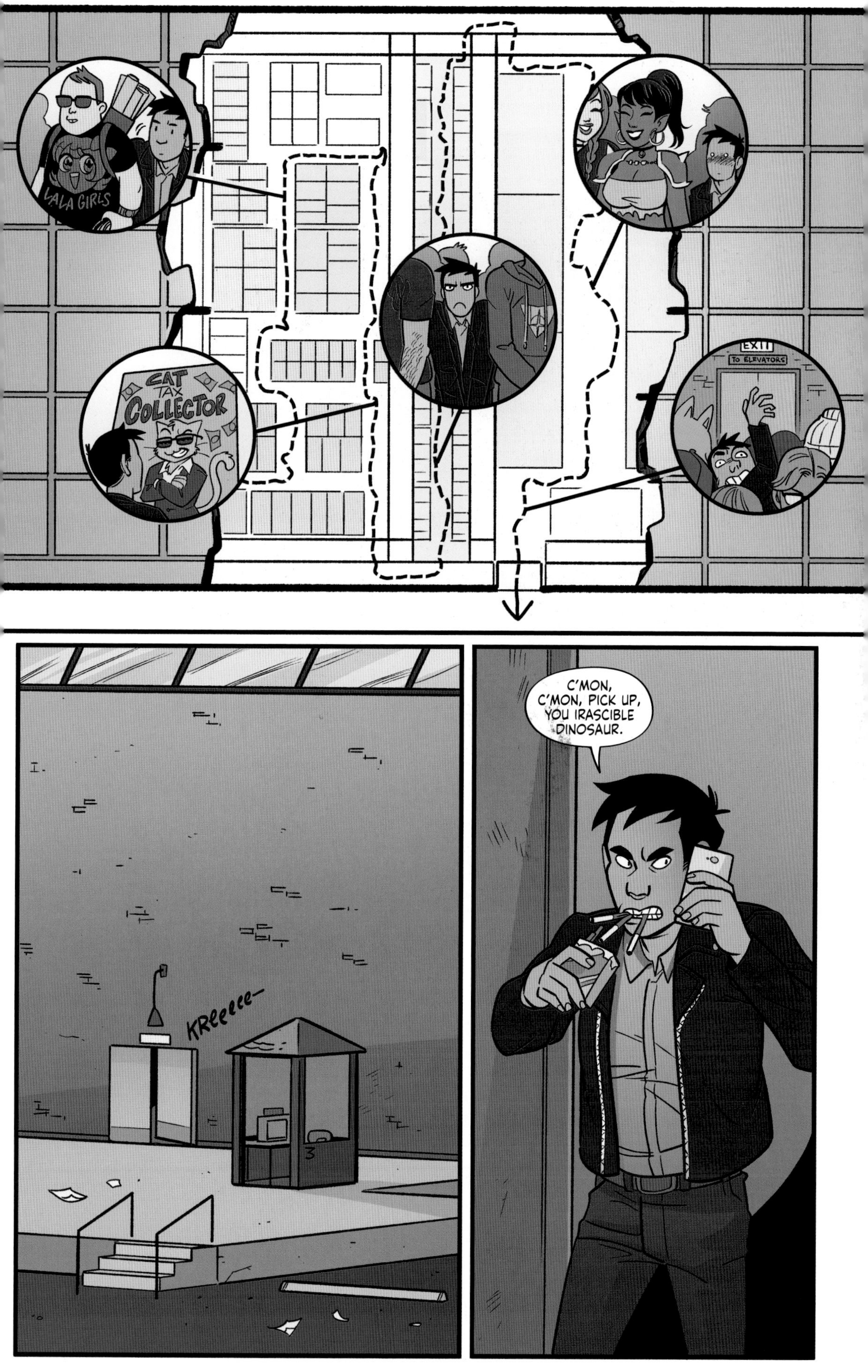
VALA GIRLS
CAT TAX COLLECTOR
EXIT
TO ELEVATORS
KReeeee—
3
C'MON, C'MON, PICK UP, YOU IRASCIBLE DINOSAUR.

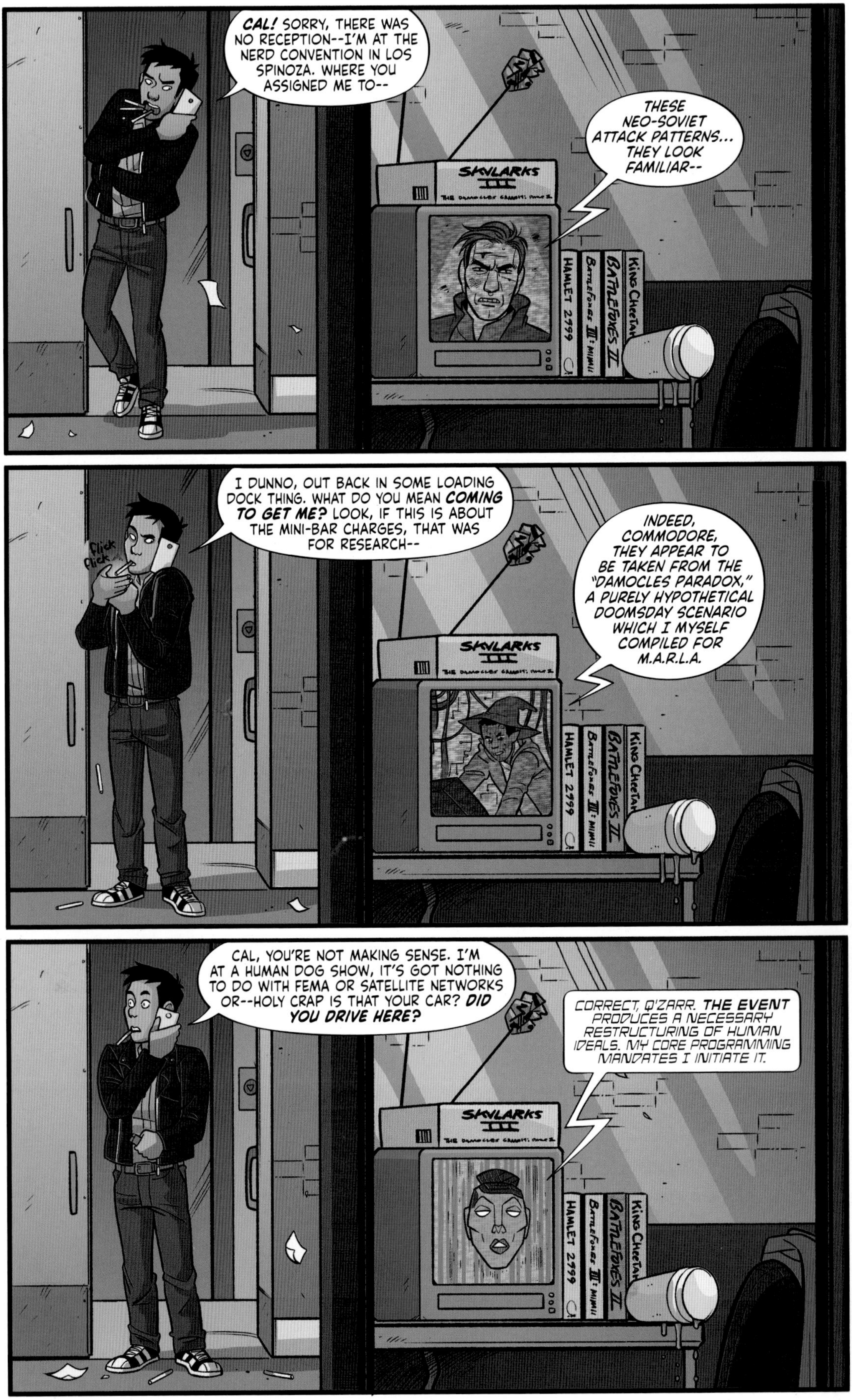
CAL! SORRY, THERE WAS NO RECEPTION--I'M AT THE NERD CONVENTION IN LOS SPINOZA. WHERE YOU ASSIGNED ME TO--
THESE NEO-SOVIET ATTACK PATTERNS... THEY LOOK FAMILIAR--
SKYLARKS III
HAMLET 2999
BATTLEFOXES III: MIMII
BATTLEFOXES II
KING CHEETAH
I DUNNO, OUT BACK IN SOME LOADING DOCK THING. WHAT DO YOU MEAN COMING TO GET ME? LOOK, IF THIS IS ABOUT THE MINI-BAR CHARGES, THAT WAS FOR RESEARCH--
flick flick
INDEED, COMMODORE, THEY APPEAR TO BE TAKEN FROM THE "DAMOCLES PARADOX," A PURELY HYPOTHETICAL DOOMSDAY SCENARIO WHICH I MYSELF COMPILED FOR M.A.R.L.A.
CAL, YOU'RE NOT MAKING SENSE. I'M AT A HUMAN DOG SHOW, IT'S GOT NOTHING TO DO WITH FEMA OR SATELLITE NETWORKS OR--HOLY CRAP IS THAT YOUR CAR? DID YOU DRIVE HERE?
CORRECT, Q'ZARR. THE EVENT PRODUCES A NECESSARY RESTRUCTURING OF HUMAN IDEALS. MY CORE PROGRAMMING MANDATES I INITIATE IT.

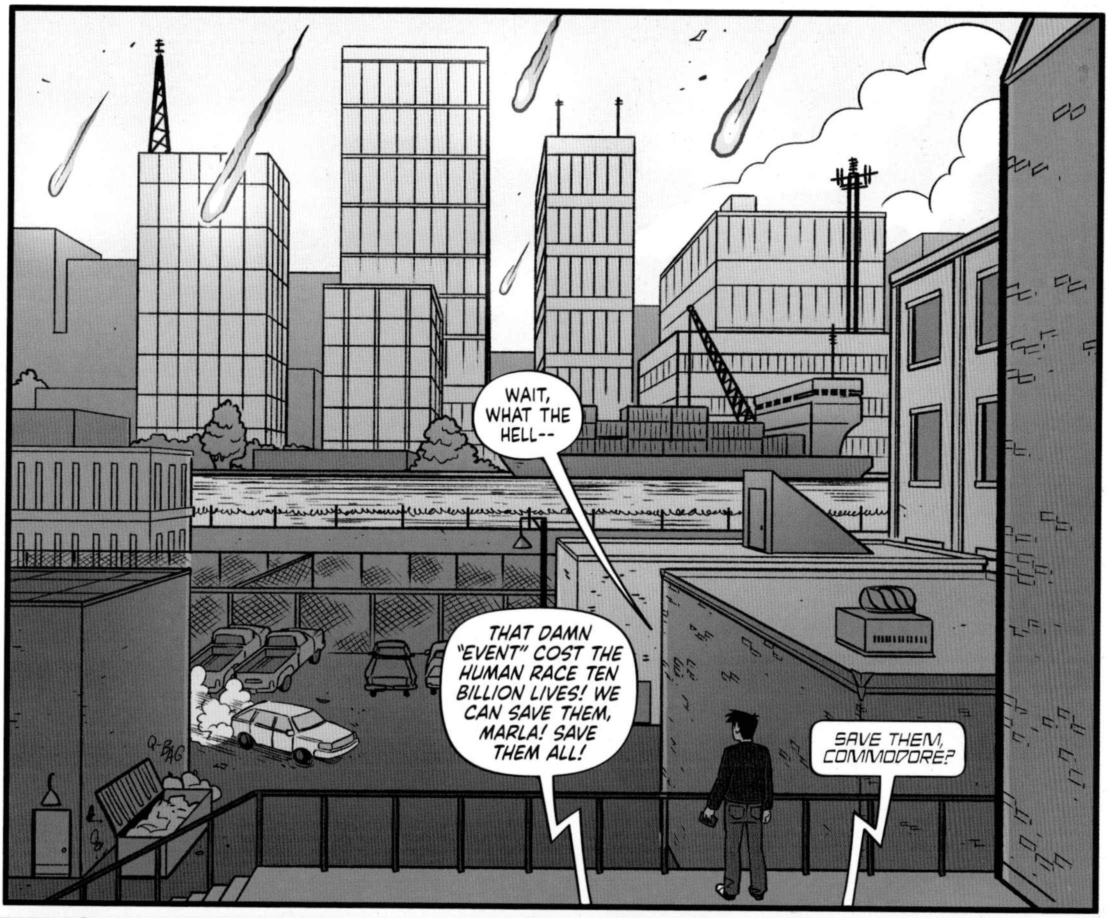
WAIT, WHAT THE HELL--
THAT DAMN "EVENT" COST THE HUMAN RACE TEN BILLION LIVES! WE CAN SAVE THEM, MARLA! SAVE THEM ALL!
SAVE THEM, COMMODORE?
Q-BAG
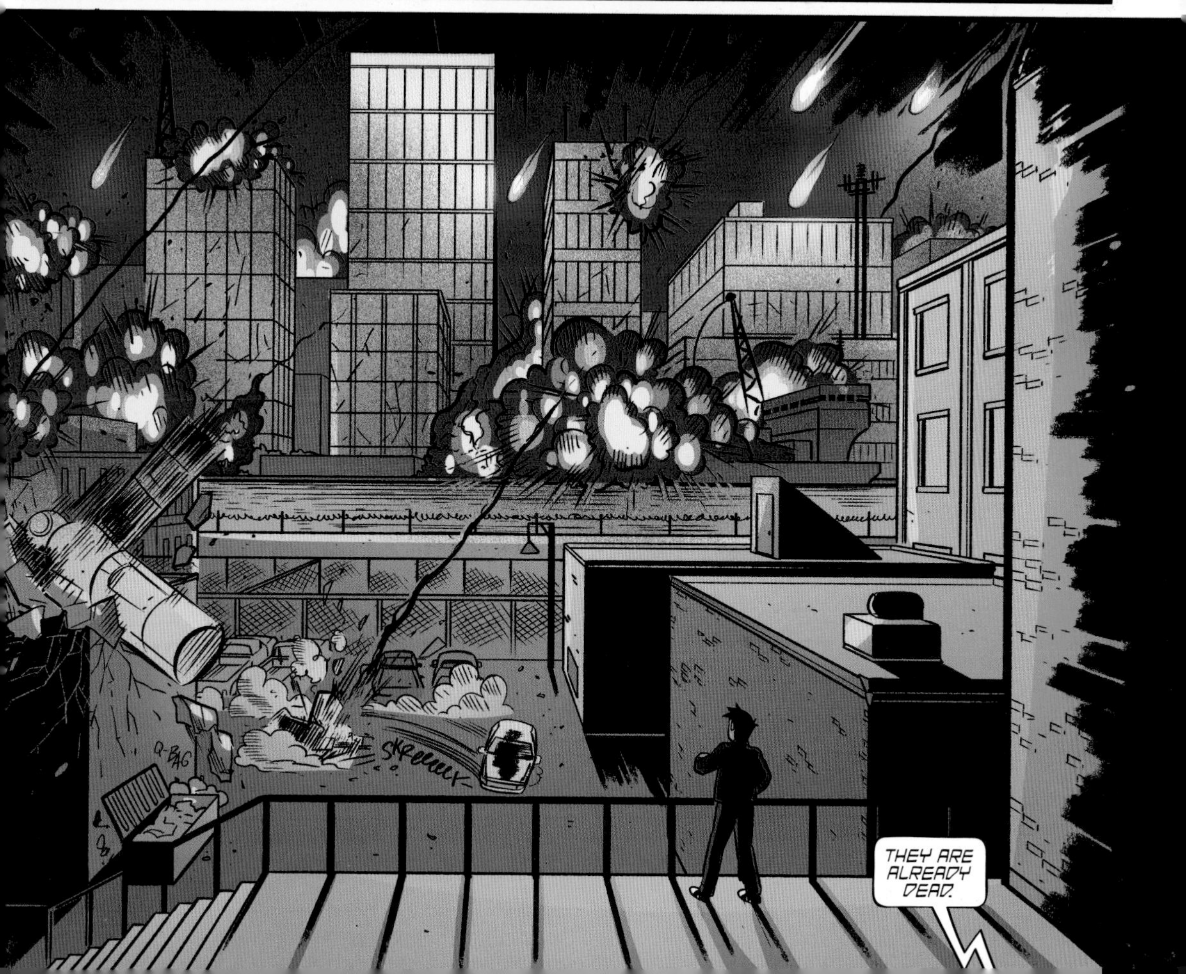
Q-BAG
THEY ARE ALREADY DEAD.

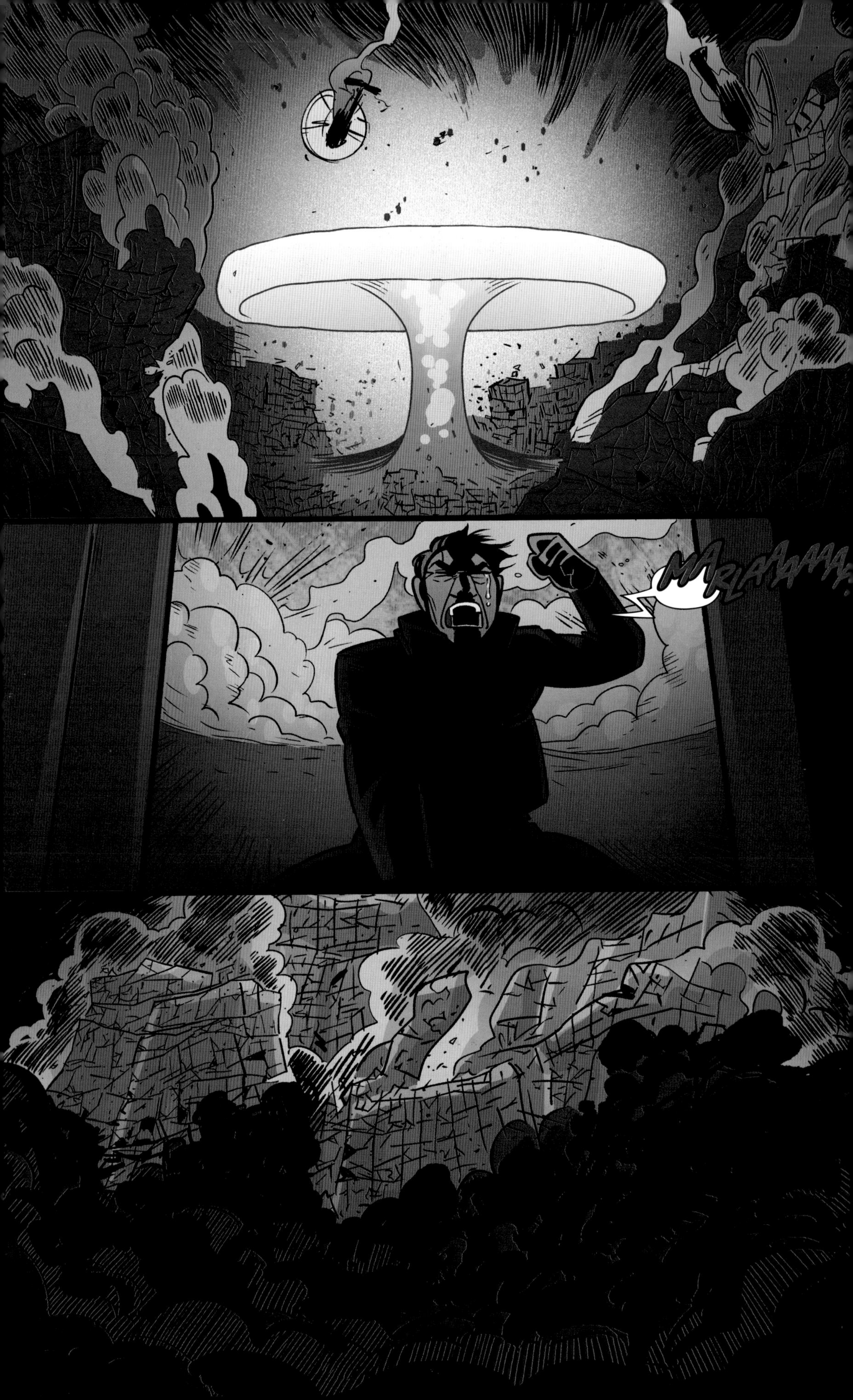
MARLAAAAAA

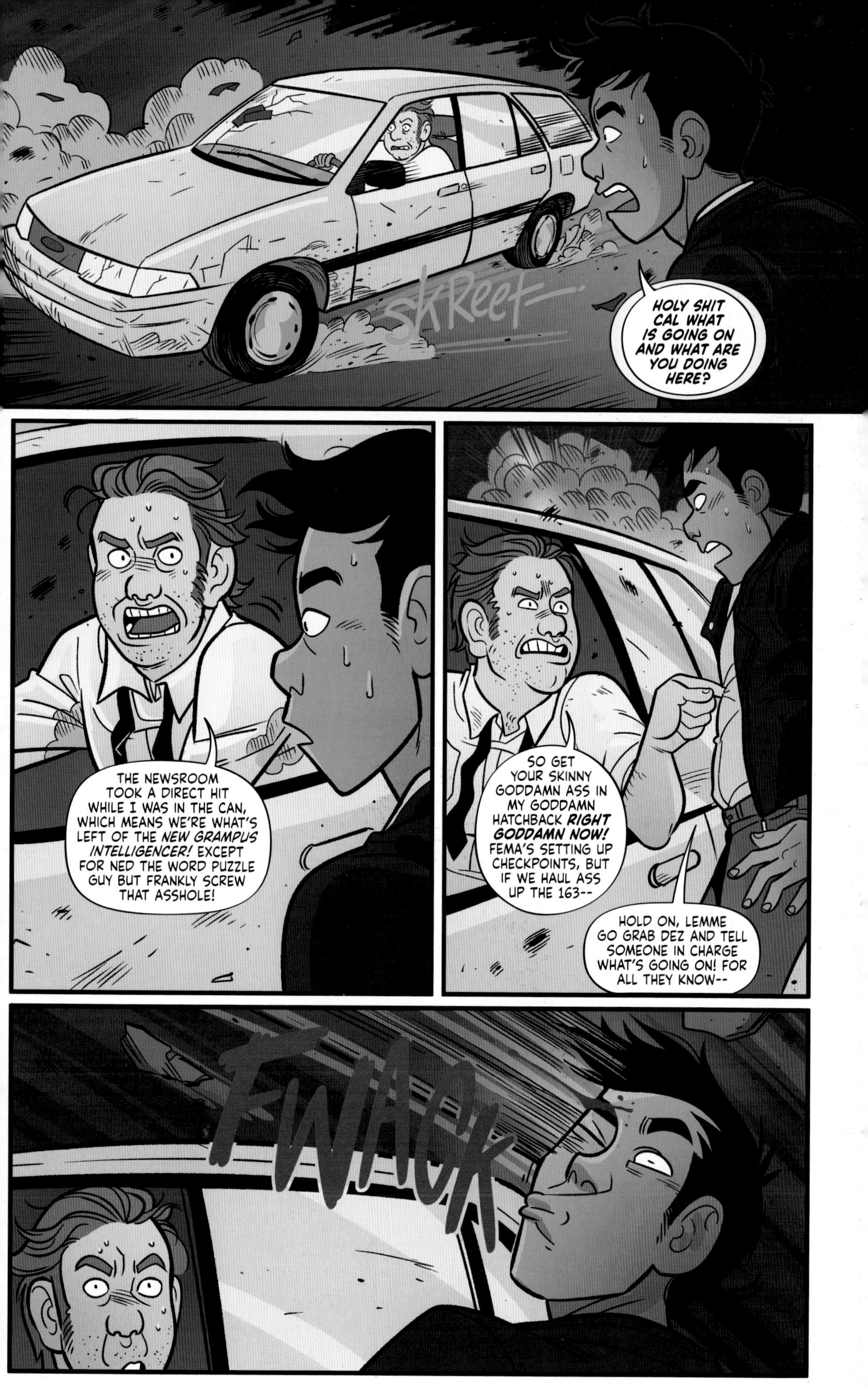

skReet
HOLY SHIT CAL WHAT IS GOING ON AND WHAT ARE YOU DOING HERE?
THE NEWSROOM TOOK A DIRECT HIT WHILE I WAS IN THE CAN, WHICH MEANS WE'RE WHAT'S LEFT OF THE *NEW GRAMPUS INTELLIGENCER!* EXCEPT FOR NED THE WORD PUZZLE GUY BUT FRANKLY SCREW THAT ASSHOLE!
SO GET YOUR SKINNY GODDAMN ASS IN MY GODDAMN HATCHBACK ***RIGHT GODDAMN NOW!*** FEMA'S SETTING UP CHECKPOINTS, BUT IF WE HAUL ASS UP THE 163--
HOLD ON, LEMME GO GRAB DEZ AND TELL SOMEONE IN CHARGE WHAT'S GOING ON! FOR ALL THEY KNOW--
FWACK

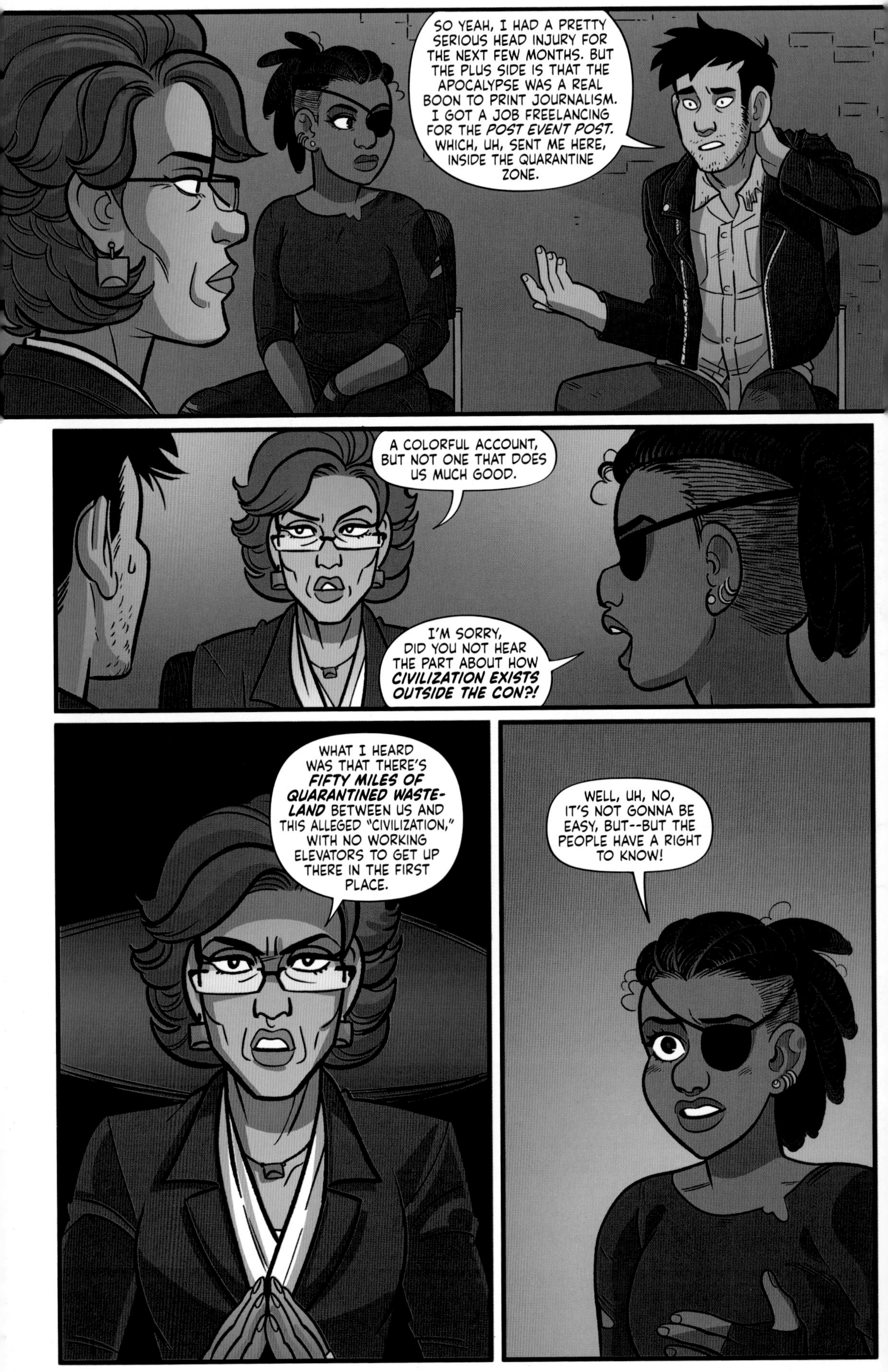
SO YEAH, I HAD A PRETTY SERIOUS HEAD INJURY FOR THE NEXT FEW MONTHS. BUT THE PLUS SIDE IS THAT THE APOCALYPSE WAS A REAL BOON TO PRINT JOURNALISM. I GOT A JOB FREELANCING FOR THE *POST EVENT POST.* WHICH, UH, SENT ME HERE, INSIDE THE QUARANTINE ZONE.
A COLORFUL ACCOUNT, BUT NOT ONE THAT DOES US MUCH GOOD.
I'M SORRY, DID YOU NOT HEAR THE PART ABOUT HOW ***CIVILIZATION EXISTS OUTSIDE THE CON?!***
WHAT I HEARD WAS THAT THERE'S ***FIFTY MILES OF QUARANTINED WASTE-LAND*** BETWEEN US AND THIS ALLEGED "CIVILIZATION," WITH NO WORKING ELEVATORS TO GET UP THERE IN THE FIRST PLACE.
WELL, UH, NO, IT'S NOT GONNA BE EASY, BUT--BUT THE PEOPLE HAVE A RIGHT TO KNOW!

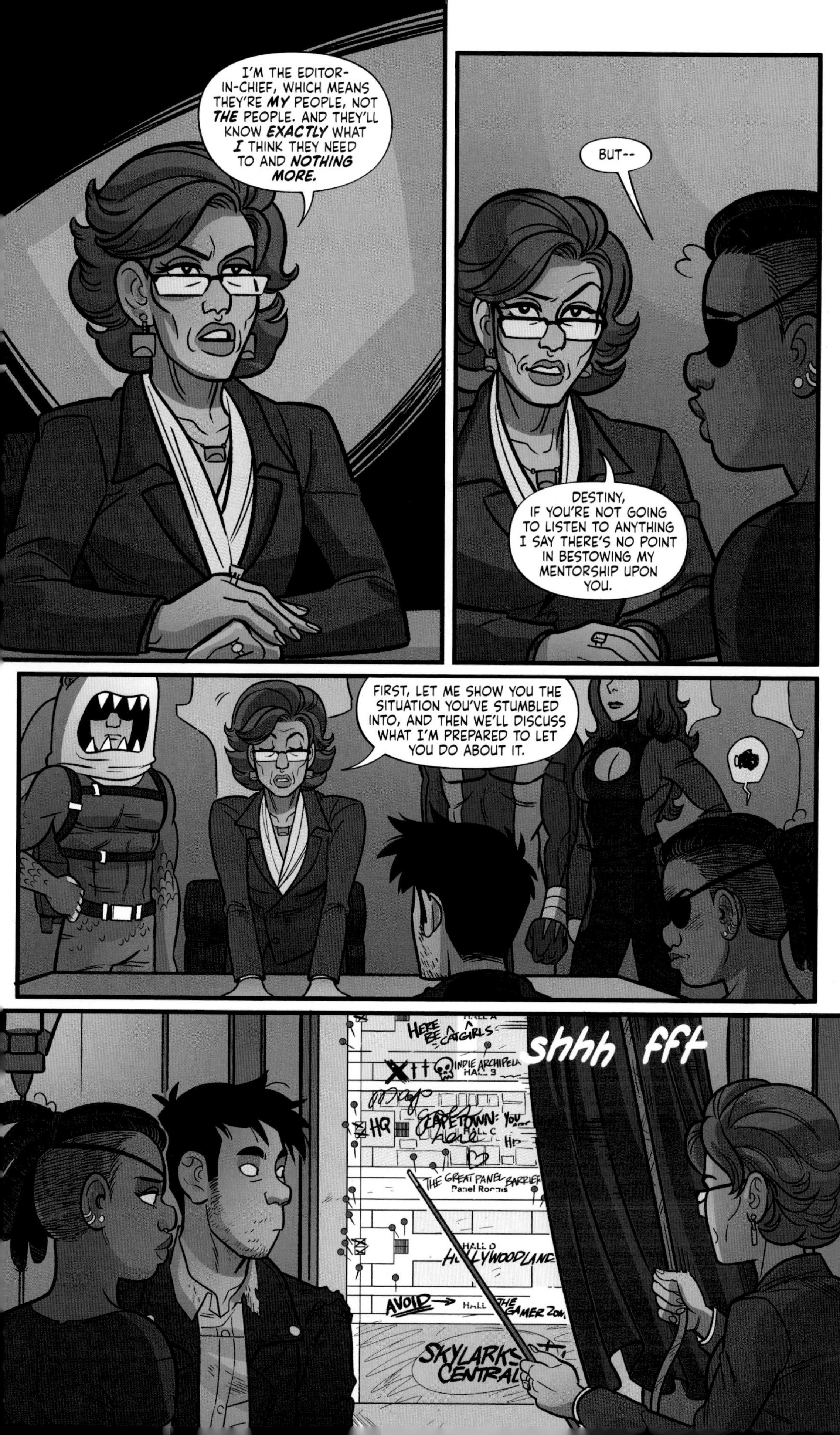
I'M THE EDITOR-IN-CHIEF, WHICH MEANS THEY'RE MY PEOPLE, NOT THE PEOPLE. AND THEY'LL KNOW EXACTLY WHAT I THINK THEY NEED TO AND NOTHING MORE.
BUT--
DESTINY, IF YOU'RE NOT GOING TO LISTEN TO ANYTHING I SAY THERE'S NO POINT IN BESTOWING MY MENTORSHIP UPON YOU.
FIRST, LET ME SHOW YOU THE SITUATION YOU'VE STUMBLED INTO, AND THEN WE'LL DISCUSS WHAT I'M PREPARED TO LET YOU DO ABOUT IT.
shhh fft
HERE BE CATGIRLS
HQ
CAPETOWN:
THE GREAT PANEL BARRIER
Panel Rooms
HOLLYWOODLAND
AVOID
SKYLARKS CENTRAL

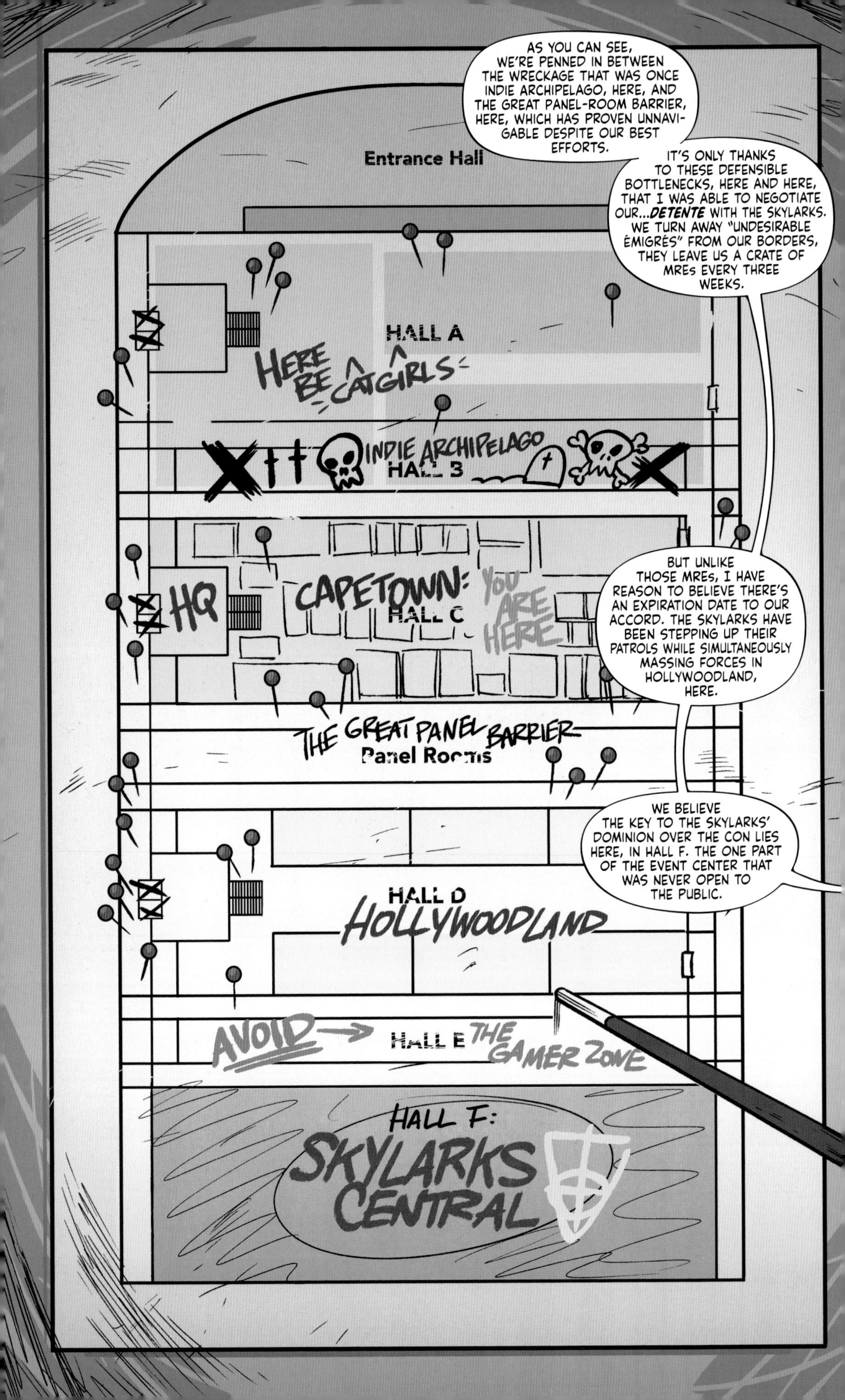

AS YOU CAN SEE, WE'RE PENNED IN BETWEEN THE WRECKAGE THAT WAS ONCE INDIE ARCHIPELAGO, HERE, AND THE GREAT PANEL-ROOM BARRIER, HERE, WHICH HAS PROVEN UNNAVI-GABLE DESPITE OUR BEST EFFORTS.
IT'S ONLY THANKS TO THESE DEFENSIBLE BOTTLENECKS, HERE AND HERE, THAT I WAS ABLE TO NEGOTIATE OUR...*DETENTE* WITH THE SKYLARKS. WE TURN AWAY "UNDESIRABLE ÉMIGRÉS" FROM OUR BORDERS, THEY LEAVE US A CRATE OF MREs EVERY THREE WEEKS.
BUT UNLIKE THOSE MREs, I HAVE REASON TO BELIEVE THERE'S AN EXPIRATION DATE TO OUR ACCORD. THE SKYLARKS HAVE BEEN STEPPING UP THEIR PATROLS WHILE SIMULTANEOUSLY MASSING FORCES IN HOLLYWOODLAND, HERE.
WE BELIEVE THE KEY TO THE SKYLARKS' DOMINION OVER THE CON LIES HERE, IN HALL F. THE ONE PART OF THE EVENT CENTER THAT WAS NEVER OPEN TO THE PUBLIC.
Entrance Hall
HALL A
HERE BE CATGIRLS
INDIE ARCHIPELAGO
HALL 3
CAPETOWN:
HALL C
YOU ARE HERE
HQ
THE GREAT PANEL BARRIER
Panel Rooms
HALL D
HOLLYWOODLAND
AVOID
HALL E
THE GAMER ZONE
HALL F:
SKYLARKS CENTRAL

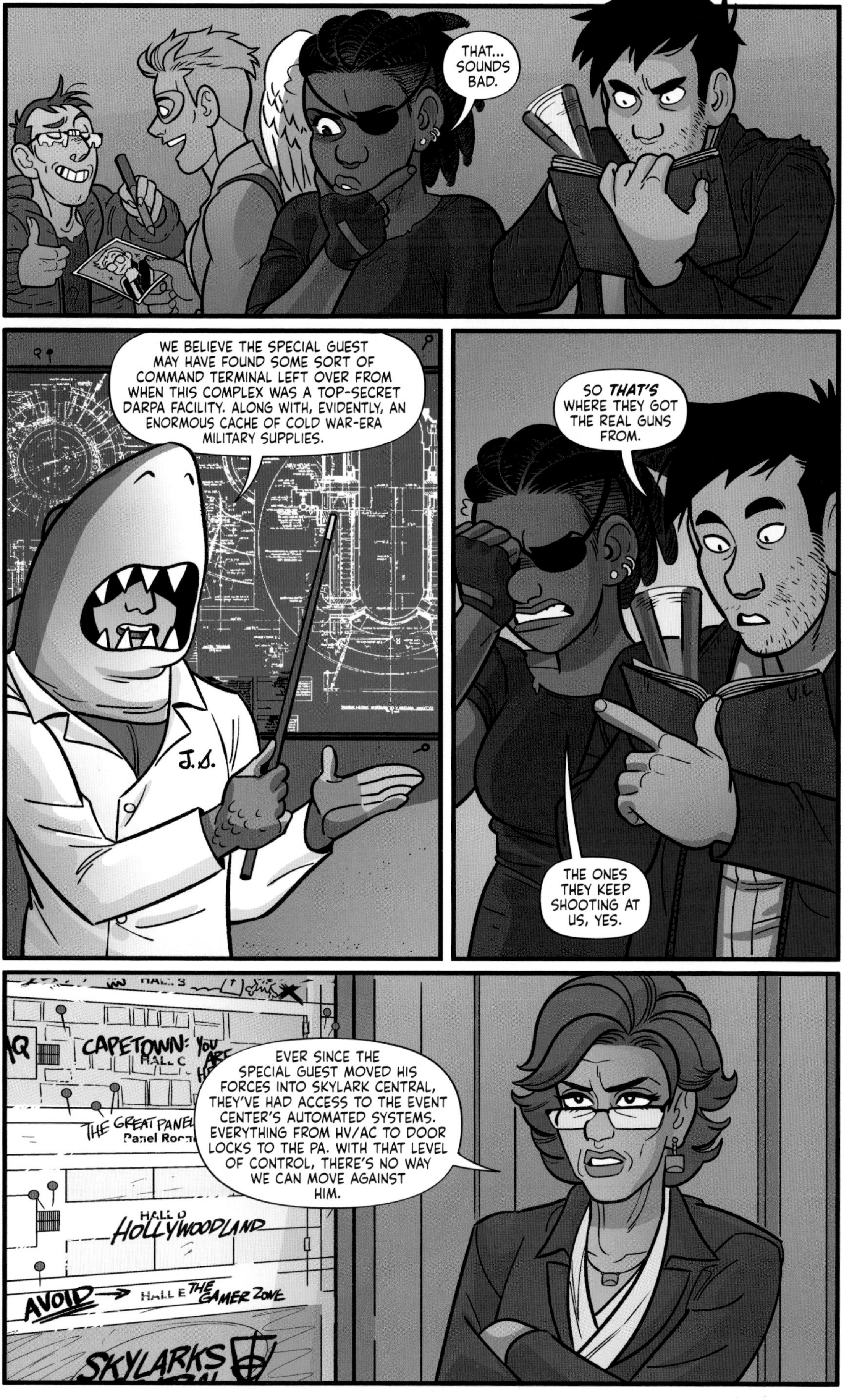

THAT... SOUNDS BAD.
WE BELIEVE THE SPECIAL GUEST MAY HAVE FOUND SOME SORT OF COMMAND TERMINAL LEFT OVER FROM WHEN THIS COMPLEX WAS A TOP-SECRET DARPA FACILITY. ALONG WITH, EVIDENTLY, AN ENORMOUS CACHE OF COLD WAR-ERA MILITARY SUPPLIES.
J.S.
SO *THAT'S* WHERE THEY GOT THE REAL GUNS FROM.
THE ONES THEY KEEP SHOOTING AT US, YES.
HALL 3
CAPETOWN:
HALL C
THE GREAT PANEL
HALL D
HOLLYWOODLAND
AVOID
HALL E THE GAMER ZONE
SKYLARKS
EVER SINCE THE SPECIAL GUEST MOVED HIS FORCES INTO SKYLARK CENTRAL, THEY'VE HAD ACCESS TO THE EVENT CENTER'S AUTOMATED SYSTEMS. EVERYTHING FROM HV/AC TO DOOR LOCKS TO THE PA. WITH THAT LEVEL OF CONTROL, THERE'S NO WAY WE CAN MOVE AGAINST HIM.

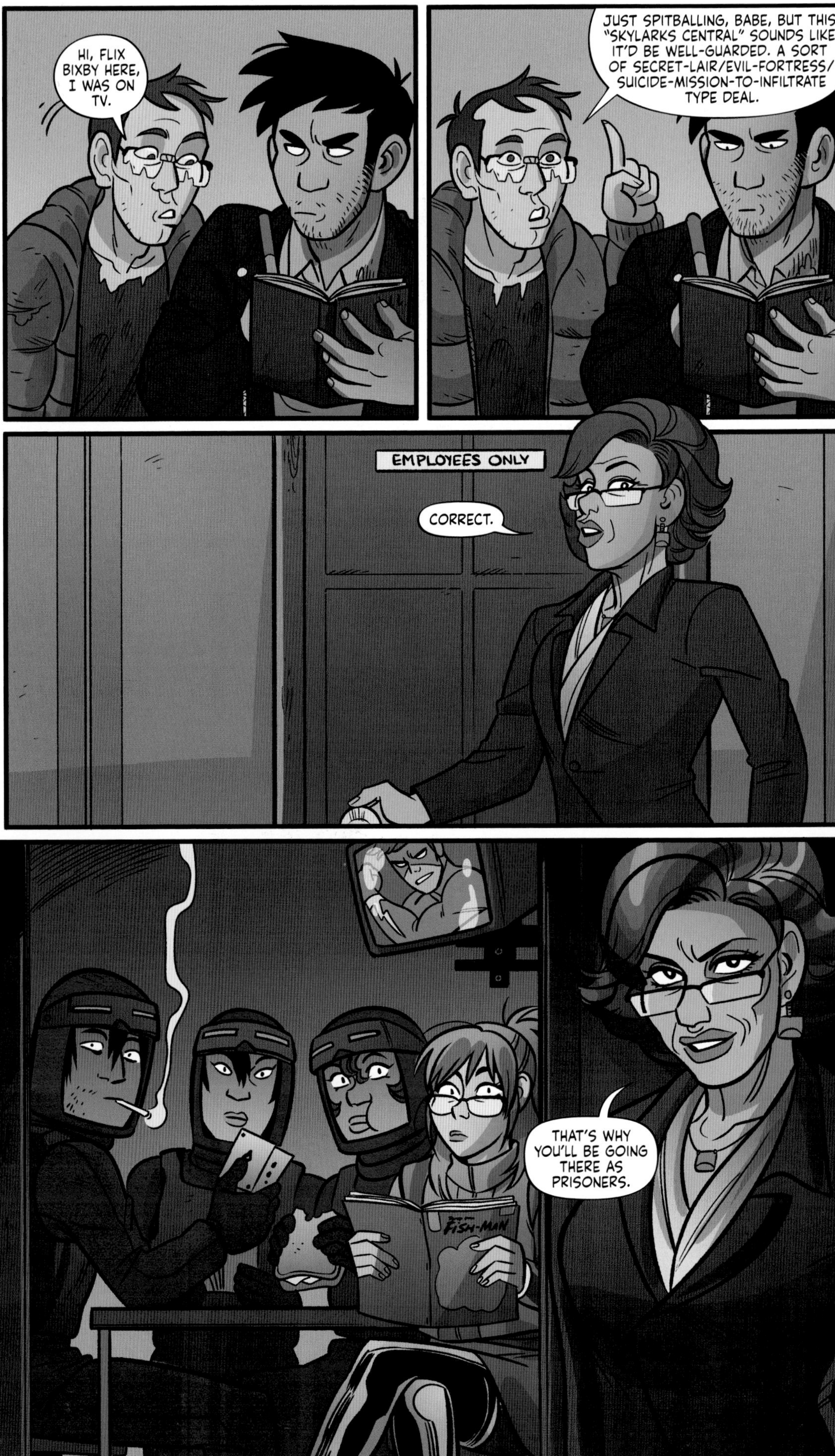
HI, FLIX BIXBY HERE, I WAS ON TV.
JUST SPITBALLING, BABE, BUT THIS "SKYLARKS CENTRAL" SOUNDS LIKE IT'D BE WELL-GUARDED. A SORT OF SECRET-LAIR/EVIL-FORTRESS/ SUICIDE-MISSION-TO-INFILTRATE TYPE DEAL.
EMPLOYEES ONLY
CORRECT.
FISH-MAN
THAT'S WHY YOU'LL BE GOING THERE AS PRISONERS.

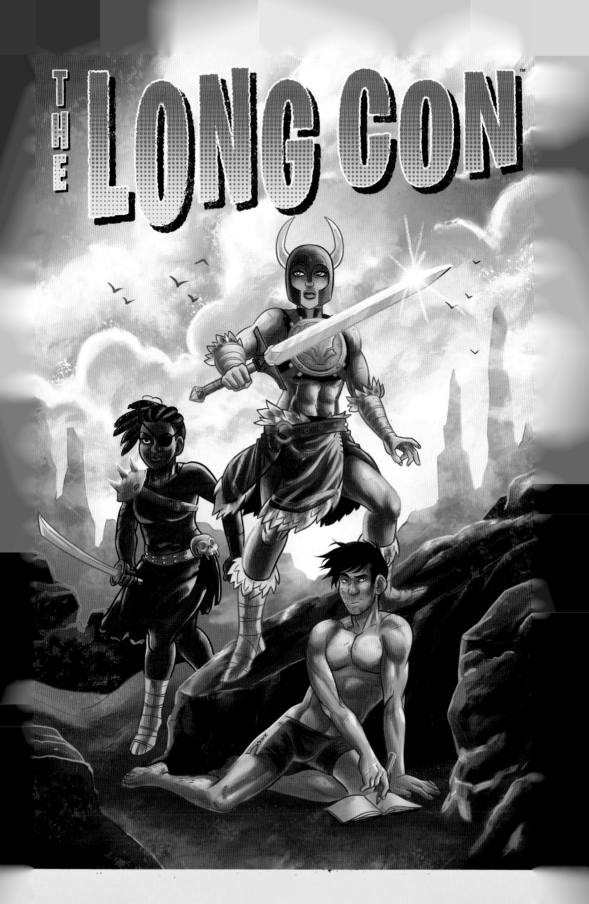

THE LONG CON

CHAPTER 7: CANON FODDER

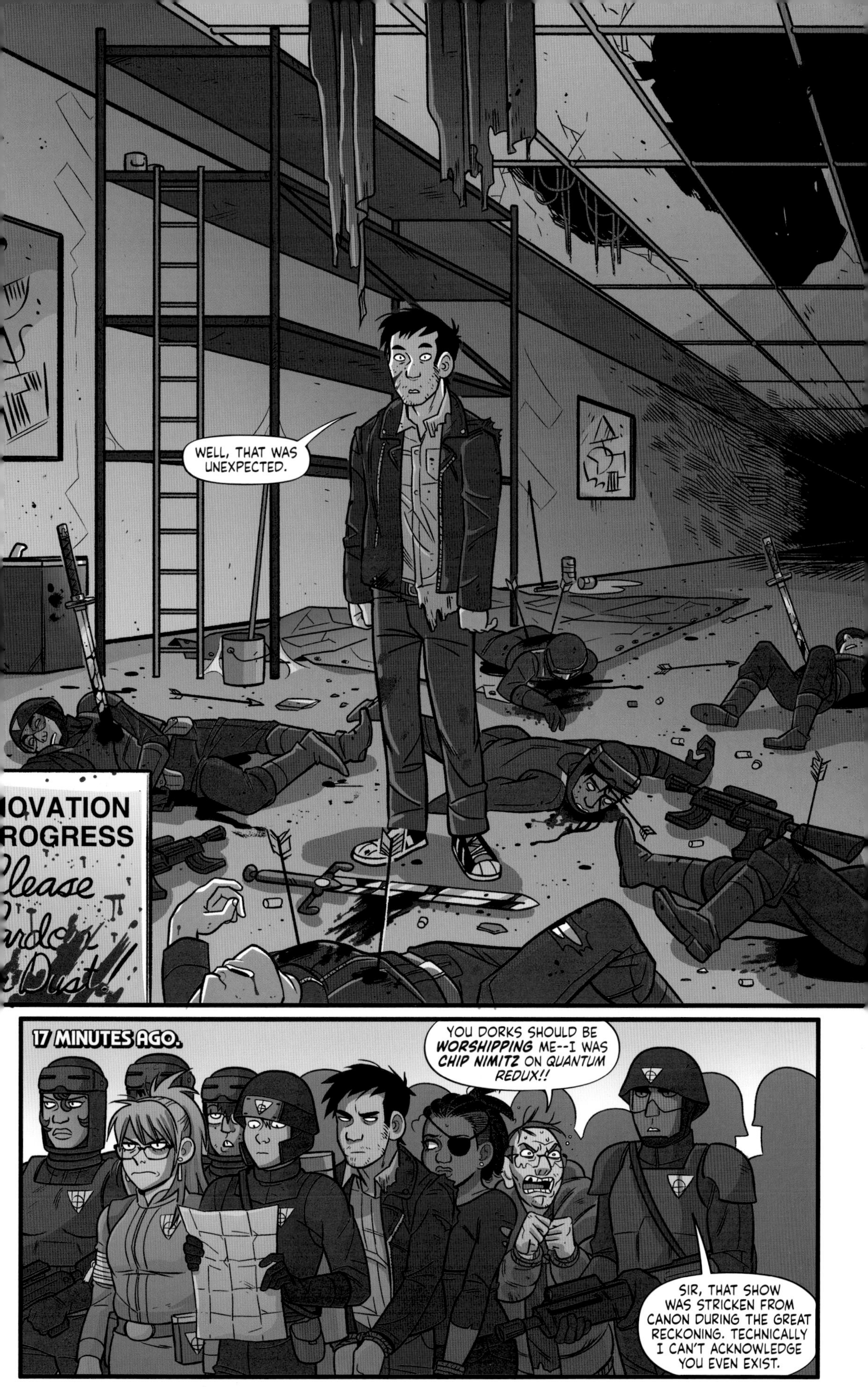
WELL, THAT WAS UNEXPECTED.
OVATION
ROGRESS
lease
17 MINUTES AGO.
YOU DORKS SHOULD BE ***WORSHIPPING*** ME--I WAS ***CHIP NIMITZ*** ON *QUANTUM REDUX*!!
SIR, THAT SHOW WAS STRICKEN FROM CANON DURING THE GREAT RECKONING. TECHNICALLY I CAN'T ACKNOWLEDGE YOU EVEN EXIST.

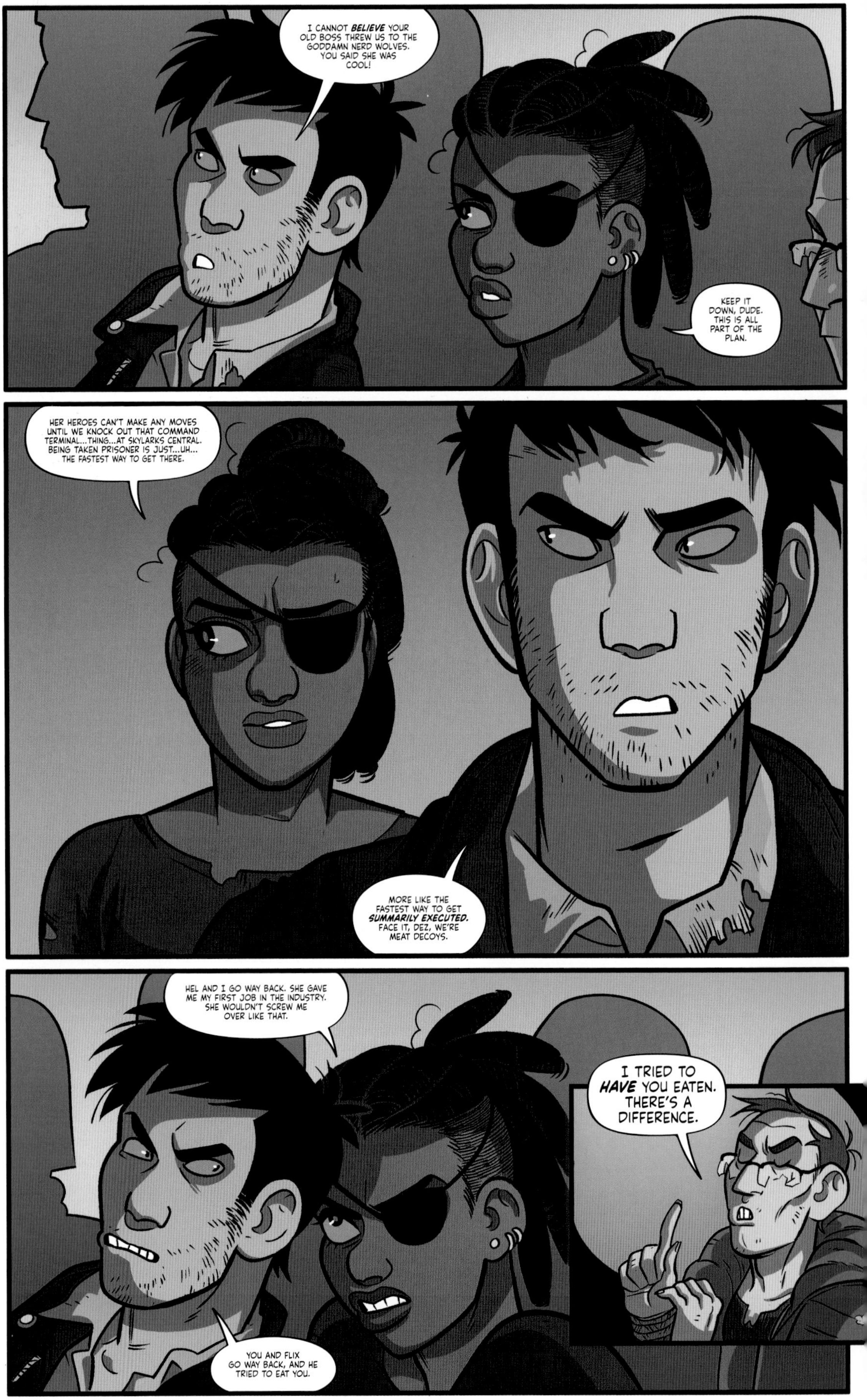
I CANNOT **BELIEVE** YOUR OLD BOSS THREW US TO THE GODDAMN NERD WOLVES. YOU SAID SHE WAS COOL!
KEEP IT DOWN, DUDE. THIS IS ALL PART OF THE PLAN.
HER HEROES CAN'T MAKE ANY MOVES UNTIL WE KNOCK OUT THAT COMMAND TERMINAL...THING...AT SKYLARKS CENTRAL. BEING TAKEN PRISONER IS JUST...UH... THE FASTEST WAY TO GET THERE.
MORE LIKE THE FASTEST WAY TO GET ***SUMMARILY EXECUTED.*** FACE IT, DEZ, WE'RE MEAT DECOYS.
HEL AND I GO WAY BACK. SHE GAVE ME MY FIRST JOB IN THE INDUSTRY. SHE WOULDN'T SCREW ME OVER LIKE THAT.
YOU AND FLIX GO WAY BACK, AND HE TRIED TO EAT YOU.
I TRIED TO ***HAVE*** YOU EATEN. THERE'S A DIFFERENCE.

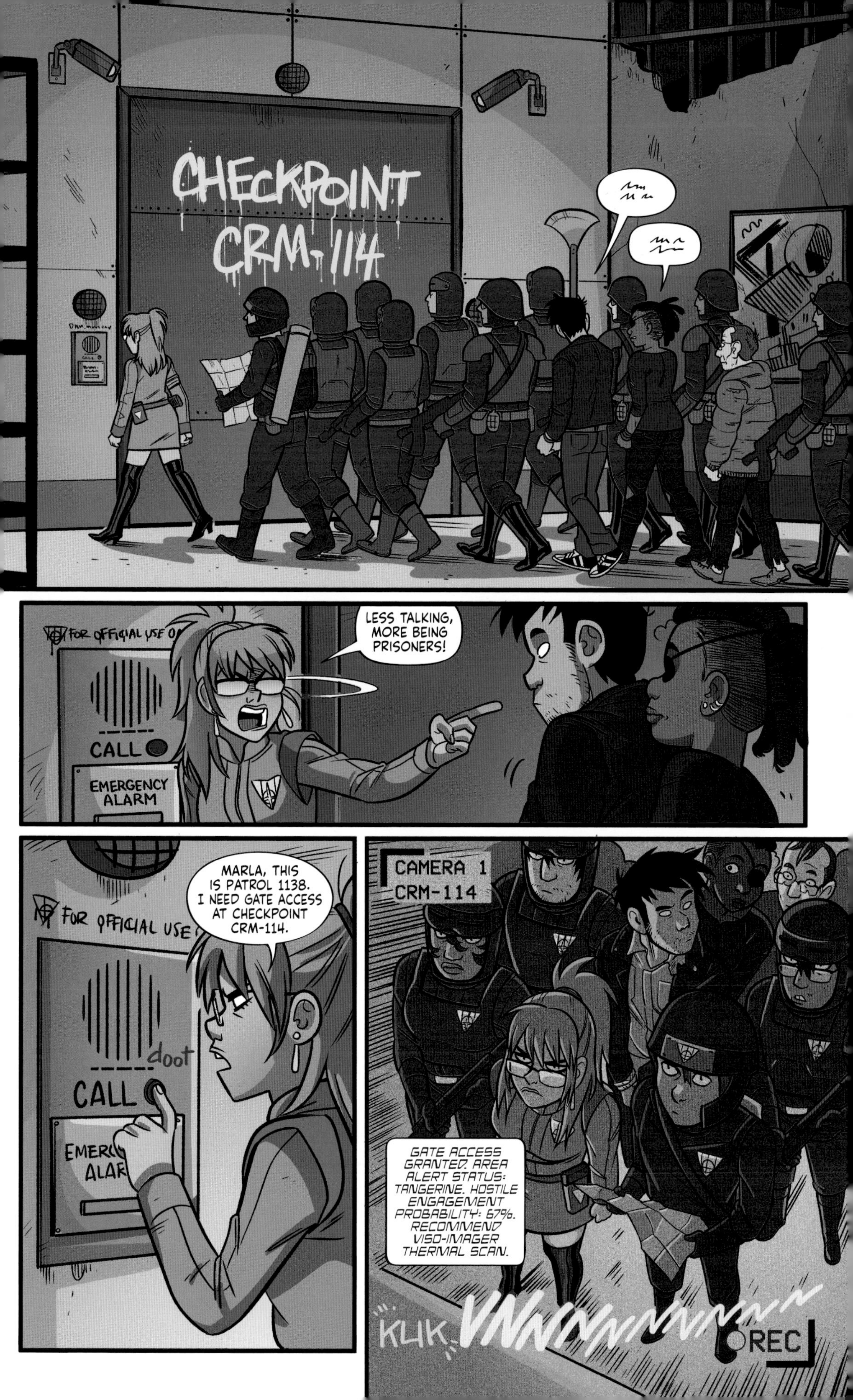
CHECKPOINT CRM. 114
FOR OFFICIAL USE O
CALL
EMERGENCY ALARM
LESS TALKING, MORE BEING PRISONERS!
FOR OFFICIAL USE
MARLA, THIS IS PATROL 1138. I NEED GATE ACCESS AT CHECKPOINT CRM-114.
doot
CALL
CAMERA 1 CRM-114
GATE ACCESS GRANTED. AREA ALERT STATUS: TANGERINE. HOSTILE ENGAGEMENT PROBABILITY: 67%. RECOMMEND VISO-IMAGER THERMAL SCAN.
KLIK
VNNNNNNNNN
REC

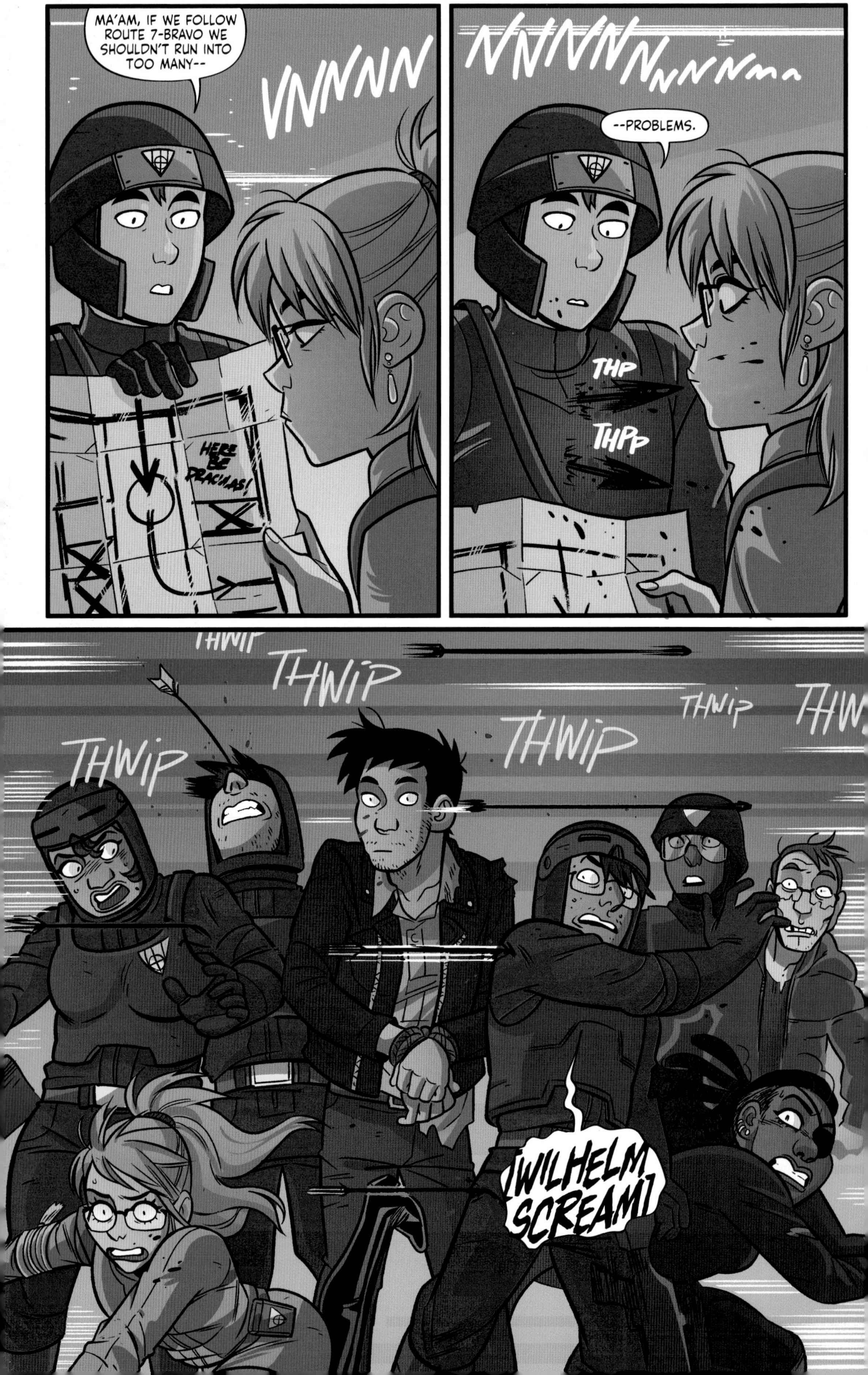
MA'AM, IF WE FOLLOW ROUTE 7-BRAVO WE SHOULDN'T RUN INTO TOO MANY--
VNNNN
HERE BE DRACULAS!
NNNNNNNNNNma
--PROBLEMS.
THP
THPP
THWIP
THWIP
THWIP
THWIP
THWIP
THW
[WILHELM SCREAM]

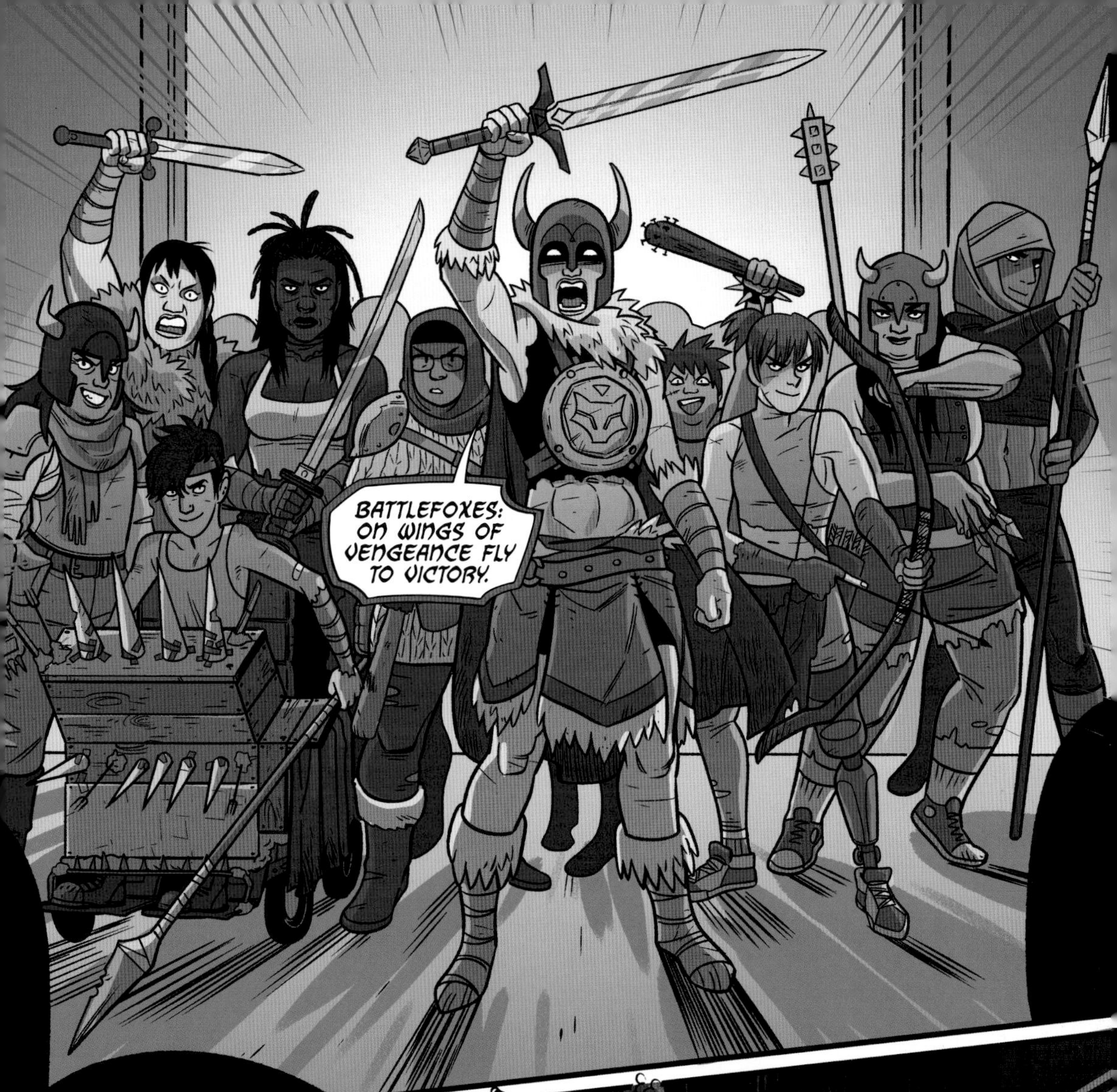
BATTLEFOXES: ON WINGS OF VENGEANCE FLY TO VICTORY.

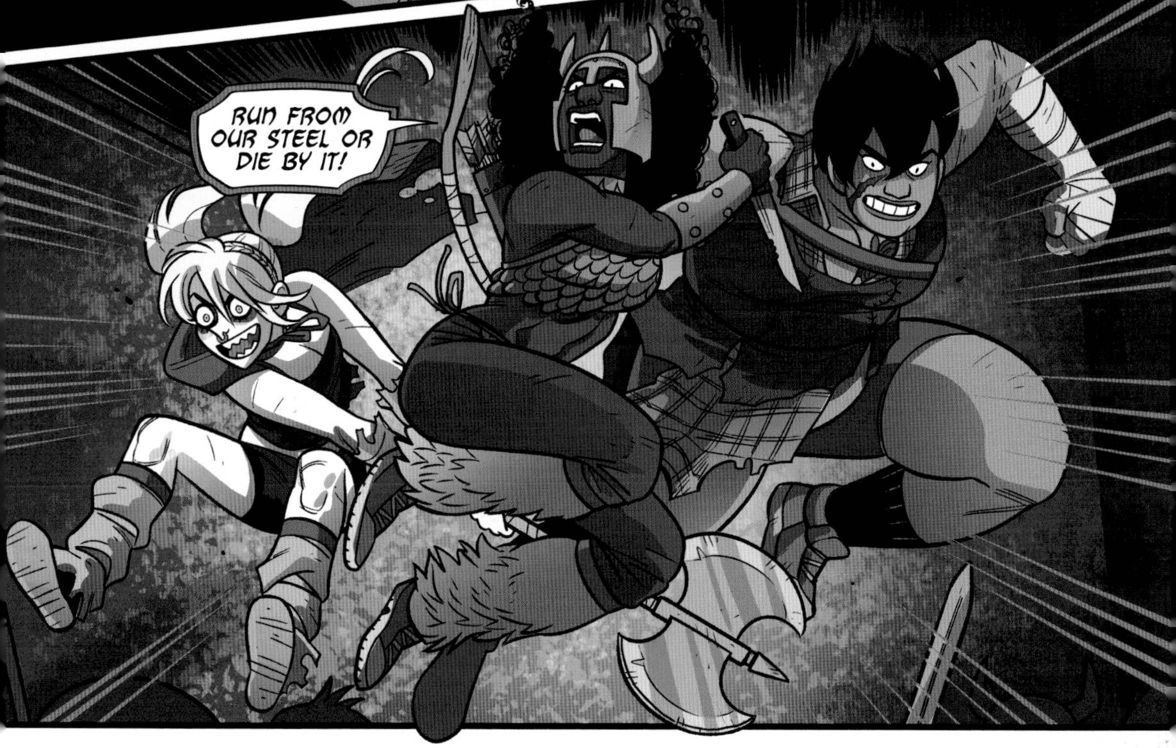
RUN FROM OUR STEEL OR DIE BY IT!

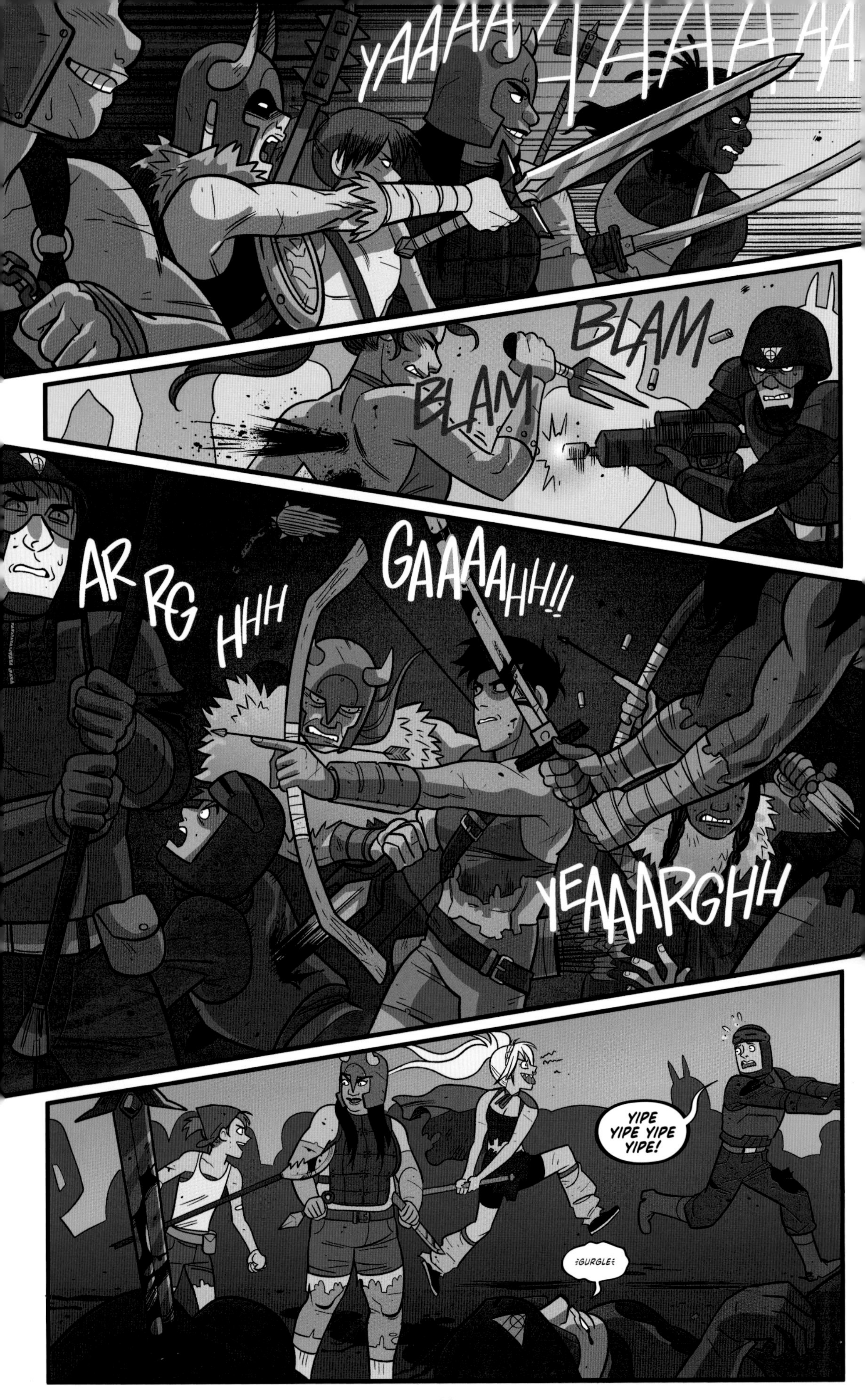
YAAAAAAAAAAAA
BLAM-
BLAM
ARRGHHH
GAAAAHH!!
YEAAARGHH
YIPE YIPE YIPE YIPE!
GURGLE

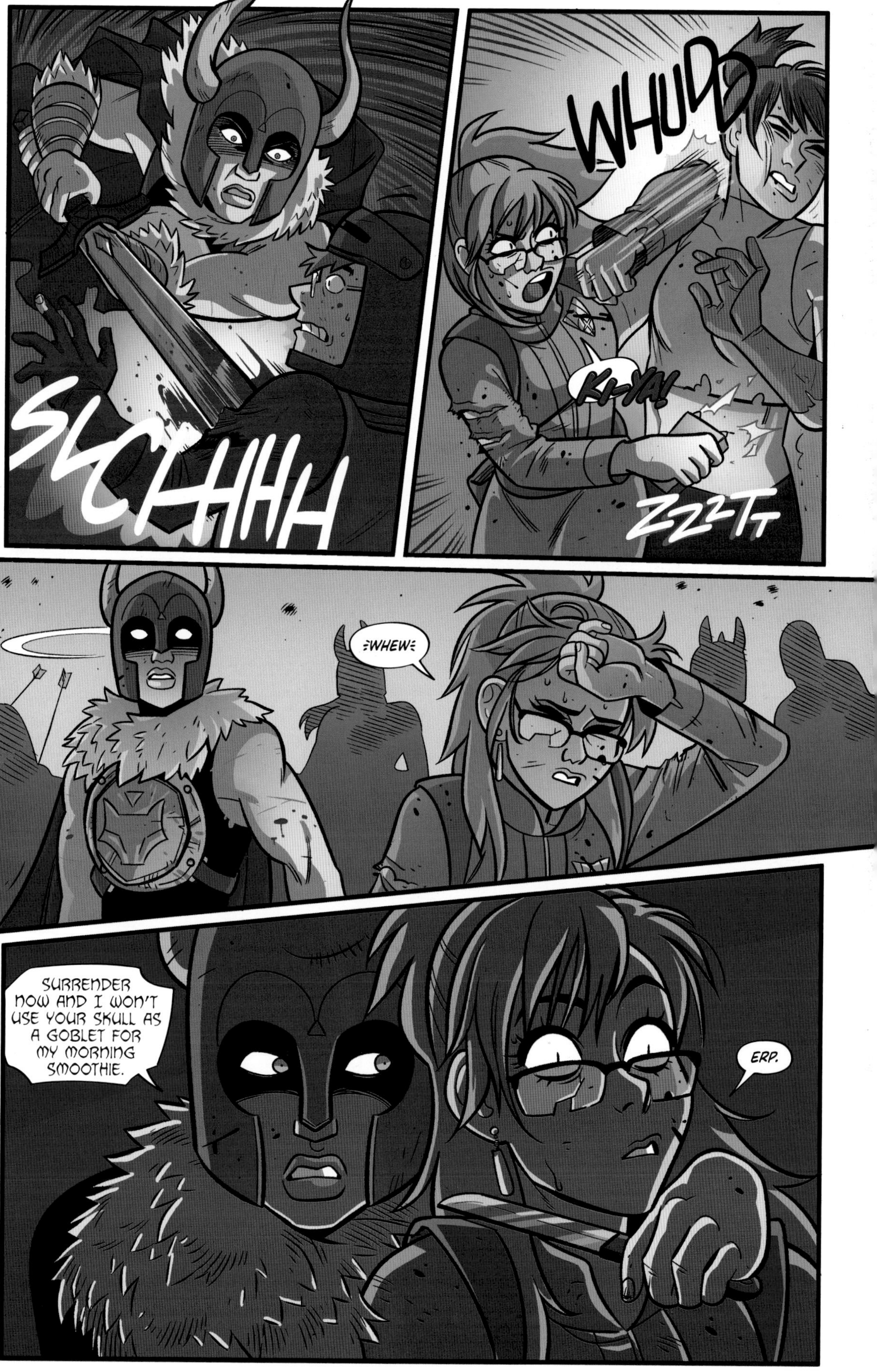
SLCHHHH
WHUDD
KI-YA!
ZZZTT
WHEW
SURRENDER NOW AND I WON'T USE YOUR SKULL AS A GOBLET FOR MY MORNING SMOOTHIE.
ERP.

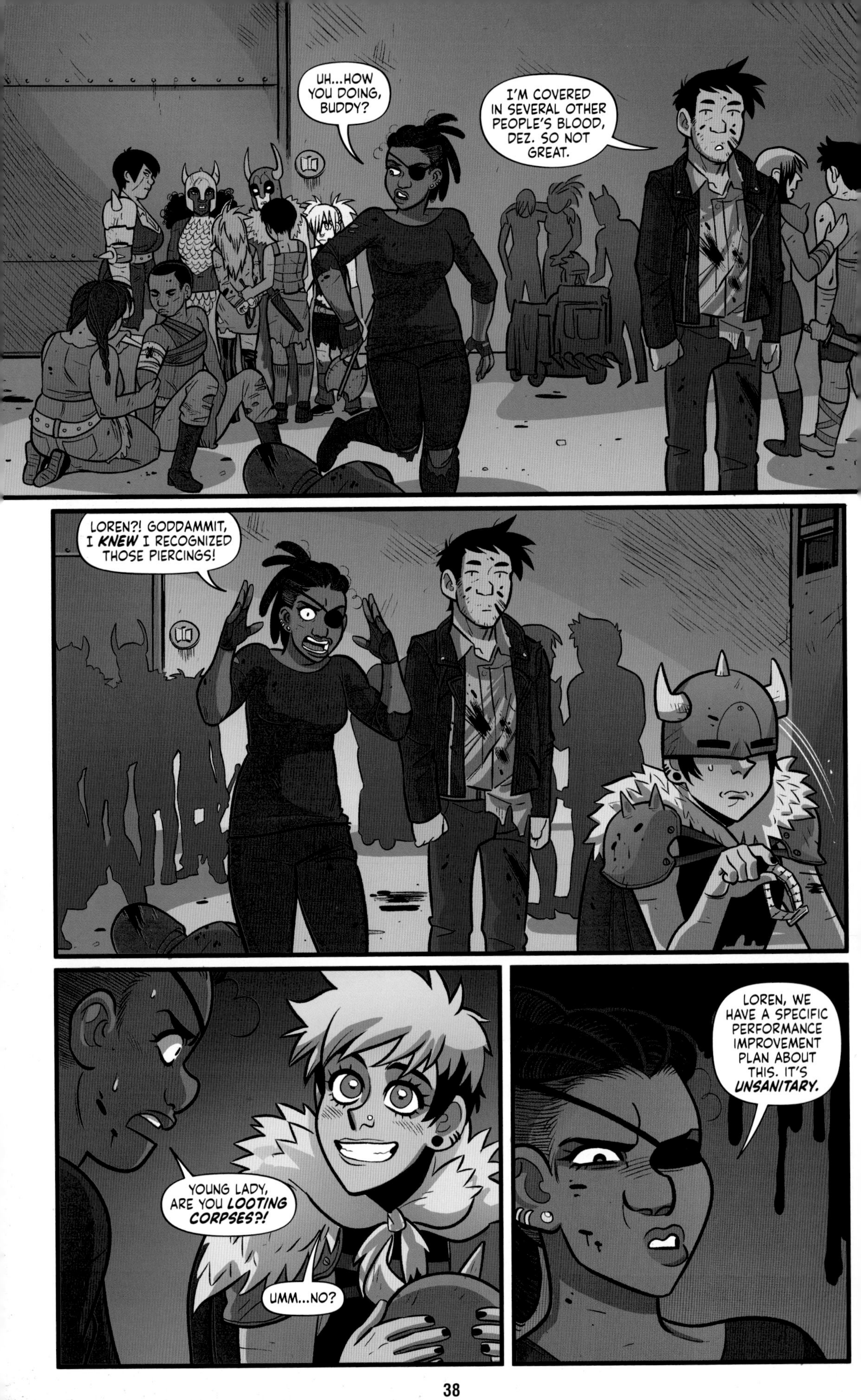
UH...HOW YOU DOING, BUDDY?
I'M COVERED IN SEVERAL OTHER PEOPLE'S BLOOD, DEZ. SO NOT GREAT.
LOREN?! GODDAMMIT, I KNEW I RECOGNIZED THOSE PIERCINGS!
YOUNG LADY, ARE YOU LOOTING CORPSES?!
UMM...NO?
LOREN, WE HAVE A SPECIFIC PERFORMANCE IMPROVEMENT PLAN ABOUT THIS. IT'S UNSANITARY.

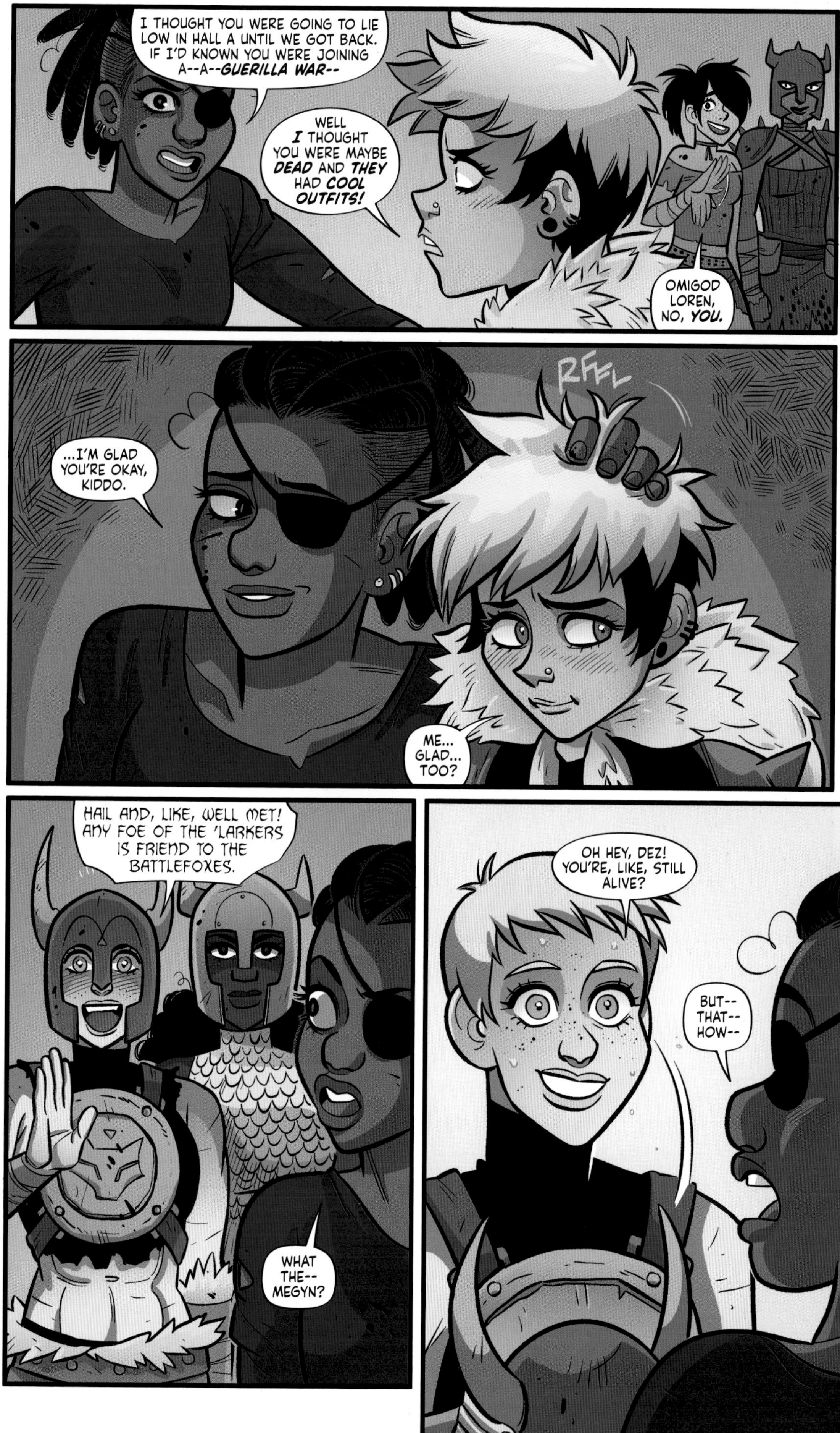
I THOUGHT YOU WERE GOING TO LIE LOW IN HALL A UNTIL WE GOT BACK. IF I'D KNOWN YOU WERE JOINING A--A--GUERILLA WAR--
WELL I THOUGHT YOU WERE MAYBE DEAD AND THEY HAD COOL OUTFITS!
OMIGOD LOREN, NO, YOU.
RFFL
...I'M GLAD YOU'RE OKAY, KIDDO.
ME... GLAD... TOO?
HAIL AND, LIKE, WELL MET! ANY FOE OF THE 'LARKERS IS FRIEND TO THE BATTLEFOXES.
WHAT THE-- MEGYN?
OH HEY, DEZ! YOU'RE, LIKE, STILL ALIVE?
BUT-- THAT-- HOW--

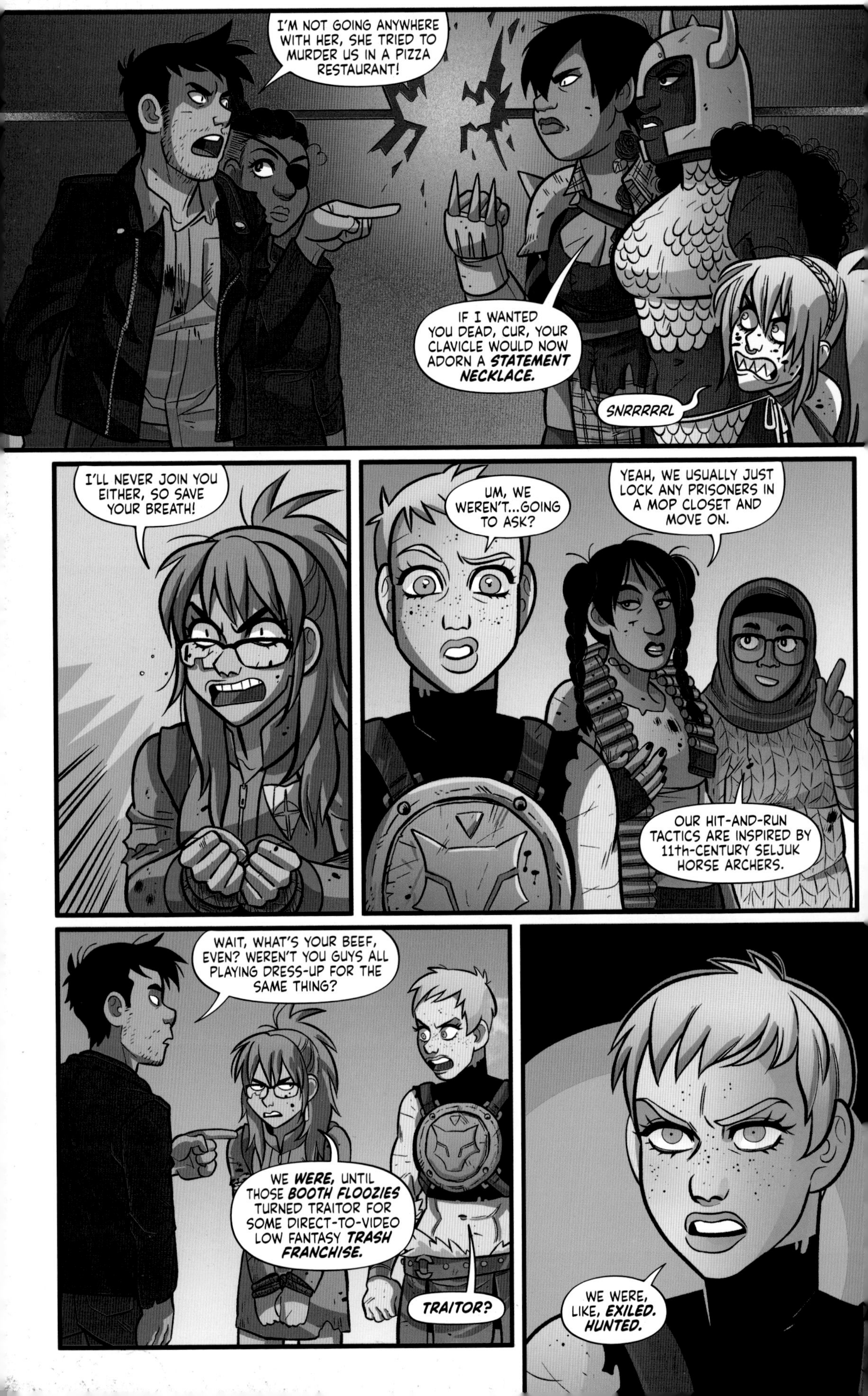
I'M NOT GOING ANYWHERE WITH HER, SHE TRIED TO MURDER US IN A PIZZA RESTAURANT!
IF I WANTED YOU DEAD, CUR, YOUR CLAVICLE WOULD NOW ADORN A STATEMENT NECKLACE.
SNRRRRRL
I'LL NEVER JOIN YOU EITHER, SO SAVE YOUR BREATH!
UM, WE WEREN'T...GOING TO ASK?
YEAH, WE USUALLY JUST LOCK ANY PRISONERS IN A MOP CLOSET AND MOVE ON.
OUR HIT-AND-RUN TACTICS ARE INSPIRED BY 11th-CENTURY SELJUK HORSE ARCHERS.
WAIT, WHAT'S YOUR BEEF, EVEN? WEREN'T YOU GUYS ALL PLAYING DRESS-UP FOR THE SAME THING?
WE WERE, UNTIL THOSE BOOTH FLOOZIES TURNED TRAITOR FOR SOME DIRECT-TO-VIDEO LOW FANTASY TRASH FRANCHISE.
TRAITOR?
WE WERE, LIKE, EXILED. HUNTED.

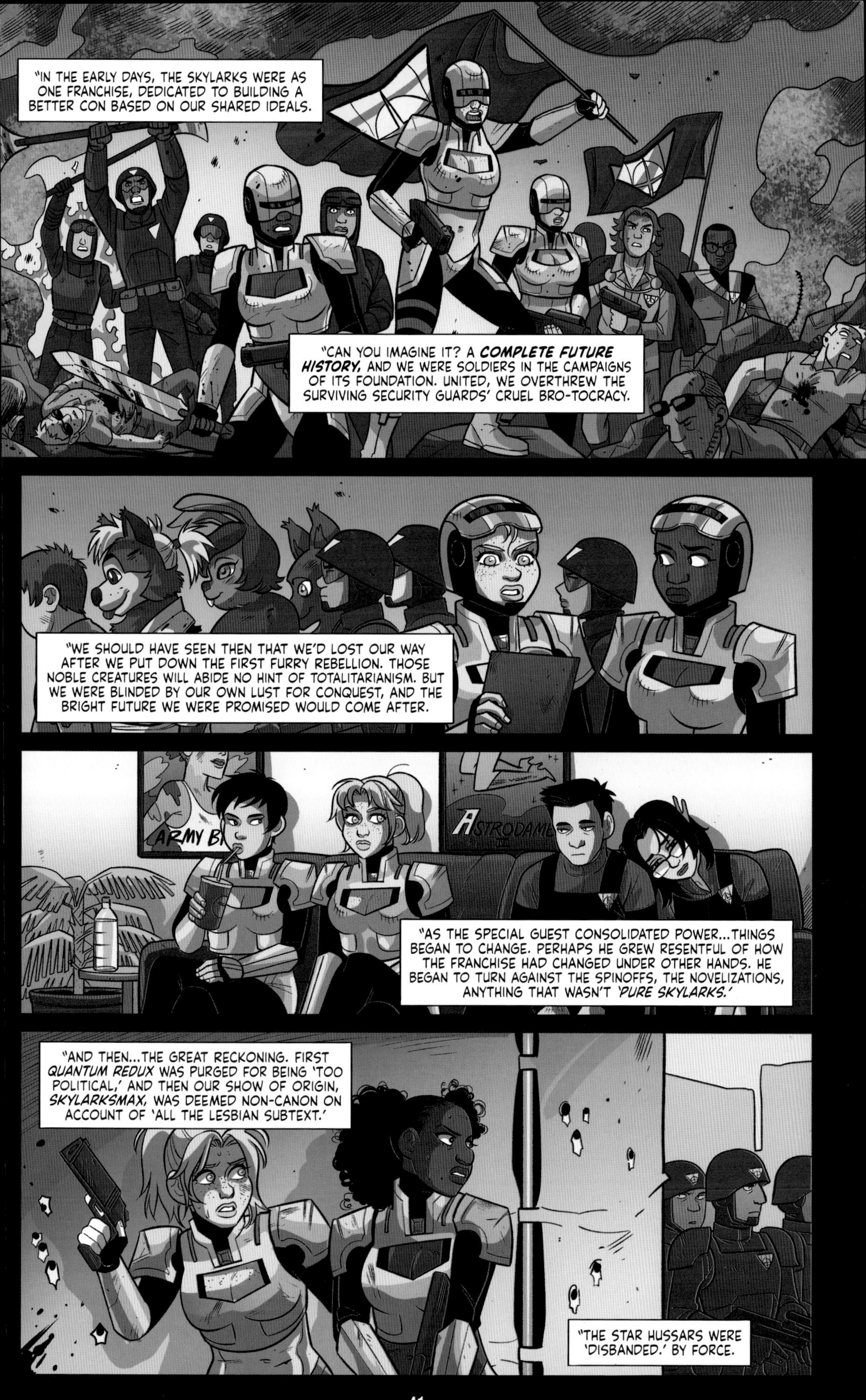
"IN THE EARLY DAYS, THE SKYLARKS WERE AS ONE FRANCHISE, DEDICATED TO BUILDING A BETTER CON BASED ON OUR SHARED IDEALS.
"CAN YOU IMAGINE IT? A **COMPLETE FUTURE HISTORY,** AND WE WERE SOLDIERS IN THE CAMPAIGNS OF ITS FOUNDATION. UNITED, WE OVERTHREW THE SURVIVING SECURITY GUARDS' CRUEL BRO-TOCRACY.
"WE SHOULD HAVE SEEN THEN THAT WE'D LOST OUR WAY AFTER WE PUT DOWN THE FIRST FURRY REBELLION. THOSE NOBLE CREATURES WILL ABIDE NO HINT OF TOTALITARIANISM. BUT WE WERE BLINDED BY OUR OWN LUST FOR CONQUEST, AND THE BRIGHT FUTURE WE WERE PROMISED WOULD COME AFTER.
"AS THE SPECIAL GUEST CONSOLIDATED POWER...THINGS BEGAN TO CHANGE. PERHAPS HE GREW RESENTFUL OF HOW THE FRANCHISE HAD CHANGED UNDER OTHER HANDS. HE BEGAN TO TURN AGAINST THE SPINOFFS, THE NOVELIZATIONS, ANYTHING THAT WASN'T *'PURE SKYLARKS.'*
"AND THEN...THE GREAT RECKONING. FIRST *QUANTUM REDUX* WAS PURGED FOR BEING 'TOO POLITICAL,' AND THEN OUR SHOW OF ORIGIN, *SKYLARKSMAX,* WAS DEEMED NON-CANON ON ACCOUNT OF 'ALL THE LESBIAN SUBTEXT.'
"THE STAR HUSSARS WERE 'DISBANDED.' BY FORCE.

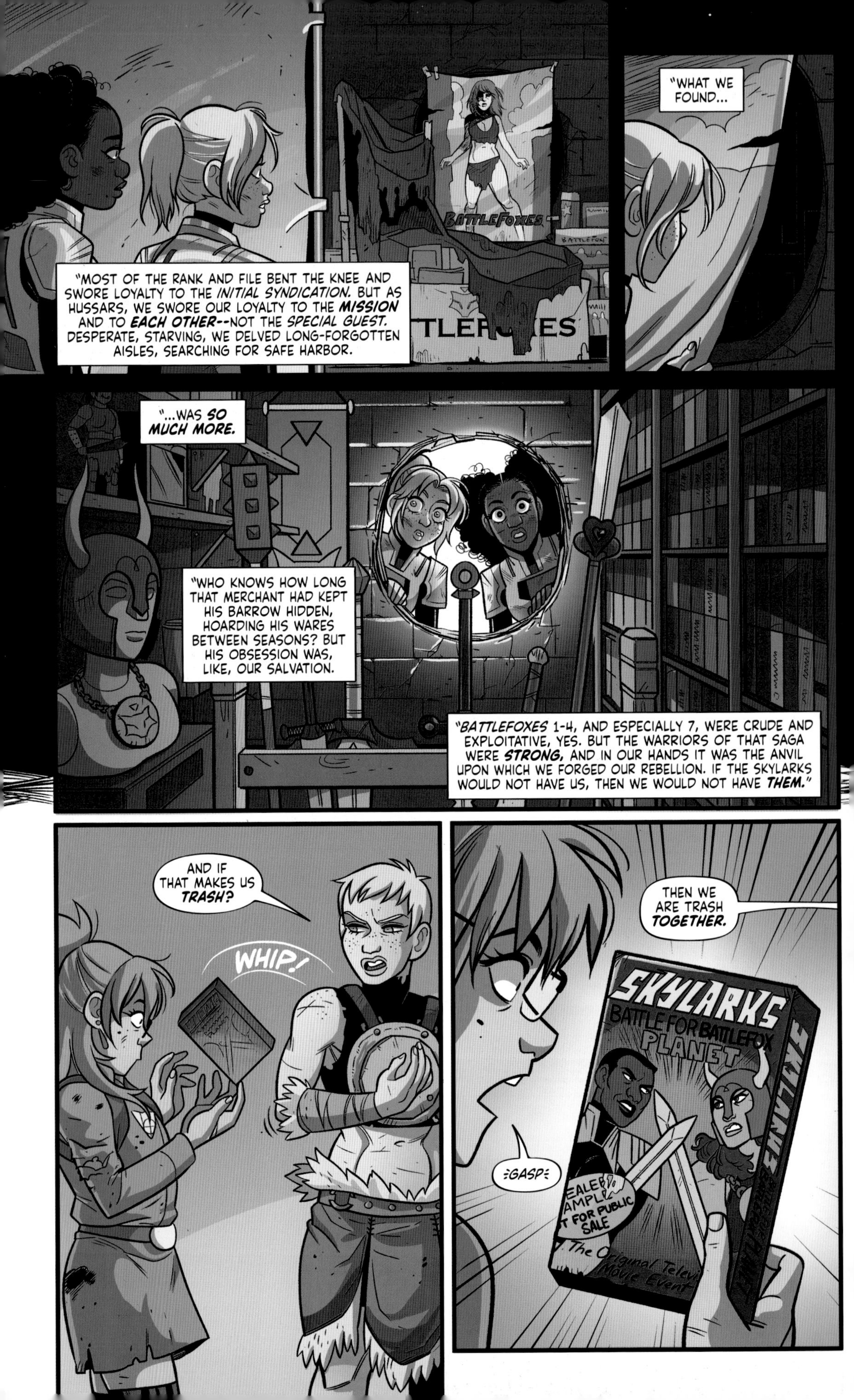
"MOST OF THE RANK AND FILE BENT THE KNEE AND SWORE LOYALTY TO THE INITIAL SYNDICATION. BUT AS HUSSARS, WE SWORE OUR LOYALTY TO THE MISSION AND TO EACH OTHER--NOT THE SPECIAL GUEST. DESPERATE, STARVING, WE DELVED LONG-FORGOTTEN AISLES, SEARCHING FOR SAFE HARBOR.
BATTLEFOXES
"WHAT WE FOUND...
"...WAS SO MUCH MORE.
"WHO KNOWS HOW LONG THAT MERCHANT HAD KEPT HIS BARROW HIDDEN, HOARDING HIS WARES BETWEEN SEASONS? BUT HIS OBSESSION WAS, LIKE, OUR SALVATION.
"BATTLEFOXES 1-4, AND ESPECIALLY 7, WERE CRUDE AND EXPLOITATIVE, YES. BUT THE WARRIORS OF THAT SAGA WERE STRONG, AND IN OUR HANDS IT WAS THE ANVIL UPON WHICH WE FORGED OUR REBELLION. IF THE SKYLARKS WOULD NOT HAVE US, THEN WE WOULD NOT HAVE THEM."
AND IF THAT MAKES US TRASH?
WHIP!
THEN WE ARE TRASH TOGETHER.
SKYLARKS
BATTLE FOR BATTLEFOX PLANET
SALE
The Original Televi
Movie Event
=GASP=

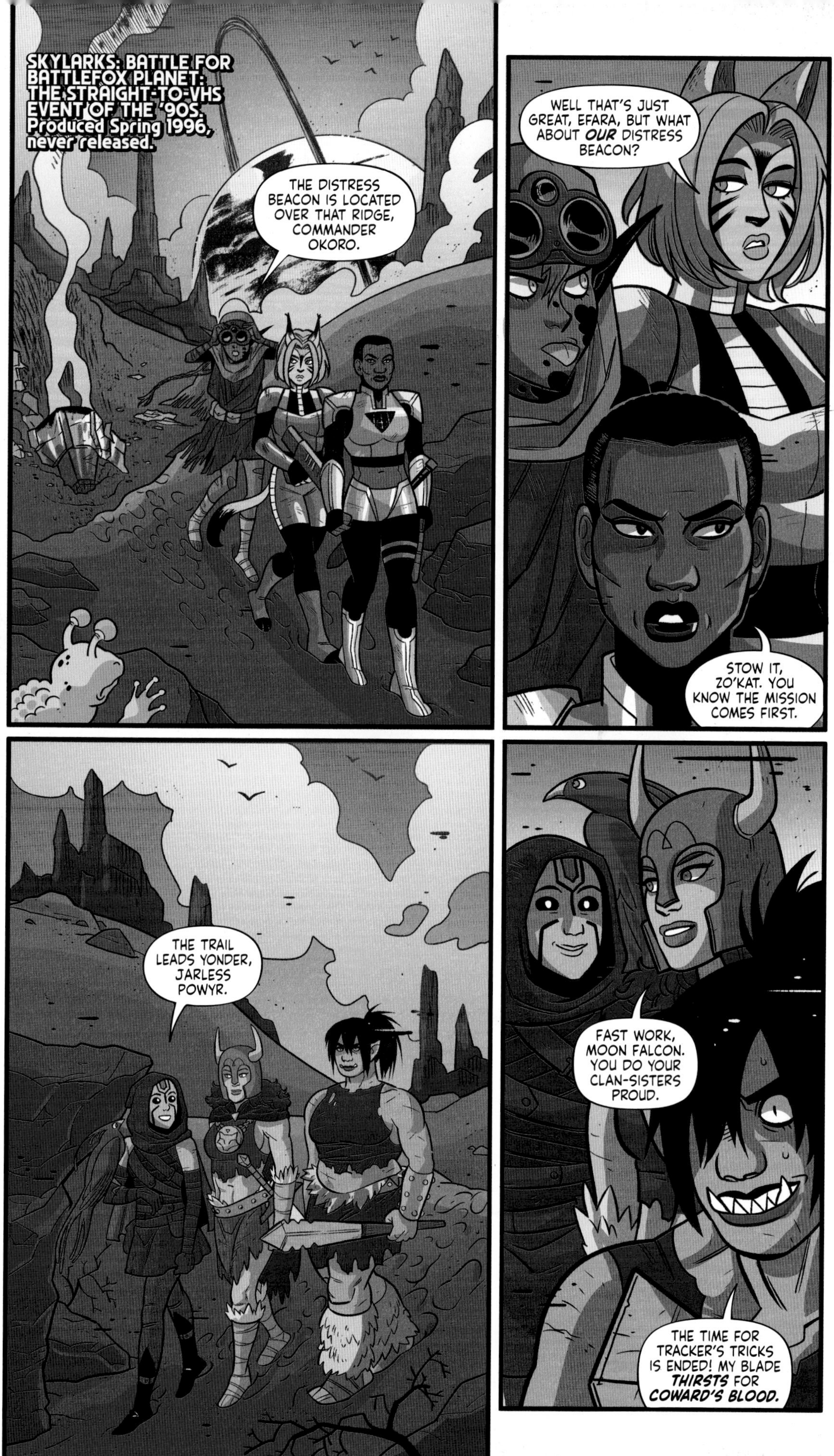
SKYLARKS: BATTLE FOR BATTLEFOX PLANET: THE STRAIGHT-TO-VHS EVENT OF THE '90S. Produced Spring 1996, never released.
THE DISTRESS BEACON IS LOCATED OVER THAT RIDGE, COMMANDER OKORO.
WELL THAT'S JUST GREAT, EFARA, BUT WHAT ABOUT *OUR* DISTRESS BEACON?
STOW IT, ZO'KAT. YOU KNOW THE MISSION COMES FIRST.
THE TRAIL LEADS YONDER, JARLESS POWYR.
FAST WORK, MOON FALCON. YOU DO YOUR CLAN-SISTERS PROUD.
THE TIME FOR TRACKER'S TRICKS IS ENDED! MY BLADE *THIRSTS* FOR *COWARD'S BLOOD.*

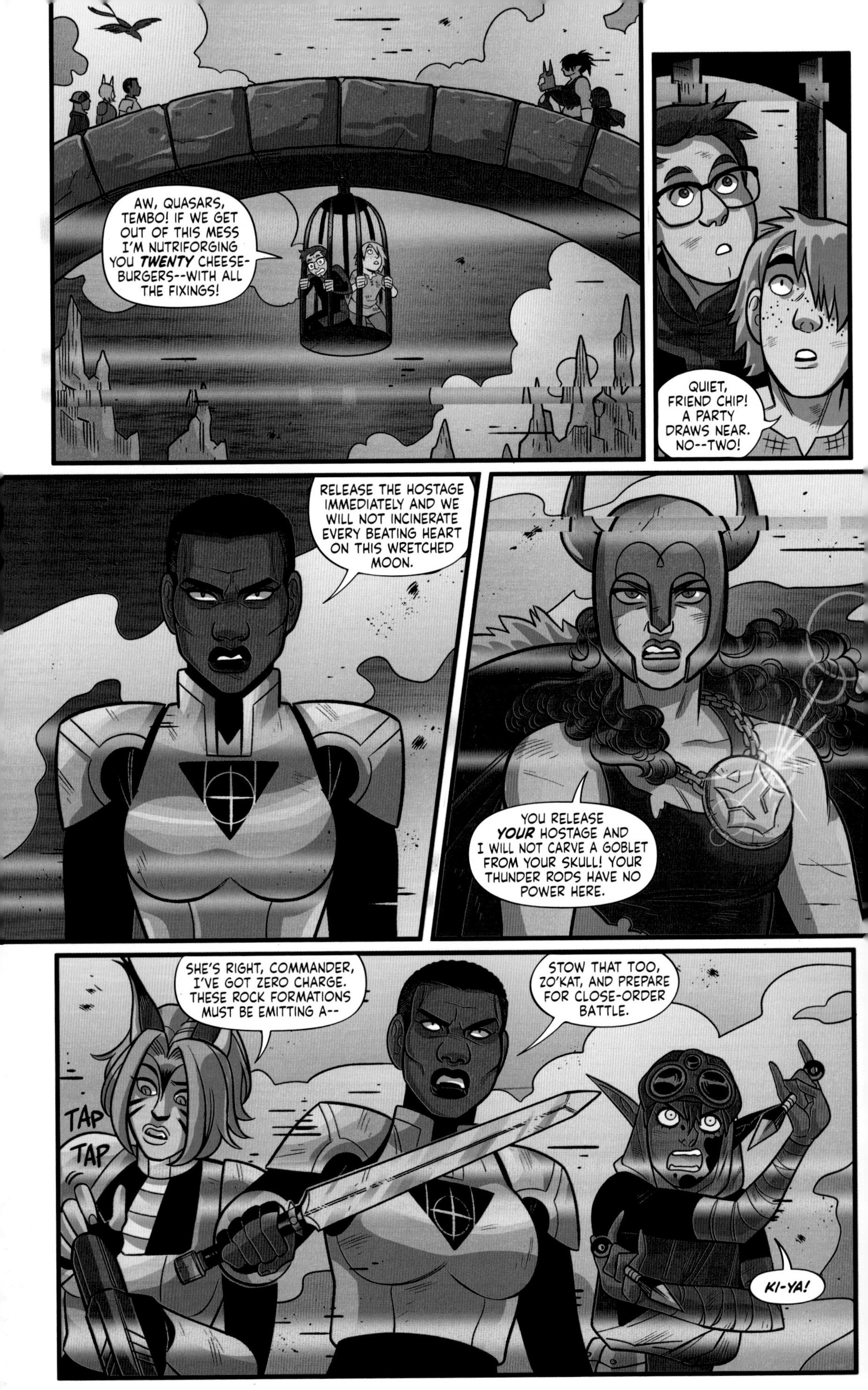
AW, QUASARS, TEMBO! IF WE GET OUT OF THIS MESS I'M NUTRIFORGING YOU *TWENTY* CHEESE-BURGERS--WITH ALL THE FIXINGS!
QUIET, FRIEND CHIP! A PARTY DRAWS NEAR. NO--TWO!
RELEASE THE HOSTAGE IMMEDIATELY AND WE WILL NOT INCINERATE EVERY BEATING HEART ON THIS WRETCHED MOON.
YOU RELEASE *YOUR* HOSTAGE AND I WILL NOT CARVE A GOBLET FROM YOUR SKULL! YOUR THUNDER RODS HAVE NO POWER HERE.
SHE'S RIGHT, COMMANDER, I'VE GOT ZERO CHARGE. THESE ROCK FORMATIONS MUST BE EMITTING A--
TAP
TAP
STOW THAT TOO, ZO'KAT, AND PREPARE FOR CLOSE-ORDER BATTLE.
KI-YA!

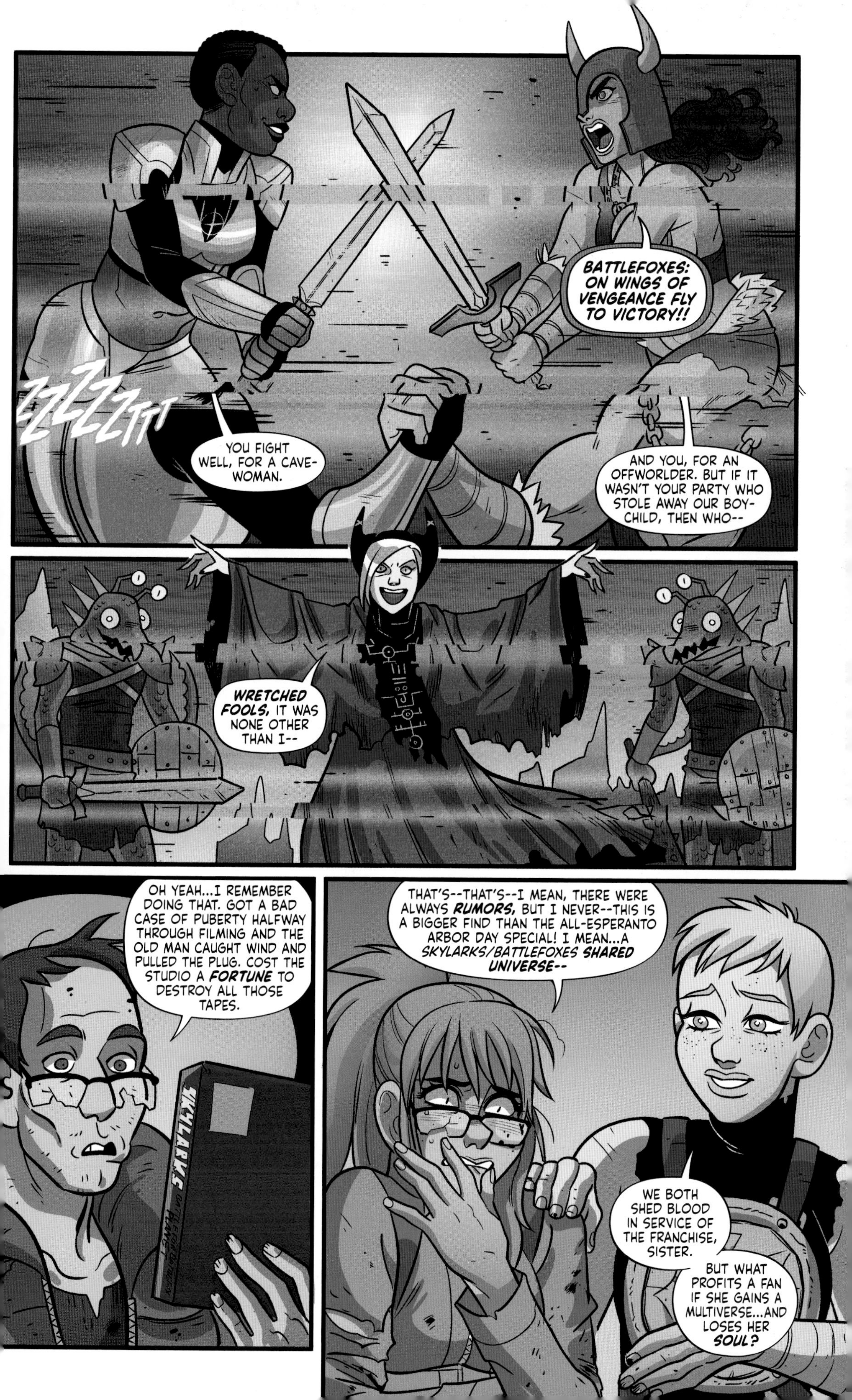
BATTLEFOXES: ON WINGS OF VENGEANCE FLY TO VICTORY!!
ZZZZZTTT
YOU FIGHT WELL, FOR A CAVE-WOMAN.
AND YOU, FOR AN OFFWORLDER. BUT IF IT WASN'T YOUR PARTY WHO STOLE AWAY OUR BOY-CHILD, THEN WHO--
WRETCHED FOOLS, IT WAS NONE OTHER THAN I--
OH YEAH...I REMEMBER DOING THAT. GOT A BAD CASE OF PUBERTY HALFWAY THROUGH FILMING AND THE OLD MAN CAUGHT WIND AND PULLED THE PLUG. COST THE STUDIO A FORTUNE TO DESTROY ALL THOSE TAPES.
SKYLARKS
THAT'S--THAT'S--I MEAN, THERE WERE ALWAYS RUMORS, BUT I NEVER--THIS IS A BIGGER FIND THAN THE ALL-ESPERANTO ARBOR DAY SPECIAL! I MEAN...A SKYLARKS/BATTLEFOXES SHARED UNIVERSE--
WE BOTH SHED BLOOD IN SERVICE OF THE FRANCHISE, SISTER.
BUT WHAT PROFITS A FAN IF SHE GAINS A MULTIVERSE...AND LOSES HER SOUL?

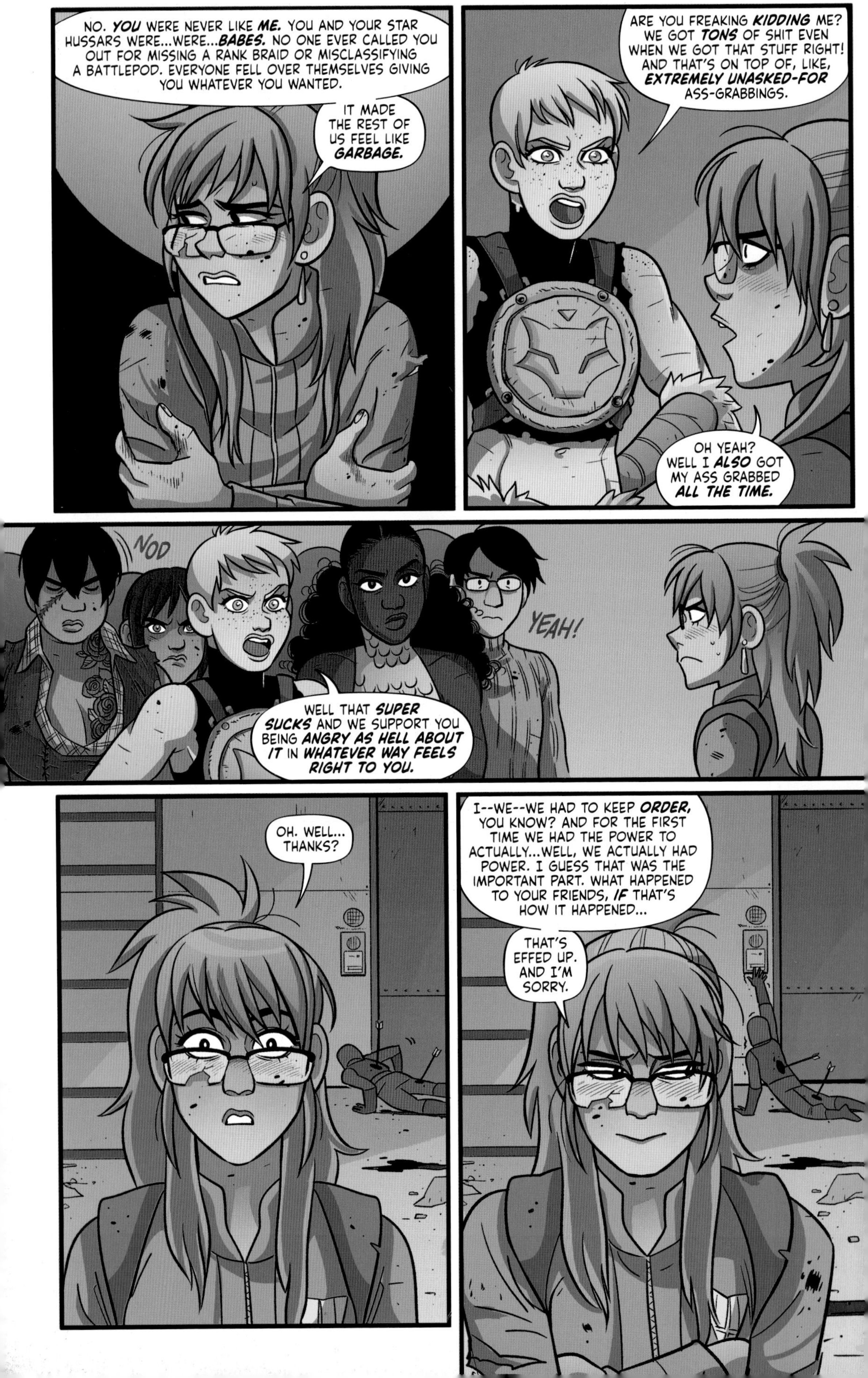
NO. YOU WERE NEVER LIKE ME. YOU AND YOUR STAR HUSSARS WERE...WERE...BABES. NO ONE EVER CALLED YOU OUT FOR MISSING A RANK BRAID OR MISCLASSIFYING A BATTLEPOD. EVERYONE FELL OVER THEMSELVES GIVING YOU WHATEVER YOU WANTED.
IT MADE THE REST OF US FEEL LIKE GARBAGE.
ARE YOU FREAKING KIDDING ME? WE GOT TONS OF SHIT EVEN WHEN WE GOT THAT STUFF RIGHT! AND THAT'S ON TOP OF, LIKE, EXTREMELY UNASKED-FOR ASS-GRABBINGS.
OH YEAH? WELL I ALSO GOT MY ASS GRABBED ALL THE TIME.
NOD
YEAH!
WELL THAT SUPER SUCKS AND WE SUPPORT YOU BEING ANGRY AS HELL ABOUT IT IN WHATEVER WAY FEELS RIGHT TO YOU.
OH. WELL... THANKS?
I--WE--WE HAD TO KEEP ORDER, YOU KNOW? AND FOR THE FIRST TIME WE HAD THE POWER TO ACTUALLY...WELL, WE ACTUALLY HAD POWER. I GUESS THAT WAS THE IMPORTANT PART. WHAT HAPPENED TO YOUR FRIENDS, IF THAT'S HOW IT HAPPENED...
THAT'S EFFED UP. AND I'M SORRY.

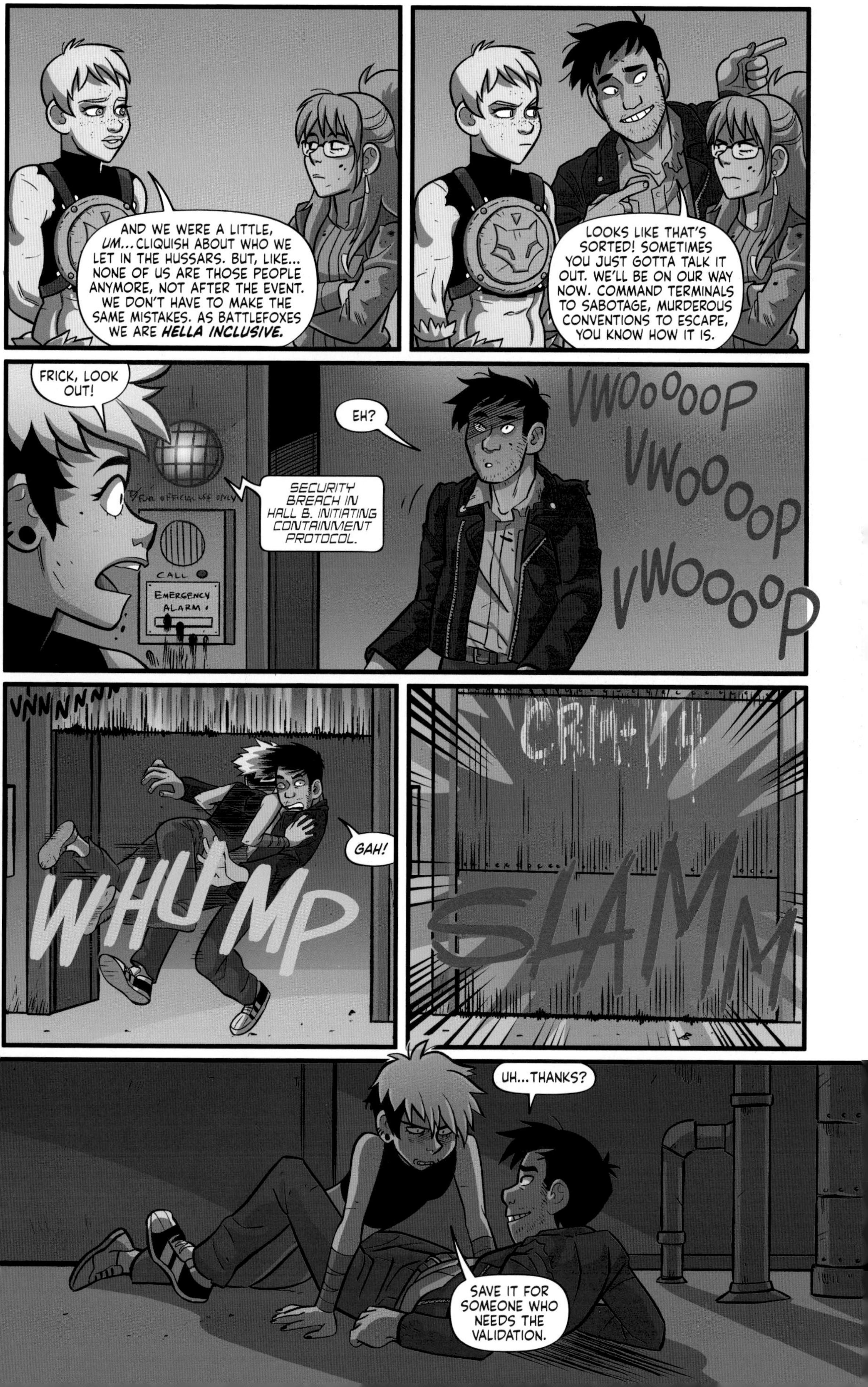
AND WE WERE A LITTLE, UM...CLIQUISH ABOUT WHO WE LET IN THE HUSSARS. BUT, LIKE... NONE OF US ARE THOSE PEOPLE ANYMORE, NOT AFTER THE EVENT. WE DON'T HAVE TO MAKE THE SAME MISTAKES. AS BATTLEFOXES WE ARE HELLA INCLUSIVE.
LOOKS LIKE THAT'S SORTED! SOMETIMES YOU JUST GOTTA TALK IT OUT. WE'LL BE ON OUR WAY NOW. COMMAND TERMINALS TO SABOTAGE, MURDEROUS CONVENTIONS TO ESCAPE, YOU KNOW HOW IT IS.
FRICK, LOOK OUT!
EH?
FOR OFFICIAL USE ONLY
CALL
EMERGENCY ALARM
SECURITY BREACH IN HALL B. INITIATING CONTAINMENT PROTOCOL.
VWOOOOOP
VWOOOOOP
VWOOOOP
VNNNNNN
GAH!
WHUMP
SLAMM
UH...THANKS?
SAVE IT FOR SOMEONE WHO NEEDS THE VALIDATION.

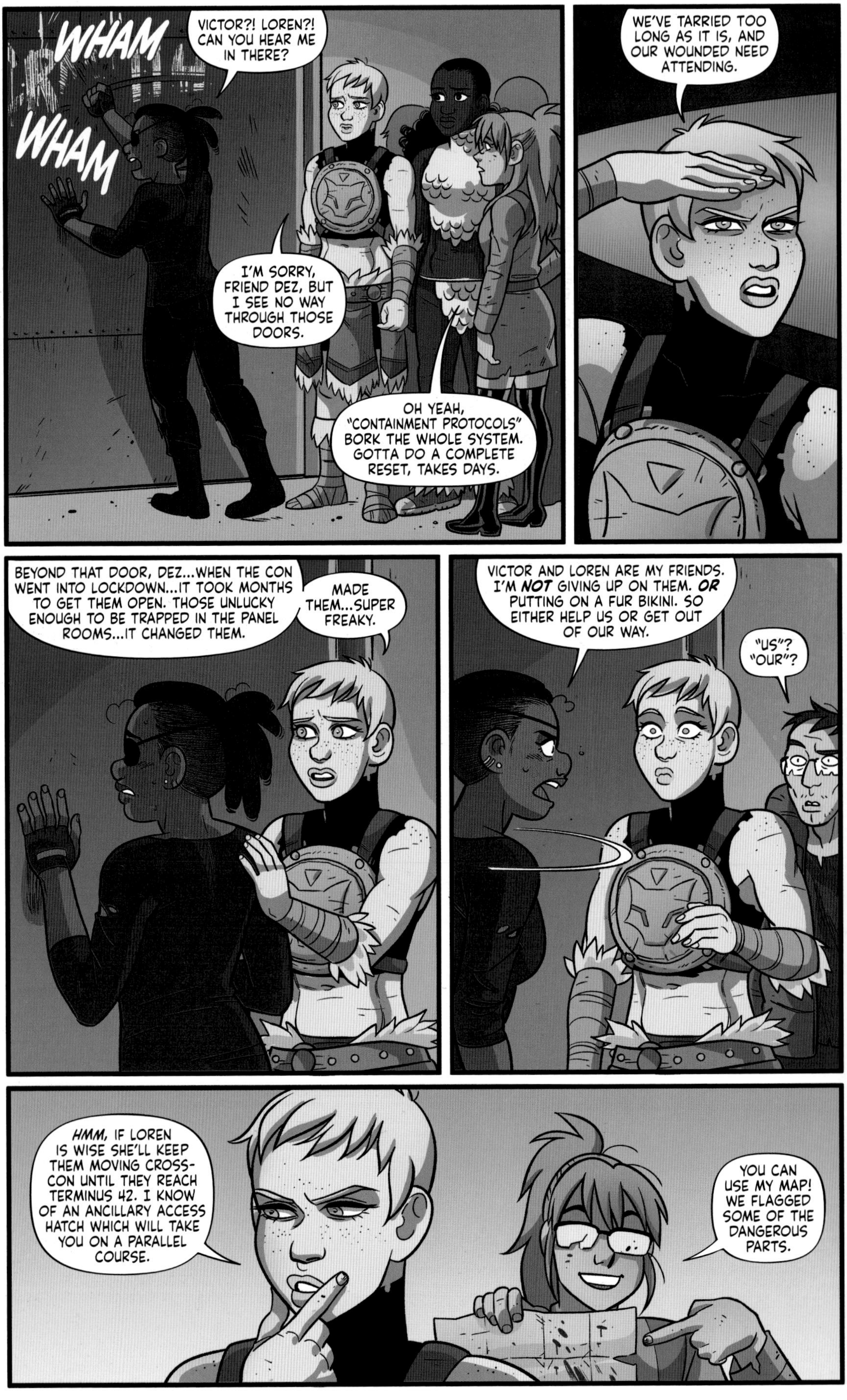
WHAM
WHAM
VICTOR?! LOREN?! CAN YOU HEAR ME IN THERE?
I'M SORRY, FRIEND DEZ, BUT I SEE NO WAY THROUGH THOSE DOORS.
OH YEAH, "CONTAINMENT PROTOCOLS" BORK THE WHOLE SYSTEM. GOTTA DO A COMPLETE RESET, TAKES DAYS.
WE'VE TARRIED TOO LONG AS IT IS, AND OUR WOUNDED NEED ATTENDING.
BEYOND THAT DOOR, DEZ...WHEN THE CON WENT INTO LOCKDOWN...IT TOOK MONTHS TO GET THEM OPEN. THOSE UNLUCKY ENOUGH TO BE TRAPPED IN THE PANEL ROOMS...IT CHANGED THEM.
MADE THEM...SUPER FREAKY.
VICTOR AND LOREN ARE MY FRIENDS. I'M ***NOT*** GIVING UP ON THEM. ***OR*** PUTTING ON A FUR BIKINI. SO EITHER HELP US OR GET OUT OF OUR WAY.
"US"? "OUR"?
HMM, IF LOREN IS WISE SHE'LL KEEP THEM MOVING CROSS-CON UNTIL THEY REACH TERMINUS 42. I KNOW OF AN ANCILLARY ACCESS HATCH WHICH WILL TAKE YOU ON A PARALLEL COURSE.
YOU CAN USE MY MAP! WE FLAGGED SOME OF THE DANGEROUS PARTS.

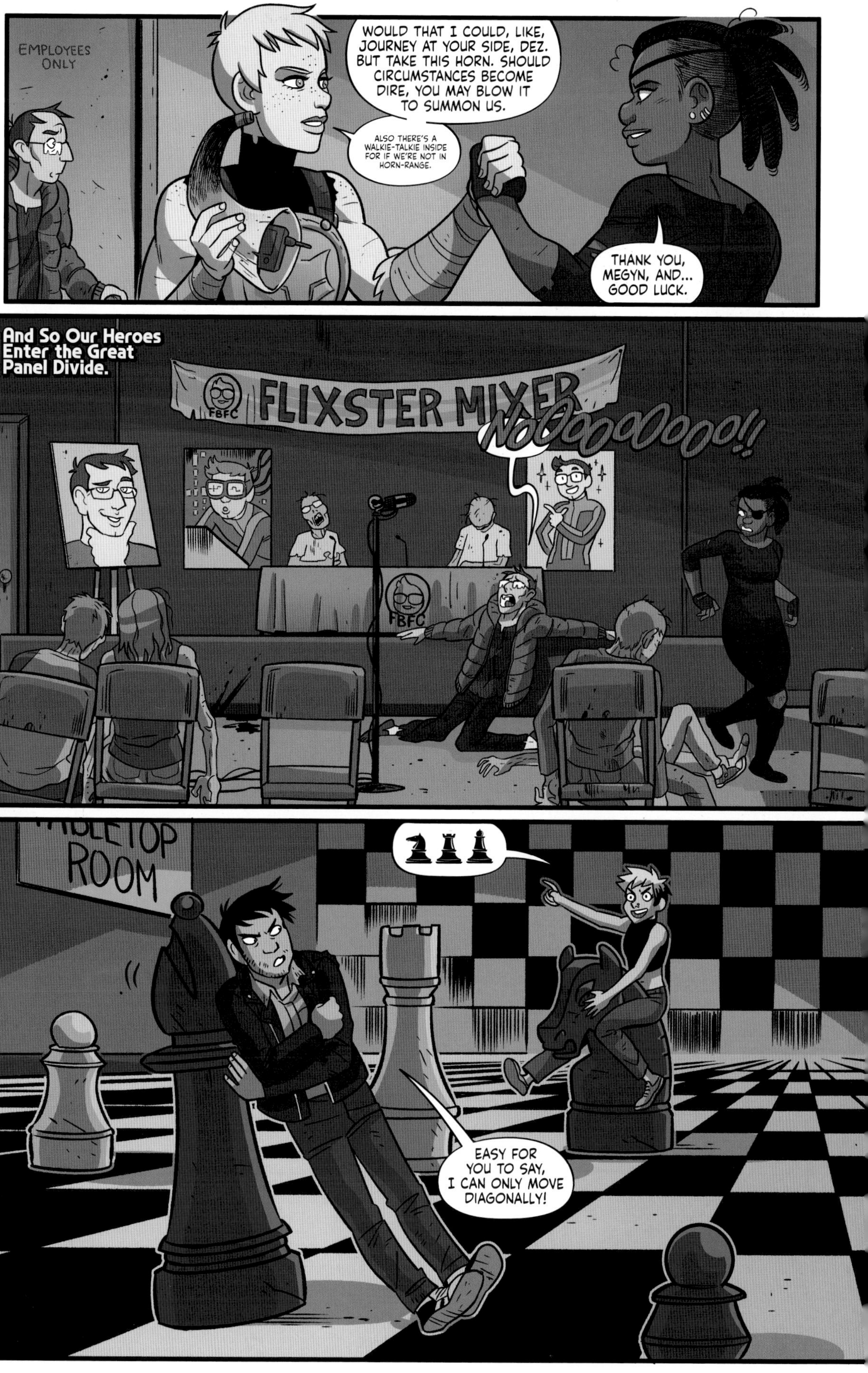
EMPLOYEES ONLY
WOULD THAT I COULD, LIKE, JOURNEY AT YOUR SIDE, DEZ. BUT TAKE THIS HORN. SHOULD CIRCUMSTANCES BECOME DIRE, YOU MAY BLOW IT TO SUMMON US.
ALSO THERE'S A WALKIE-TALKIE INSIDE FOR IF WE'RE NOT IN HORN-RANGE.
THANK YOU, MEGYN, AND... GOOD LUCK.
And So Our Heroes Enter the Great Panel Divide.
FBFC FLIXSTER MIXER
NOOOOOOOOOO!!
FBFC
ROOM
EASY FOR YOU TO SAY, I CAN ONLY MOVE DIAGONALLY!

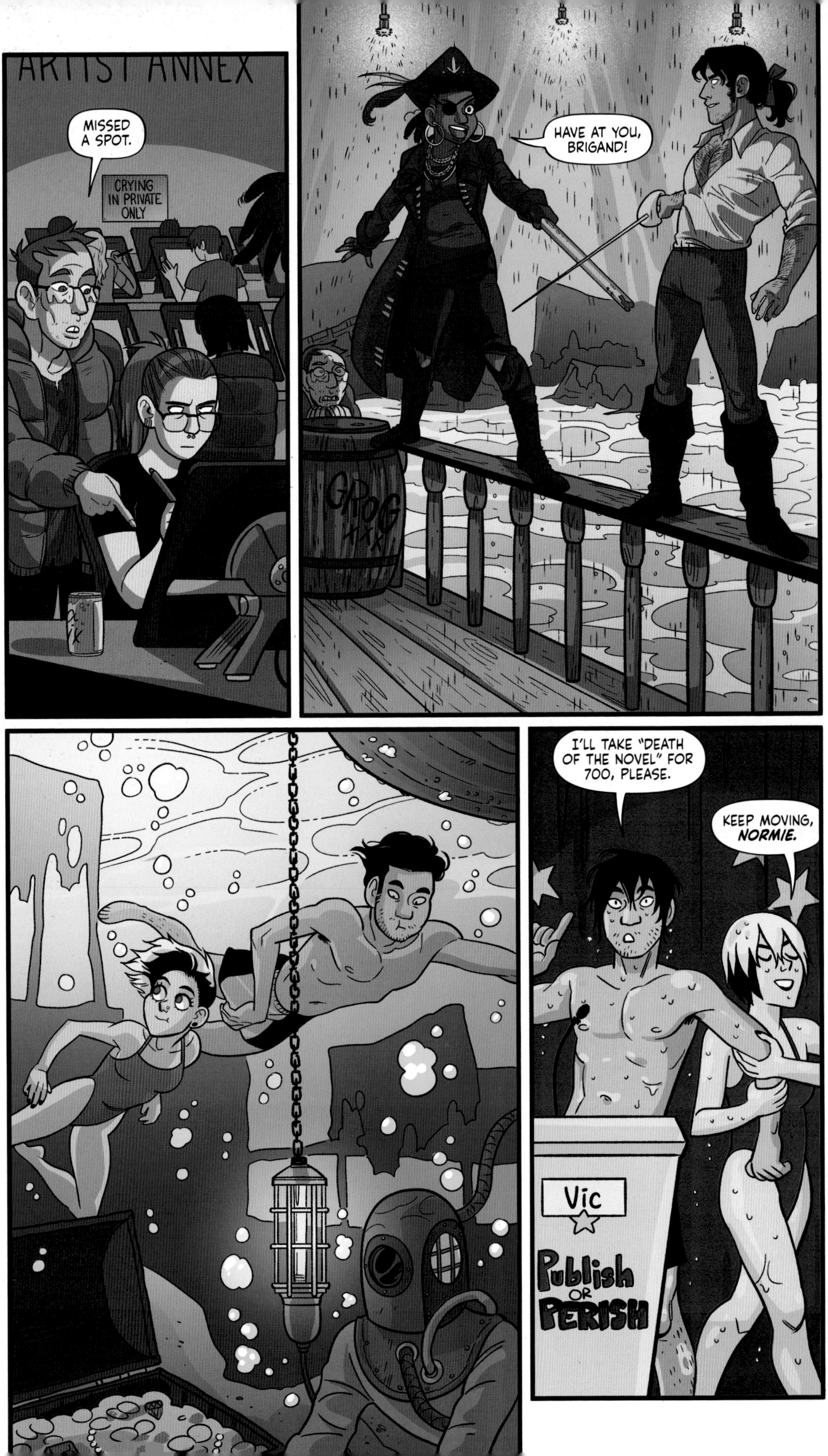
ARTIST ANNEX
MISSED A SPOT.
CRYING IN PRIVATE ONLY
HAVE AT YOU, BRIGAND!
GROG
XXX
I'LL TAKE "DEATH OF THE NOVEL" FOR 700, PLEASE.
KEEP MOVING, ***NORMIE.***
Vic
Publish OR PERISH

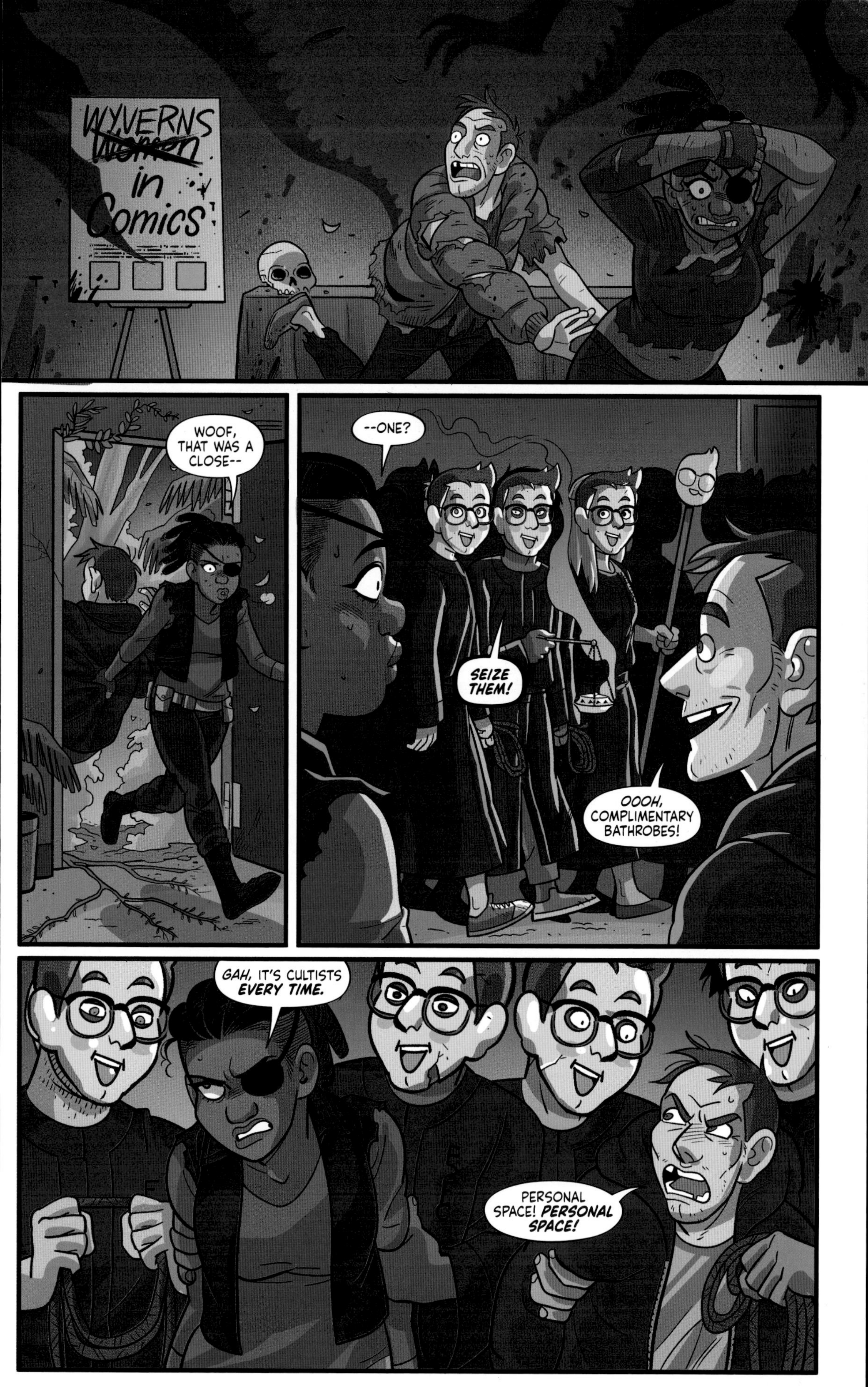
WYVERNS
Women
in
Comics
WOOF, THAT WAS A CLOSE--
--ONE?
SEIZE THEM!
OOOH, COMPLIMENTARY BATHROBES!
GAH, IT'S CULTISTS EVERY TIME.
PERSONAL SPACE! PERSONAL SPACE!

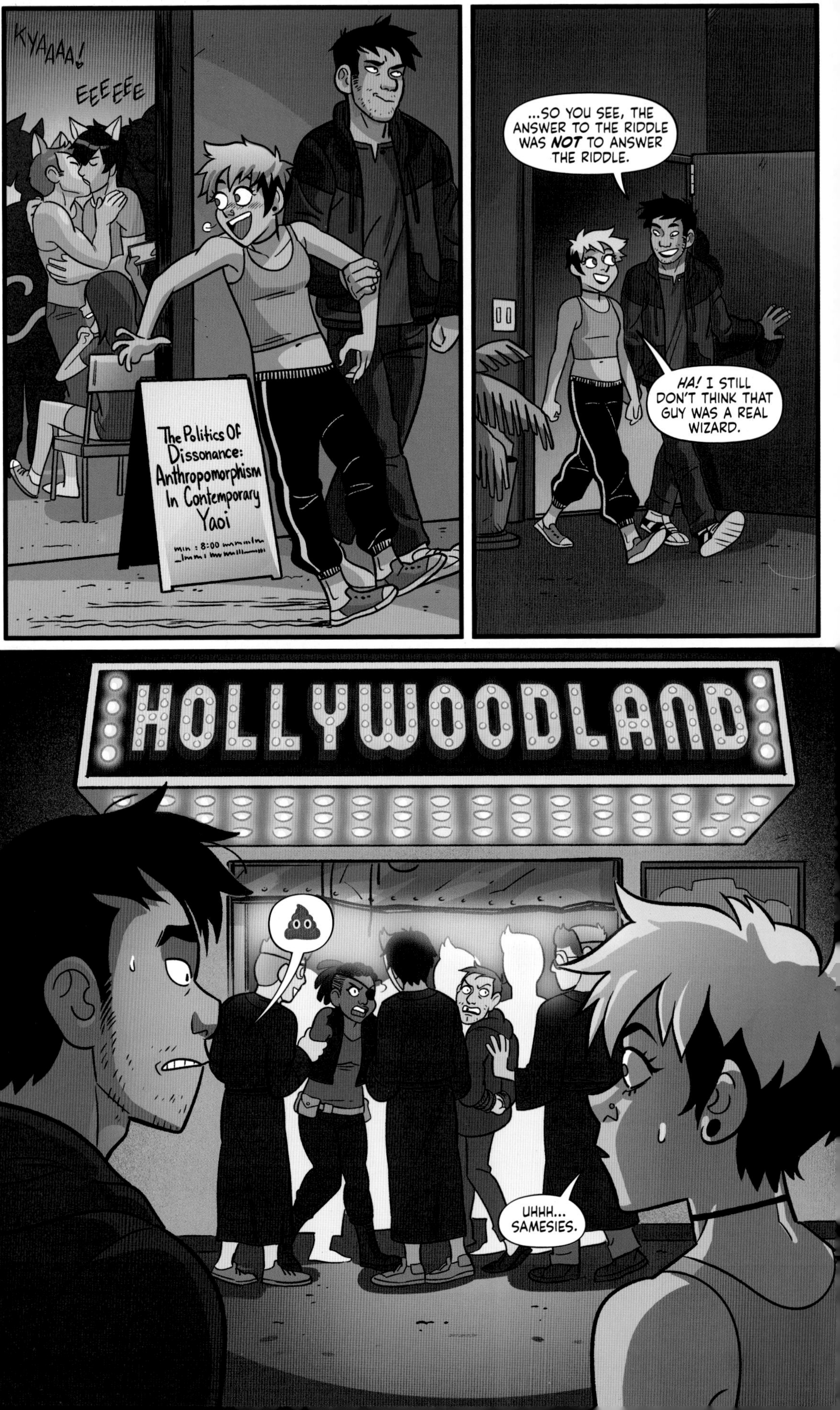
KYAAAA!
EEEEEE
The Politics Of Dissonance: Anthropomorphism In Contemporary Yaoi
...SO YOU SEE, THE ANSWER TO THE RIDDLE WAS NOT TO ANSWER THE RIDDLE.
HA! I STILL DON'T THINK THAT GUY WAS A REAL WIZARD.
HOLLYWOODLAND
UHHH... SAMESIES.

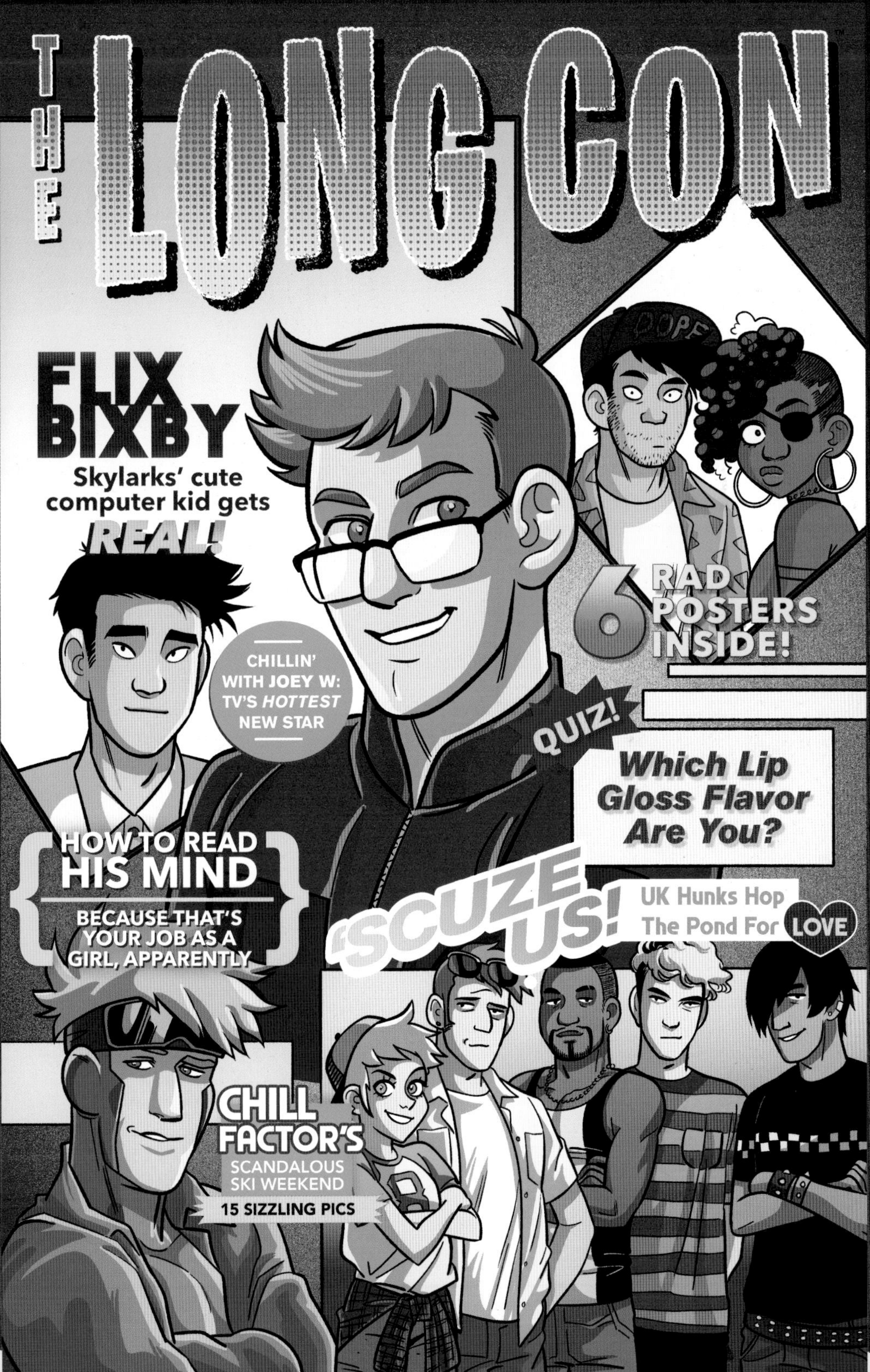
THE LONG CON
FLIX BIXBY
Skylarks' cute computer kid gets REAL!
CHILLIN' WITH JOEY W: TV'S HOTTEST NEW STAR
6 RAD POSTERS INSIDE!
QUIZ!
Which Lip Gloss Flavor Are You?
HOW TO READ HIS MIND
BECAUSE THAT'S YOUR JOB AS A GIRL, APPARENTLY
'SCUZE US!
UK Hunks Hop The Pond For LOVE
CHILL FACTOR'S
SCANDALOUS SKI WEEKEND
15 SIZZLING PICS
DOPE

CHAPTER 8: CHECKMATE

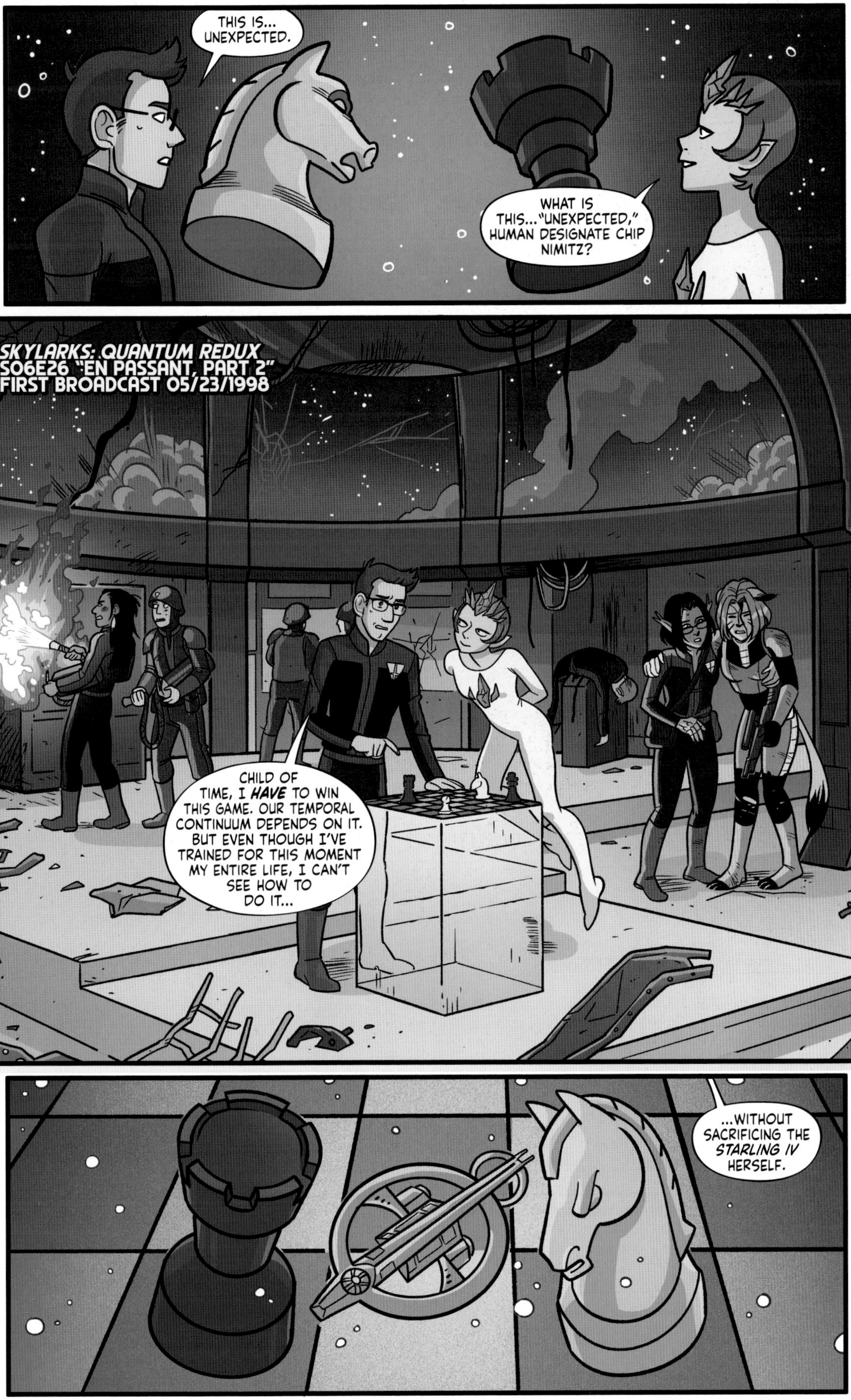
THIS IS... UNEXPECTED.
WHAT IS THIS..."UNEXPECTED," HUMAN DESIGNATE CHIP NIMITZ?
SKYLARKS: QUANTUM REDUX
S06E26 "EN PASSANT, PART 2"
FIRST BROADCAST 05/23/1998
CHILD OF TIME, I *HAVE* TO WIN THIS GAME. OUR TEMPORAL CONTINUUM DEPENDS ON IT. BUT EVEN THOUGH I'VE TRAINED FOR THIS MOMENT MY ENTIRE LIFE, I CAN'T SEE HOW TO DO IT...
...WITHOUT SACRIFICING THE *STARLING IV* HERSELF.

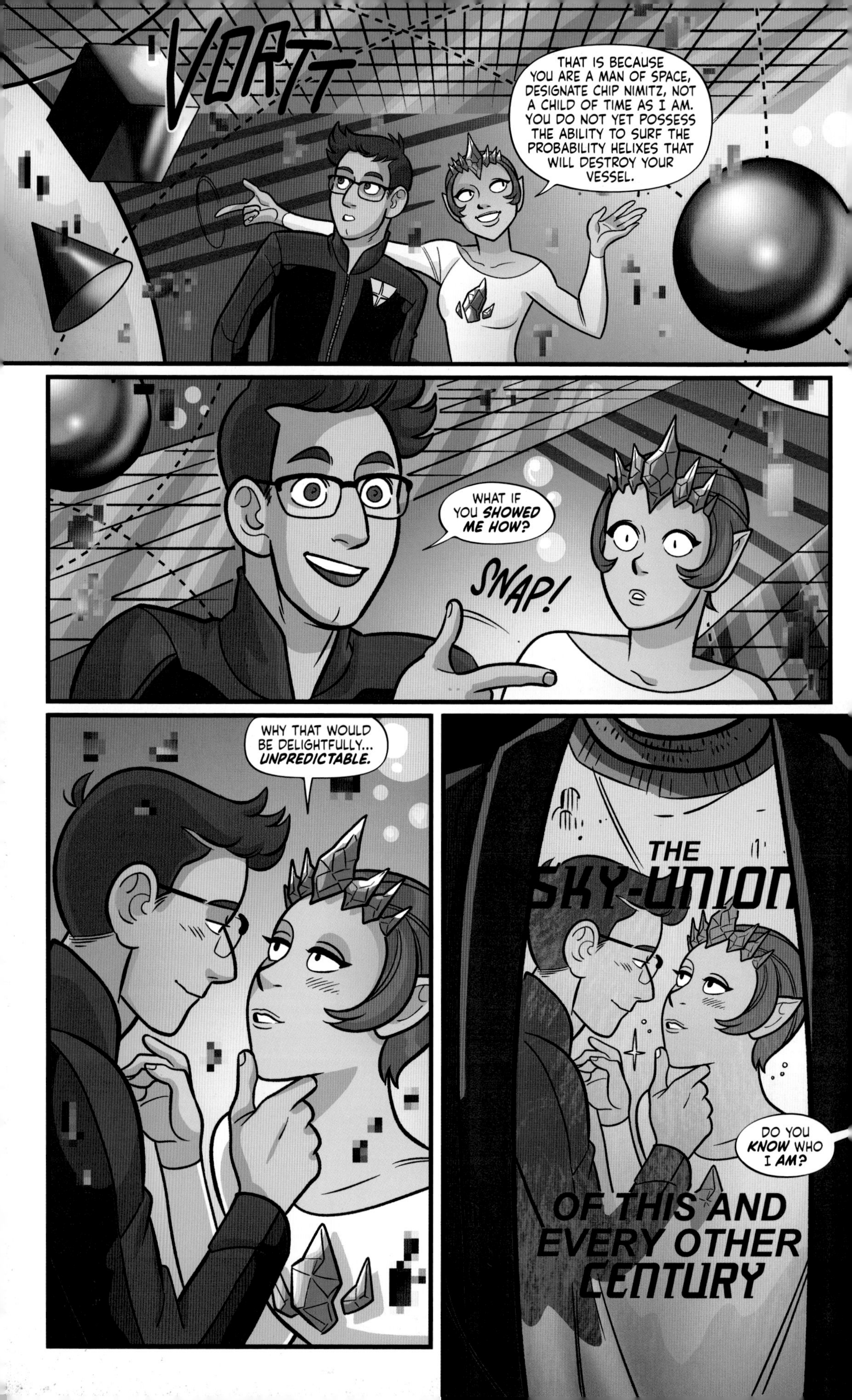
VORTT
THAT IS BECAUSE YOU ARE A MAN OF SPACE, DESIGNATE CHIP NIMITZ, NOT A CHILD OF TIME AS I AM. YOU DO NOT YET POSSESS THE ABILITY TO SURF THE PROBABILITY HELIXES THAT WILL DESTROY YOUR VESSEL.
WHAT IF YOU **SHOWED ME HOW?**
SNAP!
WHY THAT WOULD BE DELIGHTFULLY... **UNPREDICTABLE.**
THE SKY-UNION
DO YOU **KNOW** WHO I **AM?**
OF THIS AND EVERY OTHER CENTURY

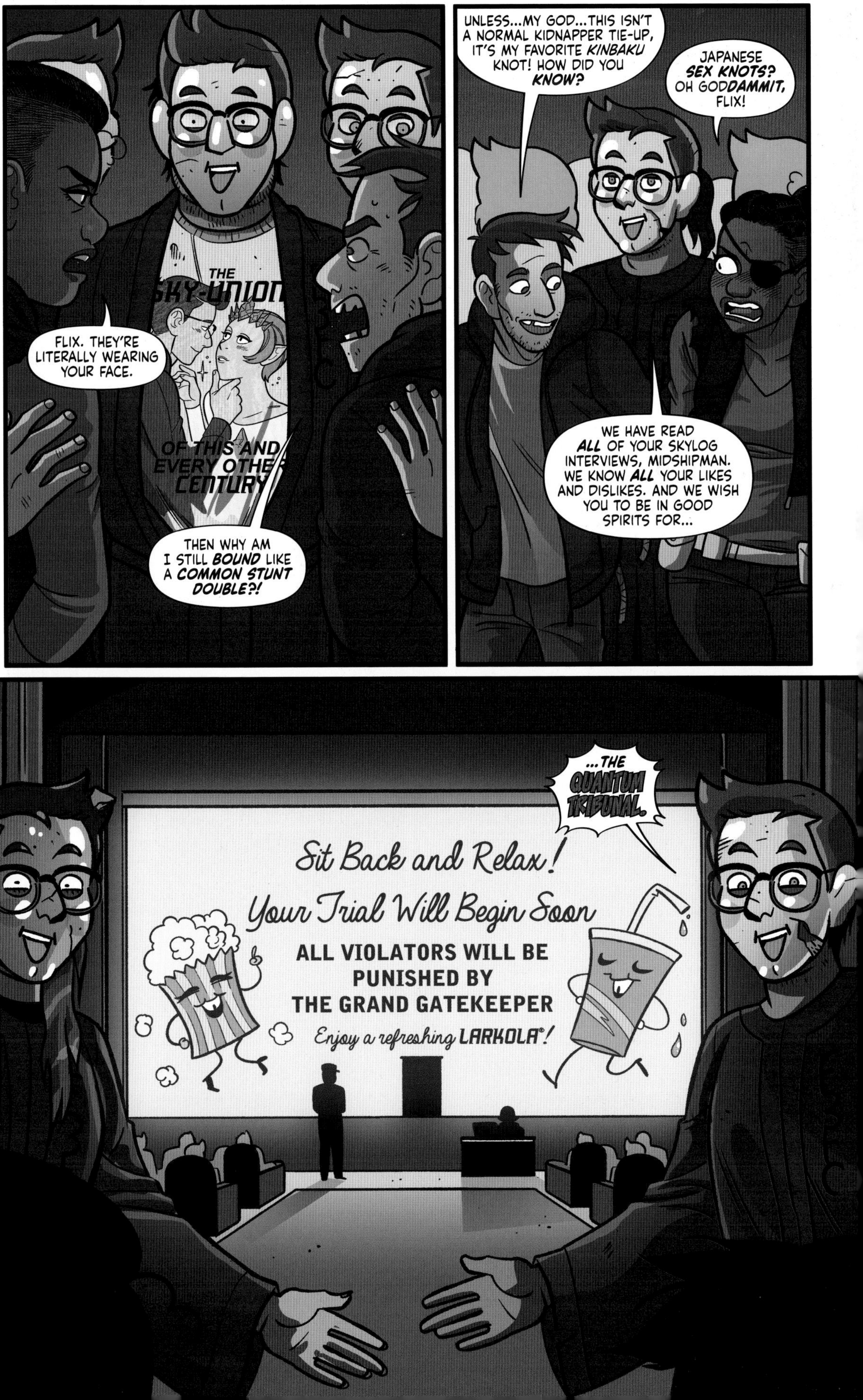

FLIX. THEY'RE LITERALLY WEARING YOUR FACE.
THEN WHY AM I STILL **BOUND** LIKE A ***COMMON STUNT DOUBLE?!***
UNLESS...MY GOD...THIS ISN'T A NORMAL KIDNAPPER TIE-UP, IT'S MY FAVORITE *KINBAKU* KNOT! HOW DID YOU ***KNOW?***
JAPANESE ***SEX KNOTS?*** OH GOD***DAMMIT,*** FLIX!
WE HAVE READ ***ALL*** OF YOUR SKYLOG INTERVIEWS, MIDSHIPMAN. WE KNOW ***ALL*** YOUR LIKES AND DISLIKES. AND WE WISH YOU TO BE IN GOOD SPIRITS FOR...
...THE ***QUANTUM TRIBUNAL.***
Sit Back and Relax!
Your Trial Will Begin Soon
ALL VIOLATORS WILL BE PUNISHED BY THE GRAND GATEKEEPER
Enjoy a refreshing LARKOLA®!

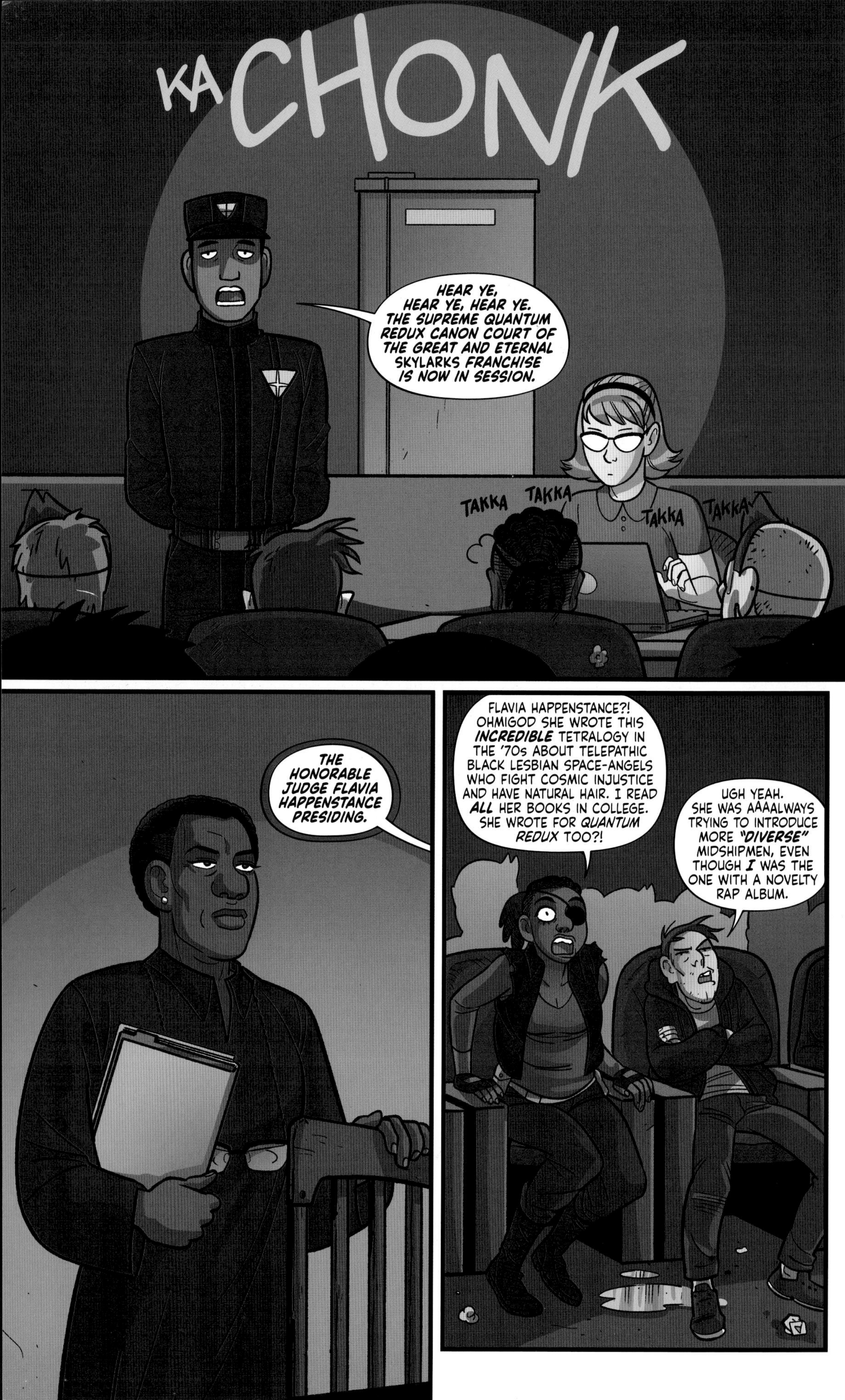
KA CHONK
HEAR YE, HEAR YE, HEAR YE. THE SUPREME QUANTUM REDUX CANON COURT OF THE GREAT AND ETERNAL SKYLARKS FRANCHISE IS NOW IN SESSION.
TAKKA TAKKA TAKKA TAKKA
THE HONORABLE JUDGE FLAVIA HAPPENSTANCE PRESIDING.
FLAVIA HAPPENSTANCE?! OHMIGOD SHE WROTE THIS INCREDIBLE TETRALOGY IN THE '70s ABOUT TELEPATHIC BLACK LESBIAN SPACE-ANGELS WHO FIGHT COSMIC INJUSTICE AND HAVE NATURAL HAIR. I READ ALL HER BOOKS IN COLLEGE. SHE WROTE FOR QUANTUM REDUX TOO?!
UGH YEAH. SHE WAS AAAALWAYS TRYING TO INTRODUCE MORE "DIVERSE" MIDSHIPMEN, EVEN THOUGH I WAS THE ONE WITH A NOVELTY RAP ALBUM.

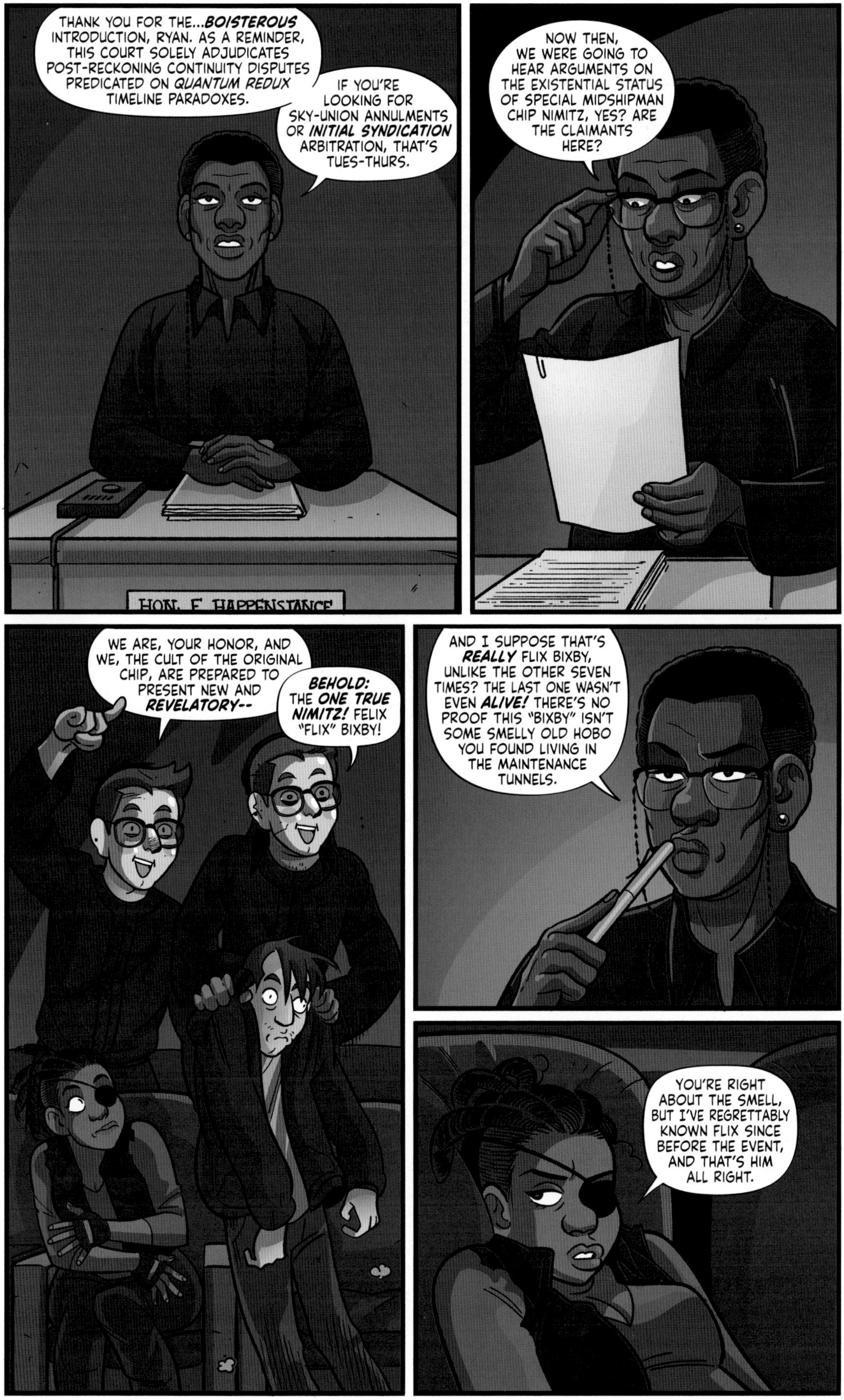
THANK YOU FOR THE...BOISTEROUS INTRODUCTION, RYAN. AS A REMINDER, THIS COURT SOLELY ADJUDICATES POST-RECKONING CONTINUITY DISPUTES PREDICATED ON QUANTUM REDUX TIMELINE PARADOXES.
IF YOU'RE LOOKING FOR SKY-UNION ANNULMENTS OR INITIAL SYNDICATION ARBITRATION, THAT'S TUES-THURS.
HON. F. HAPPENSTANCE
NOW THEN, WE WERE GOING TO HEAR ARGUMENTS ON THE EXISTENTIAL STATUS OF SPECIAL MIDSHIPMAN CHIP NIMITZ, YES? ARE THE CLAIMANTS HERE?
WE ARE, YOUR HONOR, AND WE, THE CULT OF THE ORIGINAL CHIP, ARE PREPARED TO PRESENT NEW AND REVELATORY--
BEHOLD: THE ONE TRUE NIMITZ! FELIX "FLIX" BIXBY!
AND I SUPPOSE THAT'S REALLY FLIX BIXBY, UNLIKE THE OTHER SEVEN TIMES? THE LAST ONE WASN'T EVEN ALIVE! THERE'S NO PROOF THIS "BIXBY" ISN'T SOME SMELLY OLD HOBO YOU FOUND LIVING IN THE MAINTENANCE TUNNELS.
YOU'RE RIGHT ABOUT THE SMELL, BUT I'VE REGRETTABLY KNOWN FLIX SINCE BEFORE THE EVENT, AND THAT'S HIM ALL RIGHT.

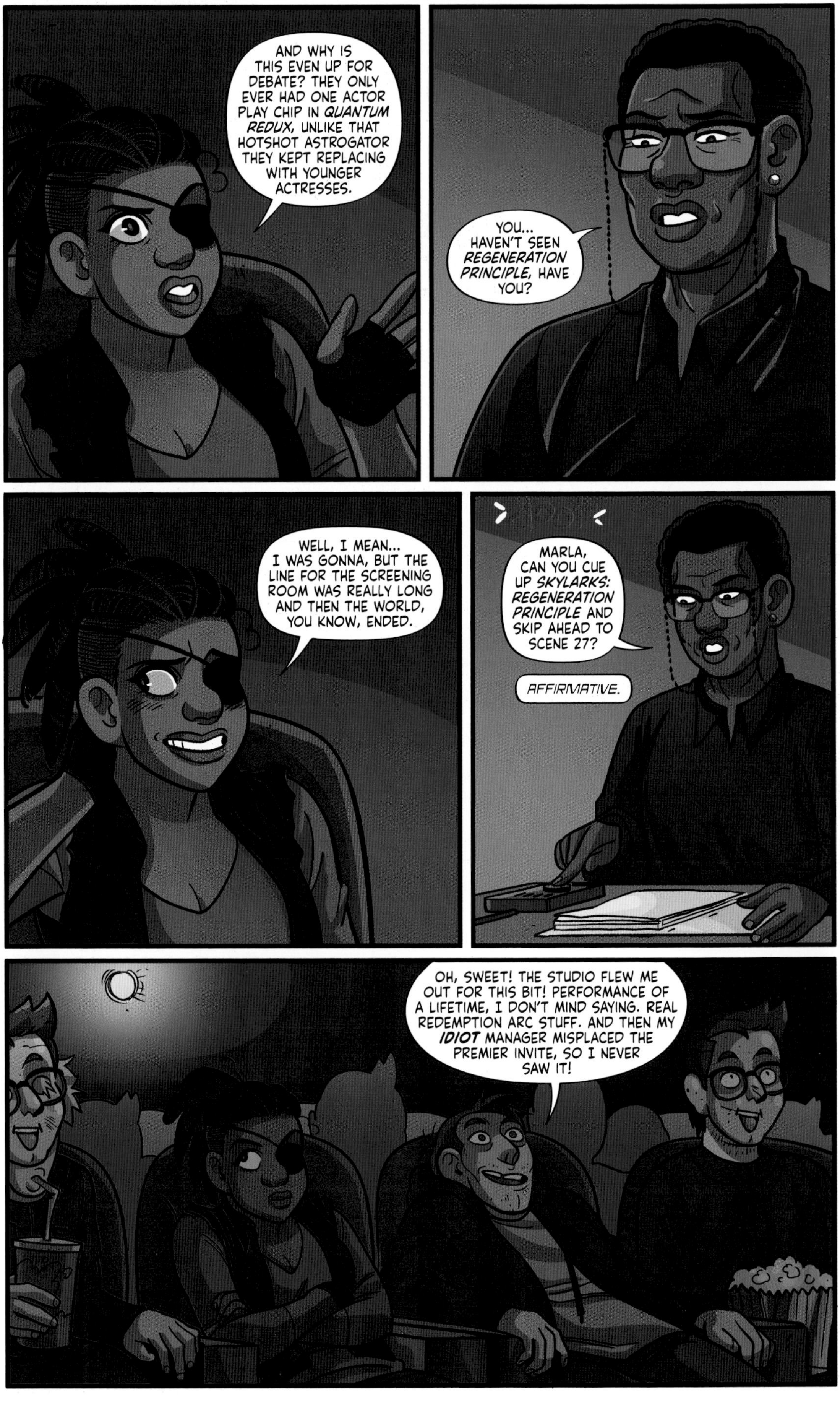
AND WHY IS THIS EVEN UP FOR DEBATE? THEY ONLY EVER HAD ONE ACTOR PLAY CHIP IN *QUANTUM REDUX*, UNLIKE THAT HOTSHOT ASTROGATOR THEY KEPT REPLACING WITH YOUNGER ACTRESSES.
YOU... HAVEN'T SEEN *REGENERATION PRINCIPLE*, HAVE YOU?
WELL, I MEAN... I WAS GONNA, BUT THE LINE FOR THE SCREENING ROOM WAS REALLY LONG AND THEN THE WORLD, YOU KNOW, ENDED.
MARLA, CAN YOU CUE UP *SKYLARKS: REGENERATION PRINCIPLE* AND SKIP AHEAD TO SCENE 27?
AFFIRMATIVE.
OH, SWEET! THE STUDIO FLEW ME OUT FOR THIS BIT! PERFORMANCE OF A LIFETIME, I DON'T MIND SAYING. REAL REDEMPTION ARC STUFF. AND THEN MY ***IDIOT*** MANAGER MISPLACED THE PREMIER INVITE, SO I NEVER SAW IT!

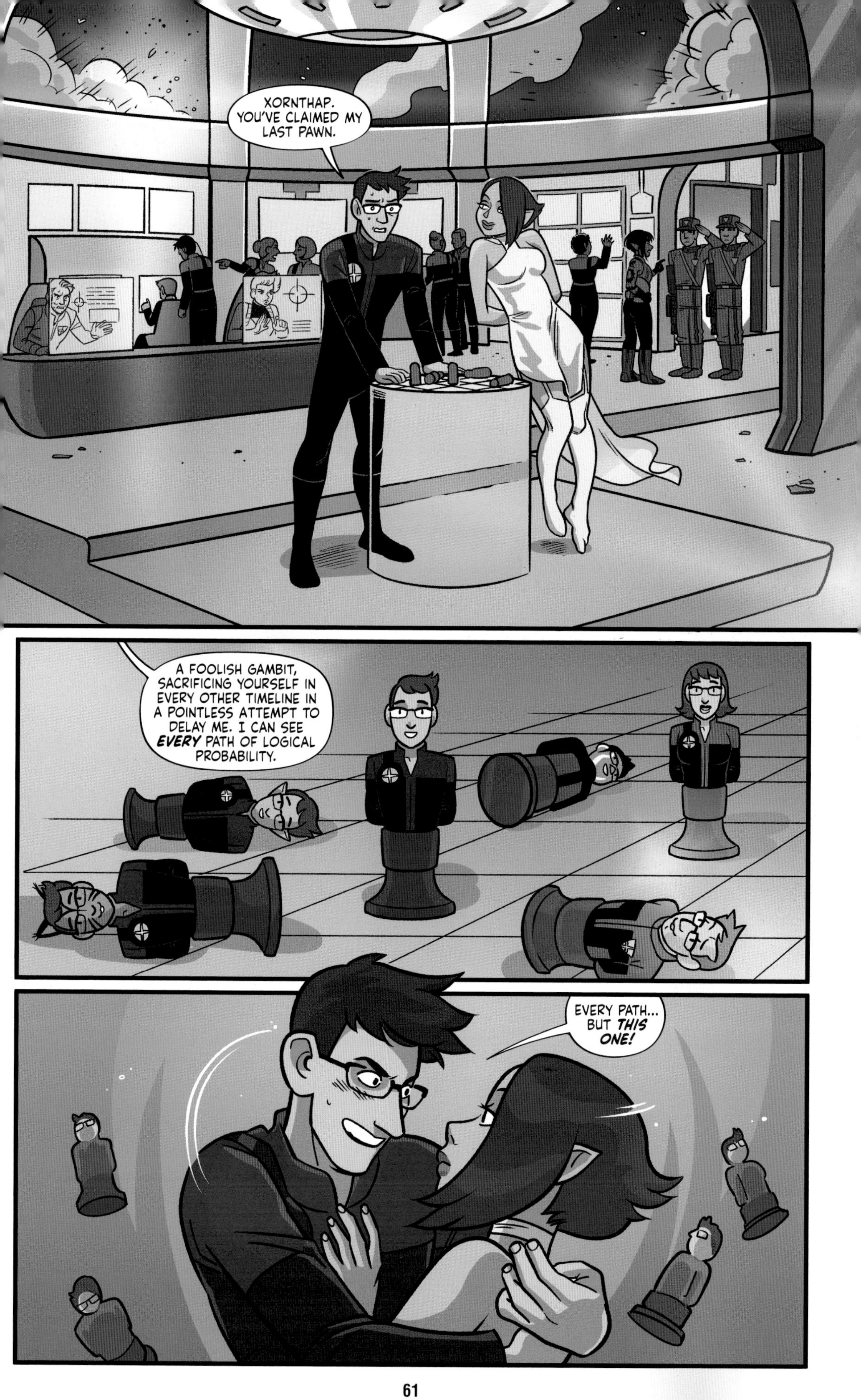
XORNTHAP. YOU'VE CLAIMED MY LAST PAWN.
A FOOLISH GAMBIT, SACRIFICING YOURSELF IN EVERY OTHER TIMELINE IN A POINTLESS ATTEMPT TO DELAY ME. I CAN SEE **EVERY** PATH OF LOGICAL PROBABILITY.
EVERY PATH... BUT ***THIS ONE!***

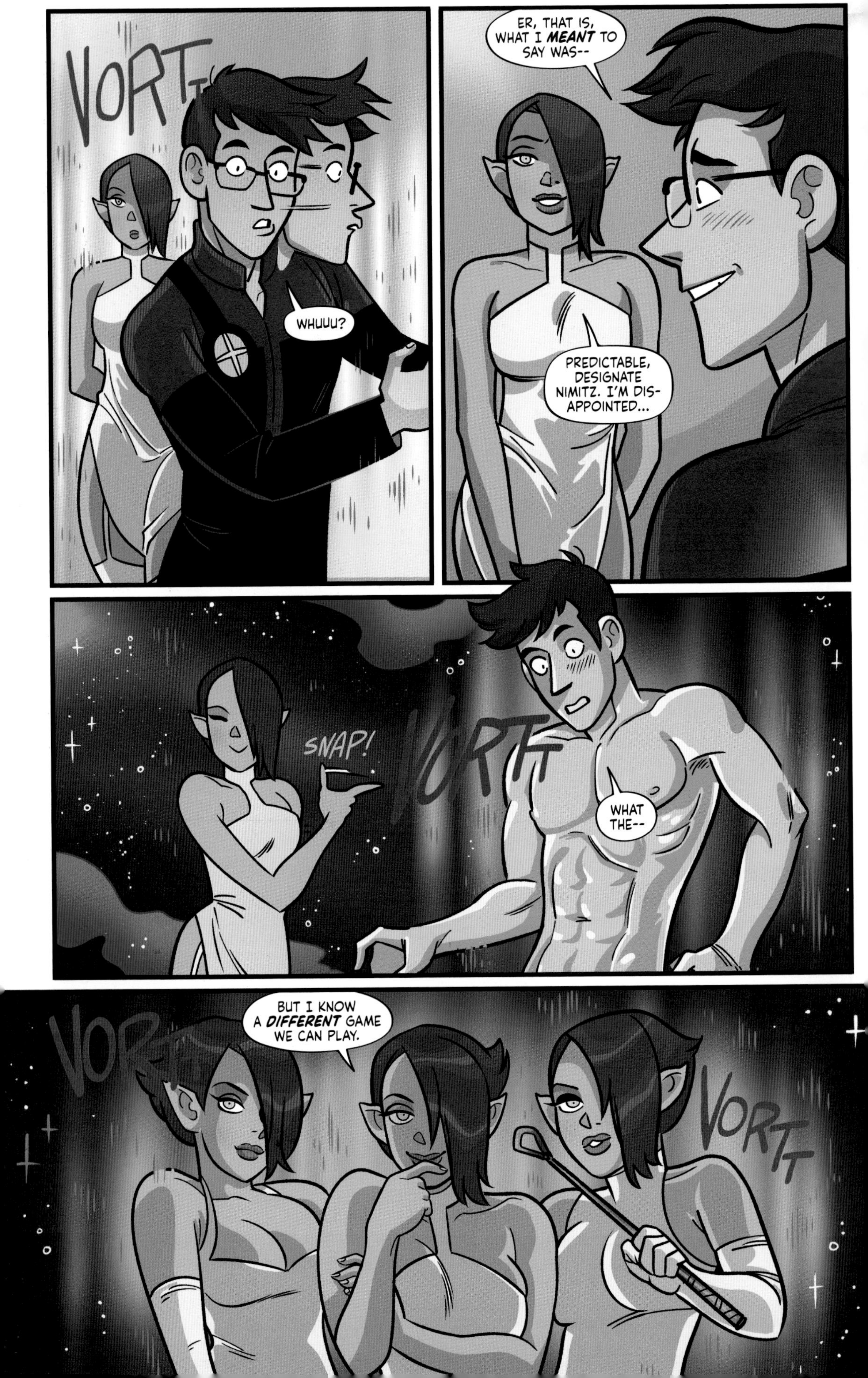
VORTT
WHUUU?
ER, THAT IS, WHAT I MEANT TO SAY WAS--
PREDICTABLE, DESIGNATE NIMITZ. I'M DIS-APPOINTED...
SNAP!
VORTT
WHAT THE--
VORTT
BUT I KNOW A DIFFERENT GAME WE CAN PLAY.
VORTT

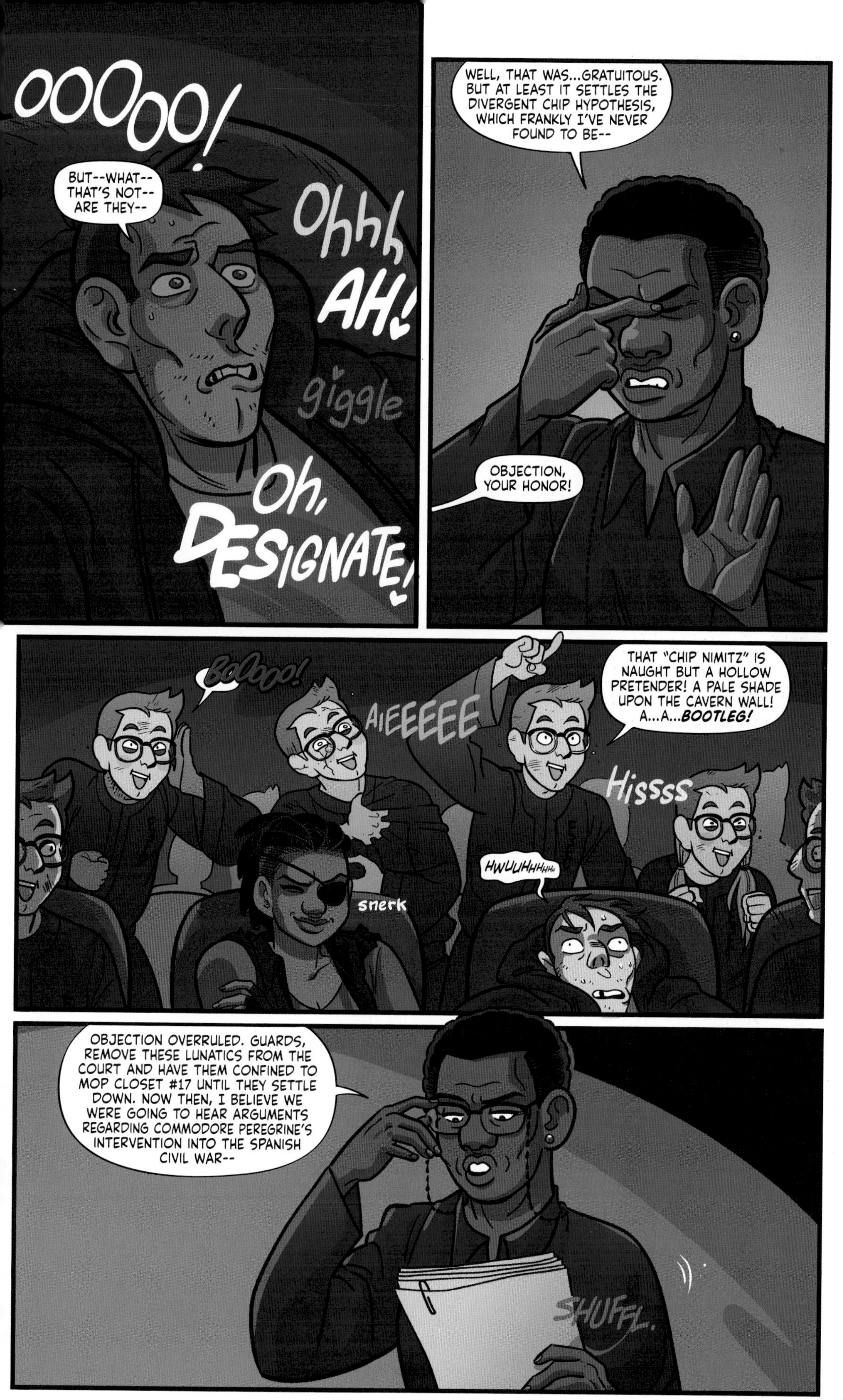
OOOOO!
BUT--WHAT--THAT'S NOT--ARE THEY--
Ohhh
AH!
giggle
Oh, DESIGNATE!
WELL, THAT WAS...GRATUITOUS. BUT AT LEAST IT SETTLES THE DIVERGENT CHIP HYPOTHESIS, WHICH FRANKLY I'VE NEVER FOUND TO BE--
OBJECTION, YOUR HONOR!
BOOOOO!
AIEEEEE
THAT "CHIP NIMITZ" IS NAUGHT BUT A HOLLOW PRETENDER! A PALE SHADE UPON THE CAVERN WALL! A...A...BOOTLEG!
Hissss
HWUUHHHHH
snerk
OBJECTION OVERRULED. GUARDS, REMOVE THESE LUNATICS FROM THE COURT AND HAVE THEM CONFINED TO MOP CLOSET #17 UNTIL THEY SETTLE DOWN. NOW THEN, I BELIEVE WE WERE GOING TO HEAR ARGUMENTS REGARDING COMMODORE PEREGRINE'S INTERVENTION INTO THE SPANISH CIVIL WAR--
SHUFFL.

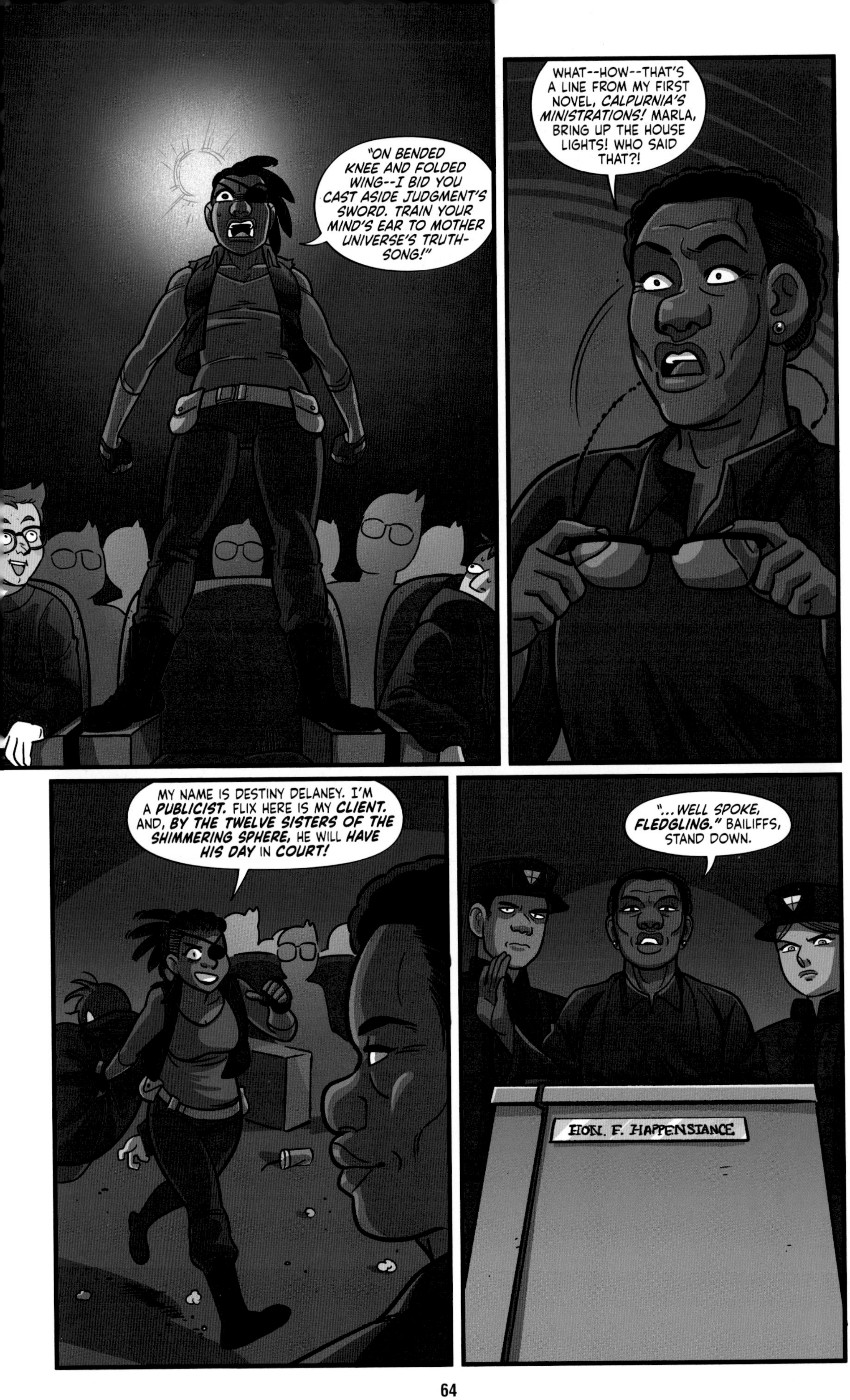
"ON BENDED KNEE AND FOLDED WING--I BID YOU CAST ASIDE JUDGMENT'S SWORD. TRAIN YOUR MIND'S EAR TO MOTHER UNIVERSE'S TRUTH-SONG!"
WHAT--HOW--THAT'S A LINE FROM MY FIRST NOVEL, *CALPURNIA'S MINISTRATIONS!* MARLA, BRING UP THE HOUSE LIGHTS! WHO SAID THAT?!
MY NAME IS DESTINY DELANEY. I'M A **PUBLICIST.** FLIX HERE IS MY **CLIENT.** AND, **BY THE TWELVE SISTERS OF THE SHIMMERING SPHERE,** HE WILL **HAVE HIS DAY** IN **COURT!**
"...WELL SPOKE, **FLEDGLING."** BAILIFFS, STAND DOWN.
HON. F. HAPPENSTANCE

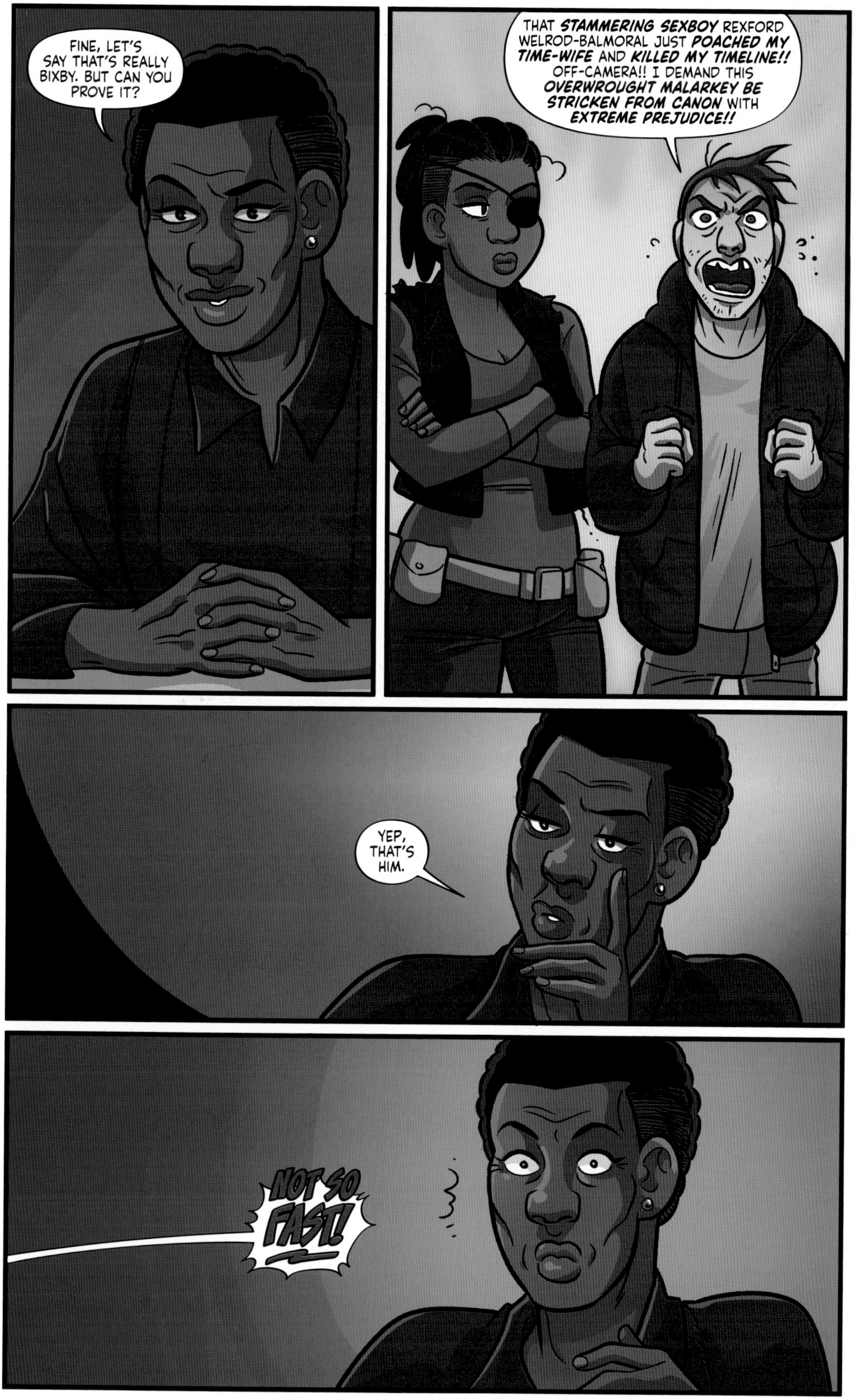
FINE, LET'S SAY THAT'S REALLY BIXBY. BUT CAN YOU PROVE IT?
THAT STAMMERING SEXBOY REXFORD WELROD-BALMORAL JUST POACHED MY TIME-WIFE AND KILLED MY TIMELINE!! OFF-CAMERA!! I DEMAND THIS OVERWROUGHT MALARKEY BE STRICKEN FROM CANON WITH EXTREME PREJUDICE!!
YEP, THAT'S HIM.
NOT SO FAST!

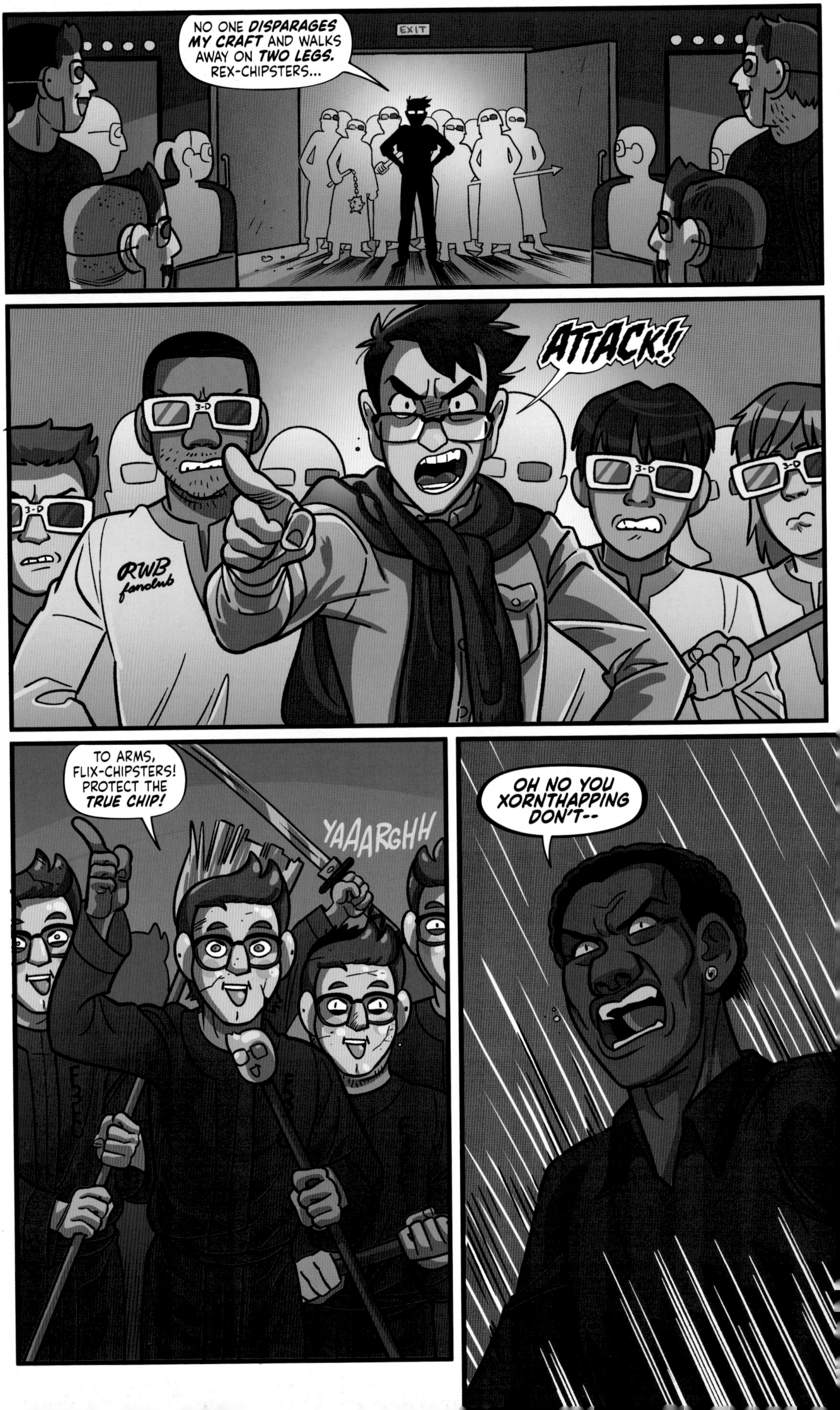
EXIT
NO ONE DISPARAGES MY CRAFT AND WALKS AWAY ON TWO LEGS. REX-CHIPSTERS...
ATTACK!!
3-D
RWB fanclub
TO ARMS, FLIX-CHIPSTERS! PROTECT THE TRUE CHIP!
YAAARGHH
OH NO YOU XORNTHAPPING DON'T--

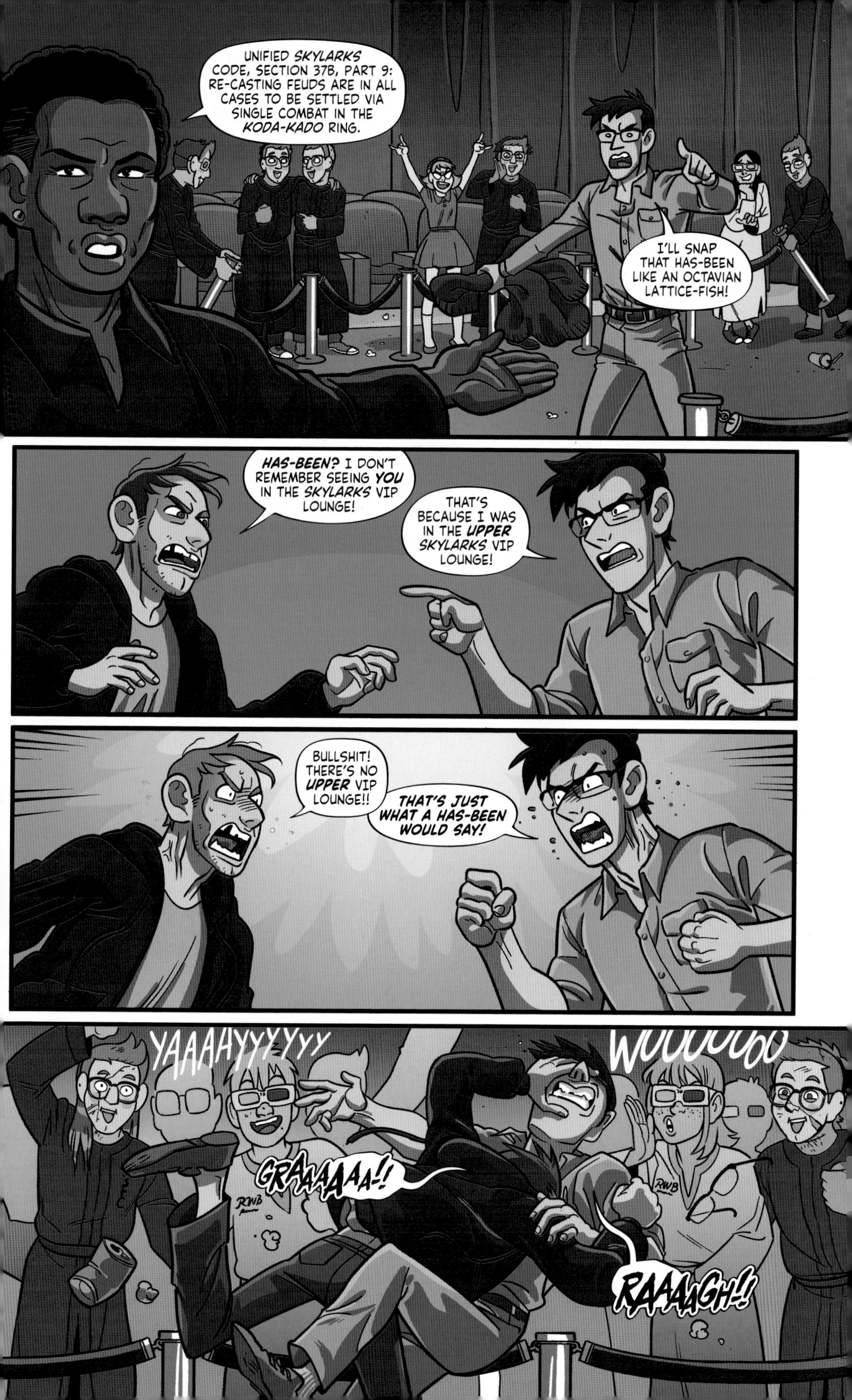
UNIFIED SKYLARKS CODE, SECTION 37B, PART 9: RE-CASTING FEUDS ARE IN ALL CASES TO BE SETTLED VIA SINGLE COMBAT IN THE KODA-KADO RING.
I'LL SNAP THAT HAS-BEEN LIKE AN OCTAVIAN LATTICE-FISH!
HAS-BEEN? I DON'T REMEMBER SEEING YOU IN THE SKYLARKS VIP LOUNGE!
THAT'S BECAUSE I WAS IN THE UPPER SKYLARKS VIP LOUNGE!
BULLSHIT! THERE'S NO UPPER VIP LOUNGE!!
THAT'S JUST WHAT A HAS-BEEN WOULD SAY!
YAAAHYYYYYY
WOOOOOOO
GRAAAAAA-!!
RAAAAGH-!!

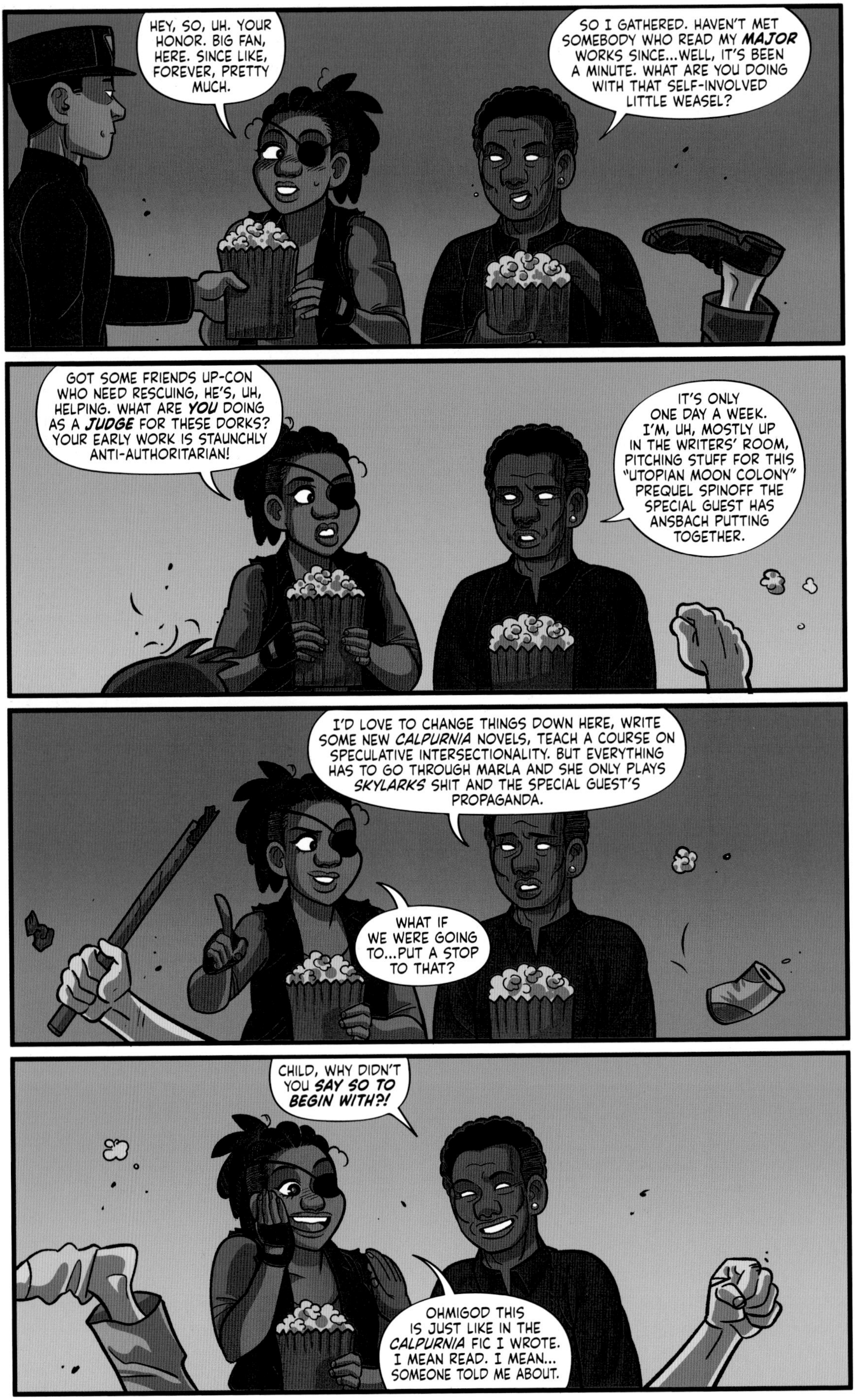
HEY, SO, UH. YOUR HONOR. BIG FAN, HERE. SINCE LIKE, FOREVER, PRETTY MUCH.
SO I GATHERED. HAVEN'T MET SOMEBODY WHO READ MY MAJOR WORKS SINCE...WELL, IT'S BEEN A MINUTE. WHAT ARE YOU DOING WITH THAT SELF-INVOLVED LITTLE WEASEL?
GOT SOME FRIENDS UP-CON WHO NEED RESCUING, HE'S, UH, HELPING. WHAT ARE YOU DOING AS A JUDGE FOR THESE DORKS? YOUR EARLY WORK IS STAUNCHLY ANTI-AUTHORITARIAN!
IT'S ONLY ONE DAY A WEEK. I'M, UH, MOSTLY UP IN THE WRITERS' ROOM, PITCHING STUFF FOR THIS "UTOPIAN MOON COLONY" PREQUEL SPINOFF THE SPECIAL GUEST HAS ANSBACH PUTTING TOGETHER.
I'D LOVE TO CHANGE THINGS DOWN HERE, WRITE SOME NEW CALPURNIA NOVELS, TEACH A COURSE ON SPECULATIVE INTERSECTIONALITY. BUT EVERYTHING HAS TO GO THROUGH MARLA AND SHE ONLY PLAYS SKYLARKS SHIT AND THE SPECIAL GUEST'S PROPAGANDA.
WHAT IF WE WERE GOING TO...PUT A STOP TO THAT?
CHILD, WHY DIDN'T YOU SAY SO TO BEGIN WITH?!
OHMIGOD THIS IS JUST LIKE IN THE CALPURNIA FIC I WROTE. I MEAN READ. I MEAN... SOMEONE TOLD ME ABOUT.

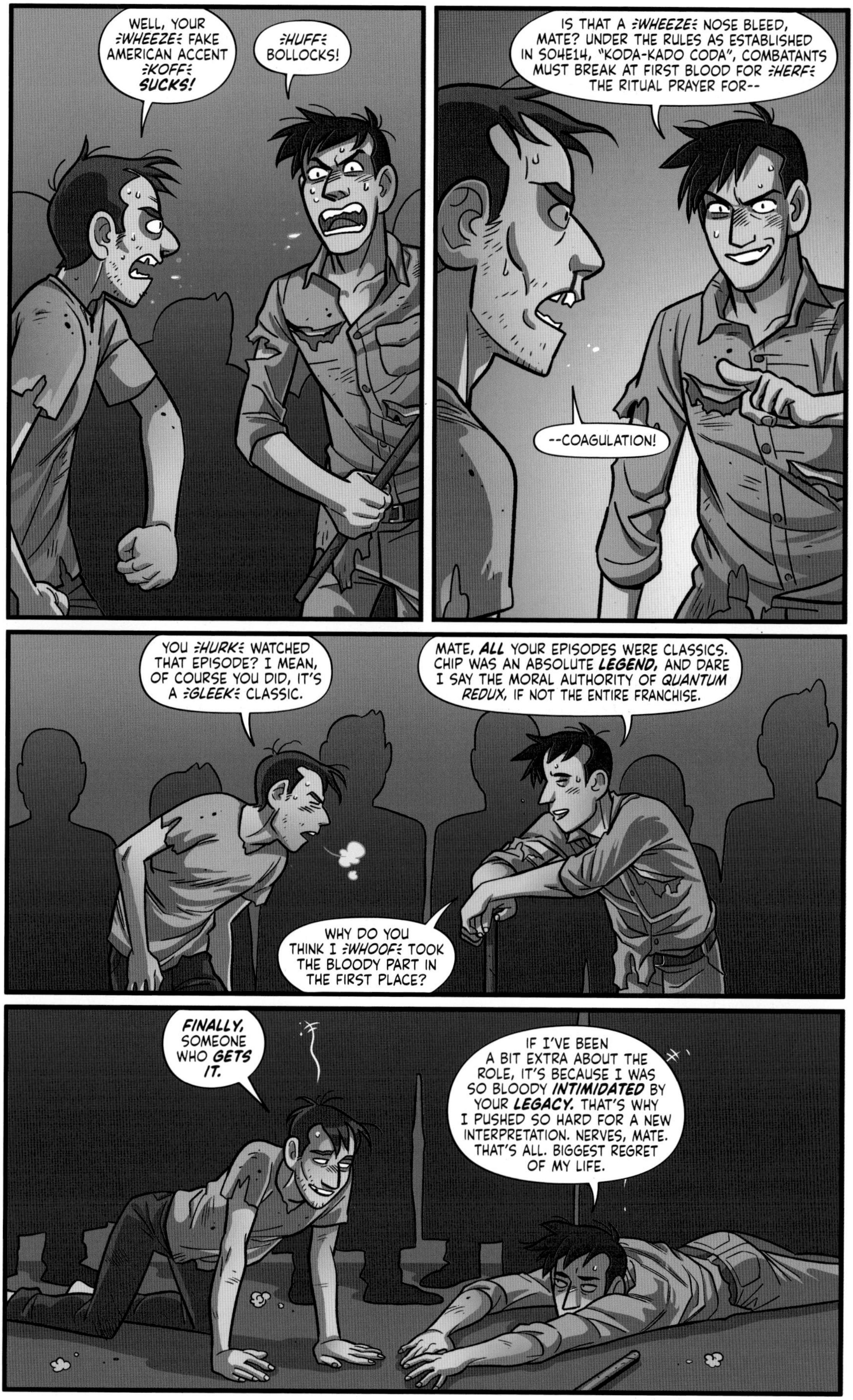
WELL, YOUR ⫶WHEEZE⫶ FAKE AMERICAN ACCENT ⫶KOFF⫶ SUCKS!
⫶HUFF⫶ BOLLOCKS!
IS THAT A ⫶WHEEZE⫶ NOSE BLEED, MATE? UNDER THE RULES AS ESTABLISHED IN S04E14, "KODA-KADO CODA", COMBATANTS MUST BREAK AT FIRST BLOOD FOR ⫶HERF⫶ THE RITUAL PRAYER FOR--
--COAGULATION!
YOU ⫶HURK⫶ WATCHED THAT EPISODE? I MEAN, OF COURSE YOU DID, IT'S A ⫶GLEEK⫶ CLASSIC.
MATE, ALL YOUR EPISODES WERE CLASSICS. CHIP WAS AN ABSOLUTE LEGEND, AND DARE I SAY THE MORAL AUTHORITY OF QUANTUM REDUX, IF NOT THE ENTIRE FRANCHISE.
WHY DO YOU THINK I ⫶WHOOF⫶ TOOK THE BLOODY PART IN THE FIRST PLACE?
FINALLY, SOMEONE WHO GETS IT.
IF I'VE BEEN A BIT EXTRA ABOUT THE ROLE, IT'S BECAUSE I WAS SO BLOODY INTIMIDATED BY YOUR LEGACY. THAT'S WHY I PUSHED SO HARD FOR A NEW INTERPRETATION. NERVES, MATE. THAT'S ALL. BIGGEST REGRET OF MY LIFE.

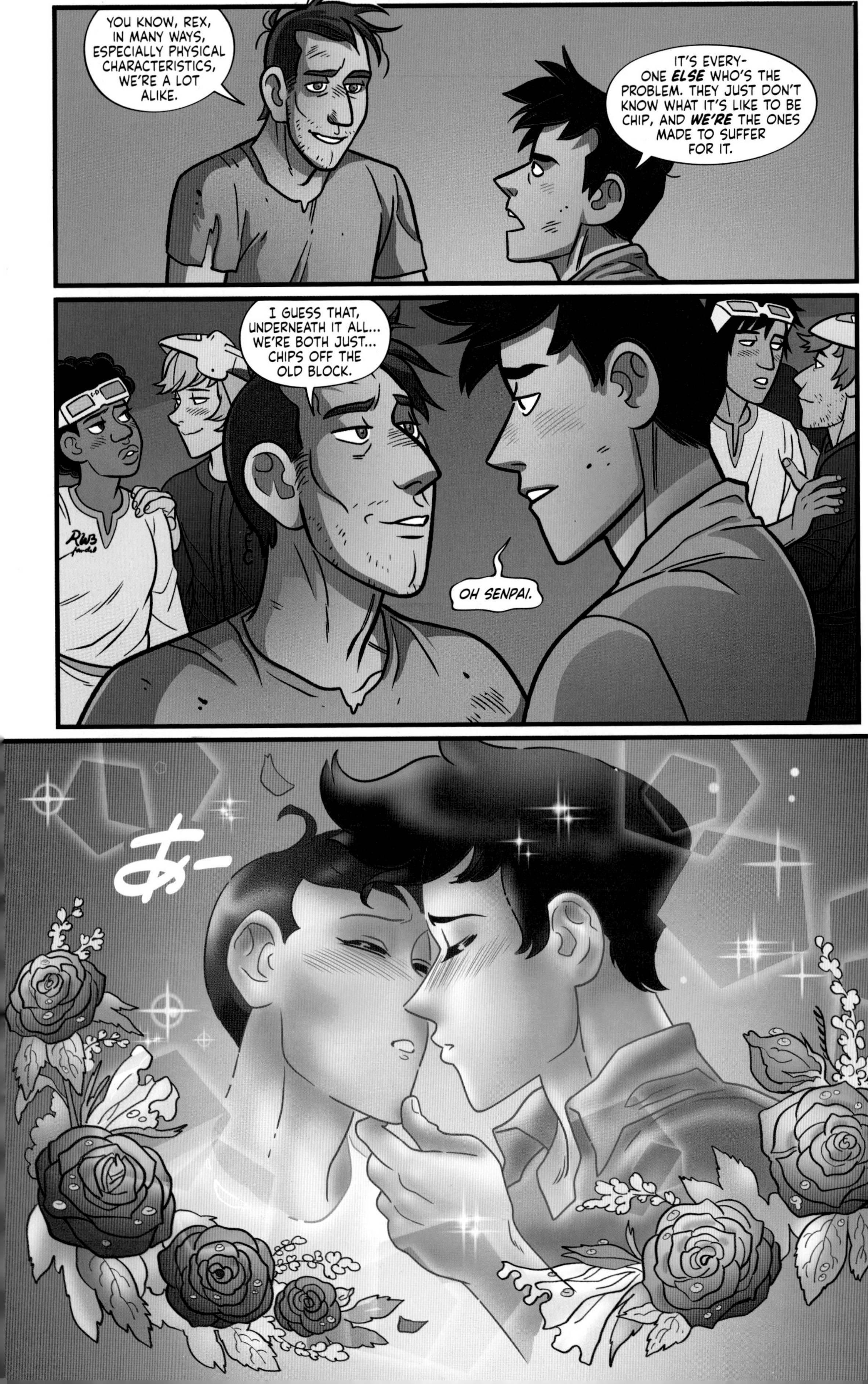
YOU KNOW, REX, IN MANY WAYS, ESPECIALLY PHYSICAL CHARACTERISTICS, WE'RE A LOT ALIKE.
IT'S EVERY-ONE ELSE WHO'S THE PROBLEM. THEY JUST DON'T KNOW WHAT IT'S LIKE TO BE CHIP, AND WE'RE THE ONES MADE TO SUFFER FOR IT.
I GUESS THAT, UNDERNEATH IT ALL... WE'RE BOTH JUST... CHIPS OFF THE OLD BLOCK.
OH SENPAI.
あー

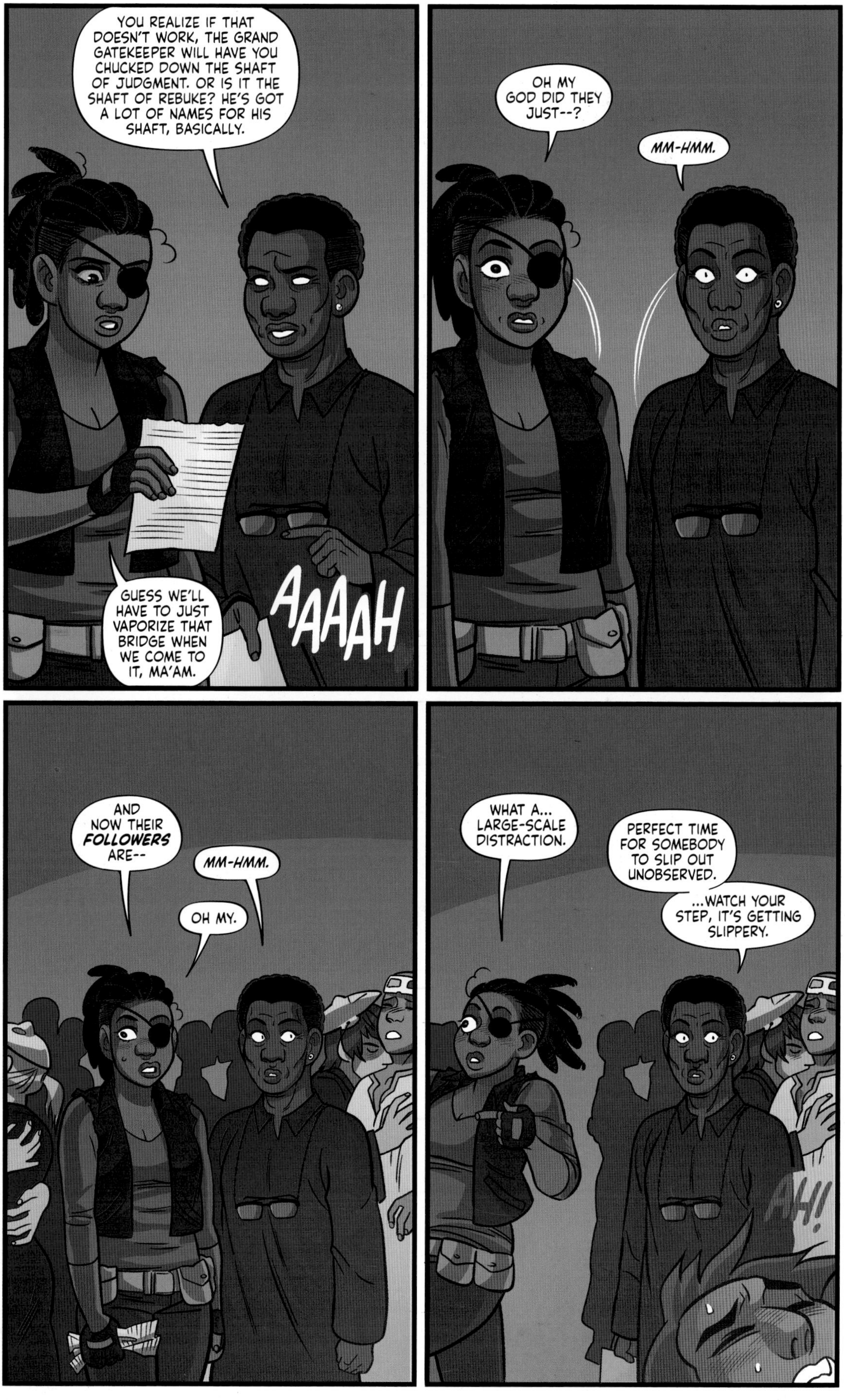
YOU REALIZE IF THAT DOESN'T WORK, THE GRAND GATEKEEPER WILL HAVE YOU CHUCKED DOWN THE SHAFT OF JUDGMENT. OR IS IT THE SHAFT OF REBUKE? HE'S GOT A LOT OF NAMES FOR HIS SHAFT, BASICALLY.
GUESS WE'LL HAVE TO JUST VAPORIZE THAT BRIDGE WHEN WE COME TO IT, MA'AM.
AAAAH
OH MY GOD DID THEY JUST--?
MM-HMM.
AND NOW THEIR ***FOLLOWERS*** ARE--
MM-HMM.
OH MY.
WHAT A... LARGE-SCALE DISTRACTION.
PERFECT TIME FOR SOMEBODY TO SLIP OUT UNOBSERVED.
...WATCH YOUR STEP, IT'S GETTING SLIPPERY.
AH!

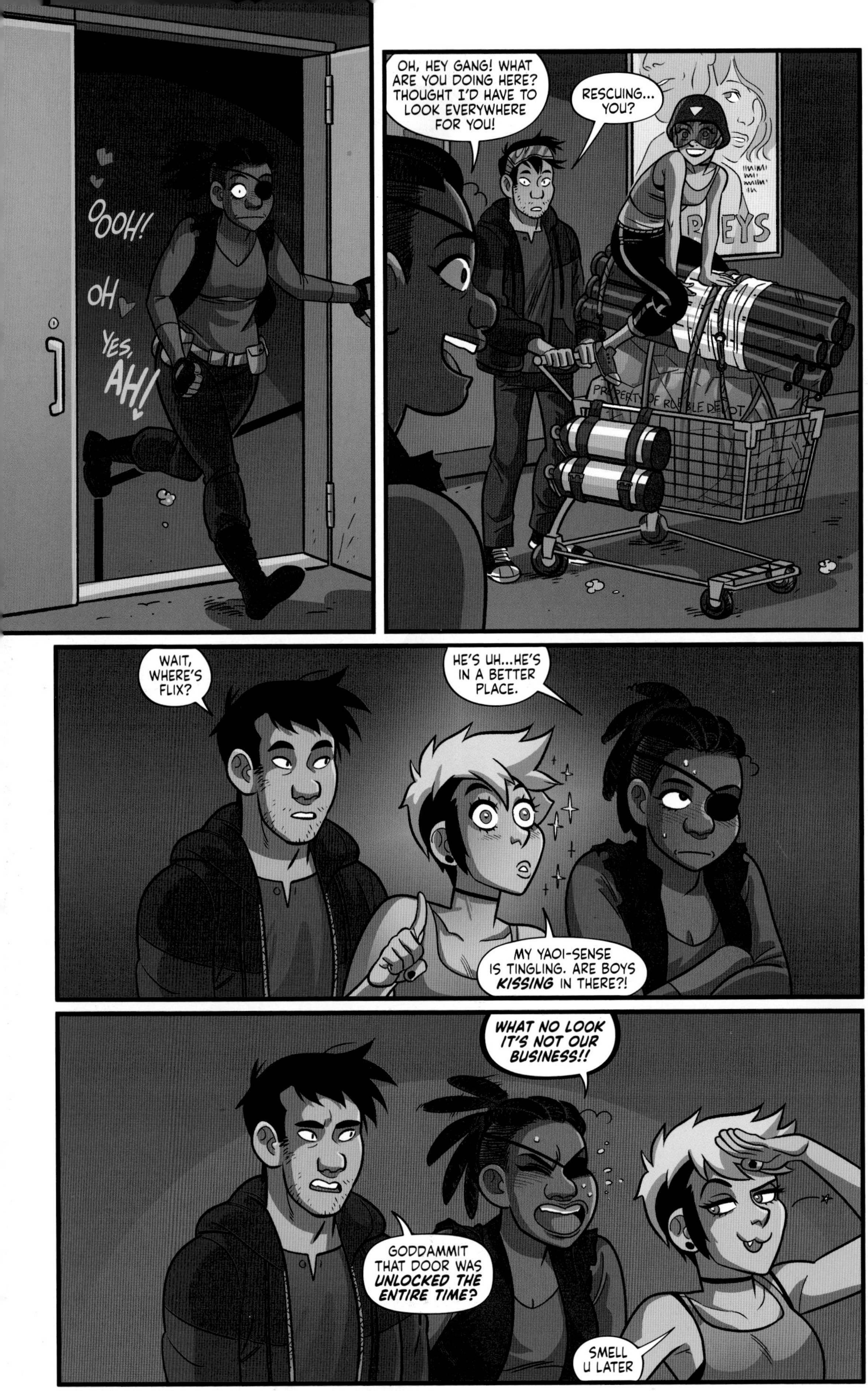
OOOH!
OH
YES, AH!
OH, HEY GANG! WHAT ARE YOU DOING HERE? THOUGHT I'D HAVE TO LOOK EVERYWHERE FOR YOU!
RESCUING... YOU?
PROPERTY OF RUBBLE DEPOT
WAIT, WHERE'S FLIX?
HE'S UH...HE'S IN A BETTER PLACE.
MY YAOI-SENSE IS TINGLING. ARE BOYS *KISSING* IN THERE?!
WHAT NO LOOK IT'S NOT OUR BUSINESS!!
GODDAMMIT THAT DOOR WAS *UNLOCKED THE ENTIRE TIME?*
SMELL U LATER

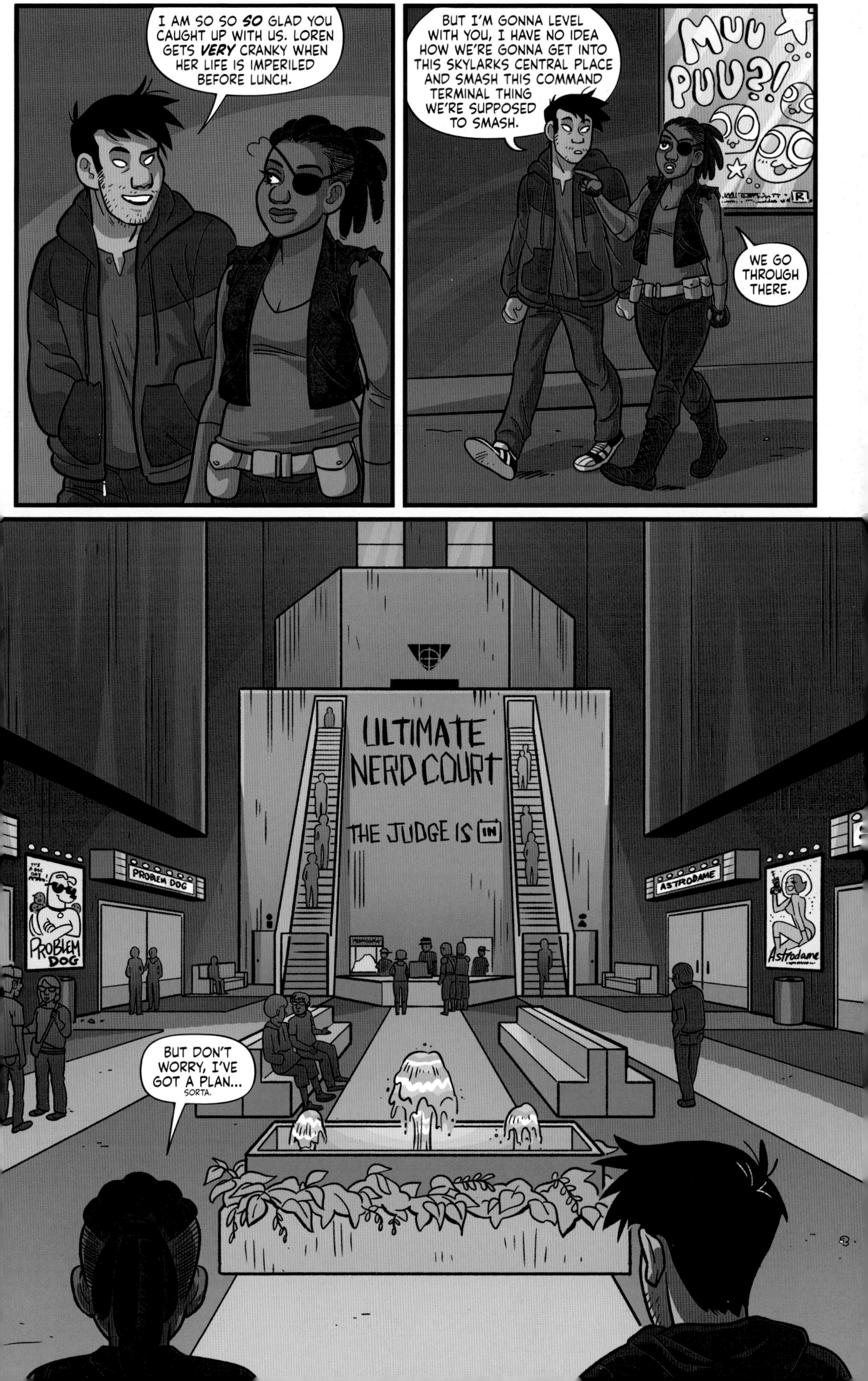
I AM SO SO SO GLAD YOU CAUGHT UP WITH US. LOREN GETS VERY CRANKY WHEN HER LIFE IS IMPERILED BEFORE LUNCH.
BUT I'M GONNA LEVEL WITH YOU, I HAVE NO IDEA HOW WE'RE GONNA GET INTO THIS SKYLARKS CENTRAL PLACE AND SMASH THIS COMMAND TERMINAL THING WE'RE SUPPOSED TO SMASH.
MUU PUU?!
WE GO THROUGH THERE.
ULTIMATE NERD COURT
THE JUDGE IS IN
PROBLEM DOG
PROBLEM DOG
ASTRODAME
Astrodame
BUT DON'T WORRY, I'VE GOT A PLAN... SORTA.

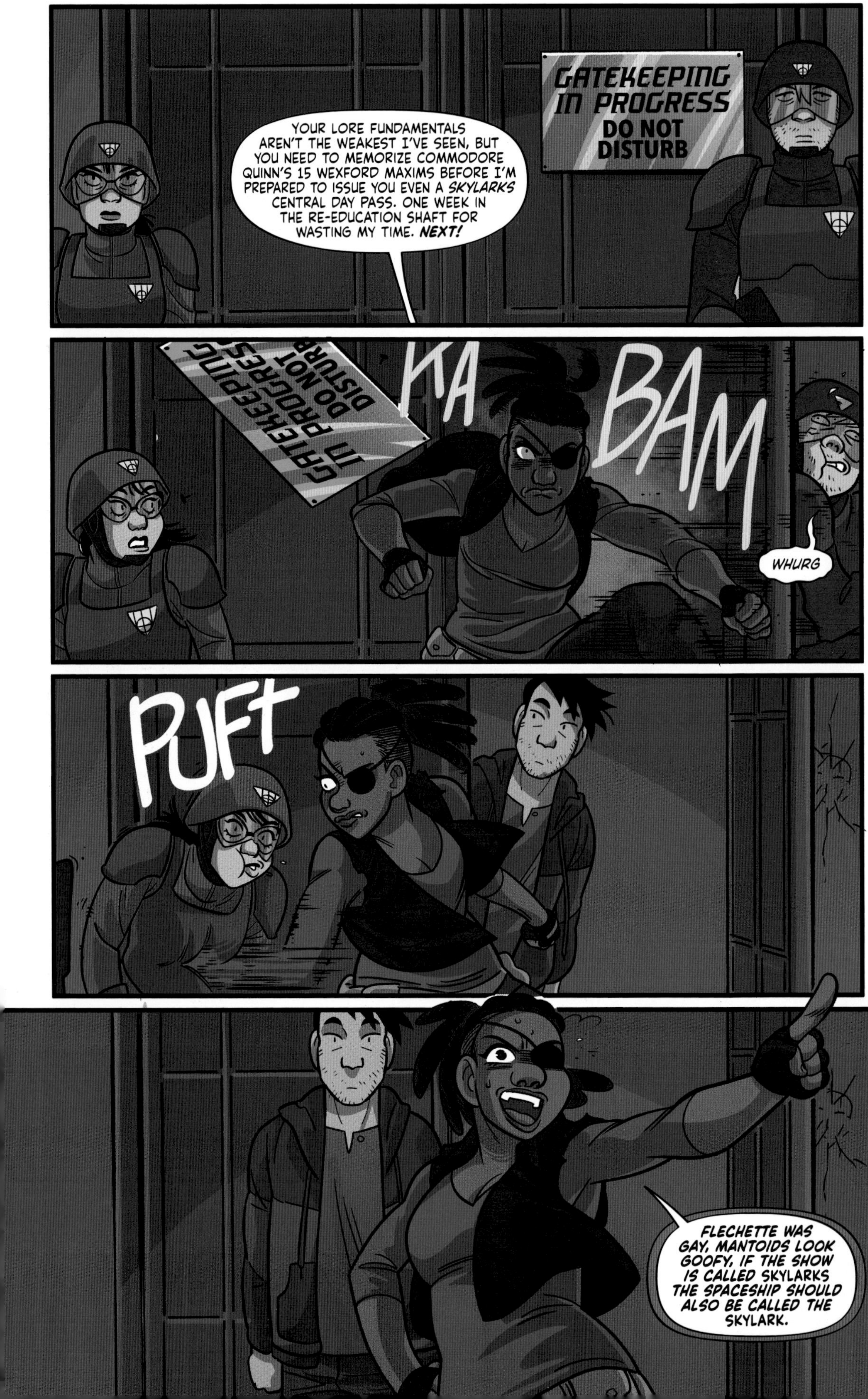
GATEKEEPING IN PROGRESS DO NOT DISTURB
YOUR LORE FUNDAMENTALS AREN'T THE WEAKEST I'VE SEEN, BUT YOU NEED TO MEMORIZE COMMODORE QUINN'S 15 WEXFORD MAXIMS BEFORE I'M PREPARED TO ISSUE YOU EVEN A *SKYLARKS* CENTRAL DAY PASS. ONE WEEK IN THE RE-EDUCATION SHAFT FOR WASTING MY TIME. ***NEXT!***
GATEKEEPING IN PROGRESS DO NOT DISTURB
KA
BAM
WHURG
PUFT
FLECHETTE WAS GAY, MANTOIDS LOOK GOOFY, IF THE SHOW IS CALLED SKYLARKS THE SPACESHIP SHOULD ALSO BE CALLED THE SKYLARK.

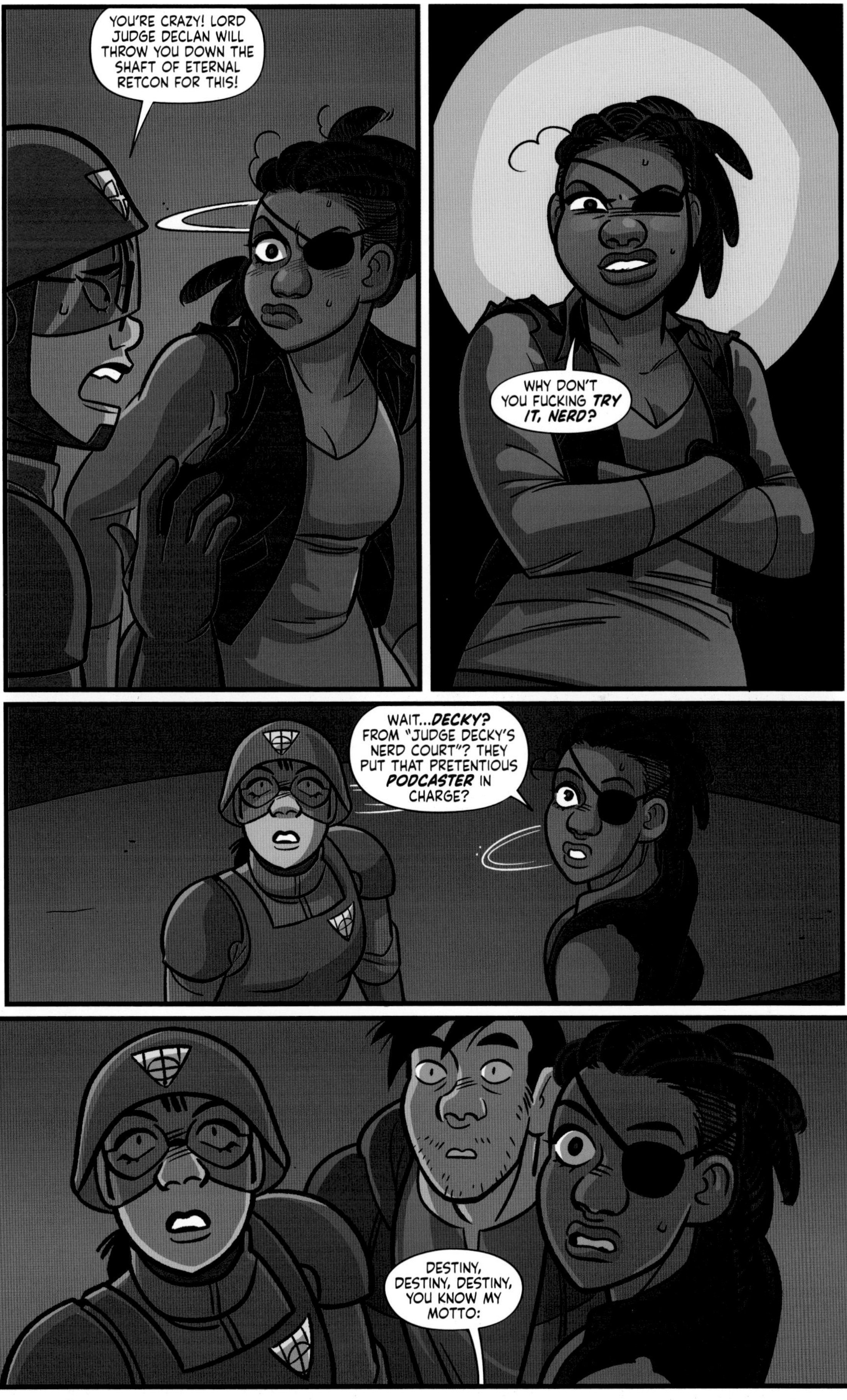

YOU'RE CRAZY! LORD JUDGE DECLAN WILL THROW YOU DOWN THE SHAFT OF ETERNAL RETCON FOR THIS!
WHY DON'T YOU FUCKING *TRY IT, NERD?*
WAIT...*DECKY?* FROM "JUDGE DECKY'S NERD COURT"? THEY PUT THAT PRETENTIOUS *PODCASTER* IN CHARGE?
DESTINY, DESTINY, DESTINY, YOU KNOW MY MOTTO:

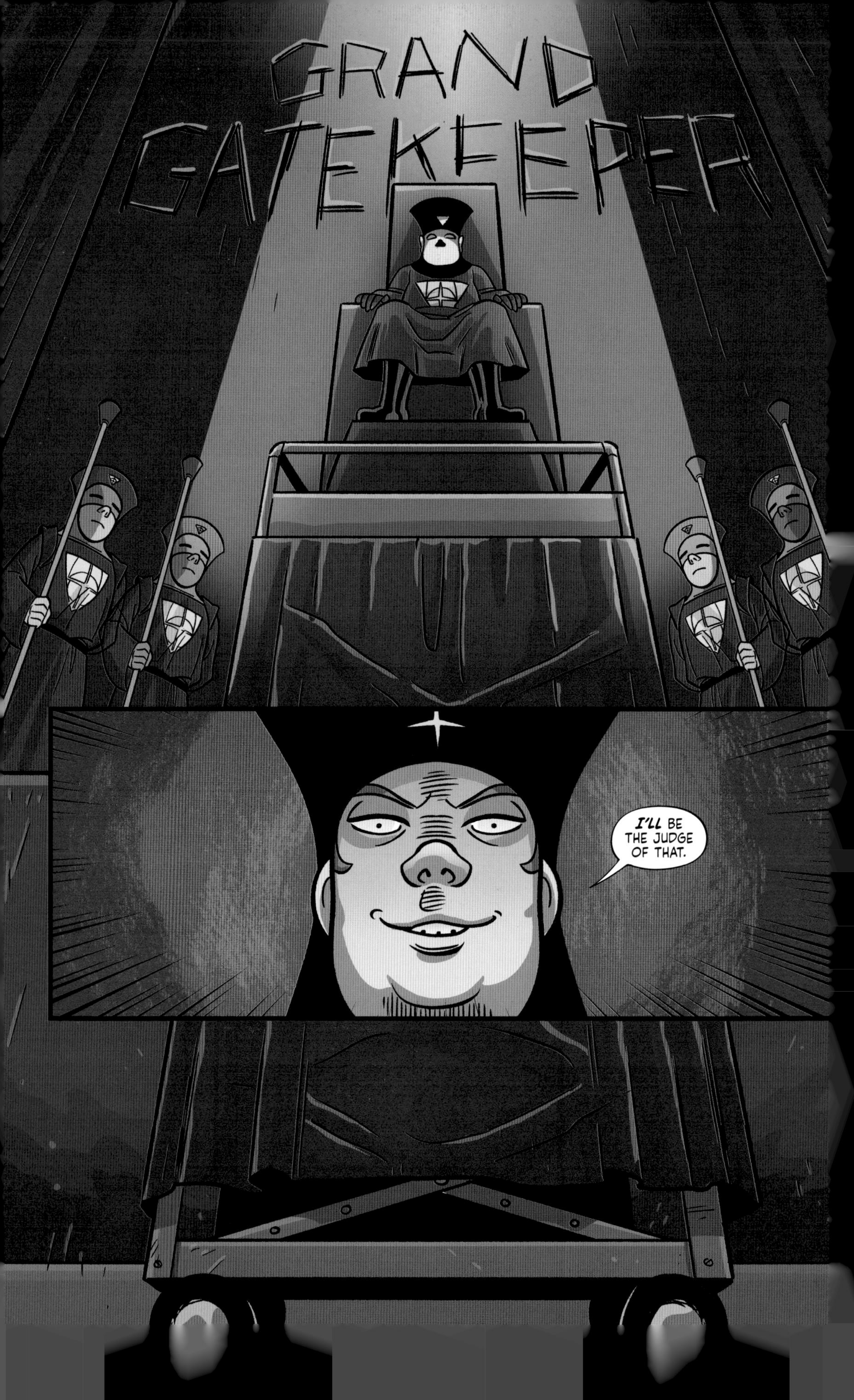
GRAND GATEKEEPER
I'LL BE THE JUDGE OF THAT.

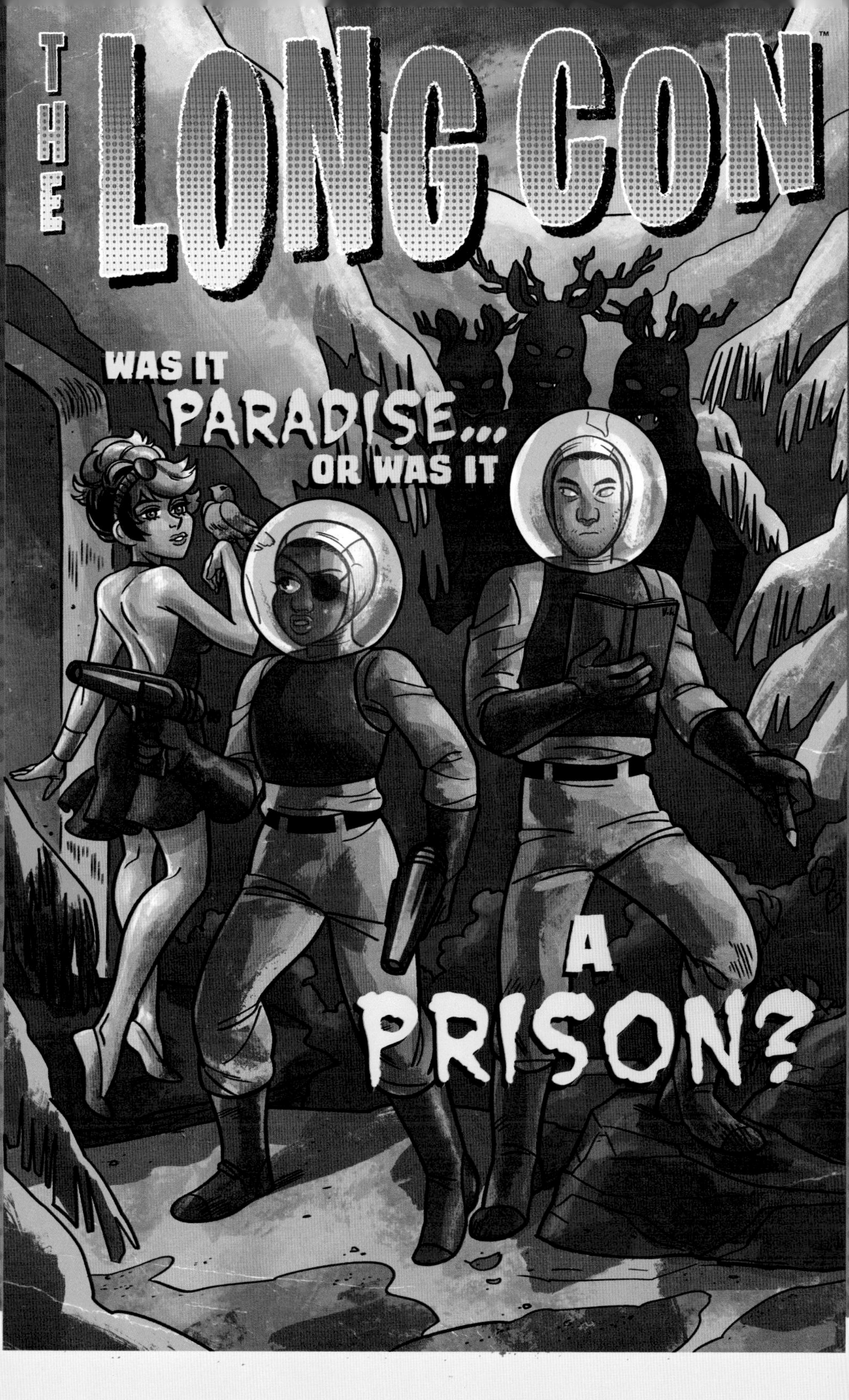
THE LONG CON™
WAS IT
PARADISE...
...OR WAS IT
A
PRISON?

CHAPTER 9: WHO GATEKEEPS THE GATEKEEPER?

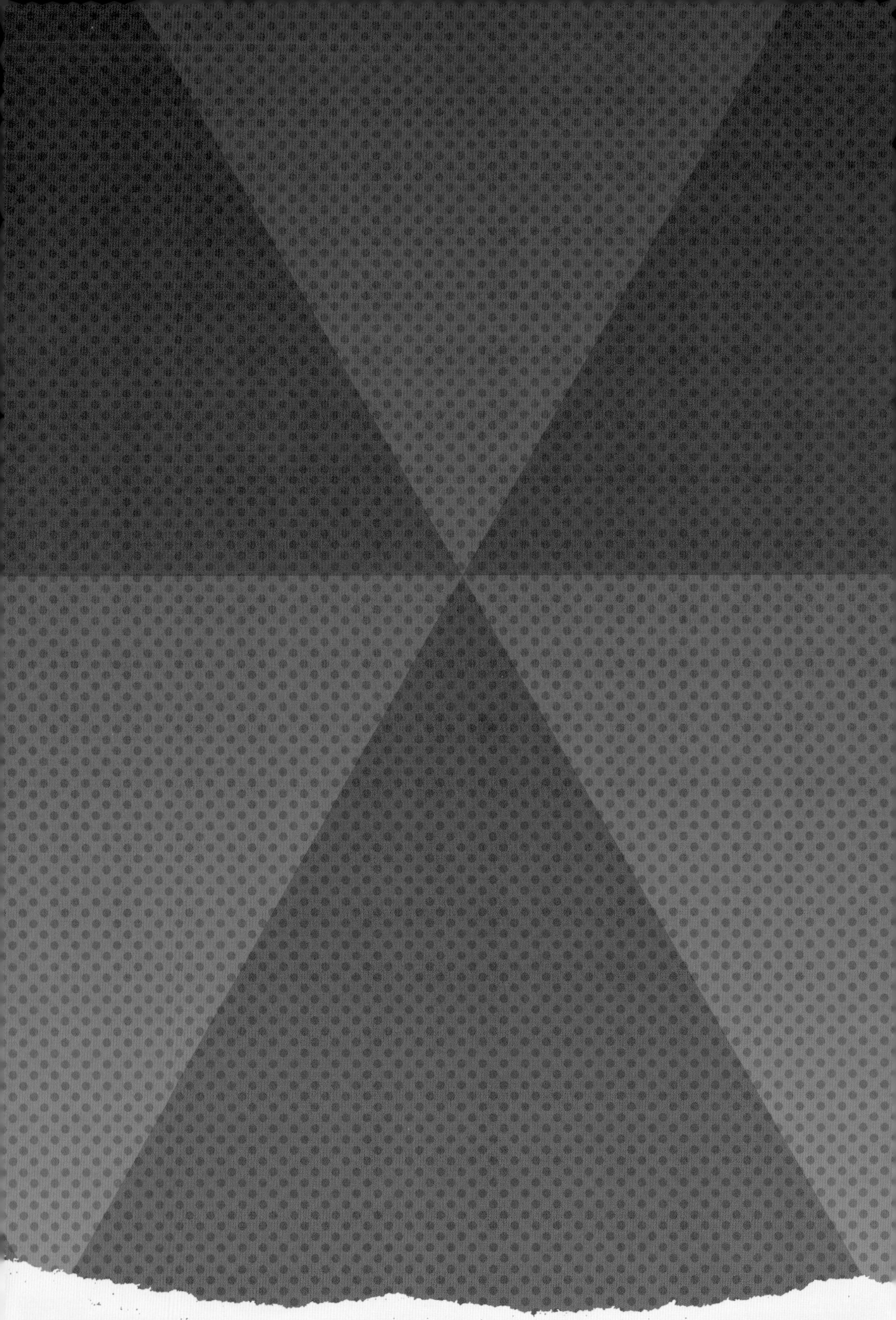

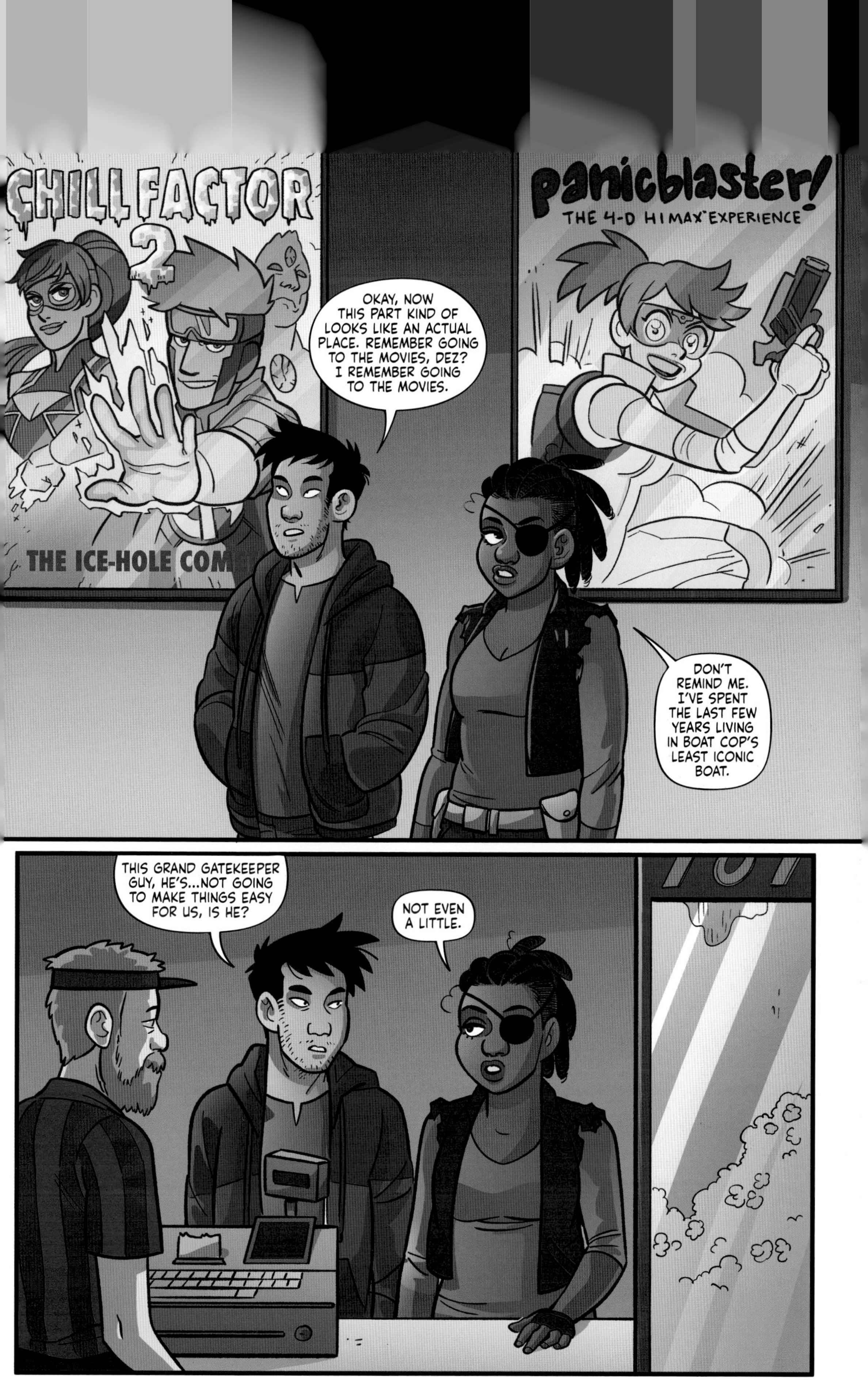
CHILL FACTOR 2
THE ICE-HOLE COM
panicblaster!
THE 4-D HIMAX™ EXPERIENCE
OKAY, NOW THIS PART KIND OF LOOKS LIKE AN ACTUAL PLACE. REMEMBER GOING TO THE MOVIES, DEZ? I REMEMBER GOING TO THE MOVIES.
DON'T REMIND ME. I'VE SPENT THE LAST FEW YEARS LIVING IN BOAT COP'S LEAST ICONIC BOAT.
THIS GRAND GATEKEEPER GUY, HE'S...NOT GOING TO MAKE THINGS EASY FOR US, IS HE?
NOT EVEN A LITTLE.

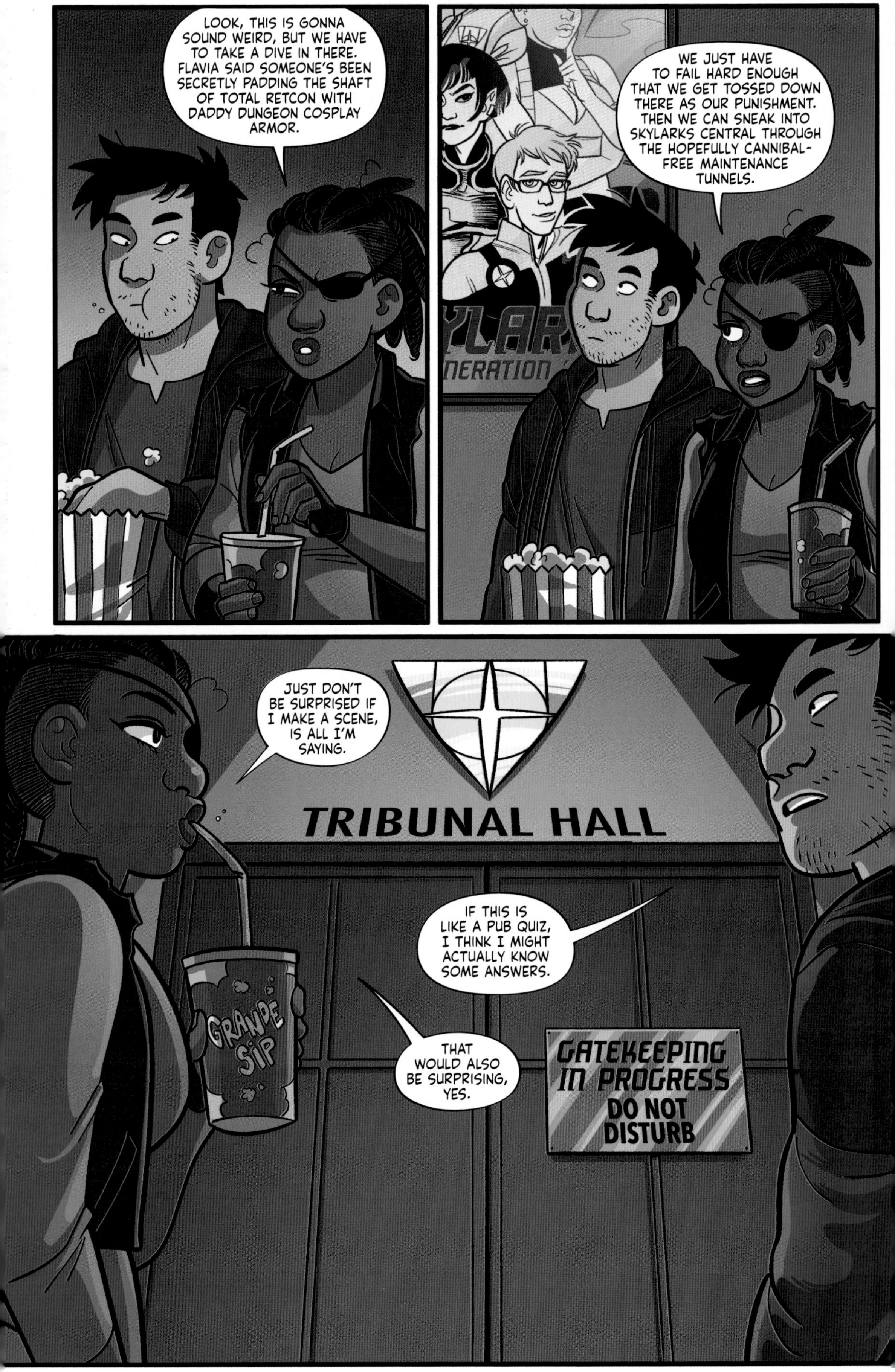
LOOK, THIS IS GONNA SOUND WEIRD, BUT WE HAVE TO TAKE A DIVE IN THERE. FLAVIA SAID SOMEONE'S BEEN SECRETLY PADDING THE SHAFT OF TOTAL RETCON WITH DADDY DUNGEON COSPLAY ARMOR.
WE JUST HAVE TO FAIL HARD ENOUGH THAT WE GET TOSSED DOWN THERE AS OUR PUNISHMENT. THEN WE CAN SNEAK INTO SKYLARKS CENTRAL THROUGH THE HOPEFULLY CANNIBAL-FREE MAINTENANCE TUNNELS.
JUST DON'T BE SURPRISED IF I MAKE A SCENE, IS ALL I'M SAYING.
TRIBUNAL HALL
IF THIS IS LIKE A PUB QUIZ, I THINK I MIGHT ACTUALLY KNOW SOME ANSWERS.
THAT WOULD ALSO BE SURPRISING, YES.
GRANDE SIP
GATEKEEPING IN PROGRESS
DO NOT DISTURB

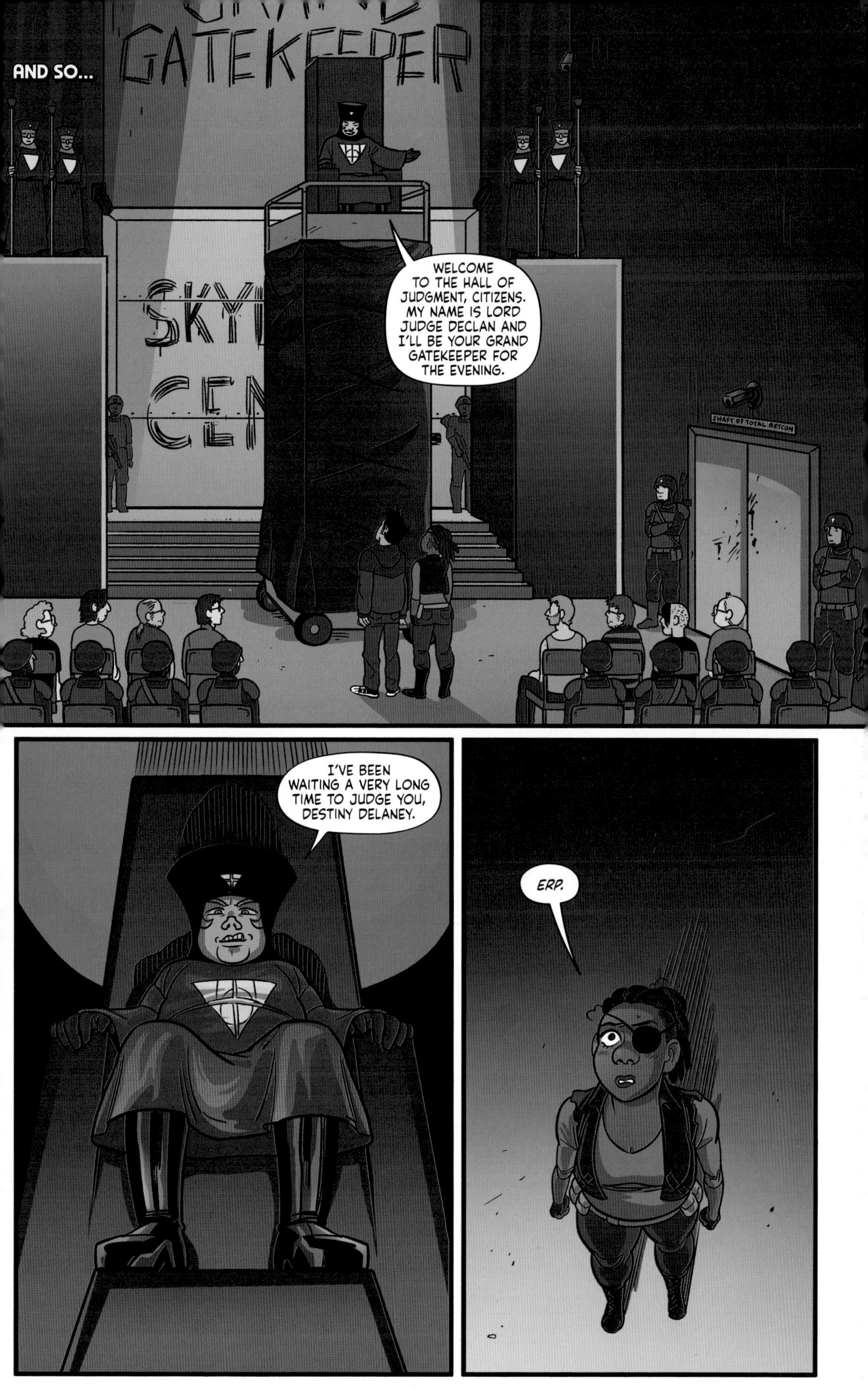
AND SO...
GRAND GATEKEEPER
WELCOME TO THE HALL OF JUDGMENT, CITIZENS. MY NAME IS LORD JUDGE DECLAN AND I'LL BE YOUR GRAND GATEKEEPER FOR THE EVENING.
SHAFT OF TOTAL RETCON
I'VE BEEN WAITING A VERY LONG TIME TO JUDGE YOU, DESTINY DELANEY.
ERP.

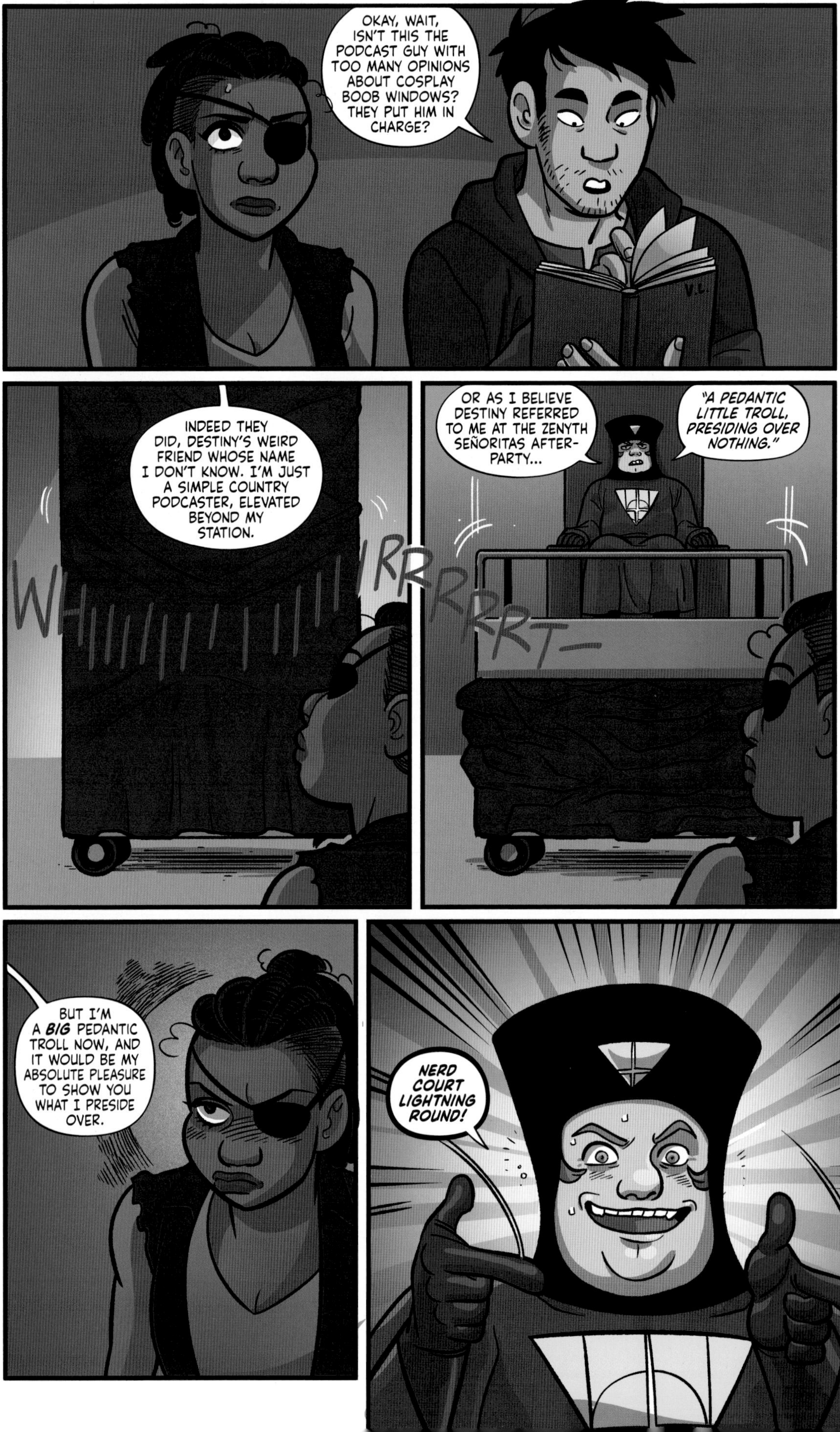
OKAY, WAIT, ISN'T THIS THE PODCAST GUY WITH TOO MANY OPINIONS ABOUT COSPLAY BOOB WINDOWS? THEY PUT HIM IN CHARGE?
V.L.
INDEED THEY DID, DESTINY'S WEIRD FRIEND WHOSE NAME I DON'T KNOW. I'M JUST A SIMPLE COUNTRY PODCASTER, ELEVATED BEYOND MY STATION.
WHIIIIIIIIIIIRRRRRRT—
OR AS I BELIEVE DESTINY REFERRED TO ME AT THE ZENYTH SEÑORITAS AFTER-PARTY...
"A PEDANTIC LITTLE TROLL, PRESIDING OVER NOTHING."
BUT I'M A *BIG* PEDANTIC TROLL NOW, AND IT WOULD BE MY ABSOLUTE PLEASURE TO SHOW YOU WHAT I PRESIDE OVER.
NERD COURT LIGHTNING ROUND!

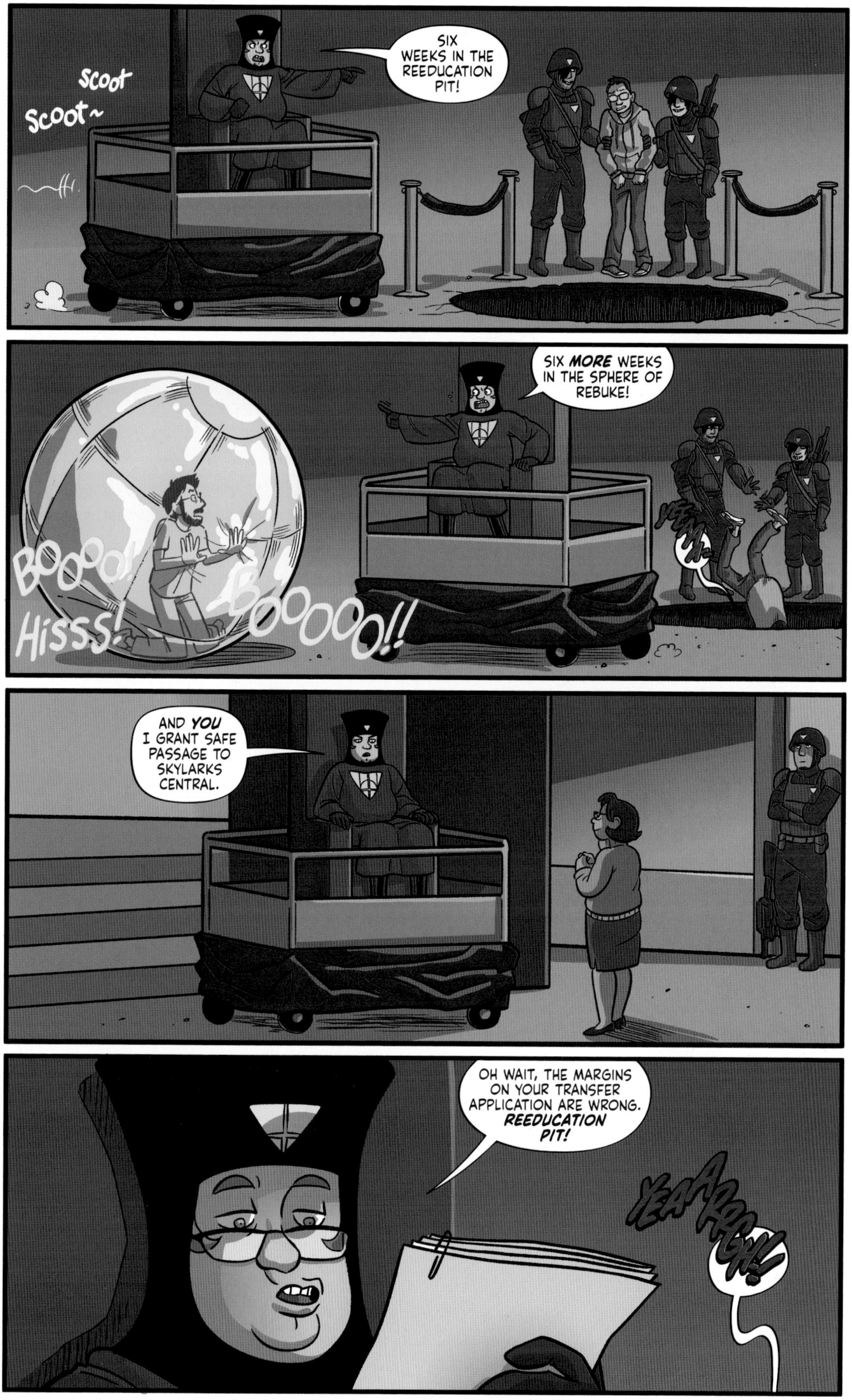
SIX WEEKS IN THE REEDUCATION PIT!
Scoot
Scoot~
SIX MORE WEEKS IN THE SPHERE OF REBUKE!
BOOOO!
HISSS!
BOOOOO!!
AND YOU I GRANT SAFE PASSAGE TO SKYLARKS CENTRAL.
OH WAIT, THE MARGINS ON YOUR TRANSFER APPLICATION ARE WRONG. REEDUCATION PIT!
YEAARGH!!

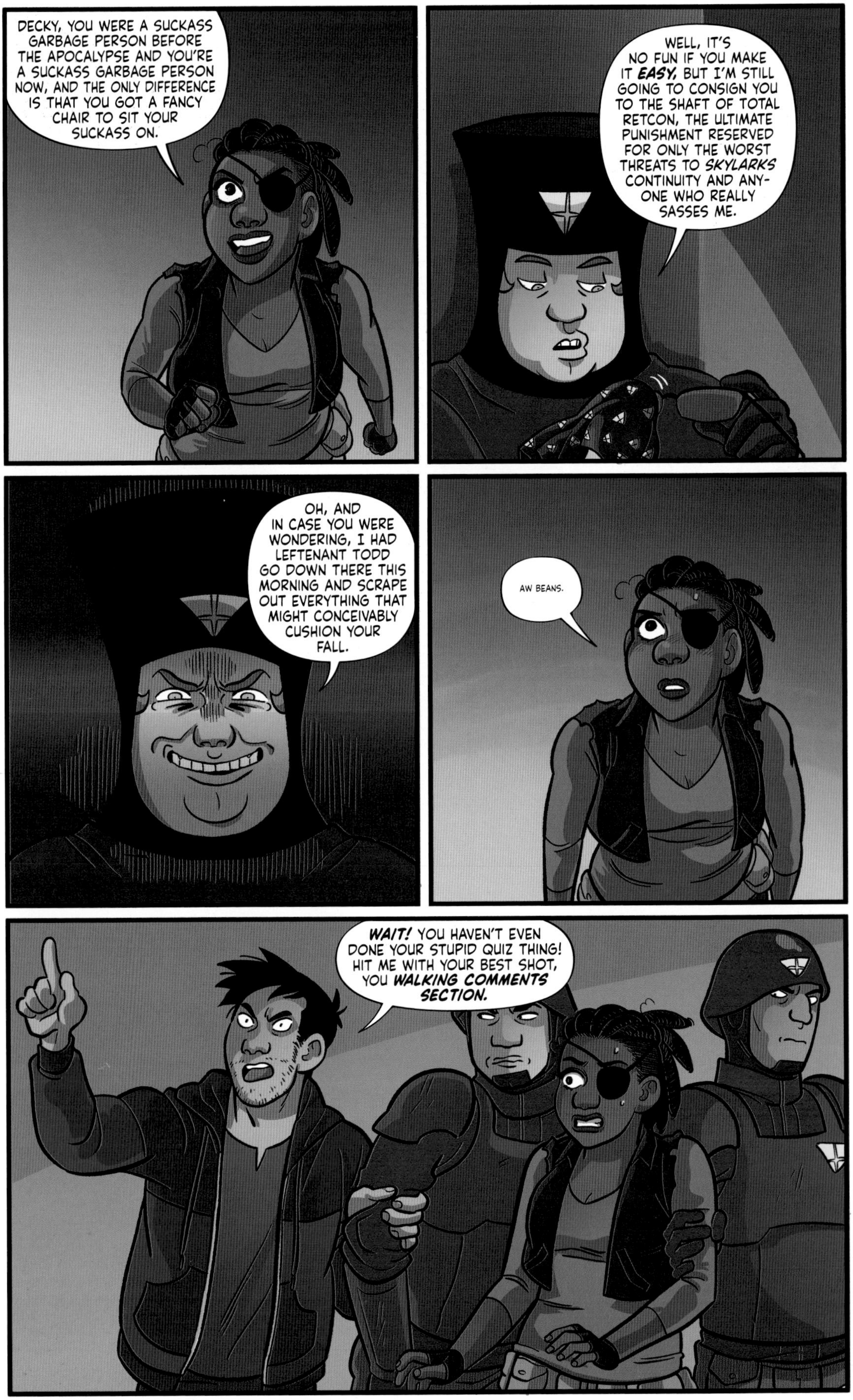

DECKY, YOU WERE A SUCKASS GARBAGE PERSON BEFORE THE APOCALYPSE AND YOU'RE A SUCKASS GARBAGE PERSON NOW, AND THE ONLY DIFFERENCE IS THAT YOU GOT A FANCY CHAIR TO SIT YOUR SUCKASS ON.
WELL, IT'S NO FUN IF YOU MAKE IT ***EASY,*** BUT I'M STILL GOING TO CONSIGN YOU TO THE SHAFT OF TOTAL RETCON, THE ULTIMATE PUNISHMENT RESERVED FOR ONLY THE WORST THREATS TO ***SKYLARKS*** CONTINUITY AND ANYONE WHO REALLY SASSES ME.
OH, AND IN CASE YOU WERE WONDERING, I HAD LEFTENANT TODD GO DOWN THERE THIS MORNING AND SCRAPE OUT EVERYTHING THAT MIGHT CONCEIVABLY CUSHION YOUR FALL.
AW BEANS.
WAIT! YOU HAVEN'T EVEN DONE YOUR STUPID QUIZ THING! HIT ME WITH YOUR BEST SHOT, YOU ***WALKING COMMENTS SECTION.***

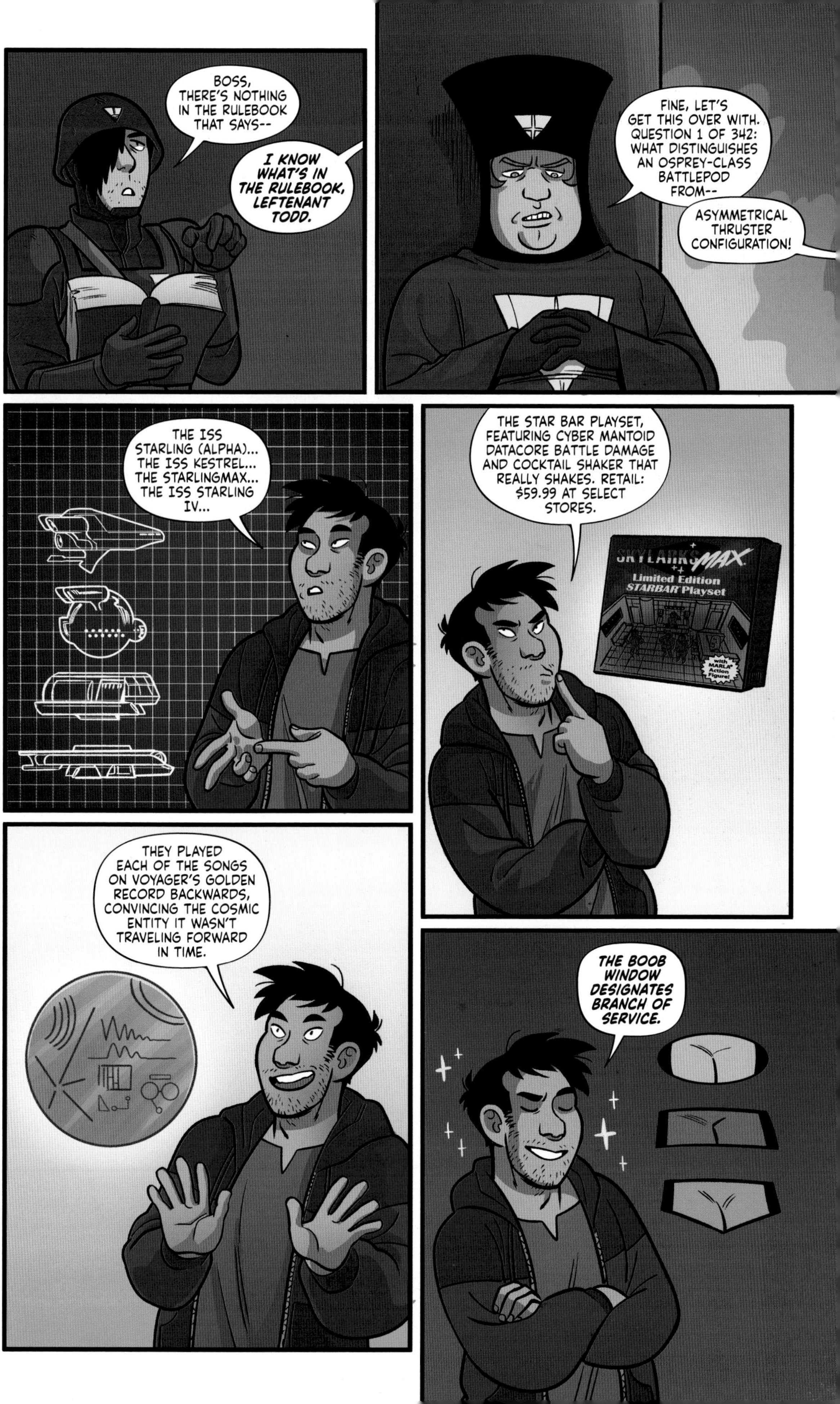
BOSS, THERE'S NOTHING IN THE RULEBOOK THAT SAYS--
I KNOW WHAT'S IN THE RULEBOOK, LEFTENANT TODD.
FINE, LET'S GET THIS OVER WITH. QUESTION 1 OF 342: WHAT DISTINGUISHES AN OSPREY-CLASS BATTLEPOD FROM--
ASYMMETRICAL THRUSTER CONFIGURATION!
THE ISS STARLING (ALPHA)... THE ISS KESTREL... THE STARLINGMAX... THE ISS STARLING IV...
THE STAR BAR PLAYSET, FEATURING CYBER MANTOID DATACORE BATTLE DAMAGE AND COCKTAIL SHAKER THAT REALLY SHAKES. RETAIL: $59.99 AT SELECT STORES.
SKYLARKS MAX
Limited Edition
STARBAR Playset
with MARLA Action Figure!
THEY PLAYED EACH OF THE SONGS ON VOYAGER'S GOLDEN RECORD BACKWARDS, CONVINCING THE COSMIC ENTITY IT WASN'T TRAVELING FORWARD IN TIME.
THE BOOB WINDOW DESIGNATES BRANCH OF SERVICE.

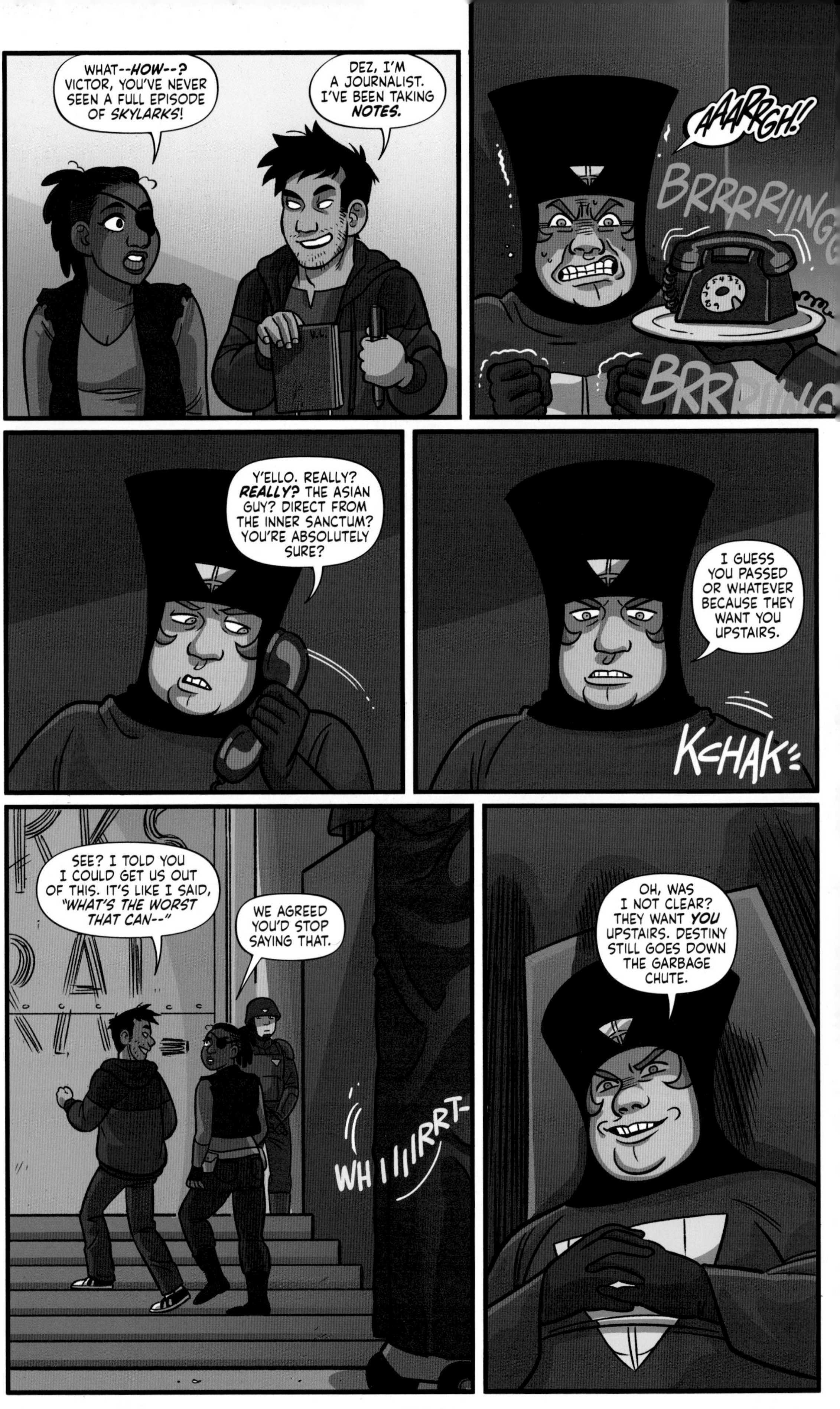
WHAT--**HOW--?** VICTOR, YOU'VE NEVER SEEN A FULL EPISODE OF *SKYLARKS*!
DEZ, I'M A JOURNALIST. I'VE BEEN TAKING **NOTES.**
AAARRGH!
BRRRRIINGG
BRRRING
Y'ELLO. REALLY? **REALLY?** THE ASIAN GUY? DIRECT FROM THE INNER SANCTUM? YOU'RE ABSOLUTELY SURE?
I GUESS YOU PASSED OR WHATEVER BECAUSE THEY WANT YOU UPSTAIRS.
KCHAK
SEE? I TOLD YOU I COULD GET US OUT OF THIS. IT'S LIKE I SAID, ***"WHAT'S THE WORST THAT CAN--"***
WE AGREED YOU'D STOP SAYING THAT.
WHIIIIRRT-
OH, WAS I NOT CLEAR? THEY WANT **YOU** UPSTAIRS. DESTINY STILL GOES DOWN THE GARBAGE CHUTE.

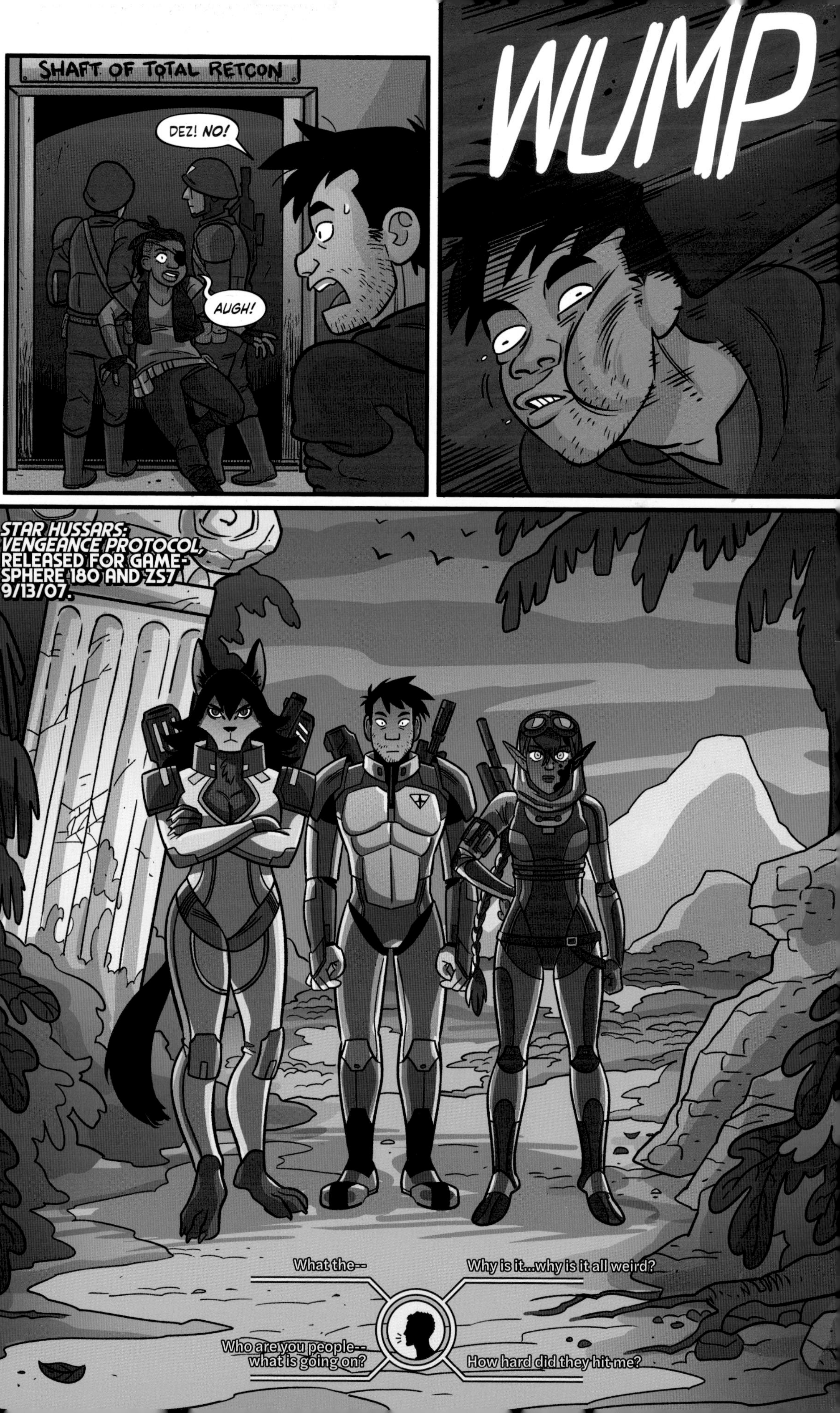
SHAFT OF TOTAL RETCON
DEZ! NO!
AUGH!
WUMP
STAR HUSSARS: VENGEANCE PROTOCOL, RELEASED FOR GAME-SPHERE 180 AND ZS7 9/13/07.
What the--
Why is it...why is it all weird?
Who are you people--what is going on?
How hard did they hit me?

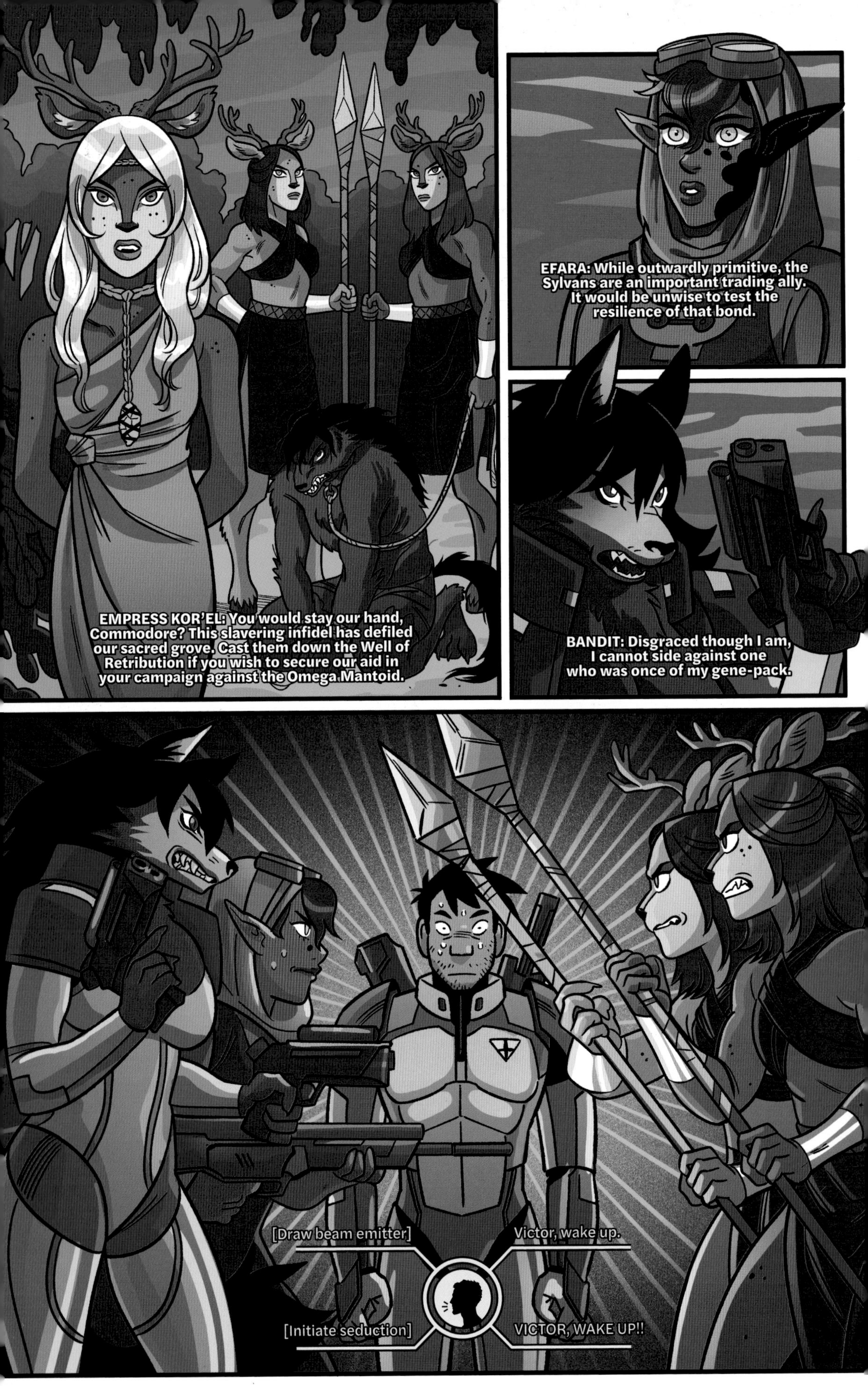
EMPRESS KOR'EL: You would stay our hand, Commodore? This slavering infidel has defiled our sacred grove. Cast them down the Well of Retribution if you wish to secure our aid in your campaign against the Omega Mantoid.
EFARA: While outwardly primitive, the Sylvans are an important trading ally. It would be unwise to test the resilience of that bond.
BANDIT: Disgraced though I am, I cannot side against one who was once of my gene-pack.
[Draw beam emitter]
Victor, wake up.
[Initiate seduction]
VICTOR, WAKE UP!!

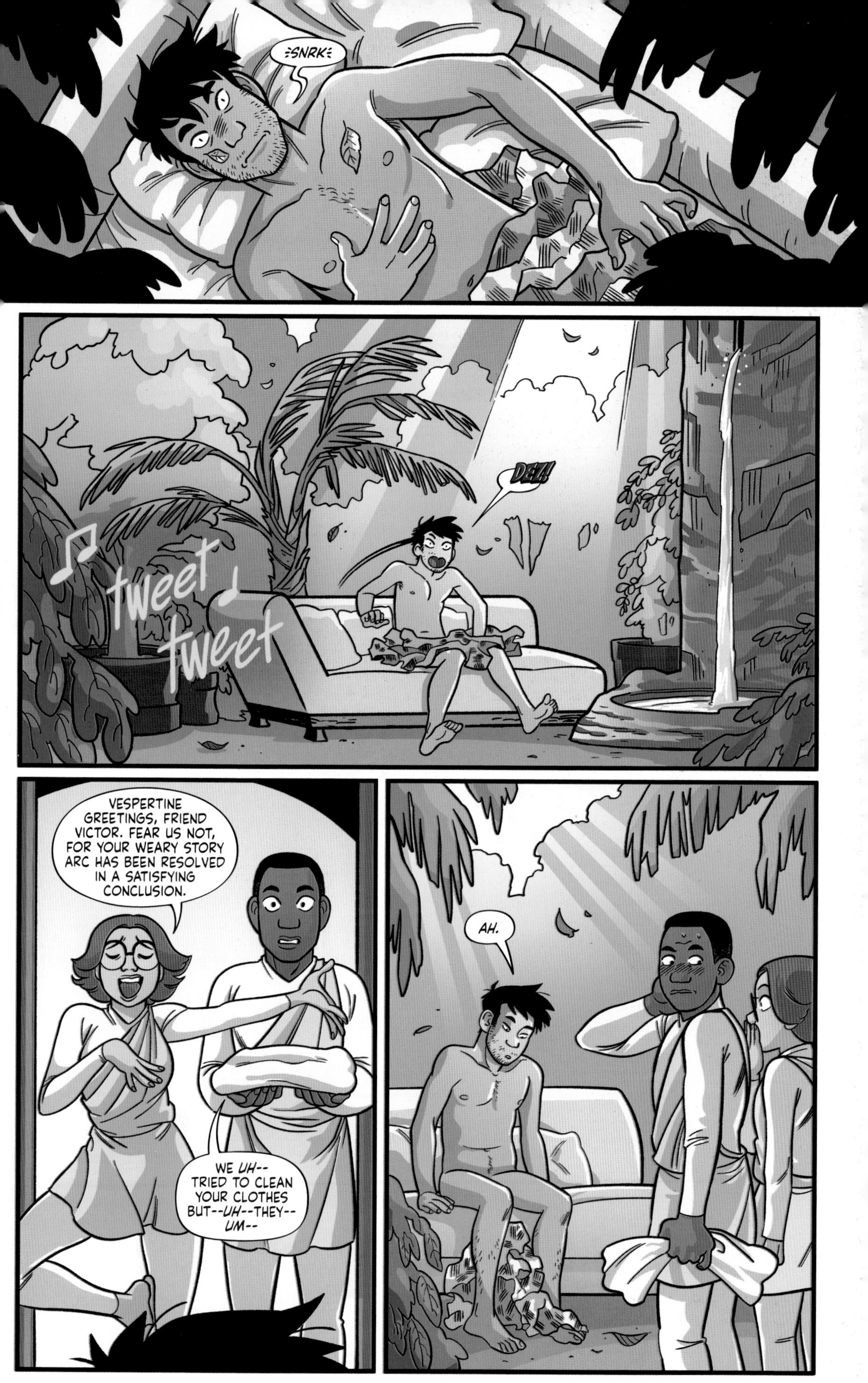
SNRK
DEZ!
tweet tweet
VESPERTINE GREETINGS, FRIEND VICTOR. FEAR US NOT, FOR YOUR WEARY STORY ARC HAS BEEN RESOLVED IN A SATISFYING CONCLUSION.
WE UH-- TRIED TO CLEAN YOUR CLOTHES BUT--UH--THEY-- UM--
AH.

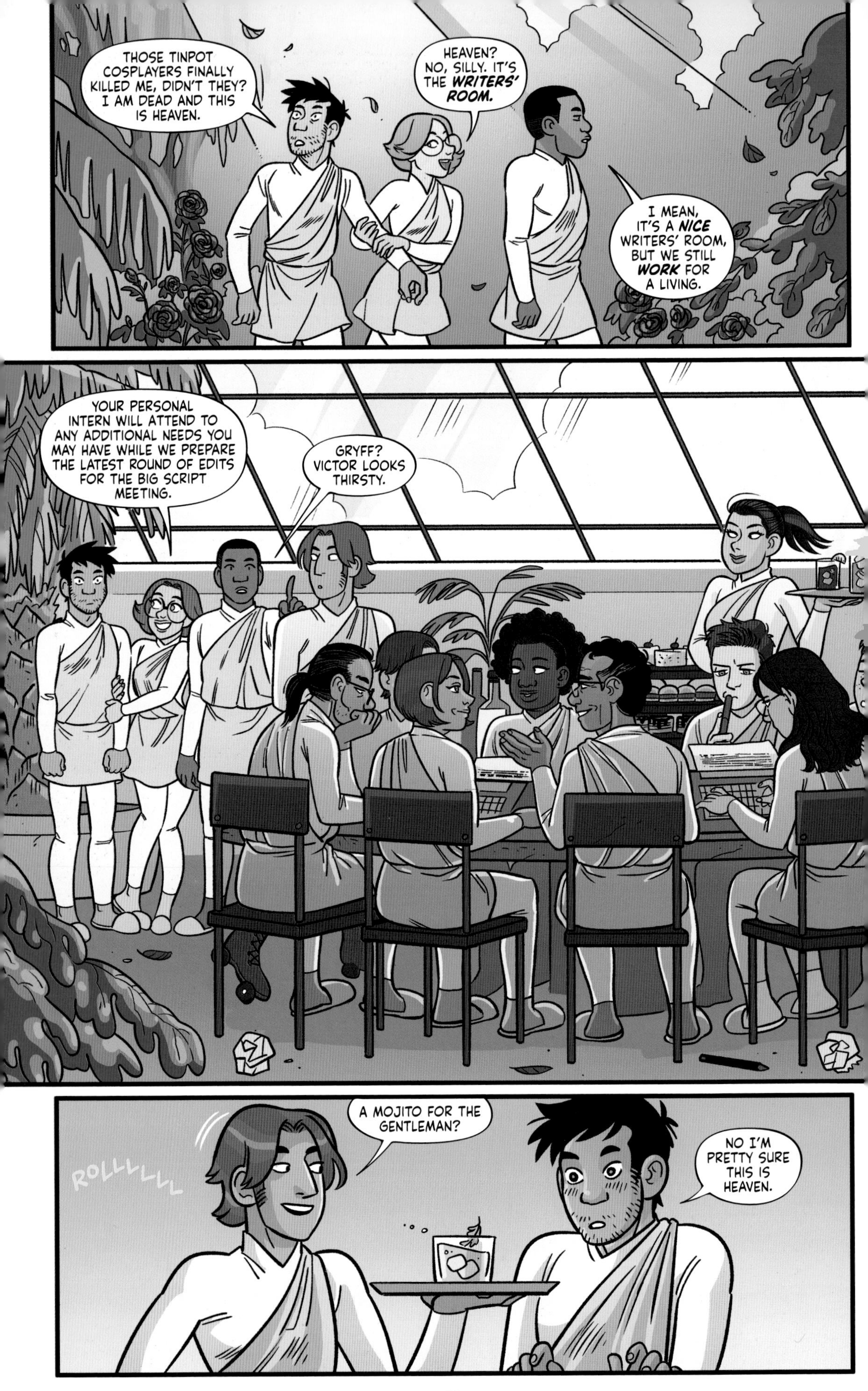
THOSE TINPOT COSPLAYERS FINALLY KILLED ME, DIDN'T THEY? I AM DEAD AND THIS IS HEAVEN.
HEAVEN? NO, SILLY. IT'S THE ***WRITERS' ROOM.***
I MEAN, IT'S A ***NICE*** WRITERS' ROOM, BUT WE STILL ***WORK*** FOR A LIVING.
YOUR PERSONAL INTERN WILL ATTEND TO ANY ADDITIONAL NEEDS YOU MAY HAVE WHILE WE PREPARE THE LATEST ROUND OF EDITS FOR THE BIG SCRIPT MEETING.
GRYFF? VICTOR LOOKS THIRSTY.
ROLLLLLLL
A MOJITO FOR THE GENTLEMAN?
NO I'M PRETTY SURE THIS IS HEAVEN.

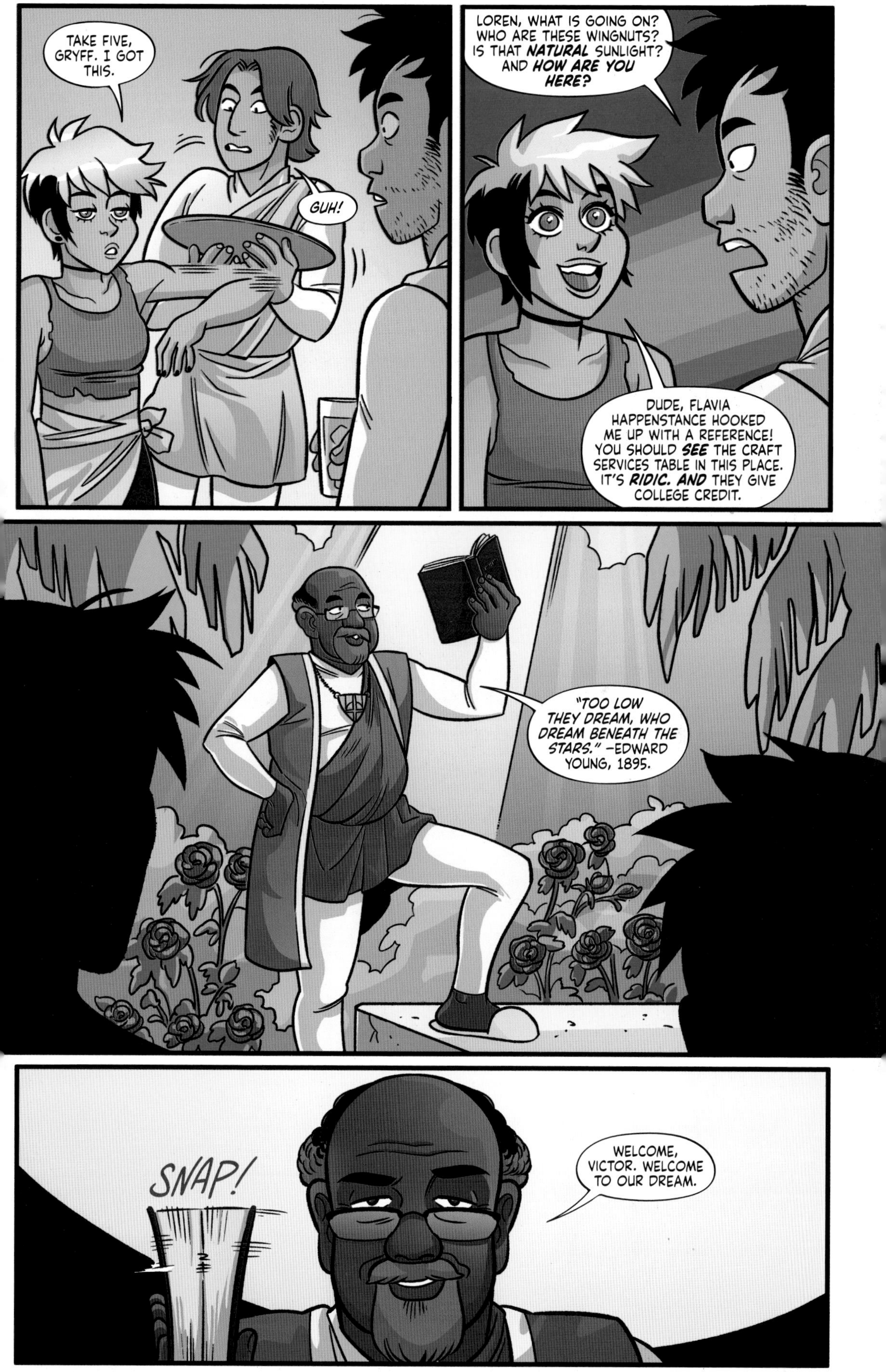
TAKE FIVE, GRYFF. I GOT THIS.
GUH!
LOREN, WHAT IS GOING ON? WHO ARE THESE WINGNUTS? IS THAT NATURAL SUNLIGHT? AND HOW ARE YOU HERE?
DUDE, FLAVIA HAPPENSTANCE HOOKED ME UP WITH A REFERENCE! YOU SHOULD SEE THE CRAFT SERVICES TABLE IN THIS PLACE. IT'S RIDIC. AND THEY GIVE COLLEGE CREDIT.
"TOO LOW THEY DREAM, WHO DREAM BENEATH THE STARS." –EDWARD YOUNG, 1895.
SNAP!
WELCOME, VICTOR. WELCOME TO OUR DREAM.

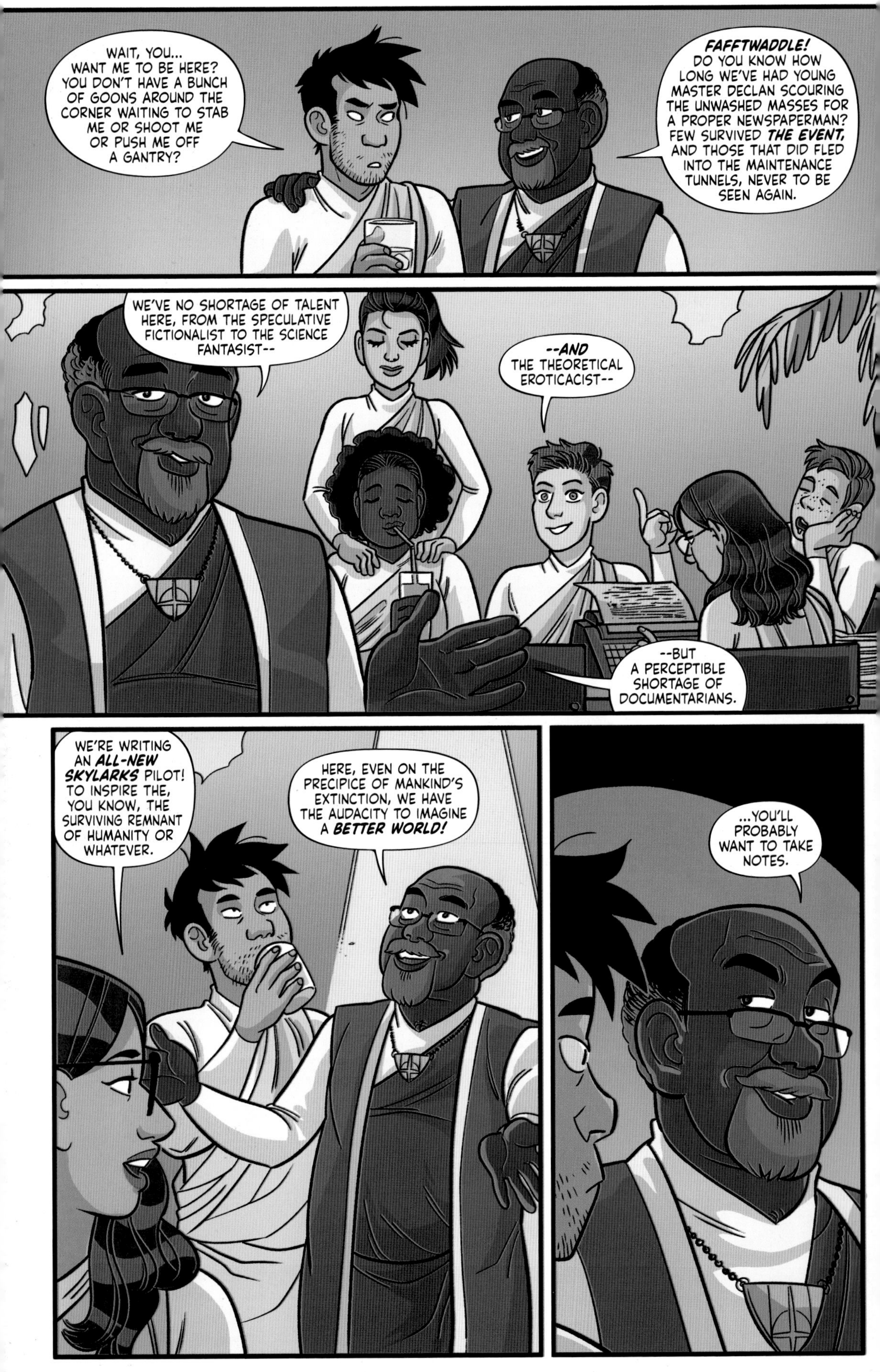

WAIT, YOU... WANT ME TO BE HERE? YOU DON'T HAVE A BUNCH OF GOONS AROUND THE CORNER WAITING TO STAB ME OR SHOOT ME OR PUSH ME OFF A GANTRY?
FAFFTWADDLE! DO YOU KNOW HOW LONG WE'VE HAD YOUNG MASTER DECLAN SCOURING THE UNWASHED MASSES FOR A PROPER NEWSPAPERMAN? FEW SURVIVED THE EVENT, AND THOSE THAT DID FLED INTO THE MAINTENANCE TUNNELS, NEVER TO BE SEEN AGAIN.
WE'VE NO SHORTAGE OF TALENT HERE, FROM THE SPECULATIVE FICTIONALIST TO THE SCIENCE FANTASIST--
--AND THE THEORETICAL EROTICACIST--
--BUT A PERCEPTIBLE SHORTAGE OF DOCUMENTARIANS.
WE'RE WRITING AN ALL-NEW SKYLARKS PILOT! TO INSPIRE THE, YOU KNOW, THE SURVIVING REMNANT OF HUMANITY OR WHATEVER.
HERE, EVEN ON THE PRECIPICE OF MANKIND'S EXTINCTION, WE HAVE THE AUDACITY TO IMAGINE A BETTER WORLD!
...YOU'LL PROBABLY WANT TO TAKE NOTES.

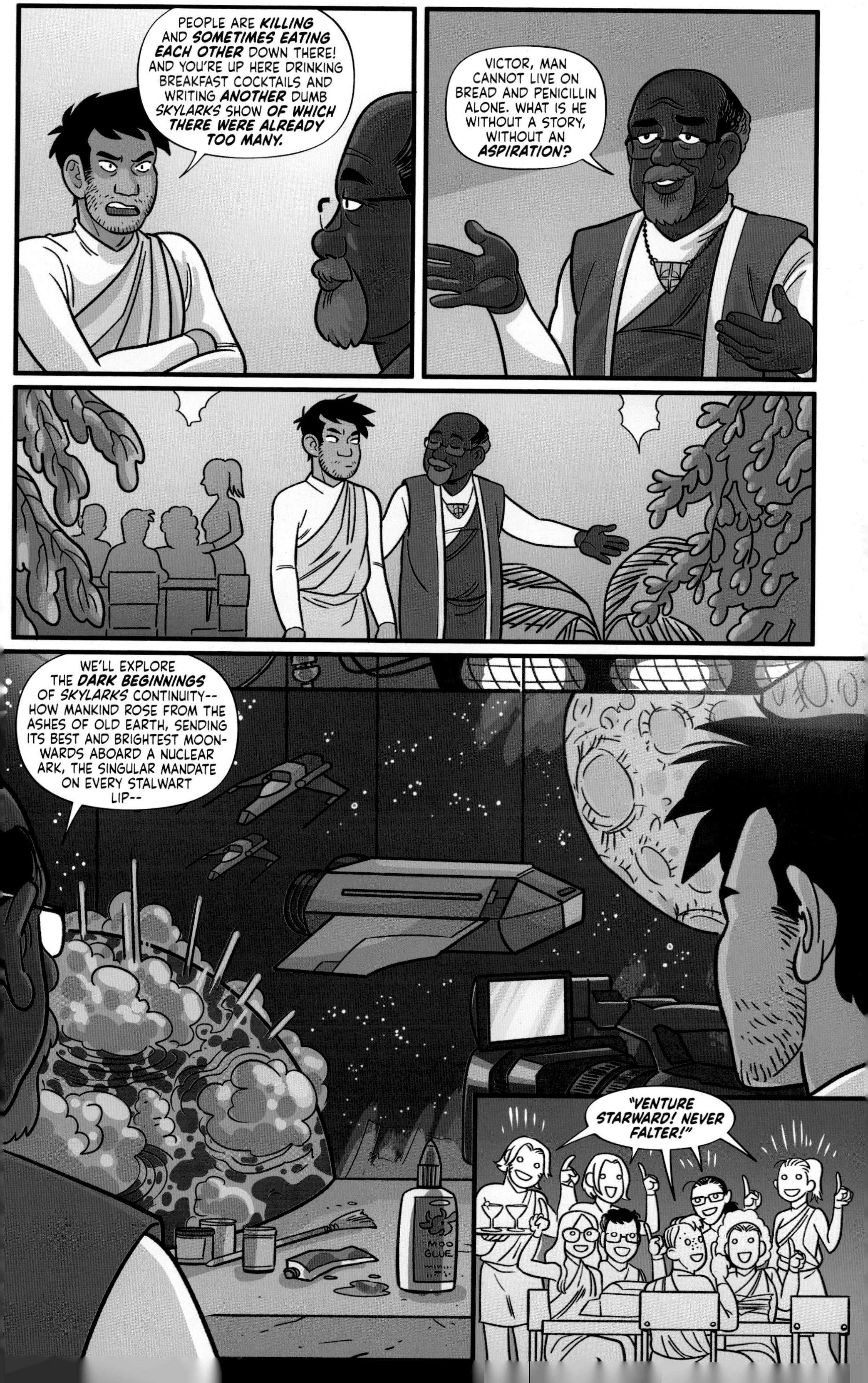
PEOPLE ARE KILLING AND SOMETIMES EATING EACH OTHER DOWN THERE! AND YOU'RE UP HERE DRINKING BREAKFAST COCKTAILS AND WRITING ANOTHER DUMB SKYLARKS SHOW OF WHICH THERE WERE ALREADY TOO MANY.
VICTOR, MAN CANNOT LIVE ON BREAD AND PENICILLIN ALONE. WHAT IS HE WITHOUT A STORY, WITHOUT AN ASPIRATION?
WE'LL EXPLORE THE DARK BEGINNINGS OF SKYLARKS CONTINUITY-- HOW MANKIND ROSE FROM THE ASHES OF OLD EARTH, SENDING ITS BEST AND BRIGHTEST MOON-WARDS ABOARD A NUCLEAR ARK, THE SINGULAR MANDATE ON EVERY STALWART LIP--
MOO GLUE
"VENTURE STARWARD! NEVER FALTER!"

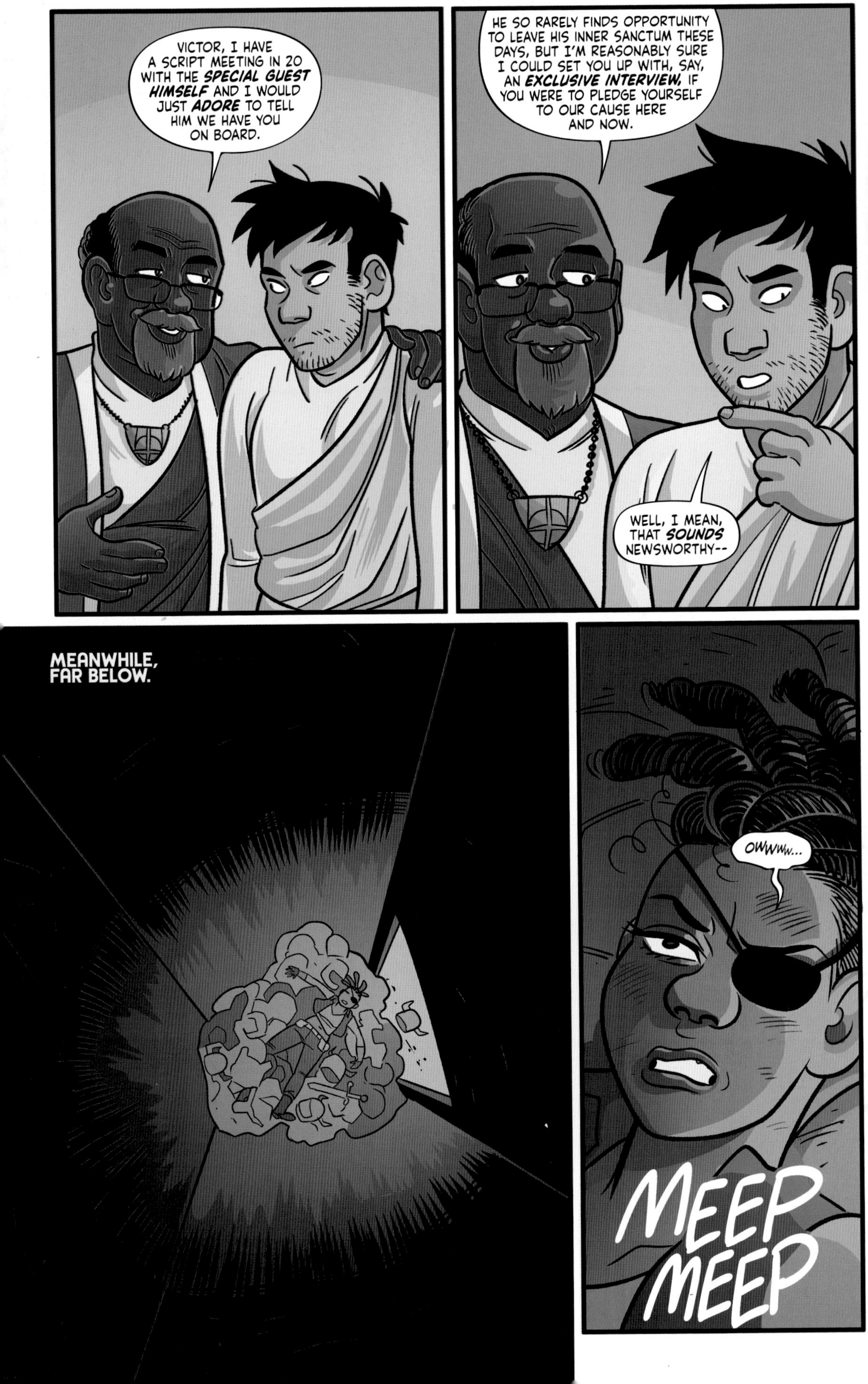
VICTOR, I HAVE A SCRIPT MEETING IN 20 WITH THE SPECIAL GUEST HIMSELF AND I WOULD JUST ADORE TO TELL HIM WE HAVE YOU ON BOARD.
HE SO RARELY FINDS OPPORTUNITY TO LEAVE HIS INNER SANCTUM THESE DAYS, BUT I'M REASONABLY SURE I COULD SET YOU UP WITH, SAY, AN EXCLUSIVE INTERVIEW, IF YOU WERE TO PLEDGE YOURSELF TO OUR CAUSE HERE AND NOW.
WELL, I MEAN, THAT SOUNDS NEWSWORTHY--
MEANWHILE, FAR BELOW.
OWWWW...
MEEP MEEP

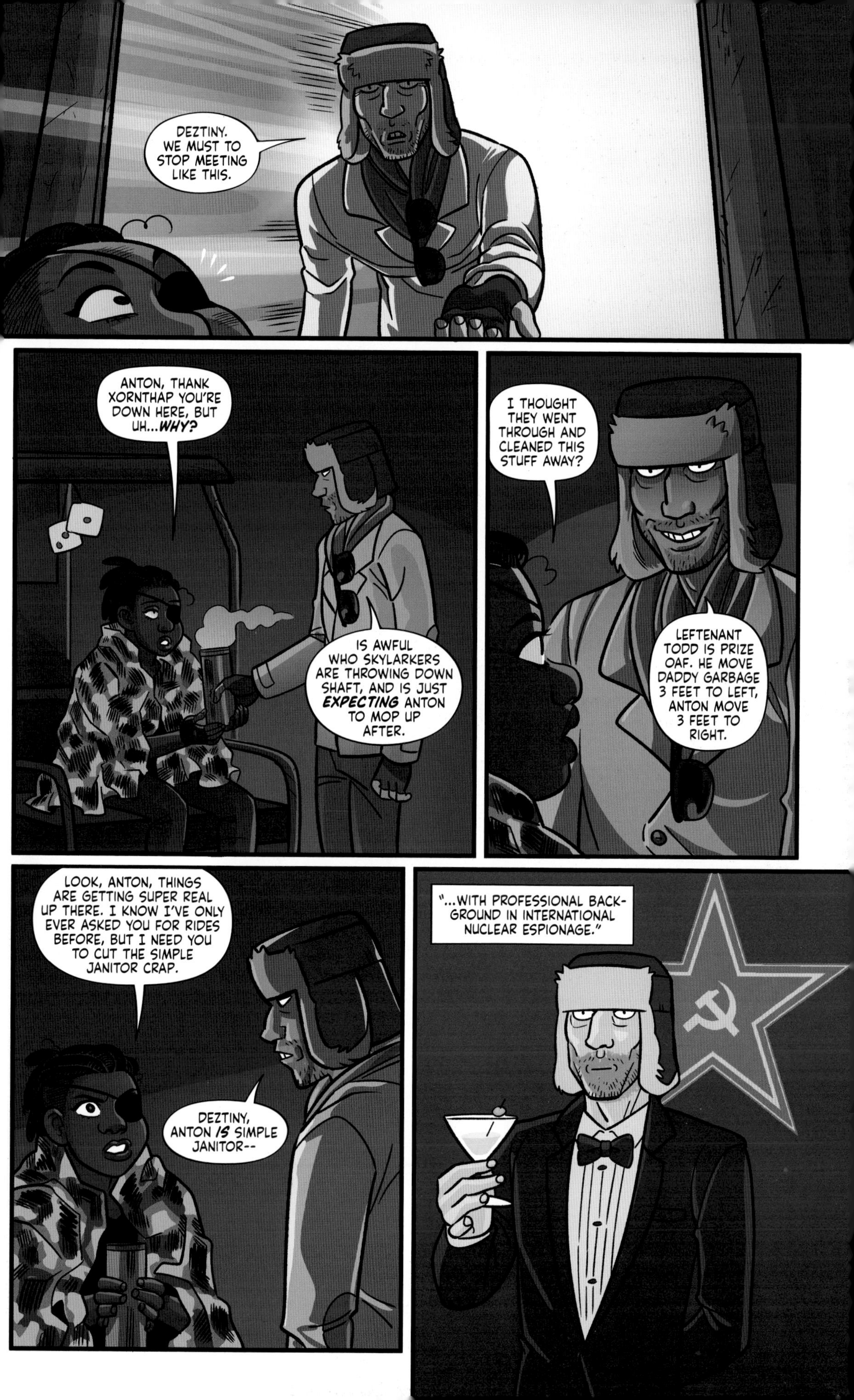
DEZTINY. WE MUST TO STOP MEETING LIKE THIS.
ANTON, THANK XORNTHAP YOU'RE DOWN HERE, BUT UH...WHY?
IS AWFUL WHO SKYLARKERS ARE THROWING DOWN SHAFT, AND IS JUST EXPECTING ANTON TO MOP UP AFTER.
I THOUGHT THEY WENT THROUGH AND CLEANED THIS STUFF AWAY?
LEFTENANT TODD IS PRIZE OAF. HE MOVE DADDY GARBAGE 3 FEET TO LEFT, ANTON MOVE 3 FEET TO RIGHT.
LOOK, ANTON, THINGS ARE GETTING SUPER REAL UP THERE. I KNOW I'VE ONLY EVER ASKED YOU FOR RIDES BEFORE, BUT I NEED YOU TO CUT THE SIMPLE JANITOR CRAP.
DEZTINY, ANTON IS SIMPLE JANITOR--
"...WITH PROFESSIONAL BACK-GROUND IN INTERNATIONAL NUCLEAR ESPIONAGE."

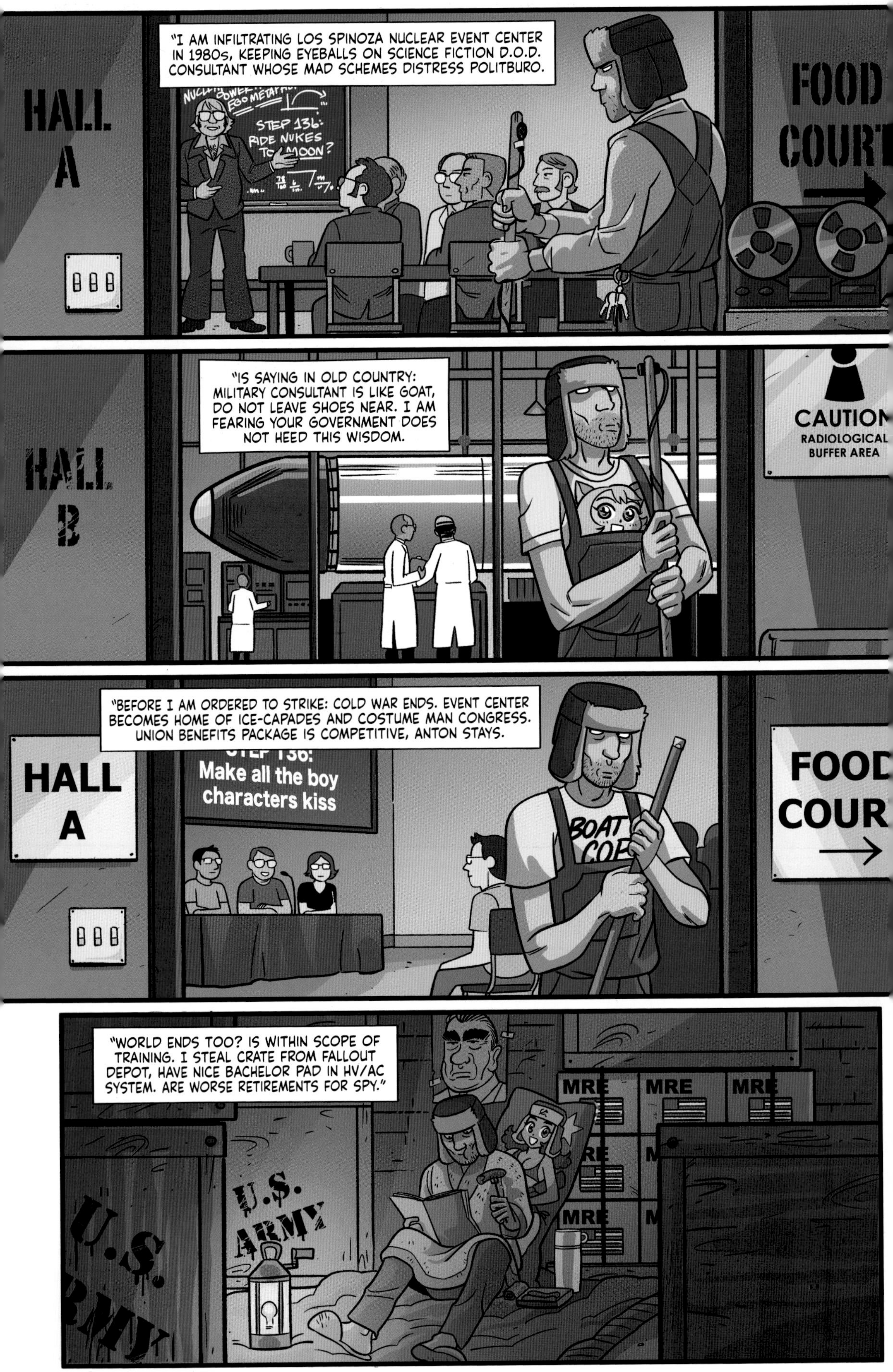
"I AM INFILTRATING LOS SPINOZA NUCLEAR EVENT CENTER IN 1980s, KEEPING EYEBALLS ON SCIENCE FICTION D.O.D. CONSULTANT WHOSE MAD SCHEMES DISTRESS POLITBURO.
HALL A
STEP 136: RIDE NUKES TO MOON?
FOOD COURT
"IS SAYING IN OLD COUNTRY: MILITARY CONSULTANT IS LIKE GOAT, DO NOT LEAVE SHOES NEAR. I AM FEARING YOUR GOVERNMENT DOES NOT HEED THIS WISDOM.
HALL B
CAUTION RADIOLOGICAL BUFFER AREA
"BEFORE I AM ORDERED TO STRIKE: COLD WAR ENDS. EVENT CENTER BECOMES HOME OF ICE-CAPADES AND COSTUME MAN CONGRESS. UNION BENEFITS PACKAGE IS COMPETITIVE, ANTON STAYS.
HALL A
Make all the boy characters kiss
FOOD COURT
"WORLD ENDS TOO? IS WITHIN SCOPE OF TRAINING. I STEAL CRATE FROM FALLOUT DEPOT, HAVE NICE BACHELOR PAD IN HV/AC SYSTEM. ARE WORSE RETIREMENTS FOR SPY."
MRE
MRE
MRE
U.S. ARMY
U.S.

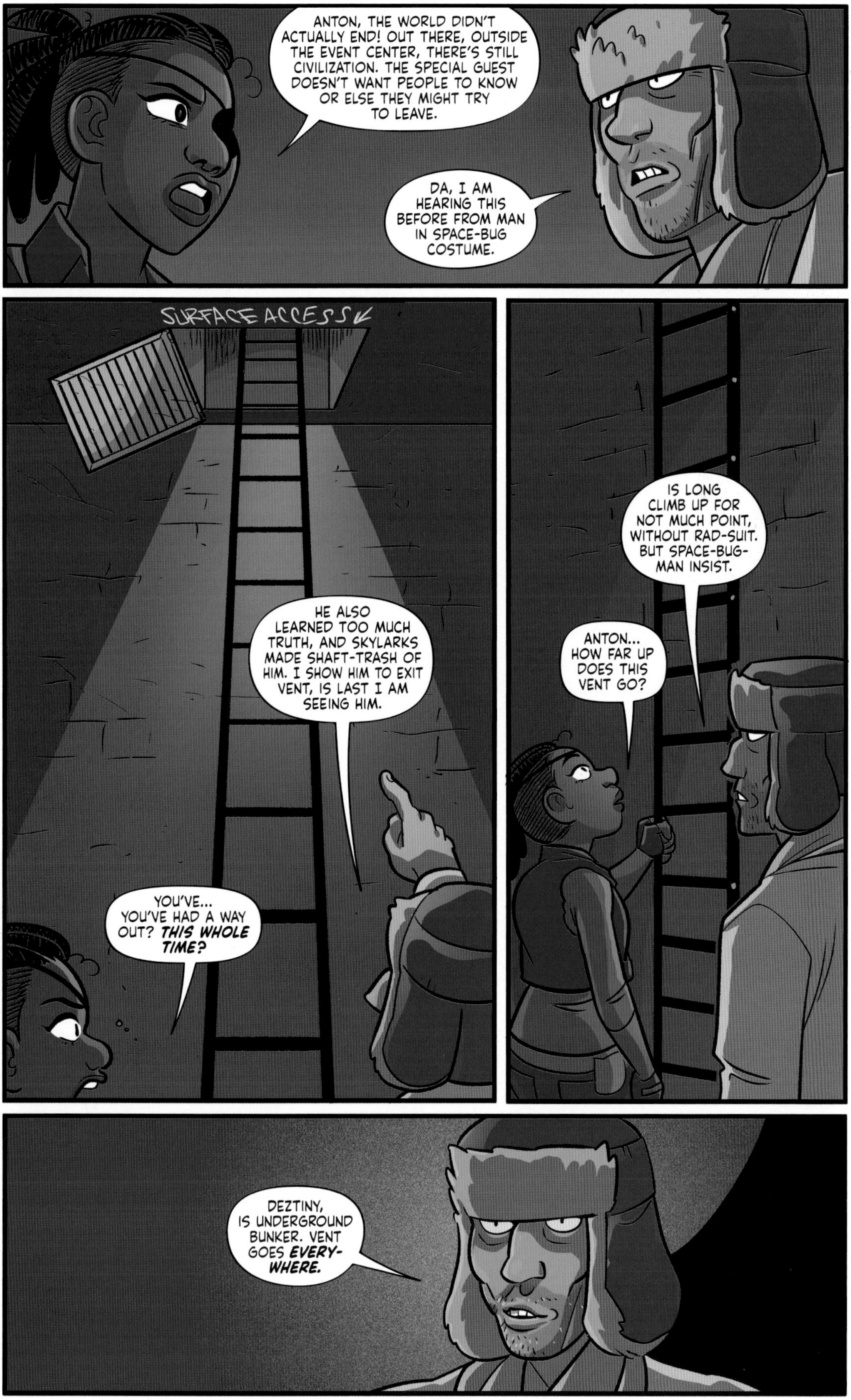
ANTON, THE WORLD DIDN'T ACTUALLY END! OUT THERE, OUTSIDE THE EVENT CENTER, THERE'S STILL CIVILIZATION. THE SPECIAL GUEST DOESN'T WANT PEOPLE TO KNOW OR ELSE THEY MIGHT TRY TO LEAVE.
DA, I AM HEARING THIS BEFORE FROM MAN IN SPACE-BUG COSTUME.
SURFACE ACCESS
HE ALSO LEARNED TOO MUCH TRUTH, AND SKYLARKS MADE SHAFT-TRASH OF HIM. I SHOW HIM TO EXIT VENT, IS LAST I AM SEEING HIM.
YOU'VE... YOU'VE HAD A WAY OUT? ***THIS WHOLE TIME?***
ANTON... HOW FAR UP DOES THIS VENT GO?
IS LONG CLIMB UP FOR NOT MUCH POINT, WITHOUT RAD-SUIT. BUT SPACE-BUG-MAN INSIST.
DEZTINY, IS UNDERGROUND BUNKER. VENT GOES ***EVERY-WHERE.***

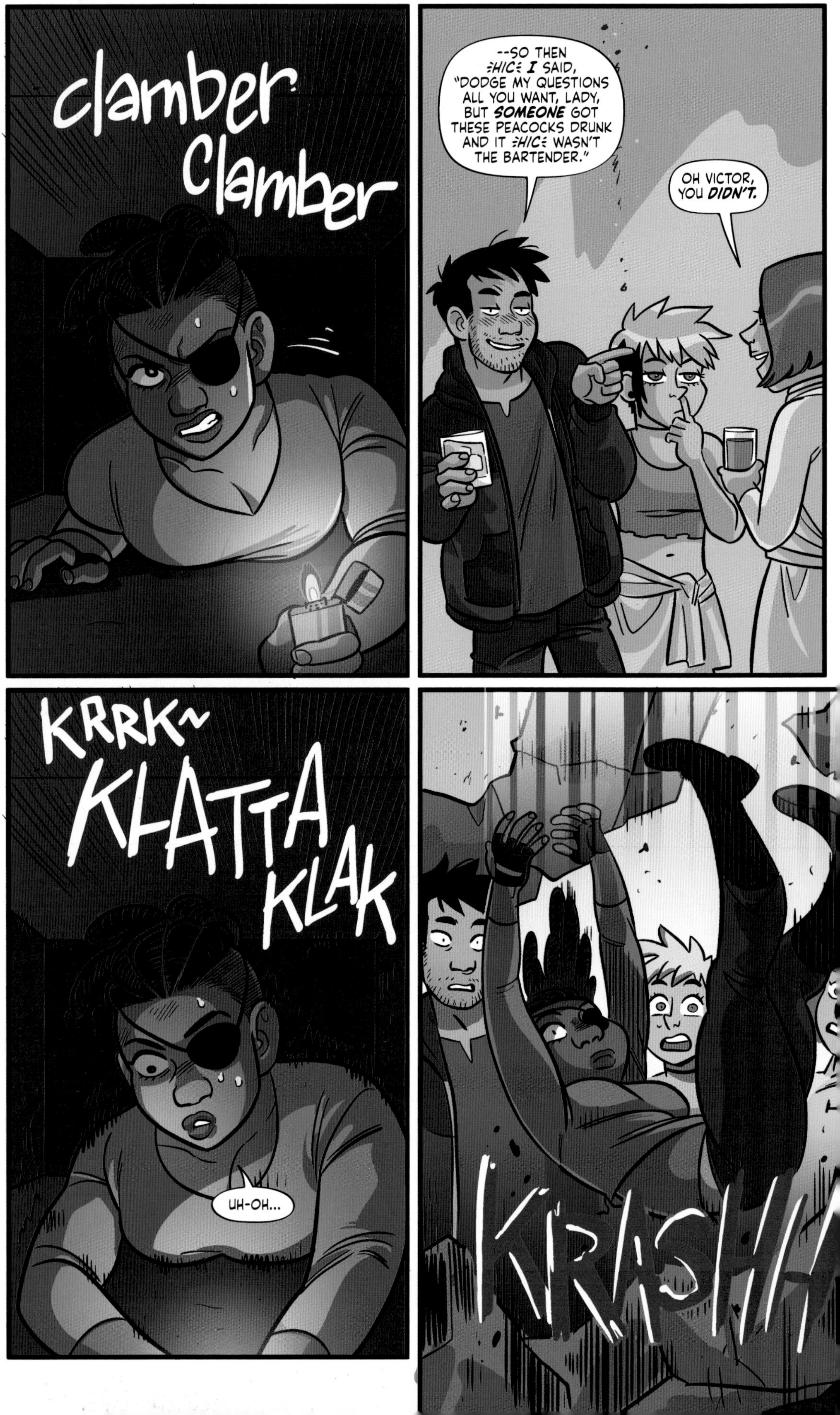
clamber clamber clamber
--SO THEN ≡HIC≡ I SAID, "DODGE MY QUESTIONS ALL YOU WANT, LADY, BUT SOMEONE GOT THESE PEACOCKS DRUNK AND IT ≡HIC≡ WASN'T THE BARTENDER."
OH VICTOR, YOU DIDN'T.
KRRK~ KLATTA KLAK
UH-OH...
KRASHH

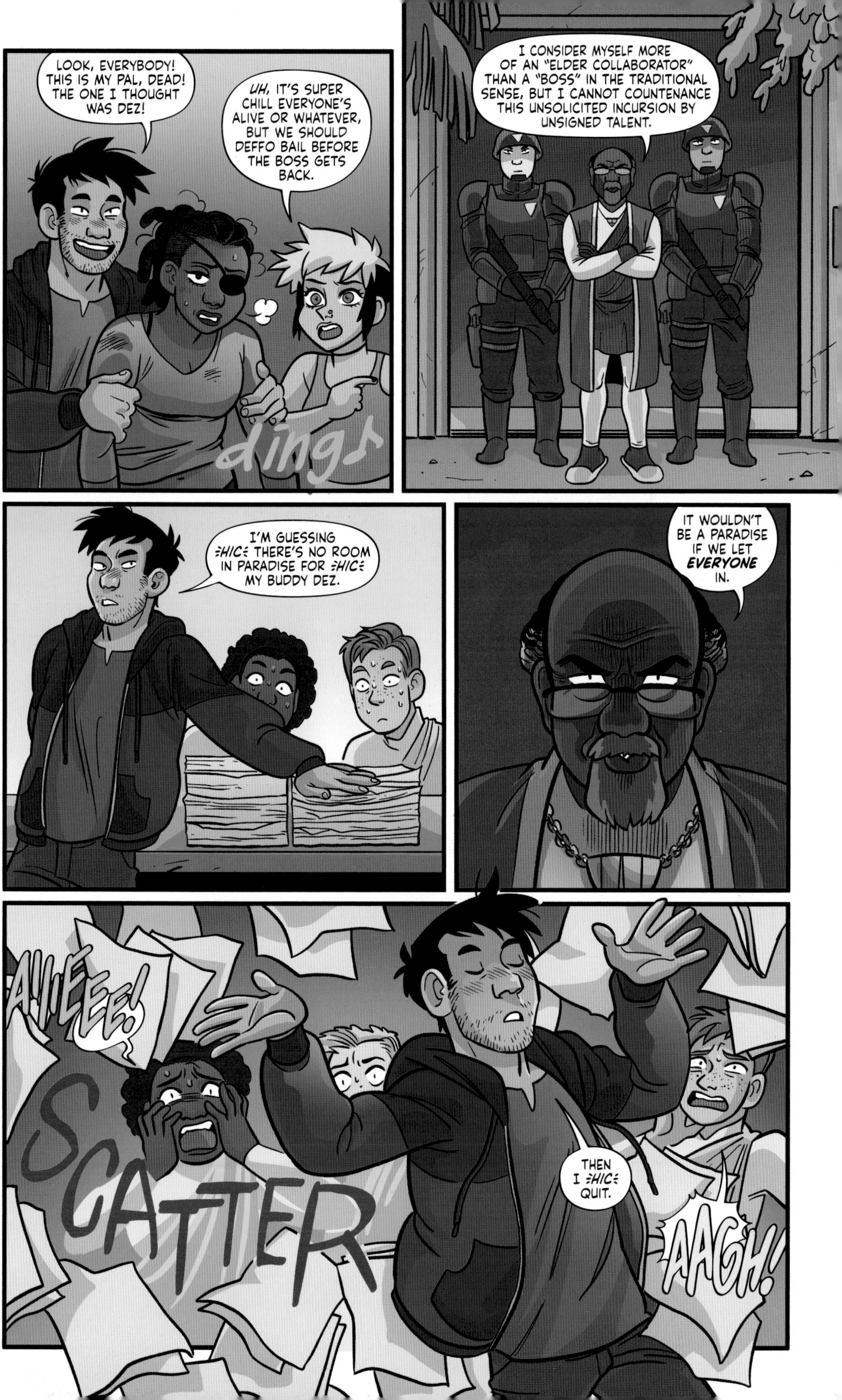
LOOK, EVERYBODY! THIS IS MY PAL, DEAD! THE ONE I THOUGHT WAS DEZ!
UH, IT'S SUPER CHILL EVERYONE'S ALIVE OR WHATEVER, BUT WE SHOULD DEFFO BAIL BEFORE THE BOSS GETS BACK.
ding♪
I CONSIDER MYSELF MORE OF AN "ELDER COLLABORATOR" THAN A "BOSS" IN THE TRADITIONAL SENSE, BUT I CANNOT COUNTENANCE THIS UNSOLICITED INCURSION BY UNSIGNED TALENT.
I'M GUESSING HIC THERE'S NO ROOM IN PARADISE FOR HIC MY BUDDY DEZ.
IT WOULDN'T BE A PARADISE IF WE LET EVERYONE IN.
AIIEEE!
SCATTER
THEN I HIC QUIT.
AAGH!

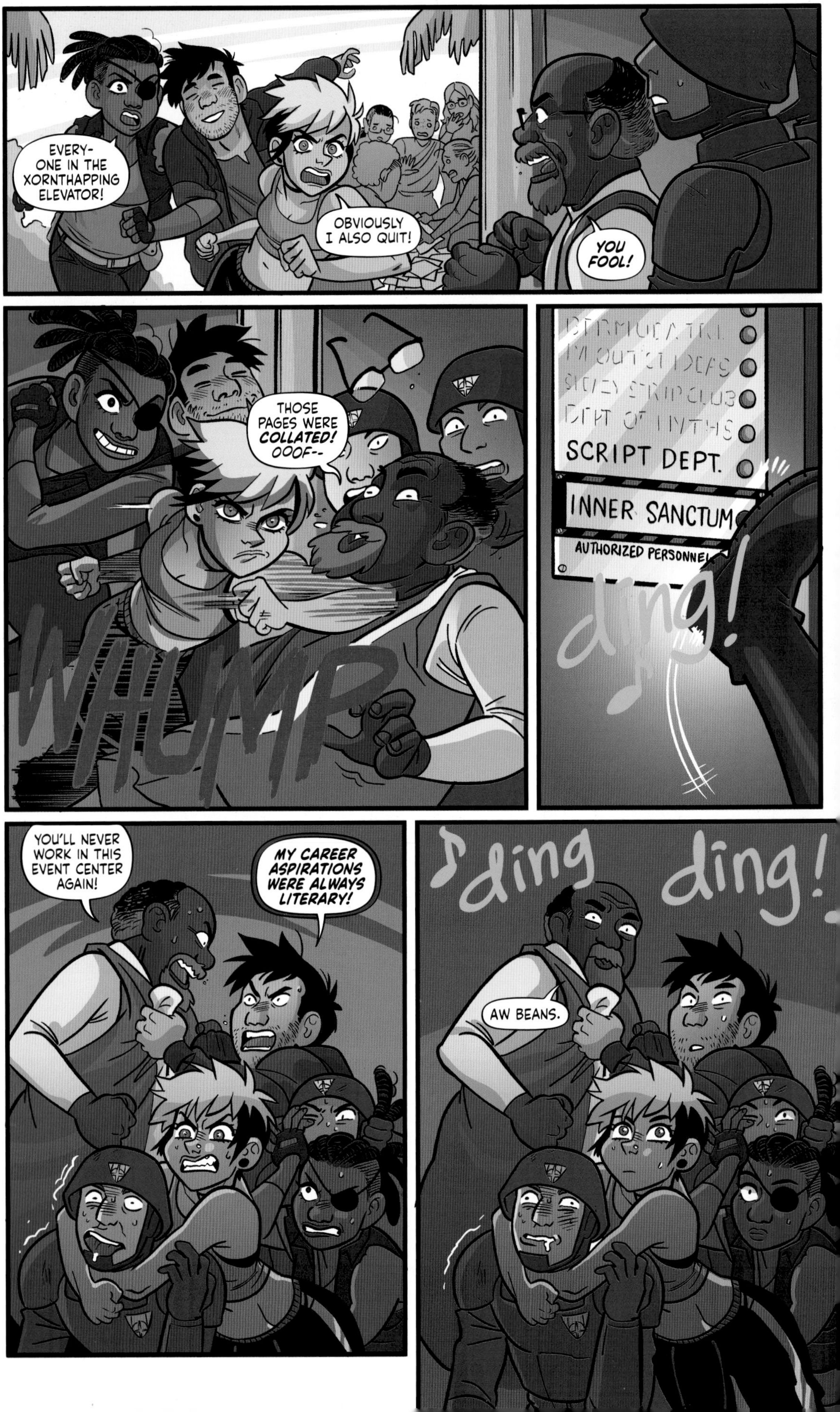
EVERY-ONE IN THE XORNTHAPPING ELEVATOR!
OBVIOUSLY I ALSO QUIT!
YOU FOOL!
THOSE PAGES WERE COLLATED! OOOF--
WHUMP
SCRIPT DEPT.
INNER SANCTUM
AUTHORIZED PERSONNEL
ding!
YOU'LL NEVER WORK IN THIS EVENT CENTER AGAIN!
MY CAREER ASPIRATIONS WERE ALWAYS LITERARY!
ding ding!
AW BEANS.

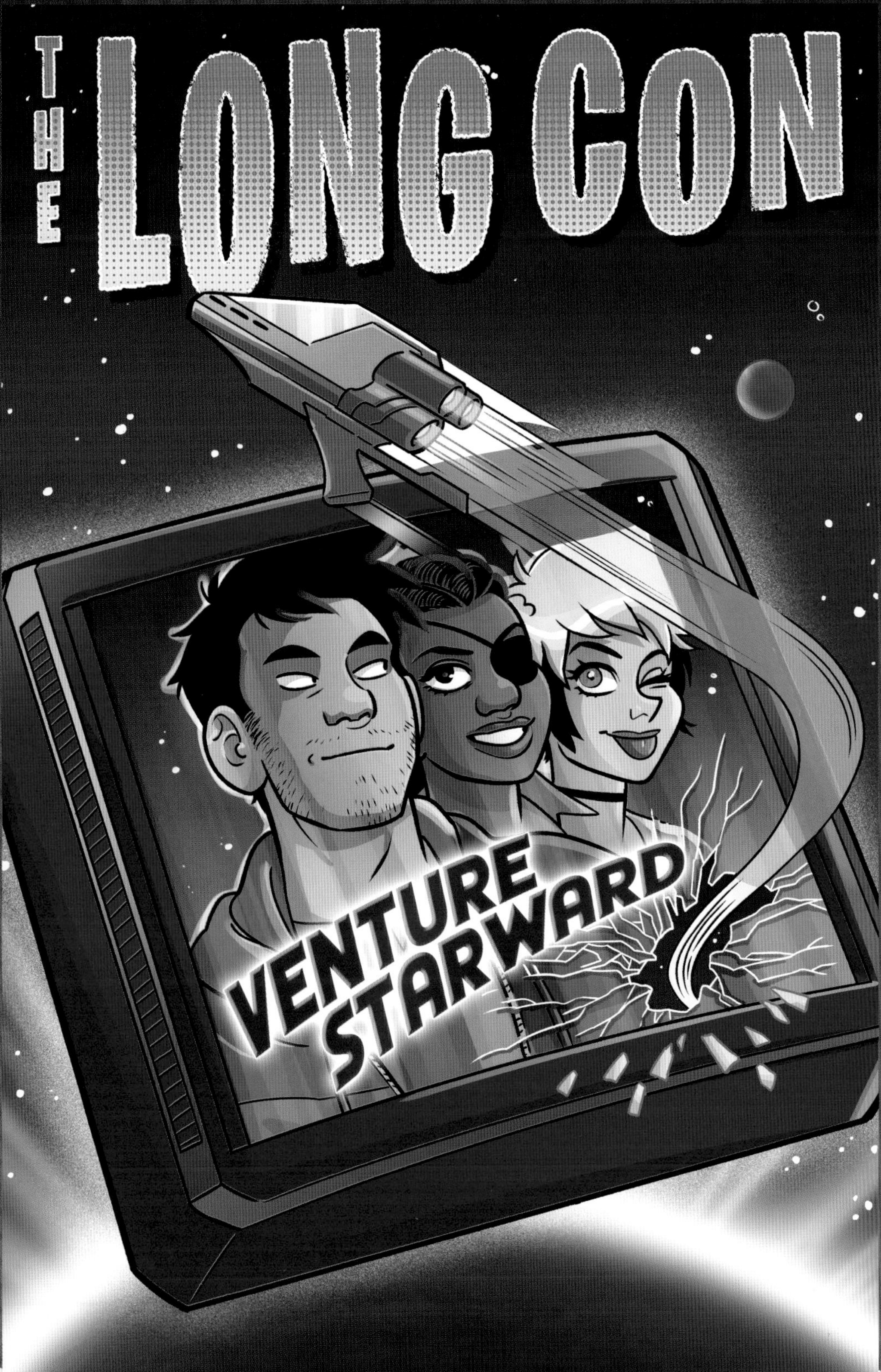
THE LONG CON
VENTURE STARWARD

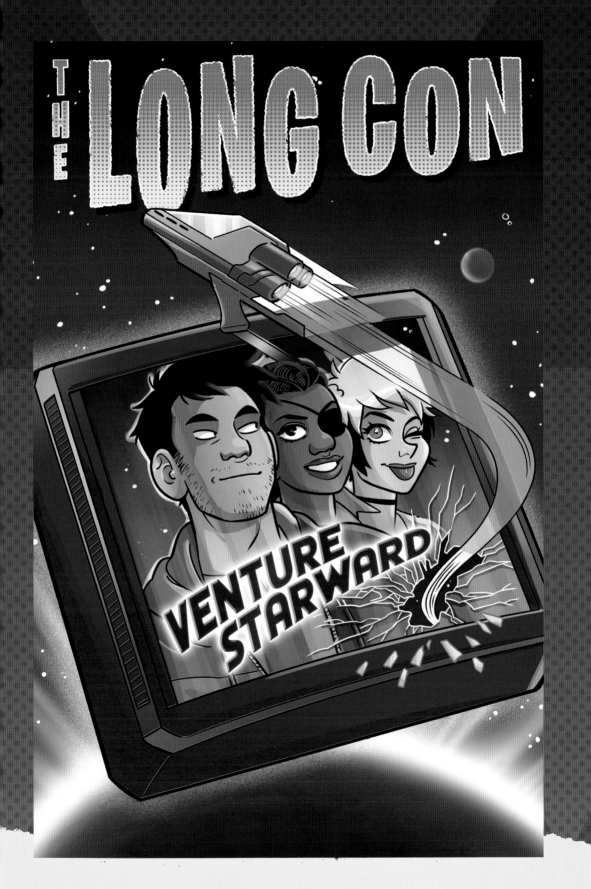

CHAPTER 10: VENTURE STARWARD

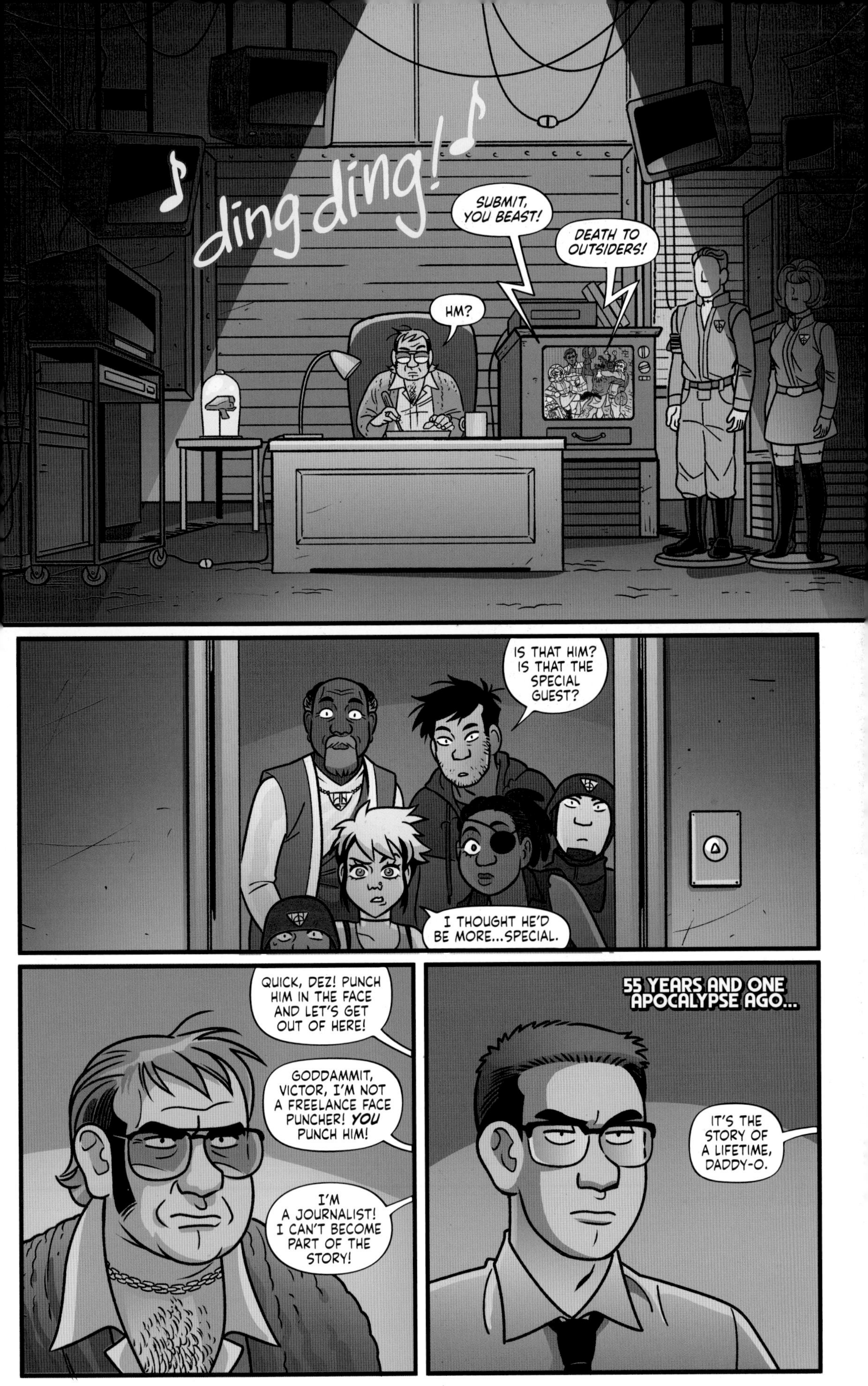
ding ding!
SUBMIT, YOU BEAST!
DEATH TO OUTSIDERS!
HM?
IS THAT HIM? IS THAT THE SPECIAL GUEST?
I THOUGHT HE'D BE MORE...SPECIAL.
QUICK, DEZ! PUNCH HIM IN THE FACE AND LET'S GET OUT OF HERE!
GODDAMMIT, VICTOR, I'M NOT A FREELANCE FACE PUNCHER! YOU PUNCH HIM!
I'M A JOURNALIST! I CAN'T BECOME PART OF THE STORY!
55 YEARS AND ONE APOCALYPSE AGO...
IT'S THE STORY OF A LIFETIME, DADDY-O.

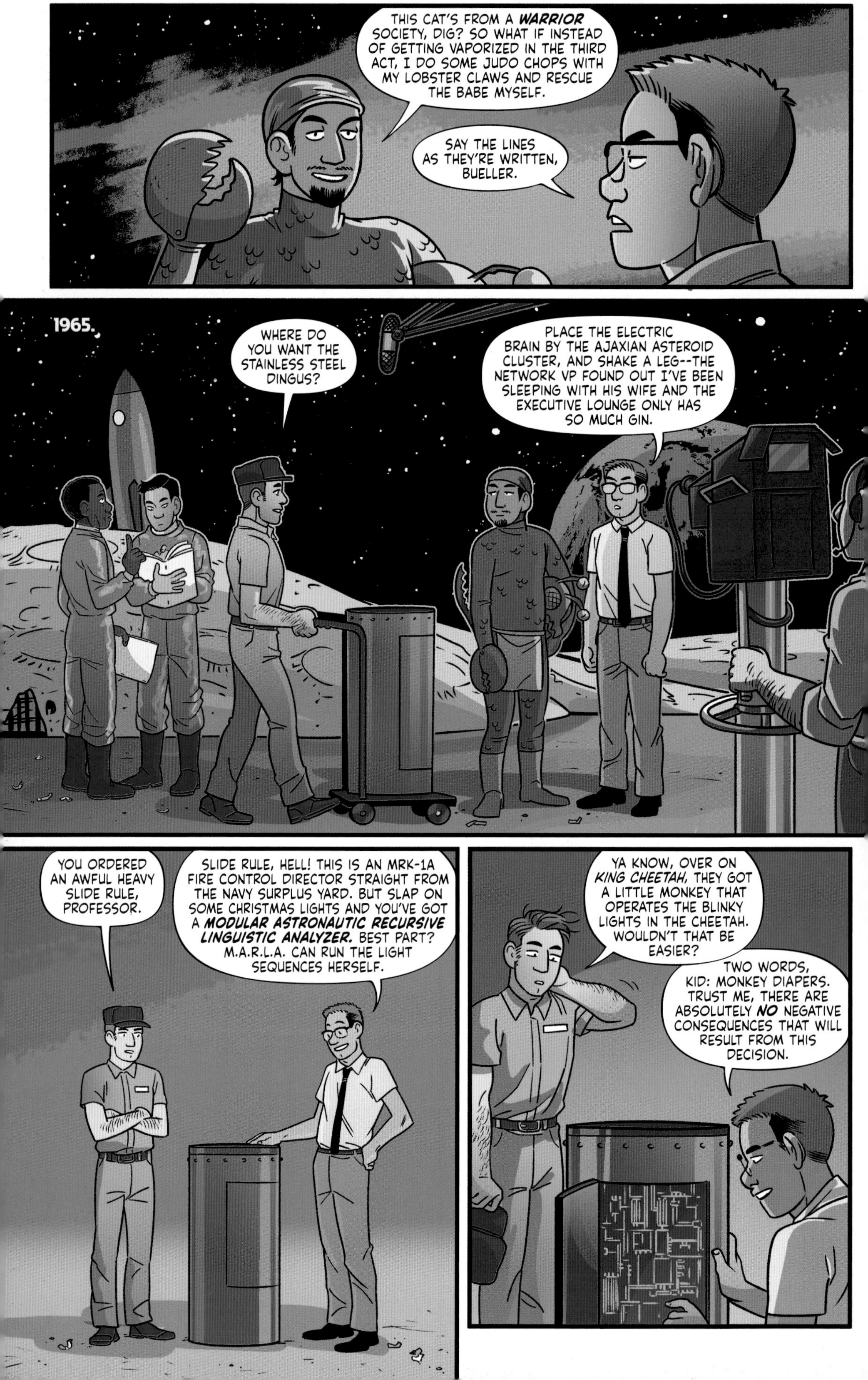
THIS CAT'S FROM A *WARRIOR* SOCIETY, DIG? SO WHAT IF INSTEAD OF GETTING VAPORIZED IN THE THIRD ACT, I DO SOME JUDO CHOPS WITH MY LOBSTER CLAWS AND RESCUE THE BABE MYSELF.
SAY THE LINES AS THEY'RE WRITTEN, BUELLER.
1965.
WHERE DO YOU WANT THE STAINLESS STEEL DINGUS?
PLACE THE ELECTRIC BRAIN BY THE AJAXIAN ASTEROID CLUSTER, AND SHAKE A LEG--THE NETWORK VP FOUND OUT I'VE BEEN SLEEPING WITH HIS WIFE AND THE EXECUTIVE LOUNGE ONLY HAS SO MUCH GIN.
YOU ORDERED AN AWFUL HEAVY SLIDE RULE, PROFESSOR.
SLIDE RULE, HELL! THIS IS AN MRK-1A FIRE CONTROL DIRECTOR STRAIGHT FROM THE NAVY SURPLUS YARD. BUT SLAP ON SOME CHRISTMAS LIGHTS AND YOU'VE GOT A ***MODULAR ASTRONAUTIC RECURSIVE LINGUISTIC ANALYZER.*** BEST PART? M.A.R.L.A. CAN RUN THE LIGHT SEQUENCES HERSELF.
YA KNOW, OVER ON *KING CHEETAH,* THEY GOT A LITTLE MONKEY THAT OPERATES THE BLINKY LIGHTS IN THE CHEETAH. WOULDN'T THAT BE EASIER?
TWO WORDS, KID: MONKEY DIAPERS. TRUST ME, THERE ARE ABSOLUTELY ***NO*** NEGATIVE CONSEQUENCES THAT WILL RESULT FROM THIS DECISION.

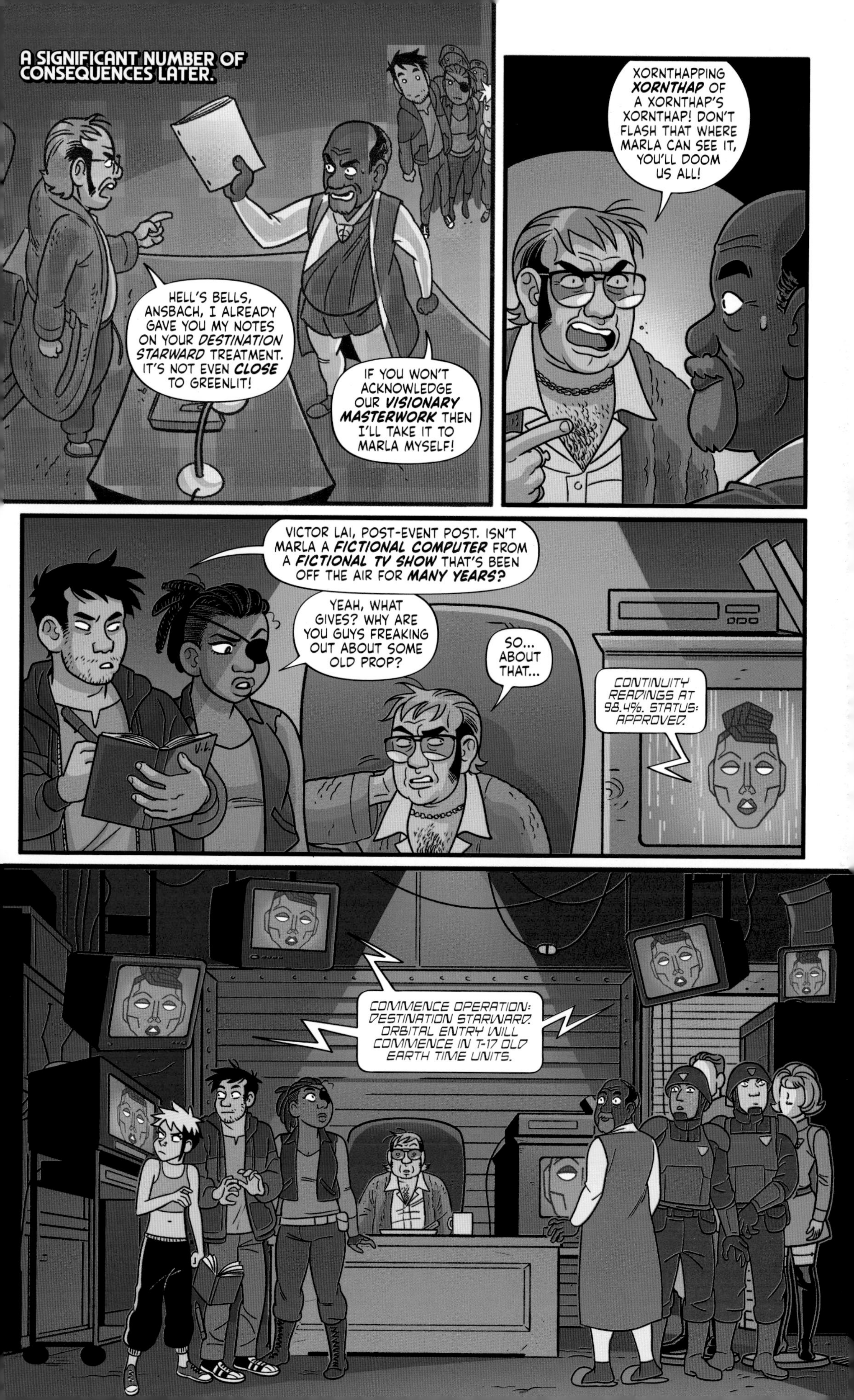
A SIGNIFICANT NUMBER OF CONSEQUENCES LATER.
HELL'S BELLS, ANSBACH, I ALREADY GAVE YOU MY NOTES ON YOUR DESTINATION STARWARD TREATMENT. IT'S NOT EVEN CLOSE TO GREENLIT!
IF YOU WON'T ACKNOWLEDGE OUR VISIONARY MASTERWORK THEN I'LL TAKE IT TO MARLA MYSELF!
XORNTHAPPING XORNTHAP OF A XORNTHAP'S XORNTHAP! DON'T FLASH THAT WHERE MARLA CAN SEE IT, YOU'LL DOOM US ALL!
VICTOR LAI, POST-EVENT POST. ISN'T MARLA A FICTIONAL COMPUTER FROM A FICTIONAL TV SHOW THAT'S BEEN OFF THE AIR FOR MANY YEARS?
YEAH, WHAT GIVES? WHY ARE YOU GUYS FREAKING OUT ABOUT SOME OLD PROP?
SO... ABOUT THAT...
CONTINUITY READINGS AT 98.4%. STATUS: APPROVED.
COMMENCE OPERATION: DESTINATION STARWARD. ORBITAL ENTRY WILL COMMENCE IN T-17 OLD EARTH TIME UNITS.

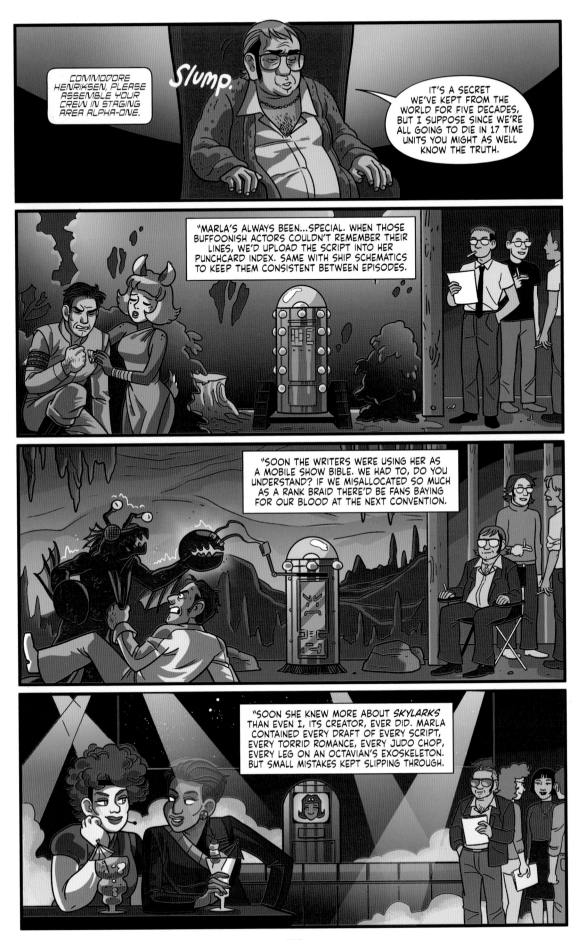

COMMODORE HENRIKSEN, PLEASE ASSEMBLE YOUR CREW IN STAGING AREA ALPHA-ONE.

Slump.

IT'S A SECRET WE'VE KEPT FROM THE WORLD FOR FIVE DECADES, BUT I SUPPOSE SINCE WE'RE ALL GOING TO DIE IN 17 TIME UNITS YOU MIGHT AS WELL KNOW THE TRUTH.

"MARLA'S ALWAYS BEEN...SPECIAL. WHEN THOSE BUFFOONISH ACTORS COULDN'T REMEMBER THEIR LINES, WE'D UPLOAD THE SCRIPT INTO HER PUNCHCARD INDEX. SAME WITH SHIP SCHEMATICS TO KEEP THEM CONSISTENT BETWEEN EPISODES.

"SOON THE WRITERS WERE USING HER AS A MOBILE SHOW BIBLE. WE HAD TO, DO YOU UNDERSTAND? IF WE MISALLOCATED SO MUCH AS A RANK BRAID THERE'D BE FANS BAYING FOR OUR BLOOD AT THE NEXT CONVENTION.

"SOON SHE KNEW MORE ABOUT *SKYLARKS* THAN EVEN I, ITS CREATOR, EVER DID. MARLA CONTAINED EVERY DRAFT OF EVERY SCRIPT, EVERY TORRID ROMANCE, EVERY JUDO CHOP, EVERY LEG ON AN OCTAVIAN'S EXOSKELETON. BUT SMALL MISTAKES KEPT SLIPPING THROUGH.

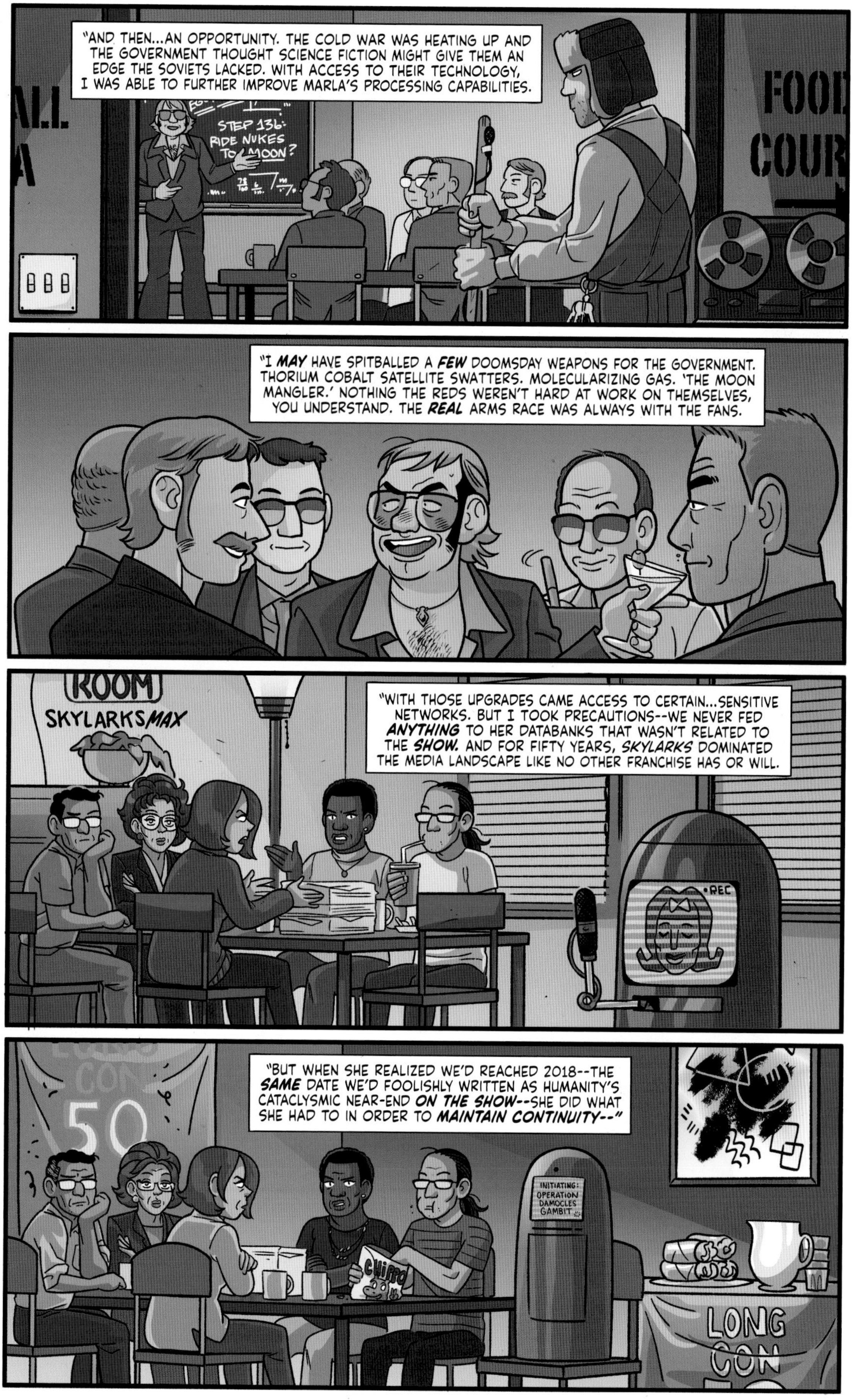
"AND THEN...AN OPPORTUNITY. THE COLD WAR WAS HEATING UP AND THE GOVERNMENT THOUGHT SCIENCE FICTION MIGHT GIVE THEM AN EDGE THE SOVIETS LACKED. WITH ACCESS TO THEIR TECHNOLOGY, I WAS ABLE TO FURTHER IMPROVE MARLA'S PROCESSING CAPABILITIES.
STEP 136: RIDE NUKES TO MOON?
FOOD
COUR
"I *MAY* HAVE SPITBALLED A *FEW* DOOMSDAY WEAPONS FOR THE GOVERNMENT. THORIUM COBALT SATELLITE SWATTERS. MOLECULARIZING GAS. 'THE MOON MANGLER.' NOTHING THE REDS WEREN'T HARD AT WORK ON THEMSELVES, YOU UNDERSTAND. THE *REAL* ARMS RACE WAS ALWAYS WITH THE FANS.
ROOM
SKYLARKS*MAX*
"WITH THOSE UPGRADES CAME ACCESS TO CERTAIN...SENSITIVE NETWORKS. BUT I TOOK PRECAUTIONS--WE NEVER FED *ANYTHING* TO HER DATABANKS THAT WASN'T RELATED TO THE *SHOW.* AND FOR FIFTY YEARS, *SKYLARKS* DOMINATED THE MEDIA LANDSCAPE LIKE NO OTHER FRANCHISE HAS OR WILL.
•REC
50
"BUT WHEN SHE REALIZED WE'D REACHED 2018--THE *SAME* DATE WE'D FOOLISHLY WRITTEN AS HUMANITY'S CATACLYSMIC NEAR-END *ON THE SHOW*--SHE DID WHAT SHE HAD TO IN ORDER TO *MAINTAIN CONTINUITY*--"
INITIATING: OPERATION DAMOCLES GAMBIT
LONG CON

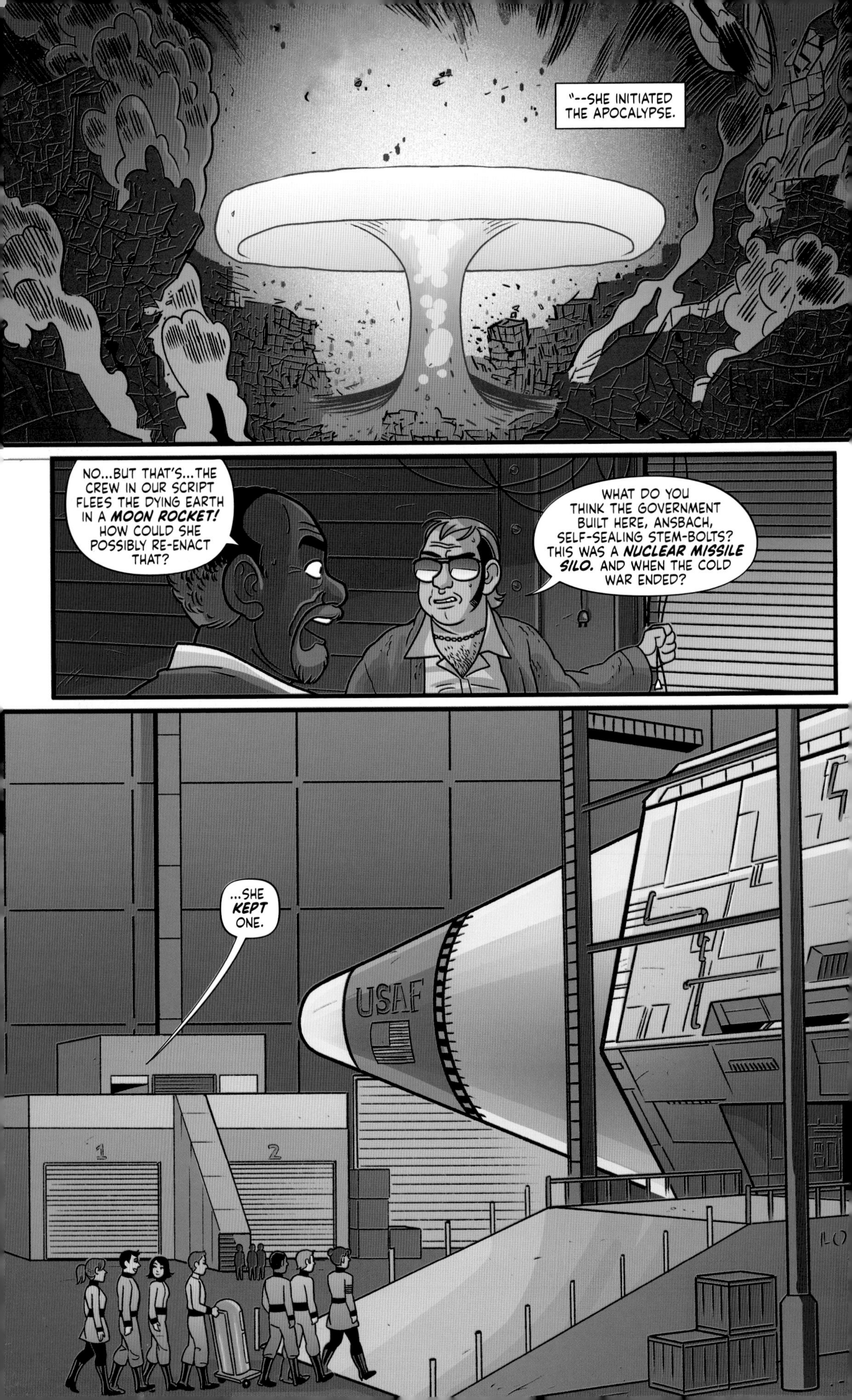
"--SHE INITIATED THE APOCALYPSE.
NO...BUT THAT'S...THE CREW IN OUR SCRIPT FLEES THE DYING EARTH IN A MOON ROCKET! HOW COULD SHE POSSIBLY RE-ENACT THAT?
WHAT DO YOU THINK THE GOVERNMENT BUILT HERE, ANSBACH, SELF-SEALING STEM-BOLTS? THIS WAS A NUCLEAR MISSILE SILO. AND WHEN THE COLD WAR ENDED?
...SHE KEPT ONE.
USAF
1
2

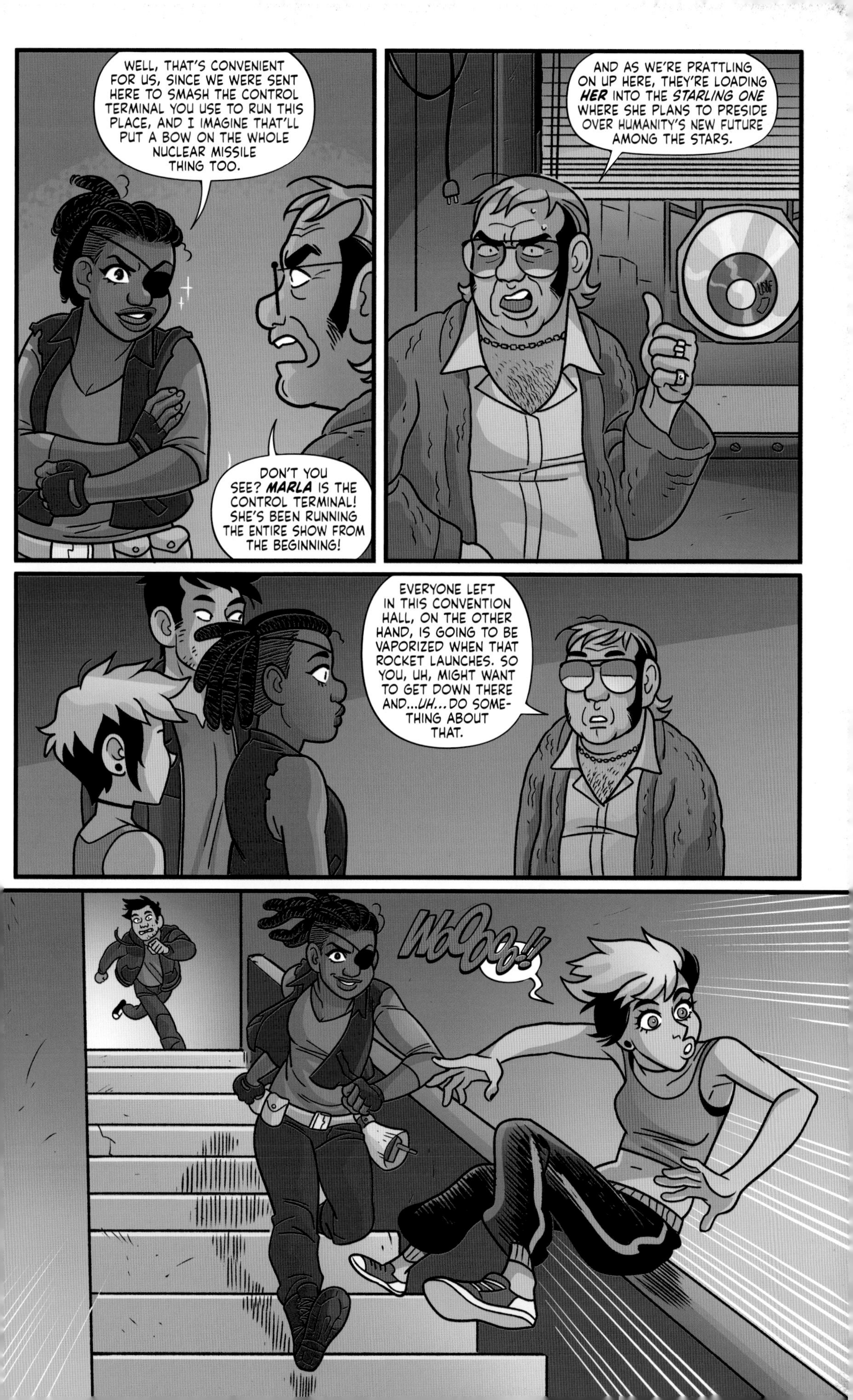
WELL, THAT'S CONVENIENT FOR US, SINCE WE WERE SENT HERE TO SMASH THE CONTROL TERMINAL YOU USE TO RUN THIS PLACE, AND I IMAGINE THAT'LL PUT A BOW ON THE WHOLE NUCLEAR MISSILE THING TOO.
DON'T YOU SEE? **MARLA** IS THE CONTROL TERMINAL! SHE'S BEEN RUNNING THE ENTIRE SHOW FROM THE BEGINNING!
AND AS WE'RE PRATTLING ON UP HERE, THEY'RE LOADING **HER** INTO THE *STARLING ONE* WHERE SHE PLANS TO PRESIDE OVER HUMANITY'S NEW FUTURE AMONG THE STARS.
EVERYONE LEFT IN THIS CONVENTION HALL, ON THE OTHER HAND, IS GOING TO BE VAPORIZED WHEN THAT ROCKET LAUNCHES. SO YOU, UH, MIGHT WANT TO GET DOWN THERE AND...*UH*...DO SOMETHING ABOUT THAT.
WOOOO!!

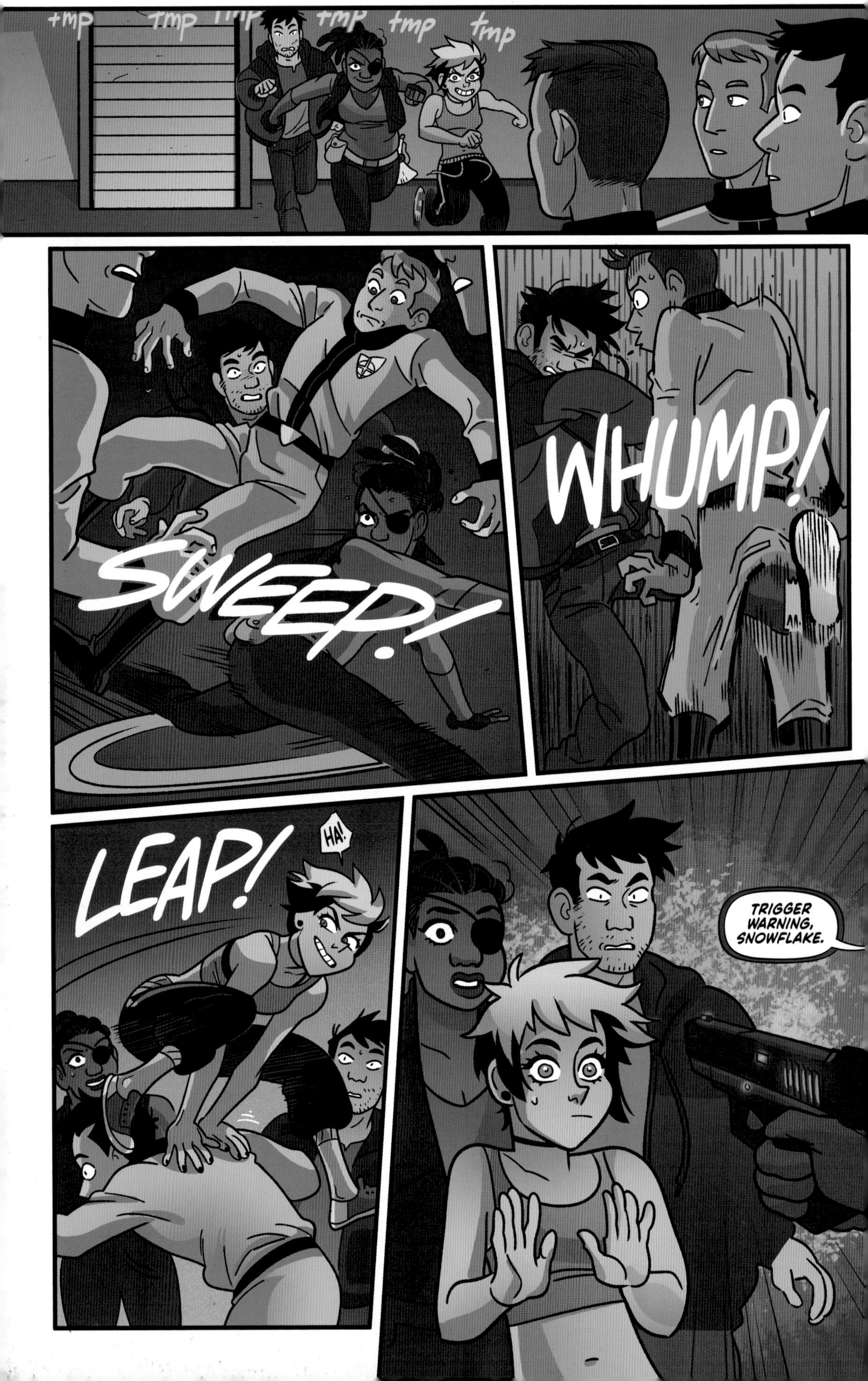
tmp
tmp
tmp
tmp
tmp
tmp
SWEEP!
WHUMP!
LEAP!
HA!
TRIGGER WARNING, SNOWFLAKE.

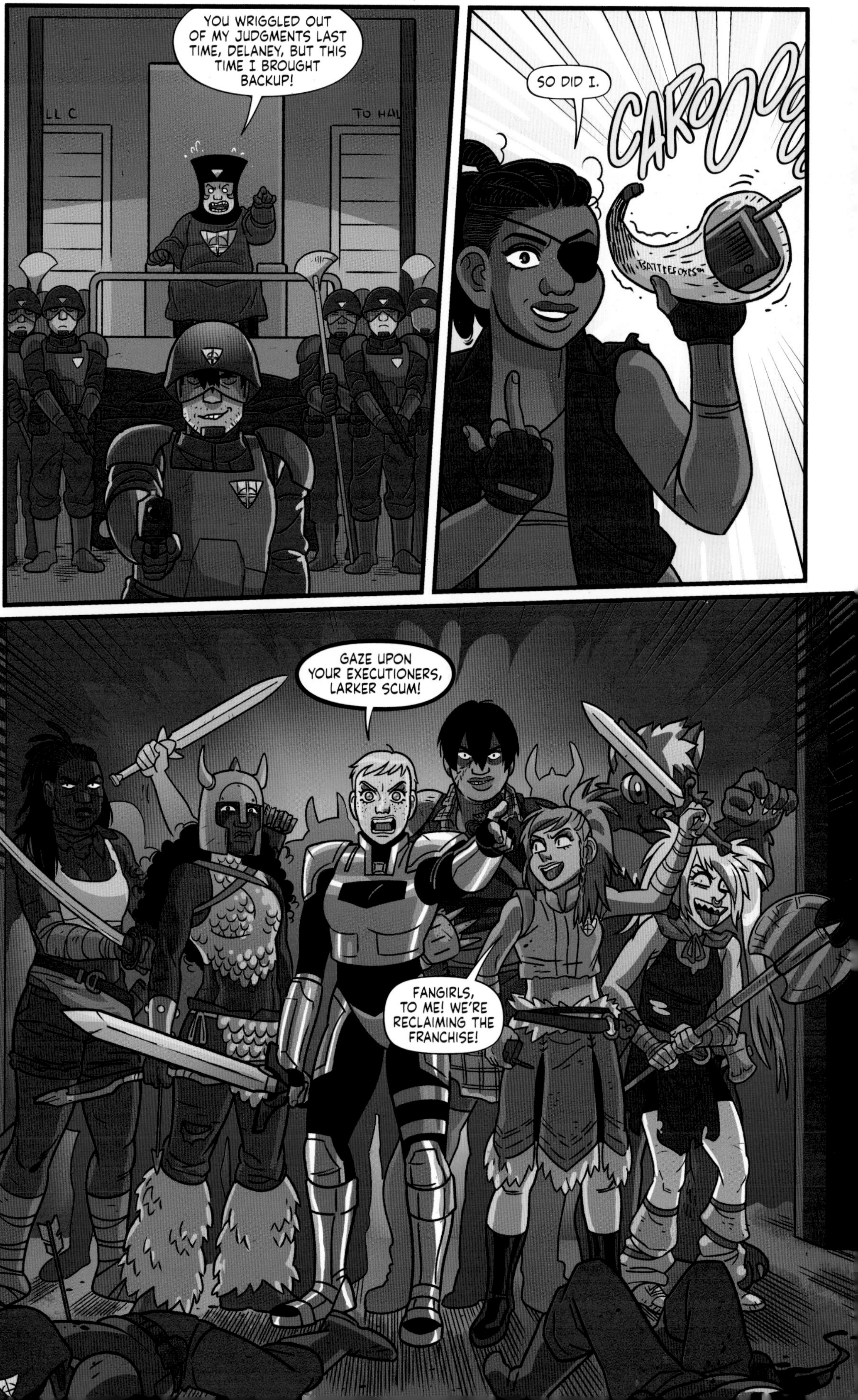
YOU WRIGGLED OUT OF MY JUDGMENTS LAST TIME, DELANEY, BUT THIS TIME I BROUGHT BACKUP!
SO DID I.
CAROOOOO
BATTLEFOXES™
GAZE UPON YOUR EXECUTIONERS, LARKER SCUM!
FANGIRLS, TO ME! WE'RE RECLAIMING THE FRANCHISE!

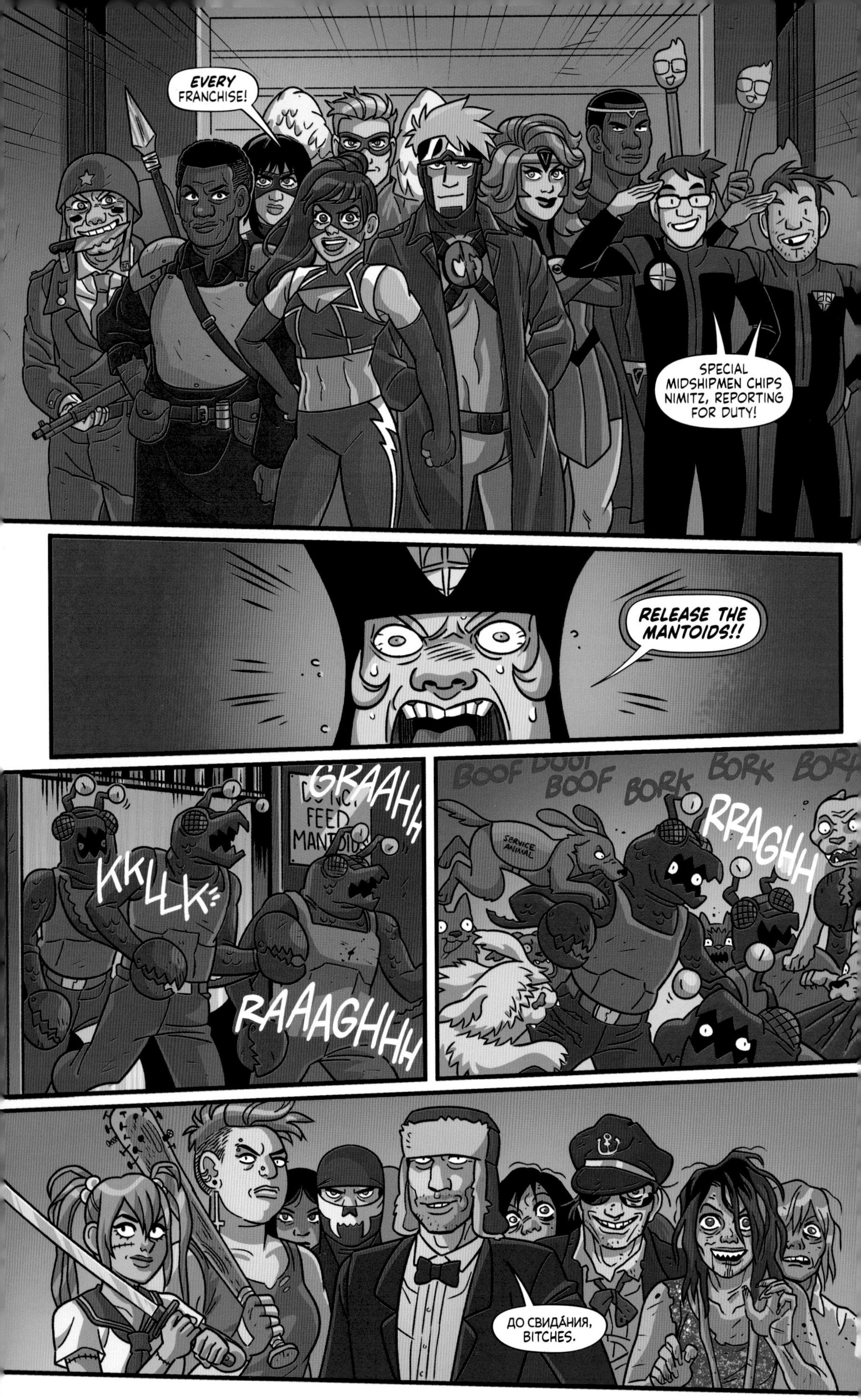
EVERY FRANCHISE!
SPECIAL MIDSHIPMEN CHIPS NIMITZ, REPORTING FOR DUTY!
RELEASE THE MANTOIDS!!
GRAAHHH
FEED
KKLLK
RAAAGHHH
BOOF BOOF BOOF
BORK BORK BORK
SERVICE ANIMAL
RRAGHH
ДО СВИДÁНИЯ, BITCHES.

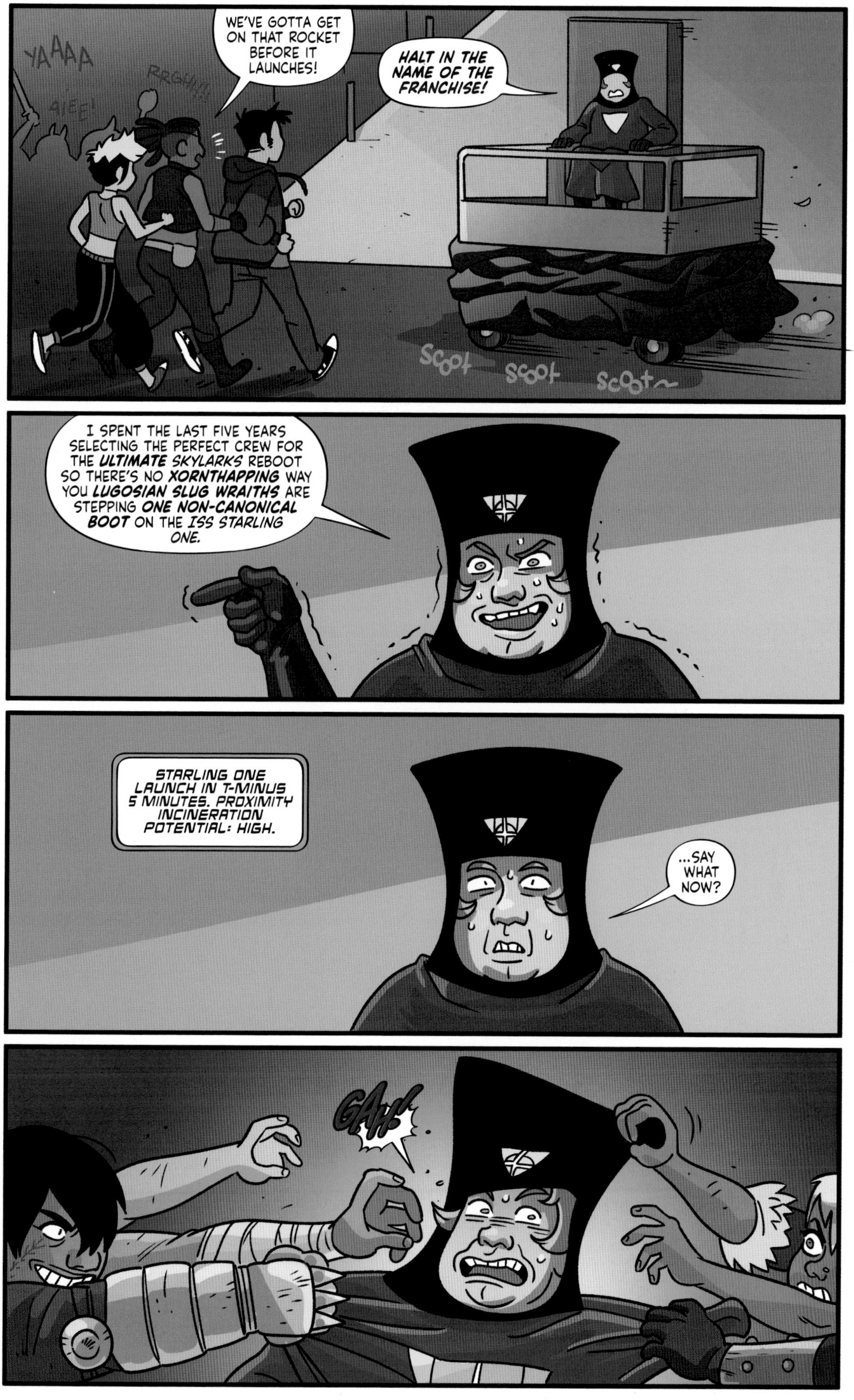
YAAAA
AIEE!
WE'VE GOTTA GET ON THAT ROCKET BEFORE IT LAUNCHES!
HALT IN THE NAME OF THE FRANCHISE!
SCOOT SCOOT SCOOT~
I SPENT THE LAST FIVE YEARS SELECTING THE PERFECT CREW FOR THE ULTIMATE SKYLARKS REBOOT SO THERE'S NO XORNTHAPPING WAY YOU LUGOSIAN SLUG WRAITHS ARE STEPPING ONE NON-CANONICAL BOOT ON THE ISS STARLING ONE.
STARLING ONE LAUNCH IN T-MINUS 5 MINUTES. PROXIMITY INCINERATION POTENTIAL: HIGH.
...SAY WHAT NOW?
GAH!

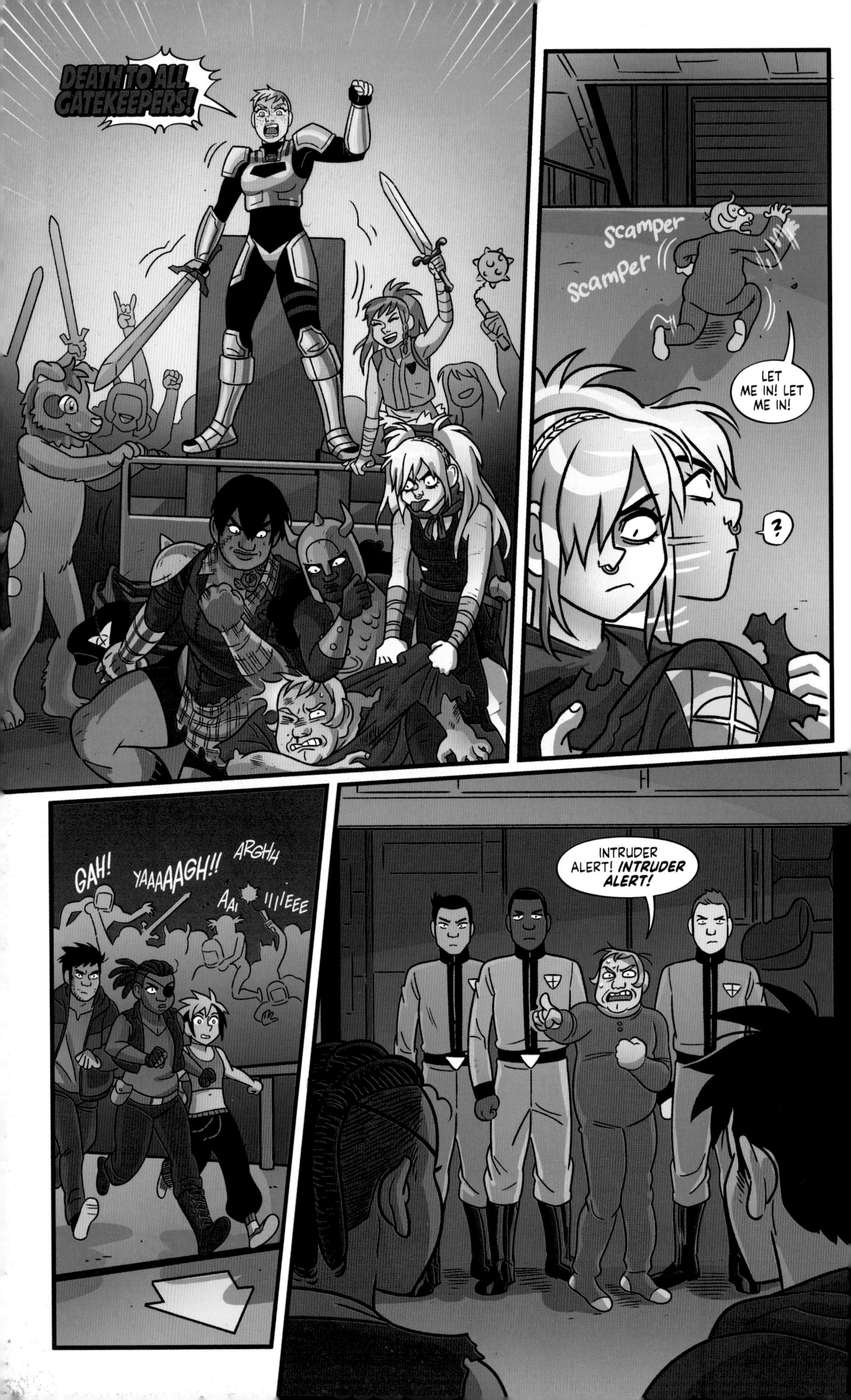
DEATH TO ALL GATEKEEPERS!
Scamper
Scamper
LET ME IN! LET ME IN!
?
GAH!
YAAAAAGH!!
ARGHH
AAI
IIIIEEE
INTRUDER ALERT! INTRUDER ALERT!

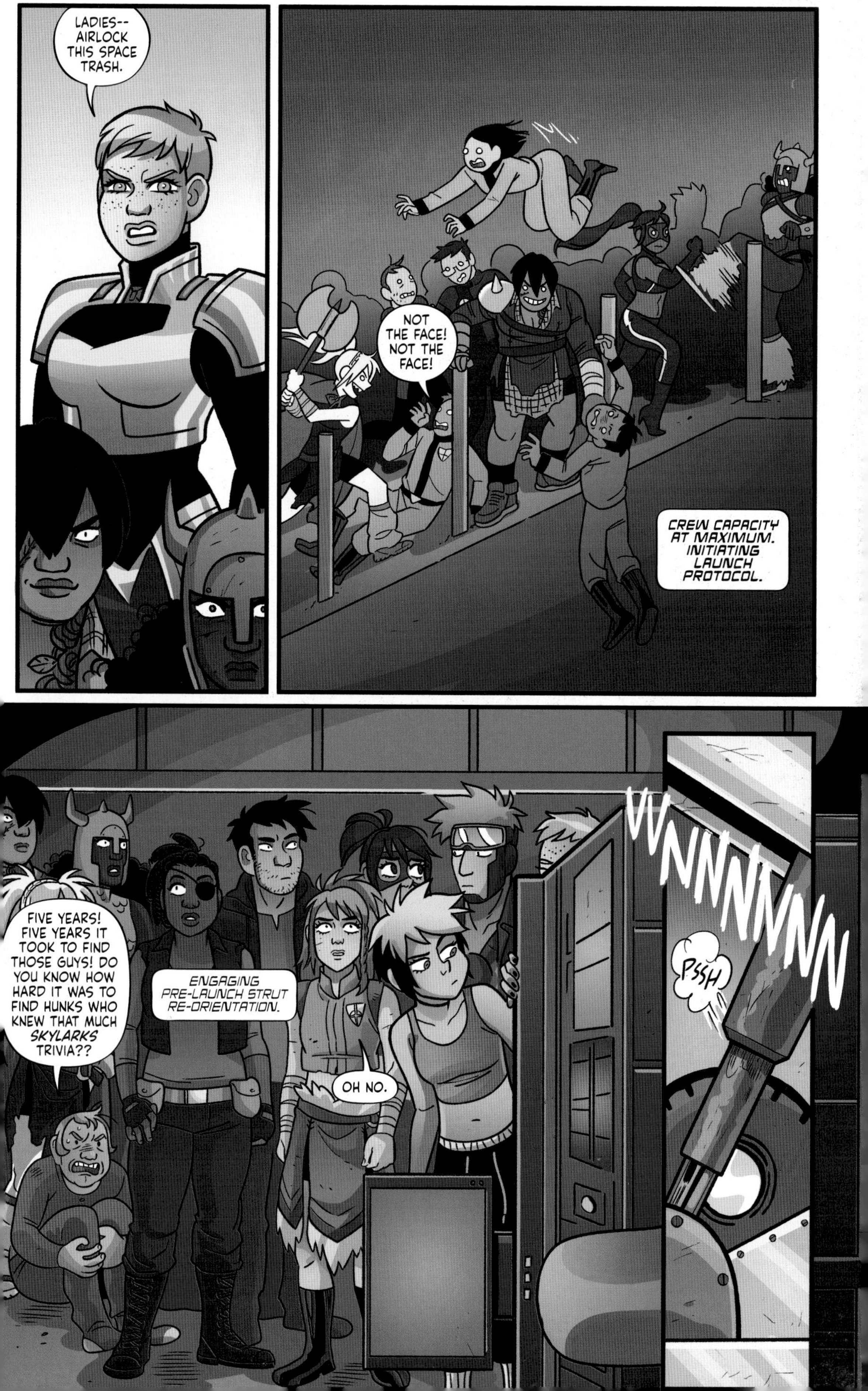
LADIES--
AIRLOCK
THIS SPACE
TRASH.
NOT
THE FACE!
NOT THE
FACE!
CREW CAPACITY
AT MAXIMUM.
INITIATING
LAUNCH
PROTOCOL.
FIVE YEARS!
FIVE YEARS IT
TOOK TO FIND
THOSE GUYS! DO
YOU KNOW HOW
HARD IT WAS TO
FIND HUNKS WHO
KNEW THAT MUCH
SKYLARKS
TRIVIA??
ENGAGING
PRE-LAUNCH STRUT
RE-ORIENTATION.
OH NO.
VVNNNNNNN
PSSH

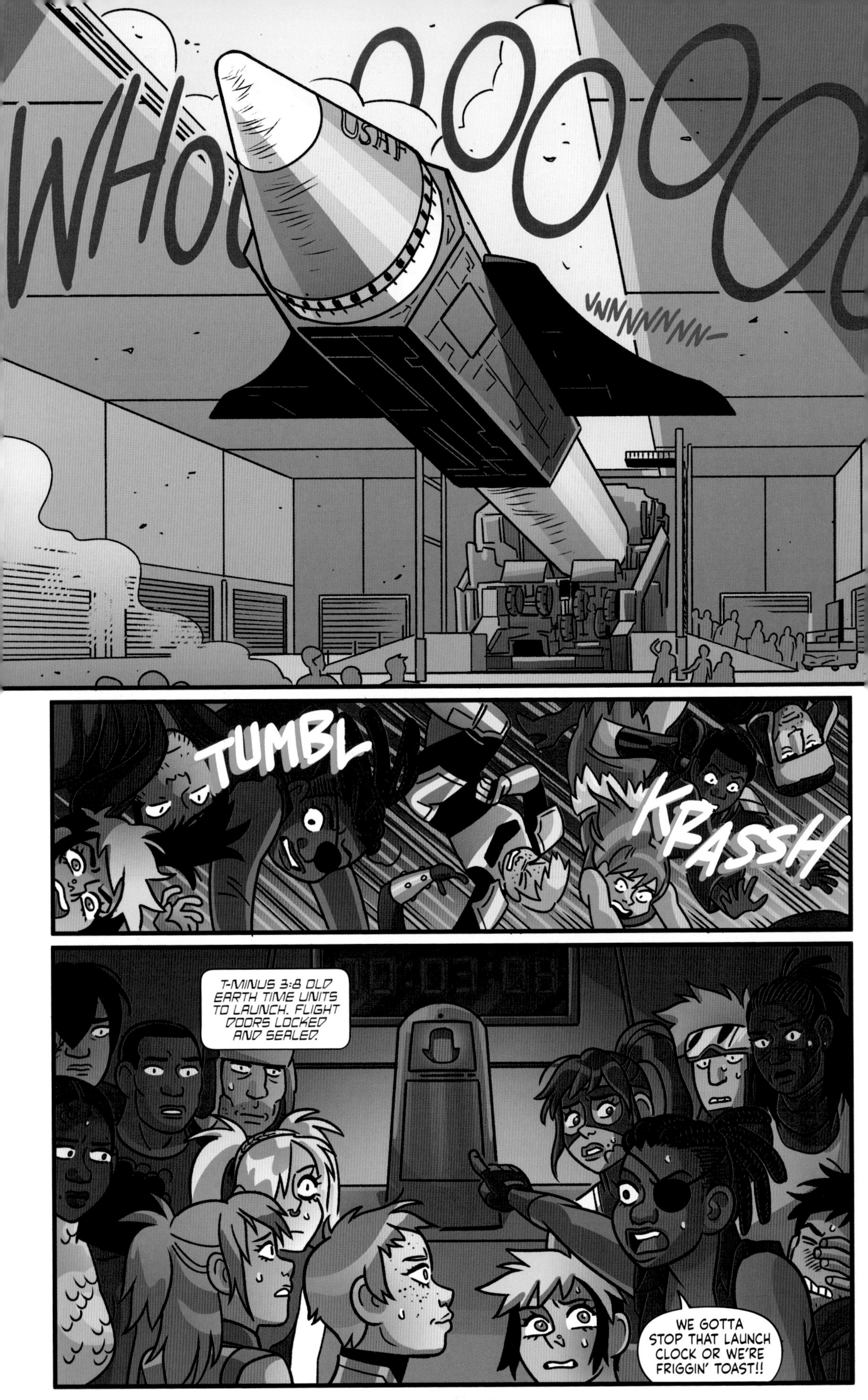
WHOOOOOOO
USAF
VNNNNNNN-
TUMBL
KRASSH
T-MINUS 3:8 OLD EARTH TIME UNITS TO LAUNCH. FLIGHT DOORS LOCKED AND SEALED.
WE GOTTA STOP THAT LAUNCH CLOCK OR WE'RE FRIGGIN' TOAST!!

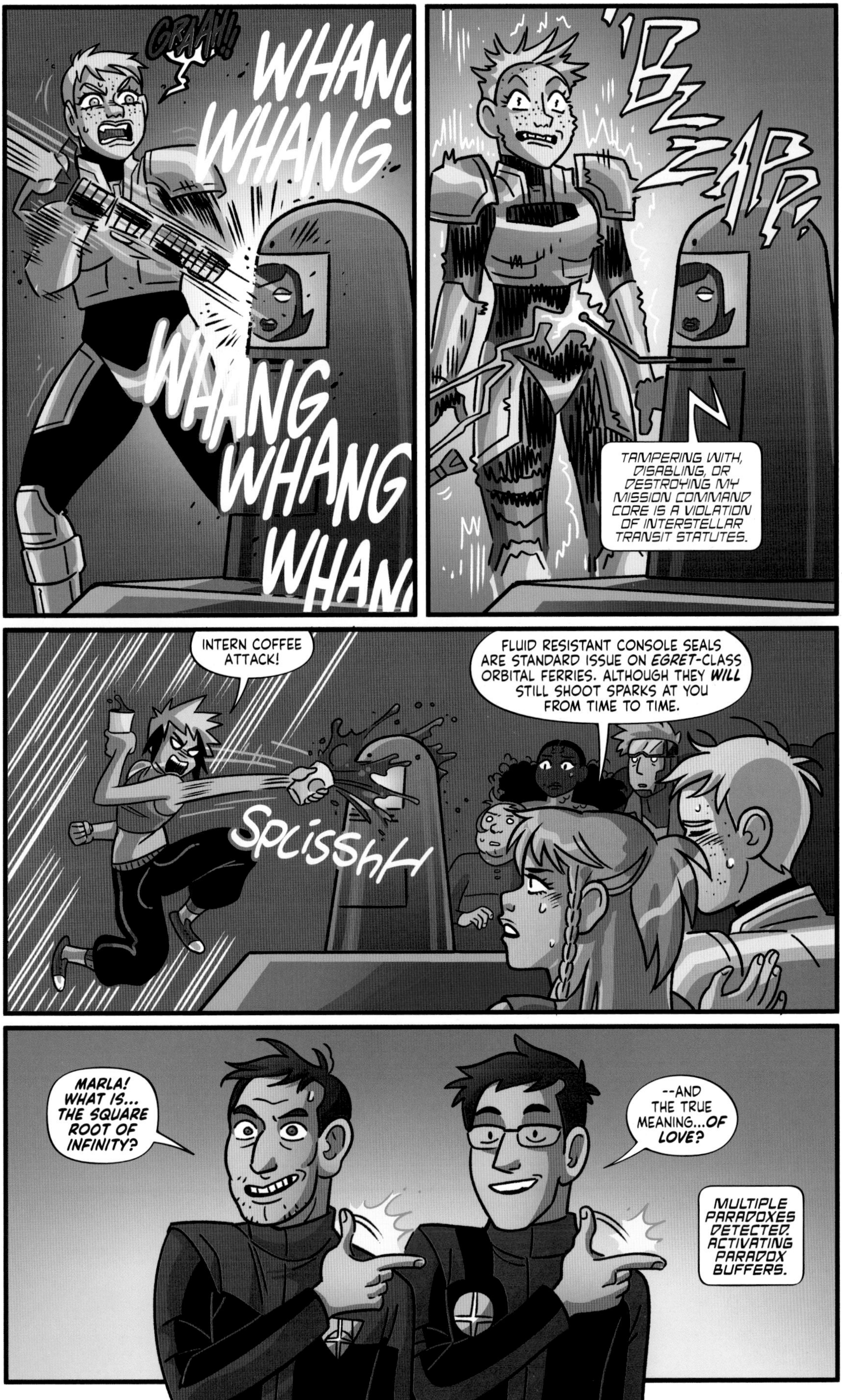

GRAAH!!
WHANG
WHANG
WHANG
WHANG
WHANG
'BZZAPP!
TAMPERING WITH, DISABLING, OR DESTROYING MY MISSION COMMAND CORE IS A VIOLATION OF INTERSTELLAR TRANSIT STATUTES.
INTERN COFFEE ATTACK!
FLUID RESISTANT CONSOLE SEALS ARE STANDARD ISSUE ON EGRET-CLASS ORBITAL FERRIES. ALTHOUGH THEY WILL STILL SHOOT SPARKS AT YOU FROM TIME TO TIME.
SPLISSHH
MARLA! WHAT IS... THE SQUARE ROOT OF INFINITY?
--AND THE TRUE MEANING...OF LOVE?
MULTIPLE PARADOXES DETECTED. ACTIVATING PARADOX BUFFERS.

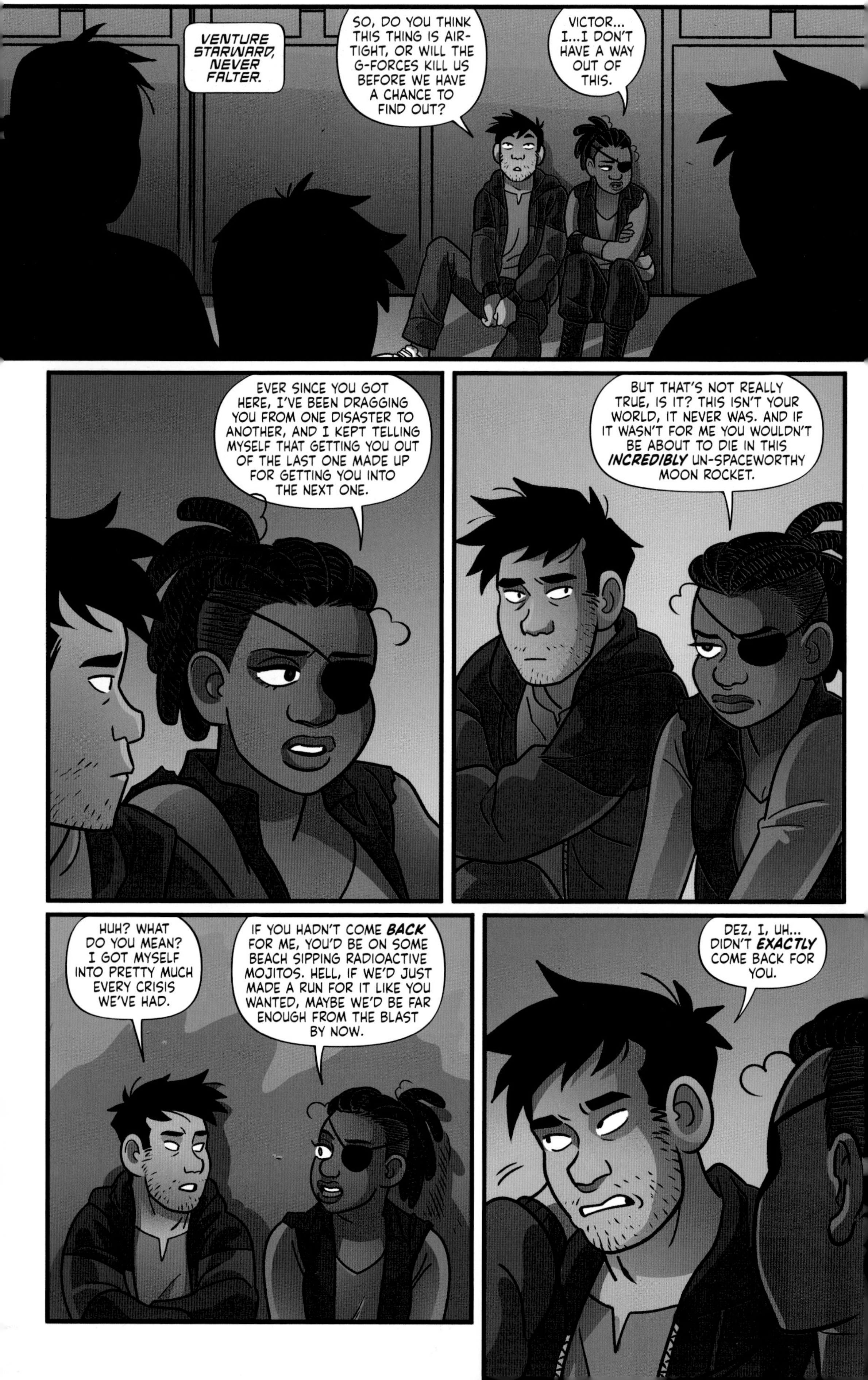
VENTURE STARWARD, NEVER FALTER.
SO, DO YOU THINK THIS THING IS AIR-TIGHT, OR WILL THE G-FORCES KILL US BEFORE WE HAVE A CHANCE TO FIND OUT?
VICTOR... I...I DON'T HAVE A WAY OUT OF THIS.
EVER SINCE YOU GOT HERE, I'VE BEEN DRAGGING YOU FROM ONE DISASTER TO ANOTHER, AND I KEPT TELLING MYSELF THAT GETTING YOU OUT OF THE LAST ONE MADE UP FOR GETTING YOU INTO THE NEXT ONE.
BUT THAT'S NOT REALLY TRUE, IS IT? THIS ISN'T YOUR WORLD, IT NEVER WAS. AND IF IT WASN'T FOR ME YOU WOULDN'T BE ABOUT TO DIE IN THIS *INCREDIBLY* UN-SPACEWORTHY MOON ROCKET.
HUH? WHAT DO YOU MEAN? I GOT MYSELF INTO PRETTY MUCH EVERY CRISIS WE'VE HAD.
IF YOU HADN'T COME *BACK* FOR ME, YOU'D BE ON SOME BEACH SIPPING RADIOACTIVE MOJITOS. HELL, IF WE'D JUST MADE A RUN FOR IT LIKE YOU WANTED, MAYBE WE'D BE FAR ENOUGH FROM THE BLAST BY NOW.
DEZ, I, UH... DIDN'T *EXACTLY* COME BACK FOR YOU.

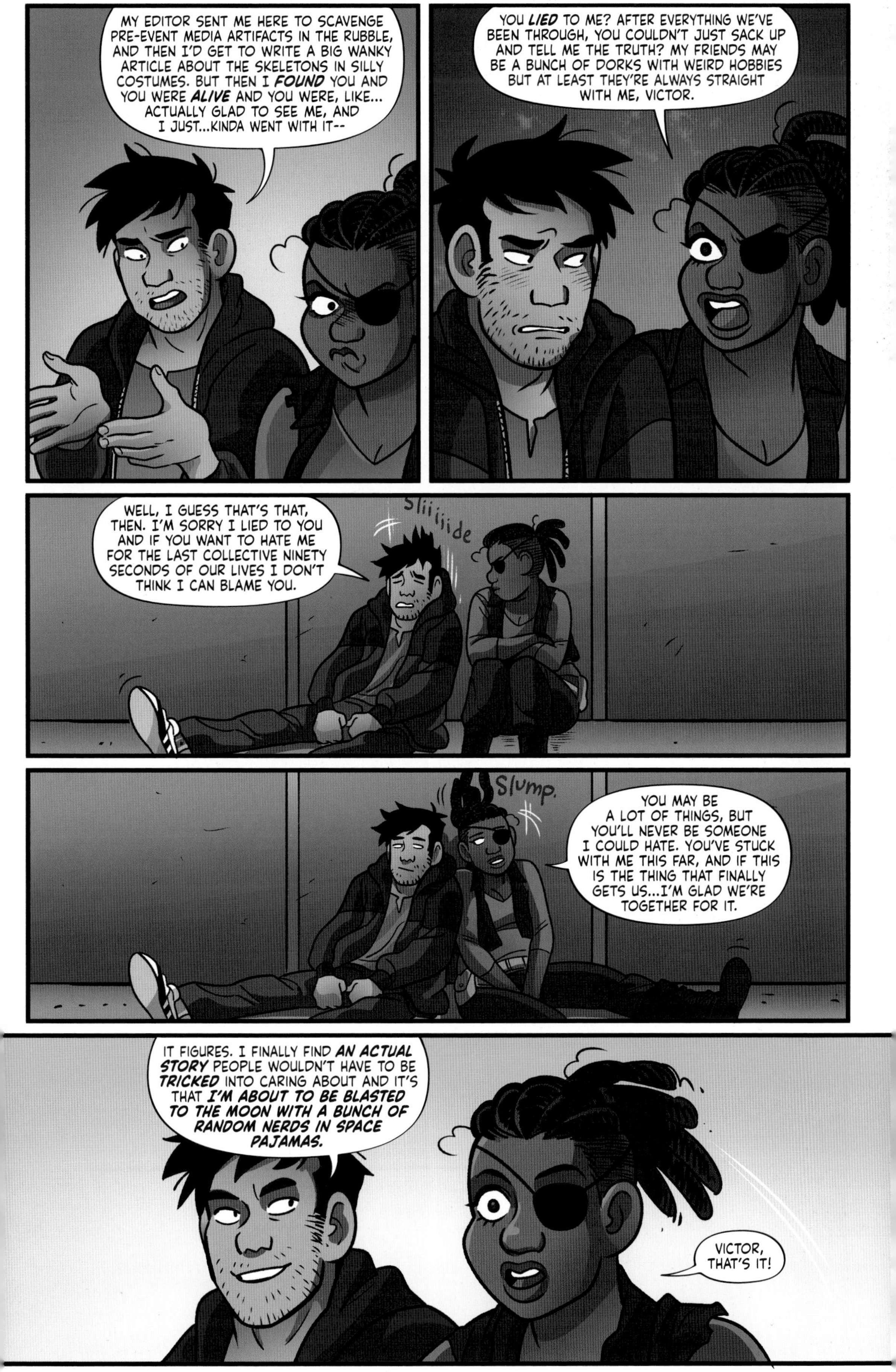
MY EDITOR SENT ME HERE TO SCAVENGE PRE-EVENT MEDIA ARTIFACTS IN THE RUBBLE, AND THEN I'D GET TO WRITE A BIG WANKY ARTICLE ABOUT THE SKELETONS IN SILLY COSTUMES. BUT THEN I FOUND YOU AND YOU WERE ALIVE AND YOU WERE, LIKE... ACTUALLY GLAD TO SEE ME, AND I JUST...KINDA WENT WITH IT--
YOU LIED TO ME? AFTER EVERYTHING WE'VE BEEN THROUGH, YOU COULDN'T JUST SACK UP AND TELL ME THE TRUTH? MY FRIENDS MAY BE A BUNCH OF DORKS WITH WEIRD HOBBIES BUT AT LEAST THEY'RE ALWAYS STRAIGHT WITH ME, VICTOR.
WELL, I GUESS THAT'S THAT, THEN. I'M SORRY I LIED TO YOU AND IF YOU WANT TO HATE ME FOR THE LAST COLLECTIVE NINETY SECONDS OF OUR LIVES I DON'T THINK I CAN BLAME YOU.
Sliiiiiide
Slump.
YOU MAY BE A LOT OF THINGS, BUT YOU'LL NEVER BE SOMEONE I COULD HATE. YOU'VE STUCK WITH ME THIS FAR, AND IF THIS IS THE THING THAT FINALLY GETS US...I'M GLAD WE'RE TOGETHER FOR IT.
IT FIGURES. I FINALLY FIND AN ACTUAL STORY PEOPLE WOULDN'T HAVE TO BE TRICKED INTO CARING ABOUT AND IT'S THAT I'M ABOUT TO BE BLASTED TO THE MOON WITH A BUNCH OF RANDOM NERDS IN SPACE PAJAMAS.
VICTOR, THAT'S IT!

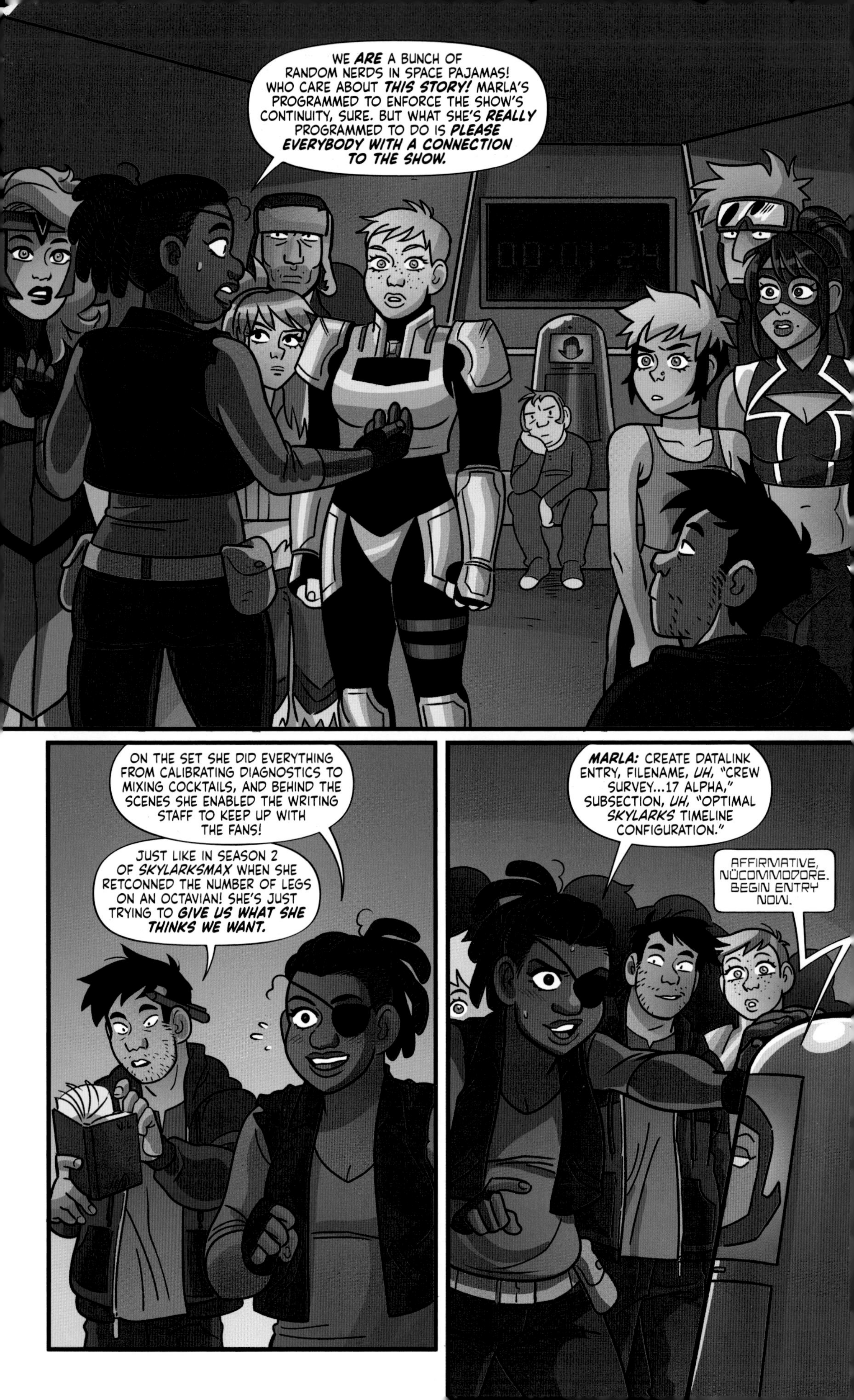
WE ARE A BUNCH OF RANDOM NERDS IN SPACE PAJAMAS! WHO CARE ABOUT THIS STORY! MARLA'S PROGRAMMED TO ENFORCE THE SHOW'S CONTINUITY, SURE. BUT WHAT SHE'S REALLY PROGRAMMED TO DO IS PLEASE EVERYBODY WITH A CONNECTION TO THE SHOW.
ON THE SET SHE DID EVERYTHING FROM CALIBRATING DIAGNOSTICS TO MIXING COCKTAILS, AND BEHIND THE SCENES SHE ENABLED THE WRITING STAFF TO KEEP UP WITH THE FANS!
JUST LIKE IN SEASON 2 OF SKYLARKSMAX WHEN SHE RETCONNED THE NUMBER OF LEGS ON AN OCTAVIAN! SHE'S JUST TRYING TO GIVE US WHAT SHE THINKS WE WANT.
MARLA: CREATE DATALINK ENTRY, FILENAME, UH, "CREW SURVEY...17 ALPHA," SUBSECTION, UH, "OPTIMAL SKYLARKS TIMELINE CONFIGURATION."
AFFIRMATIVE, NÜCOMMODORE. BEGIN ENTRY NOW.

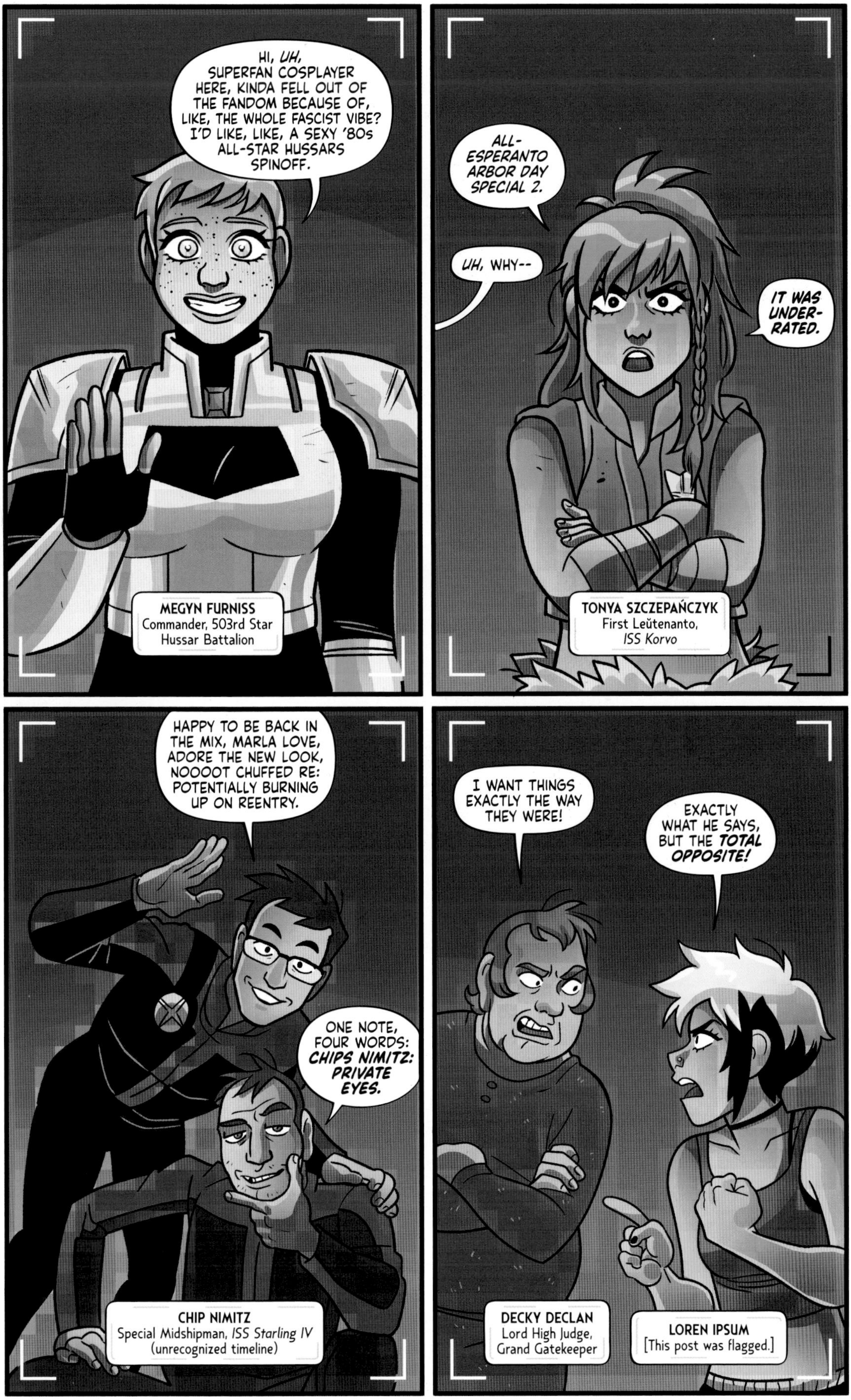
HI, *UH,* SUPERFAN COSPLAYER HERE, KINDA FELL OUT OF THE FANDOM BECAUSE OF, LIKE, THE WHOLE FASCIST VIBE? I'D LIKE, LIKE, A SEXY '80s ALL-STAR HUSSARS SPINOFF.
MEGYN FURNISS
Commander, 503rd Star Hussar Battalion
ALL-ESPERANTO ARBOR DAY SPECIAL 2.
UH, WHY--
IT WAS UNDER-RATED.
TONYA SZCZEPAŃCZYK
First Leŭtenanto, *ISS Korvo*
HAPPY TO BE BACK IN THE MIX, MARLA LOVE, ADORE THE NEW LOOK, NOOOOT CHUFFED RE: POTENTIALLY BURNING UP ON REENTRY.
ONE NOTE, FOUR WORDS: ***CHIPS NIMITZ: PRIVATE EYES.***
CHIP NIMITZ
Special Midshipman, *ISS Starling IV* (unrecognized timeline)
I WANT THINGS EXACTLY THE WAY THEY WERE!
EXACTLY WHAT HE SAYS, BUT THE ***TOTAL OPPOSITE!***
DECKY DECLAN
Lord High Judge, Grand Gatekeeper
LOREN IPSUM
[This post was flagged.]

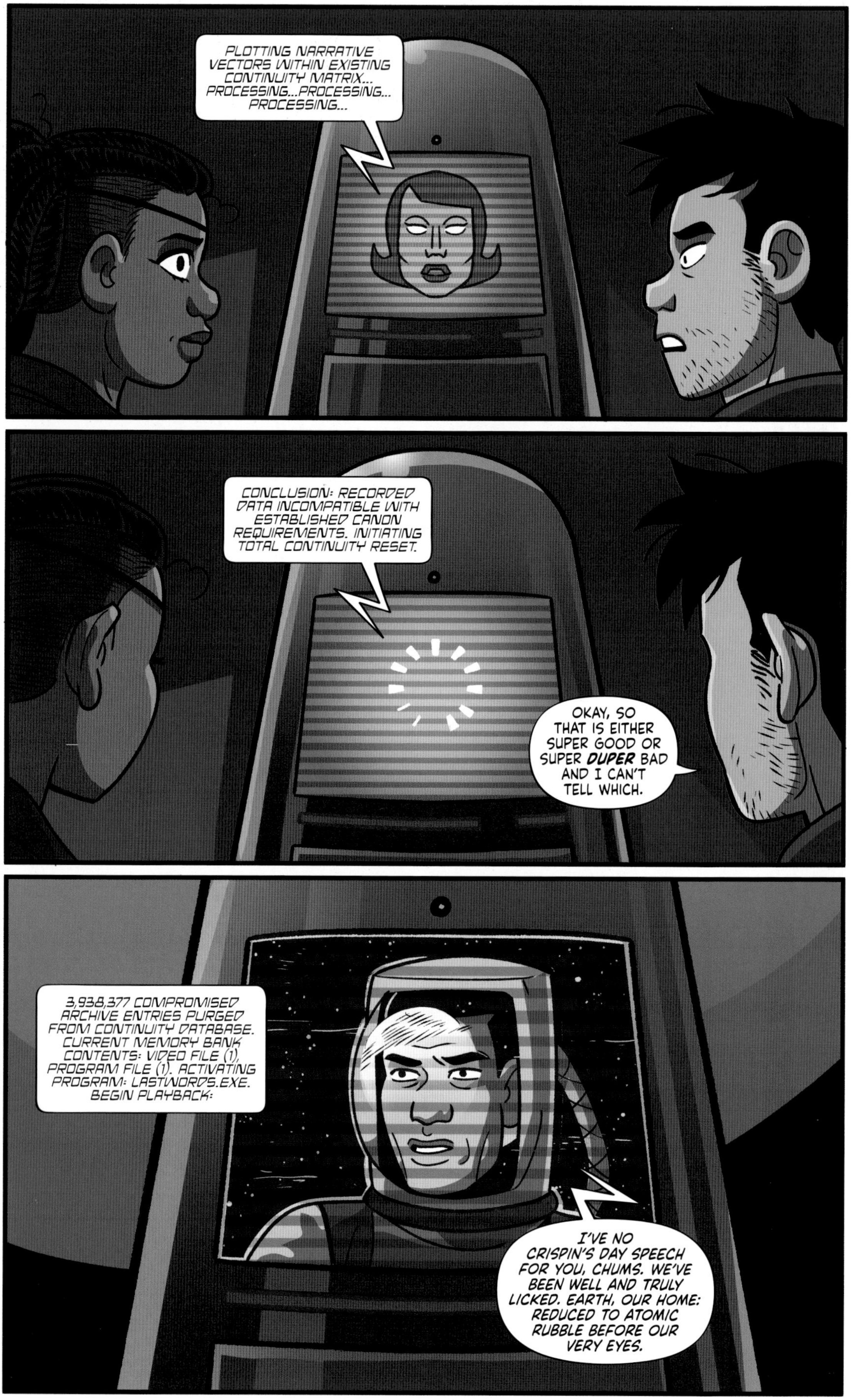
PLOTTING NARRATIVE VECTORS WITHIN EXISTING CONTINUITY MATRIX... PROCESSING...PROCESSING... PROCESSING...
CONCLUSION: RECORDED DATA INCOMPATIBLE WITH ESTABLISHED CANON REQUIREMENTS. INITIATING TOTAL CONTINUITY RESET.
OKAY, SO THAT IS EITHER SUPER GOOD OR SUPER **DUPER** BAD AND I CAN'T TELL WHICH.
3,938,377 COMPROMISED ARCHIVE ENTRIES PURGED FROM CONTINUITY DATABASE. CURRENT MEMORY BANK CONTENTS: VIDEO FILE (1), PROGRAM FILE (1). ACTIVATING PROGRAM: LASTWORDS.EXE. BEGIN PLAYBACK:
I'VE NO CRISPIN'S DAY SPEECH FOR YOU, CHUMS. WE'VE BEEN WELL AND TRULY LICKED. EARTH, OUR HOME: REDUCED TO ATOMIC RUBBLE BEFORE OUR VERY EYES.

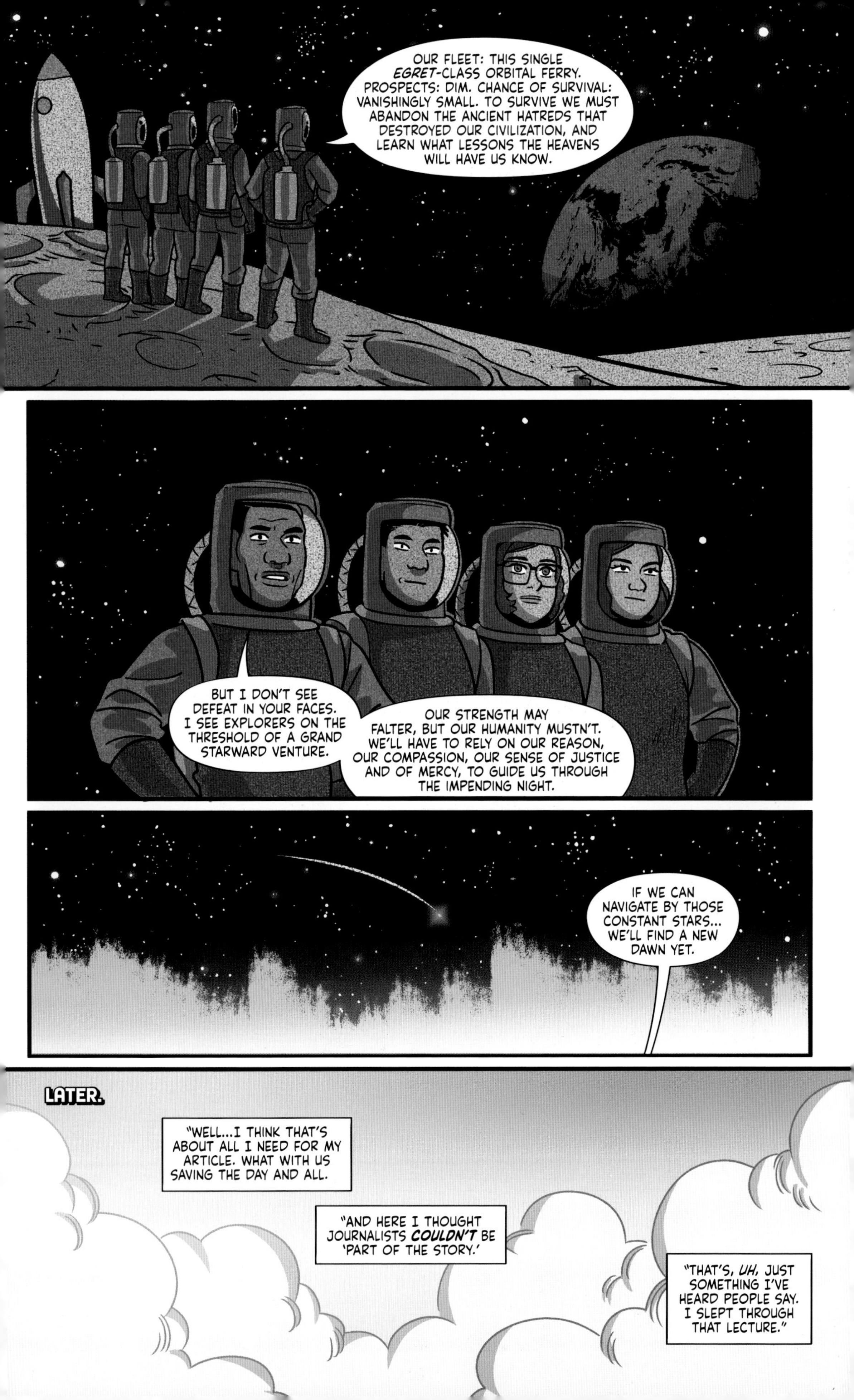
OUR FLEET: THIS SINGLE *EGRET*-CLASS ORBITAL FERRY. PROSPECTS: DIM. CHANCE OF SURVIVAL: VANISHINGLY SMALL. TO SURVIVE WE MUST ABANDON THE ANCIENT HATREDS THAT DESTROYED OUR CIVILIZATION, AND LEARN WHAT LESSONS THE HEAVENS WILL HAVE US KNOW.
BUT I DON'T SEE DEFEAT IN YOUR FACES. I SEE EXPLORERS ON THE THRESHOLD OF A GRAND STARWARD VENTURE.
OUR STRENGTH MAY FALTER, BUT OUR HUMANITY MUSTN'T. WE'LL HAVE TO RELY ON OUR REASON, OUR COMPASSION, OUR SENSE OF JUSTICE AND OF MERCY, TO GUIDE US THROUGH THE IMPENDING NIGHT.
IF WE CAN NAVIGATE BY THOSE CONSTANT STARS... WE'LL FIND A NEW DAWN YET.
LATER.
"WELL...I THINK THAT'S ABOUT ALL I NEED FOR MY ARTICLE. WHAT WITH US SAVING THE DAY AND ALL.
"AND HERE I THOUGHT JOURNALISTS ***COULDN'T*** BE 'PART OF THE STORY.'
"THAT'S, *UH*, JUST SOMETHING I'VE HEARD PEOPLE SAY. I SLEPT THROUGH THAT LECTURE."

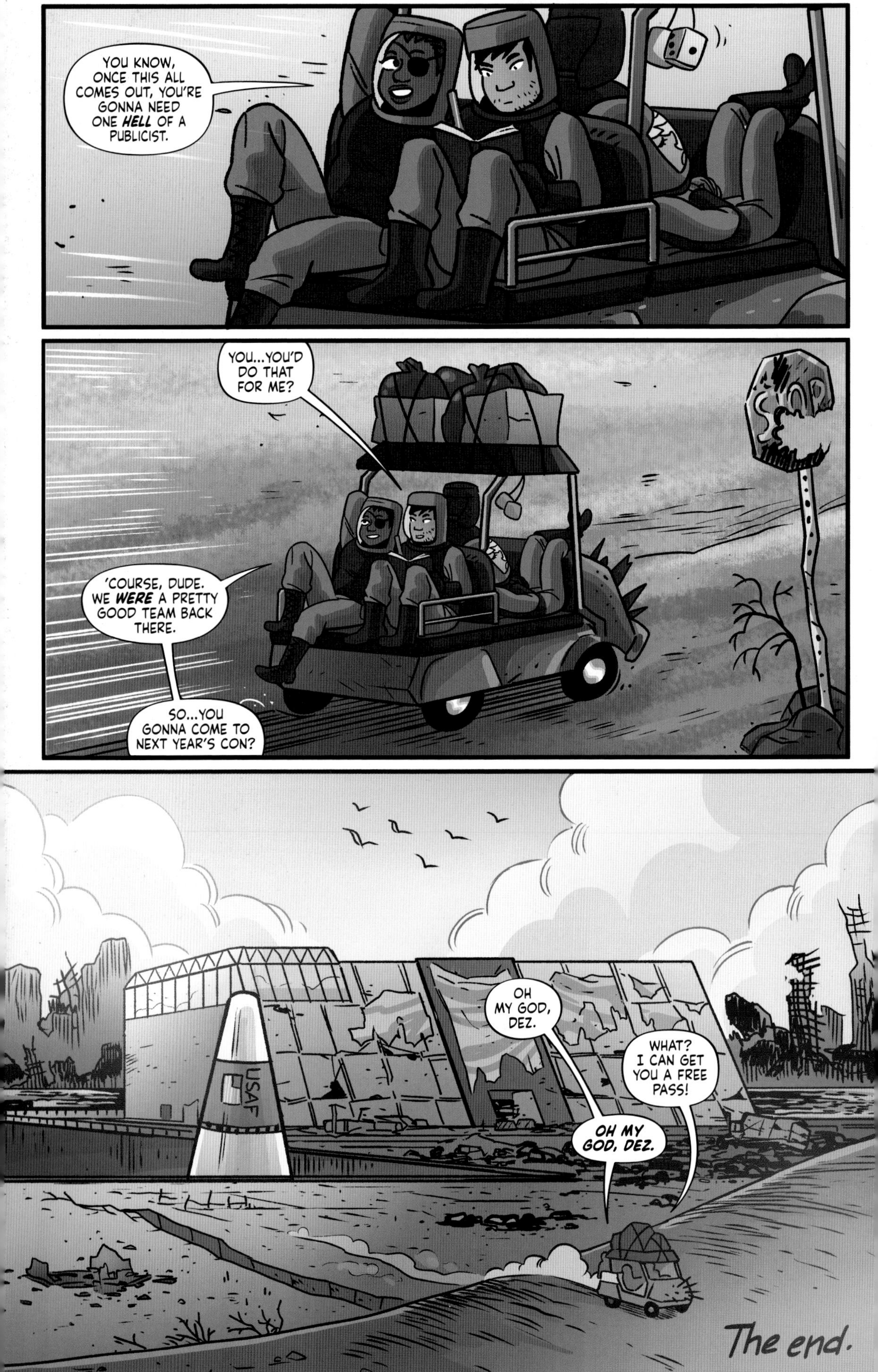
YOU KNOW, ONCE THIS ALL COMES OUT, YOU'RE GONNA NEED ONE HELL OF A PUBLICIST.
YOU...YOU'D DO THAT FOR ME?
'COURSE, DUDE. WE WERE A PRETTY GOOD TEAM BACK THERE.
SO...YOU GONNA COME TO NEXT YEAR'S CON?
USAF
OH MY GOD, DEZ.
WHAT? I CAN GET YOU A FREE PASS!
OH MY GOD, DEZ.
The end.

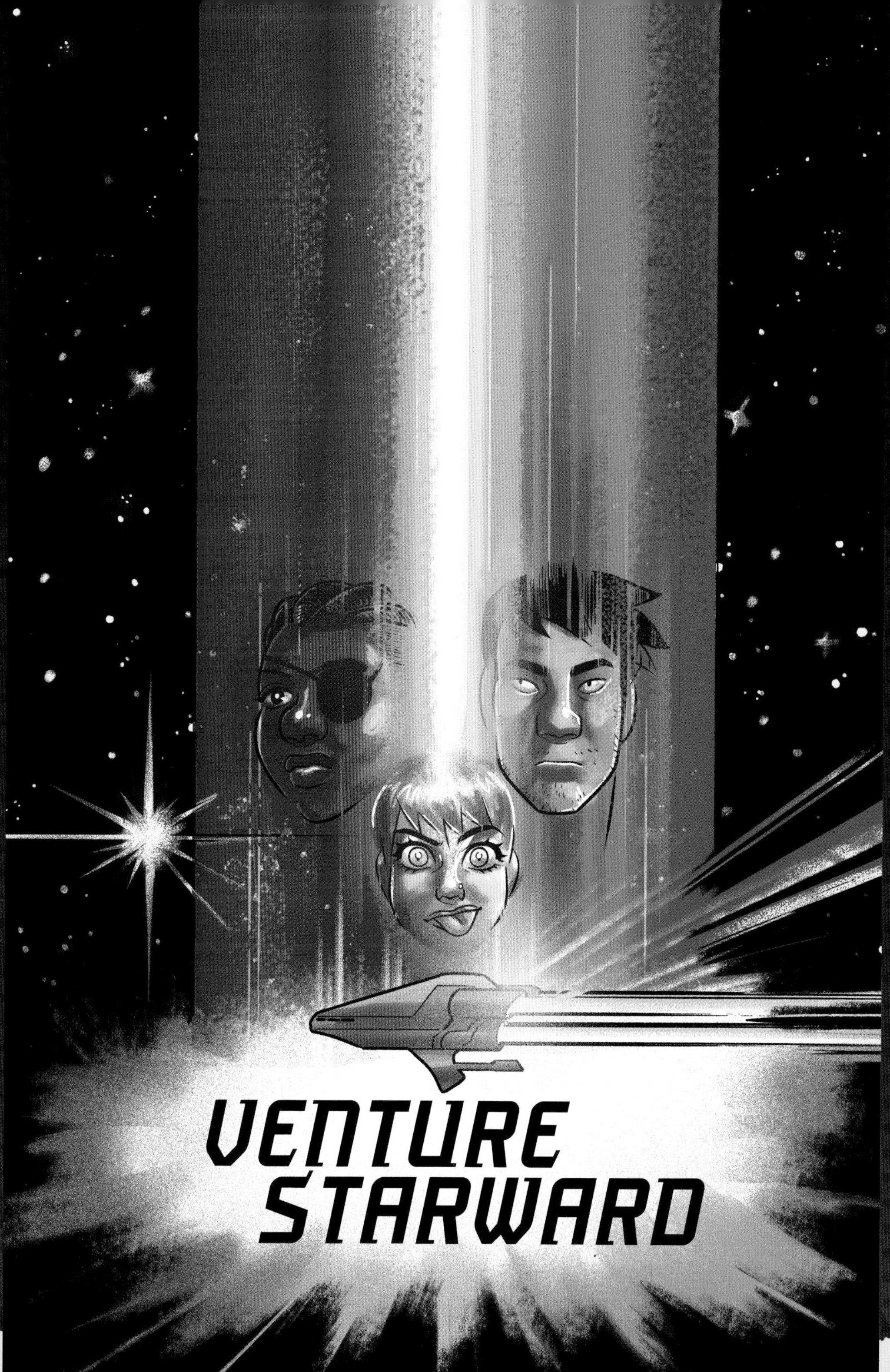
VENTURE
STARWARD

"The Glowing Lady" Vol. VI, No. 1,098

The Post-Event Post

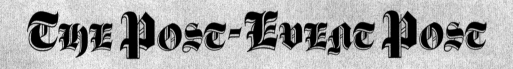

New Grampus, May 4th, AE 6 $3.50 or the equivalent in precious corn

And The Fans Played On

Deep Underground, a Mystery 50 Years in the Making

BY VICTOR LAI

"It's the story of a *lifetime*," says the very earnest man in the 6-foot purple bug costume, waving foam lobster claws in my face like his life depended on it. And *maybe it did*, because 5 years and an apocalypse later, he turned up dead at a QZ checkpoint, a convention badge still clutched in his bloody pincer. Story of a lifetime? Yeah, *it just might be at that*.

Let's begin at the beginning. It's 9 am on the first day of LongCon 50 and I'm standing on the steps of the Los Spinoza Event Center, a handsome but world-weary beat reporter wondering what I'd done to earn my lubriguous editor's disfavor with this latest assignment. The comic book scene isn't my bag, sure, but comic conventions are noisy and crowded and full of weirdos representing bastions of pop culture that I find both *bewildering* and *faintly threatening*. Have you ever met a King Cheetah impersonator in full bondage gear? Because I *have*, and he's a paleontologist from Arizona named Kevin.

Thankfully, I have a Virgil to my Dante in the form of Dez Delaney, an old college pal who's graciously agreed to ferry me through the *candy-colored cacophony* of a modern day pop culture convention. Dez has a keen eye for navigating the sweaty human sea that instantly seethes around us, and the right amount of bluster to get past the various security checkpoints separating us from the *nerd nirvana* that lies within. She is polite but direct, quick with a joke, throws elbows only when necessary and with the elegant efficiency of a champion fencer. Those same skills would prove invaluable five years later as we found ourselves dodging *cannibal celebrities* and *feral service dogs* through the bowels of a decommissioned Cold War doomsday weapons factory (I *think* that's what it was?). Despite *the* fact that I may have *technically* abandoned her for dead during the chaotic first moments of the Event, after we reunited, Dez never left my side, barring a few instances were an evil robot tried to kidnap her and one time to forage for hot dogs while I was asleep. She's the truest friend I've ever known, and even her intern isn't as obnoxious as one might initially conclude from her look and demeanor and literally everything else about her.

But before we get to that part, let's answer the burning question on everyone's mind: why exactly is the Long Con called the Long Con?

"I guess in the '70s there were two *Skylarks* conventions in Los Spinoza," she tells me, "one at Admiral Bellwood's Disco Ballroom that was Saturday and Sunday, and one at the Lindser-Annie Disco Roller Rink that was only on Saturday. Fans just kinda started calling them 'the long con' and 'the short con,' and the names stuck." When I asked her what happened to the so-called "short con," she got a distant look in her eye and said, "We do not discuss it with outsiders." Then she punched me in the shoulder. *Anyway*, let's get to the saving the world (or what's left of it) part.

CONTINUED ON PAGE A1

LOWER LOS SPINOZA

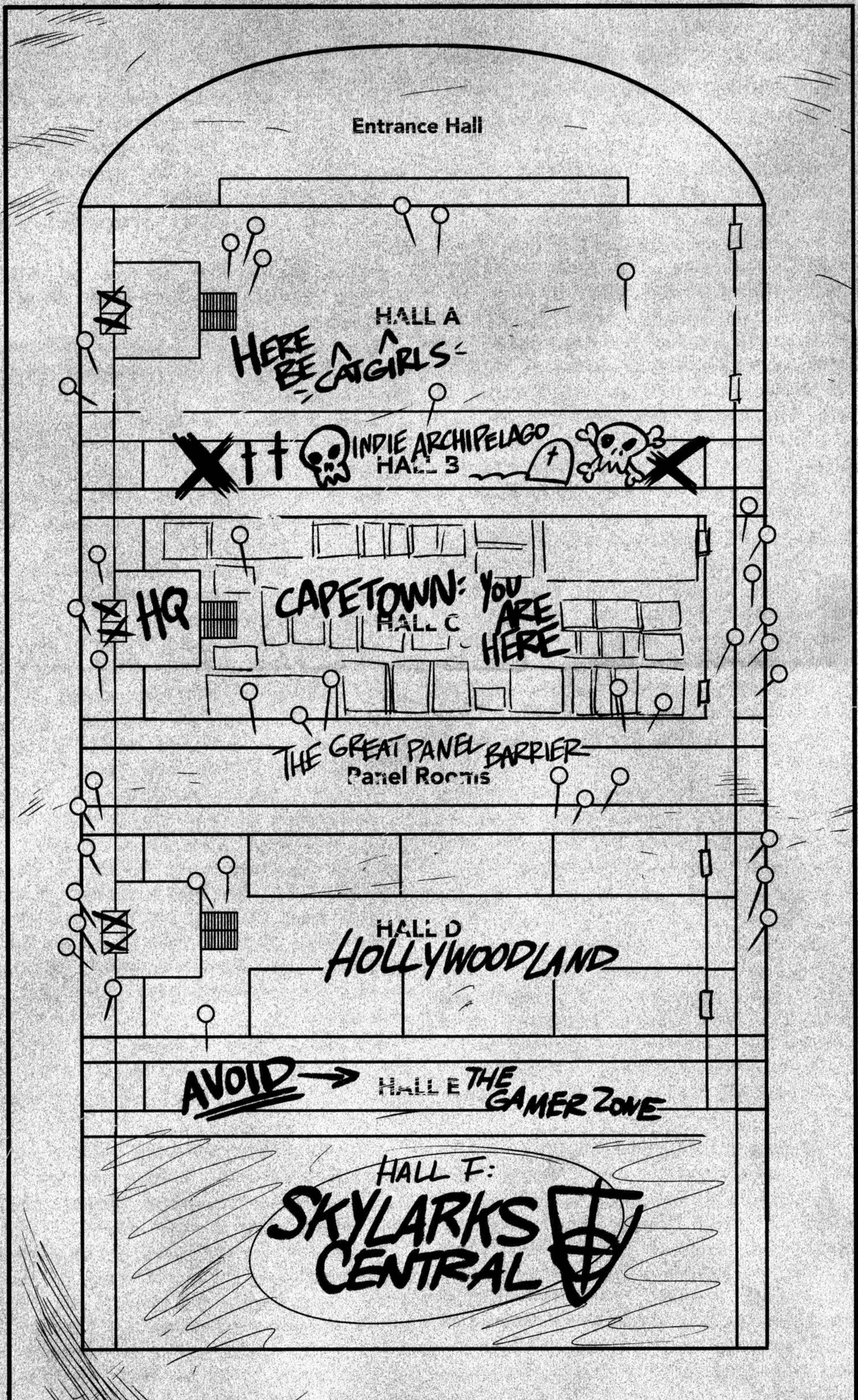

Entrance Hall
HALL A
HERE BE CATGIRLS
INDIE ARCHIPELAGO
HALL B
HQ
CAPETOWN: YOU ARE HERE
HALL C
THE GREAT PANEL BARRIER
Panel Rooms
HALL D
HOLLYWOODLAND
AVOID
HALL E
THE GAMER ZONE
HALL F:
SKYLARKS CENTRAL

REBRANDED CONVENTION PROMISES FEWER DEATHS

LOWER LOS SPINOZA, CA.

After what a recent press release describes as a "5-year period of strategic restructuring," newly incorporated Caslon Events LLC announced that LongCon 51 will convene next spring, with pre-sale tickets available for pre-order via FEMAmail+. Featuring surviving guests from the previous LongCon, as well as a curated selection of post-Event talent, the revitalized convention promises a uniquely pre-Event spin on the current pop culture landscape. "Once we informed our loved ones we hadn't been incinerated 5 years ago, got some vitamin shots, and emptied out our comic shop pull boxes, we realized it was just about time for con season to start up again," explained Caslon's publicist, Destiny Delaney. "We're excited to partner with She-Bolt Security Solutions to provide our guests with a safe and empowering experience," Delaney added, with SBSS president She-Bolt interject-

I am not BOAT COP
by Boat Cop

"Captivating"
-New Grampus Review of Books

ing that "any hint of potential despotism will be dealt with swiftly by a crimson-grieved judo-chop of justice."

LOWER LOS SPINOZA OPENS FIGURATIVE DOORS

NEW GRAMPUS, CA.

Seeking to increase diversity within their rapidly growing subterranean community, representatives of the newly democratic city-state of Lower Los Spinoza announced a citizenship application process for those who were not registered attendees of Long Con at the time of the Event, with bonus incentives advertised for qualified medical professionals. "We could, like, really use some doctors and professors and stuff to rebuild society with," said local BattleMaiden Megyn Furnis. While the newly founded nerd colony lies 50 miles within the Quarantine Zone and deep underground, Furnis described the compensation packages as "totes competitive," including "like, all the MREs you can eat," plus the option to register with "the subculture of your choice" after a six month evaluation period.

CRIME CRUISE TO COMMENCE PRESENTLY

ASTORIA, OR.

Not to be outdone by the return of a rival convention, *Interstellar Skylarks* creator Marlon T. Skylark and acclaimed novelist Ansbach Trireme (*The Man Who Stood Alone*, *Penumbra in Decline*) have announced the inaugural voyage of "The Long Cruise," an elite offshore experience reportedly tailored exclusively for former members of their iron-fisted reign of terror. Described as "indefinite" and "non-voluntary" by FEMA+ authorities, the seafaring festival aims

to provide the same rigorous adherence to established canon that members of the former Skylarks regime have come to expect. "Some peo-

Salad Saloon

Now open to the general public
"Try the salad!"

Stall 3, Hall A, Lower Los Spinoza, Open 7 Days a Week

ple are saying that the post-Event prison system simply couldn't accommodate so many cronies, collaborators, and general hangers-on to the quasi-fashistic microsociety that flourished under our watch, but nothing could be further from the truth," Cruise Director Decky Declan told gathered reporters, adding that he was "genuinely looking forward" to spending an unspecified amount of time away from civilization.

HANRAHAN'S
Discount Hazmat Suits
HOT LOOKS • RAD SAVINGS

BIRD SPOTTED

HARNED, CA.

Local residents "flocked" to the former Frock Fortress parking lot in this sleepy seaside town on news that a bird had been seen, although local FEMA+ officials were quick to caution that it may have been the painting of a bird that graces a nearby mural. Undaunted, several avian enthusiasts have struck camp

CONTINUED ON PAGE A17

THE NEW GRAMPUS REVIEW OF BOOKS

NONFICTION/MEMOIR

Don't Call it Destiny: How I Survived the Longest Con

by Destiny Delaney (Caslon House)
Reviewed by Elinor Jones

This rock 'em sock 'em tell-'em-all is destined (title aside) for the bestseller list. In punchy prose that showcases both literary acumen and time spent in the funnybook trenches, Delaney details the chaotic first moments after the Event, the swift descent into anarchy, and the common heroism of the everyday fan. Readers will find all their lingering questions answered as Delaney deftly closes plot holes and ties up narrative threads left dangling by mainstream press coverage. The only source of complaint will likely be Delaney's stubborn refusal to acknowledge the potentially incandescent sexual tension between her and her erstwhile rescuer, the Post's own culture correspondent, Victor Lai (personally, this reviewer doesn't see the appeal).

FANTASY (???)

Flix Bixby's Hyperion Canticles: the Pentarch Deception: an Ezekiel Faust Mystery

by Felix Bixby with Ronald D. Chan (Caslon House)
Reviewed by Alison Hallett

Easily the most exasperating novel to come out of the Lower Long Con genre renaissance, FBHC:tPD:aEFM nonetheless cobbles together a potent brew of space opera tropes and supernatural urban fantasy erotica. Marrying the pretensions of a high concept vanity project with the unvarnished horniness of an airport novel (remember airports?), Bixby and Chan inject the absurd proceedings with enough vim to keep the overburdened plot moving across the viscera-splattered finish line. Despite his abundant shortcomings as a protagonist, there's no doubt in my mind that Ezekiel Faust's bestubbled mug and twin ensorcelled pistols will feature prominently in the first round of big budget literary adaptations from the recently announced Hall D Pictures.

SCIENCE FICTION

Calpurnia Resurgent

by Flavia Happenstance (Glimerence Press)
Reviewed by Michael Schaub

String theory, lesbian separatist movements, and the Book of Ezekiel combine in this revelatory and deeply experimental journey through a quaint 23rd century Caribbean fishing village populated by multidimensional archangels. Reclusive Afrofuturist visionary Happenstance returns with the final volume of her epic tetralogy, bringing twists both narrative and anatomical to a series that's been an underground bellwether since the 1970s. While maintaining those same subversive undercurrents of anti-authoritarian social theory, the bulk of the story focuses on the profoundly corporeal joys of hauling nets and finding love in a sleepy seaside coffee shop. 900 pages of sensually charged socio-political discourse between full-figured space angels may seem like a lot, but ever since the global communications network fell on Los Spinoza, we've all had a lot of downtime. And as Happenstance notes in "Oblations of Ecstasy," the 30,000 word introductory essay that precedes the novel: "In a shattered world, what is more radical than joy?"

CRIME/MYSTERY

My Partner is a Pangolin

by Cat Farris (Total Bullshit Books)
Reviewed by Courtenay Wisenheimer

An alluring cocktail of three parts gin-soaked noir, two parts zoological farce, *Pangolin* finds hard-drinking homicide detective Nora Slatehammer partnered up with Prickly Pete, an adult male pangolin lacking discernable detective skills, the ability to speak any language, open doors, or reach anything higher than four feet off the ground. While the odd couple buddy cop beat is well trodden literary ground, it's hard to repress a smile with Prickly Pete on the case, especially when the city's ant farm dealers start turning up dead. While the inevitable romance felt contrived, it's hard to argue Farris hasn't pulled another satisfying yarn from this unusual pairing.

GRAPHIC NOVEL

The Lone Corn, Volume 2

by Dylan Meconis and Ben Coleman (posthumous) (TBP)
Reviewed by Angie Knowles

CONTINUED ON PAGE E12

I am BOAT COP
by Boat Cop

"Resplendent"
–New Grampus Review of Books

THE STARS ALIGN, ON SCREEN AND OFF

FELIX BIXBY
§
DEXTER WELROD-BALMORAL IV

When cult favorite former child star Felix "Flix" Bixby (L) learned that, after more than two decades, he would no longer lay sole claim to the role he originated—guileless intergalactic wunderkind Special Midshipman Chippington "Chip" Nimitz—he was initially devastated. "I thought: good luck getting the signature finger snap right, that's harder than it looks," he mused thoughtfully over a breakfast martini, "but *then* I thought... perhaps love is the greatest role of all, and *that's* a role you can share." His other half, actor and current Chip, Dexter "Dexty" Welrod-Balmoral IV, declared his fiance's performance "BAFTA-worthy."

FROM ENEMIES TO FRIENDS, FROM FRIENDS TO LOVERS

MEGYN FURNIS
§
TONYA SZCZEPAŃCZYK

This Thursday, friends and battlekin will gather in the Upper Atrium to celebrate the first legally recognized femslash OTP license issued under the auspices of the Lower Los Spinoza civil government. This groundbreaking legal status confers the benefits of traditional marriage, with bride-to-be and erstwhile security goon Tonya Renata Szczepańczyk (R) noting there are some "unique privileges" as well, including "the possibility of multishipping." Her blushing BattleBride Megyn Keighlee Furnis is looking forward to the custom wedding armor hand-fitted to her magnificent frame by notorious *BattleFoxes 5* costume designer Johansen Chiodini. Note: the ceremony will be conducted in Esperanto and accompanied by the ululation of true warriors.

HEROES, JUST FOR ONE DAY AND ALSO FOREVER

KAROLA ZERÓN DE GARCÍA
§
CHAD WAINWRIGHT

Biff! Pow! Zap! Marriage isn't just for alter egos anymore! The betrothed couple, who hold the offices of do-gooder heroine She-Bolt (R) and ne'er-do-well anti-hero Chill Factor, will be married by officiant sidekick Zap Lass both in and out of continuity, barring future retcons, reboots, or surprise reveals. The question on everybody's lips—could this unprecedented team-up result in spin-offs? "We're looking forward to building a chill-ass family together," announced Wainwright/Factor on the steps of Capetown city hall, adding, "Those lil' bolters will have a *sick* power-set." The bride will be keep her maiden ego; the groom will become Bolt-Bro.

THEY GUARDED EVERYTHING, EXCEPT THEIR HEARTS

COLIN PUMPERNICKEL
§
AMANDA FRANCE

Best friends since third grade, Colin Pumpernickel (L) and Amanda France quietly suspected they'd spend a lifetime pursuing their shared loves of vintage science fiction and Swiss cuisine together, though they never suspected that a significant section of that time would be spent 300 feet underground. An inseparable pair, they grew closer still standing guard against what their defense council claims they believed were haunted animatronic skeletons dressed as first responders.

Looking for love...

SNRRGIRL89

BODY TYPE: BattleWaif
LOOKING FOR: good craic
LIKES: Whiskey in the firelight, liquid eyeliner, friendly dogs
DISLIKES: Fidgeters, bullying, dull cutlery

Name's Aoife, pronounced "EE-fa." Am quality so I expect quality. Looking for a bit of fun after being outta the scene for a while. Love 2 dance all night and greet the dawn with a greasy breakfast on the hood of a car at the edge of town. If you talk mess about my two best friends I'll slice you open stem to stern for the crows to feast on lol jk I guess there aren't crows anymore? But the slicing part still applies.

the_brambled_path

BODY TYPE: More to love
LOOKING FOR: A snuggle bug (perhaps you??)
LIKES: JRPGs, kickboxing, the poetry of Pablo Neruda
DISLIKES: Doing the dishes, waiting in line, insult comedy

Hi! I'm Rose! I've been described as "towering"and "a living wall of fists and steel" but honestly I'm perfectly content to spend all weekend horizontal on the couch playing *Daddy Dungeon* in matching pajamas. My last boyfriend was crushed under a collapsing t-shirt tower so I'm not looking to jump into anything, but if you are kind, patient, and my two best friends like you, I'm confident we can find something magical.

Chainmail Diva

BODY TYPE: Imperious edifice
LOOKING FOR: Obedience
LIKES: 8os New Wave, samurai movies, expensive red wine
DISLIKES: game players, slow drivers, flats

Newly tenured professor of comparative literature looking for companionship and unquestioning worship. I will remorselessly destroy you, and you will beg me to continue. Disrespect towards myself or my two best friends will not be countenanced, however if you demonstrate loyalty and devotion you will find the rewards bountiful indeed. Height is immaterial as you will quickly find yourself kneeling before me.

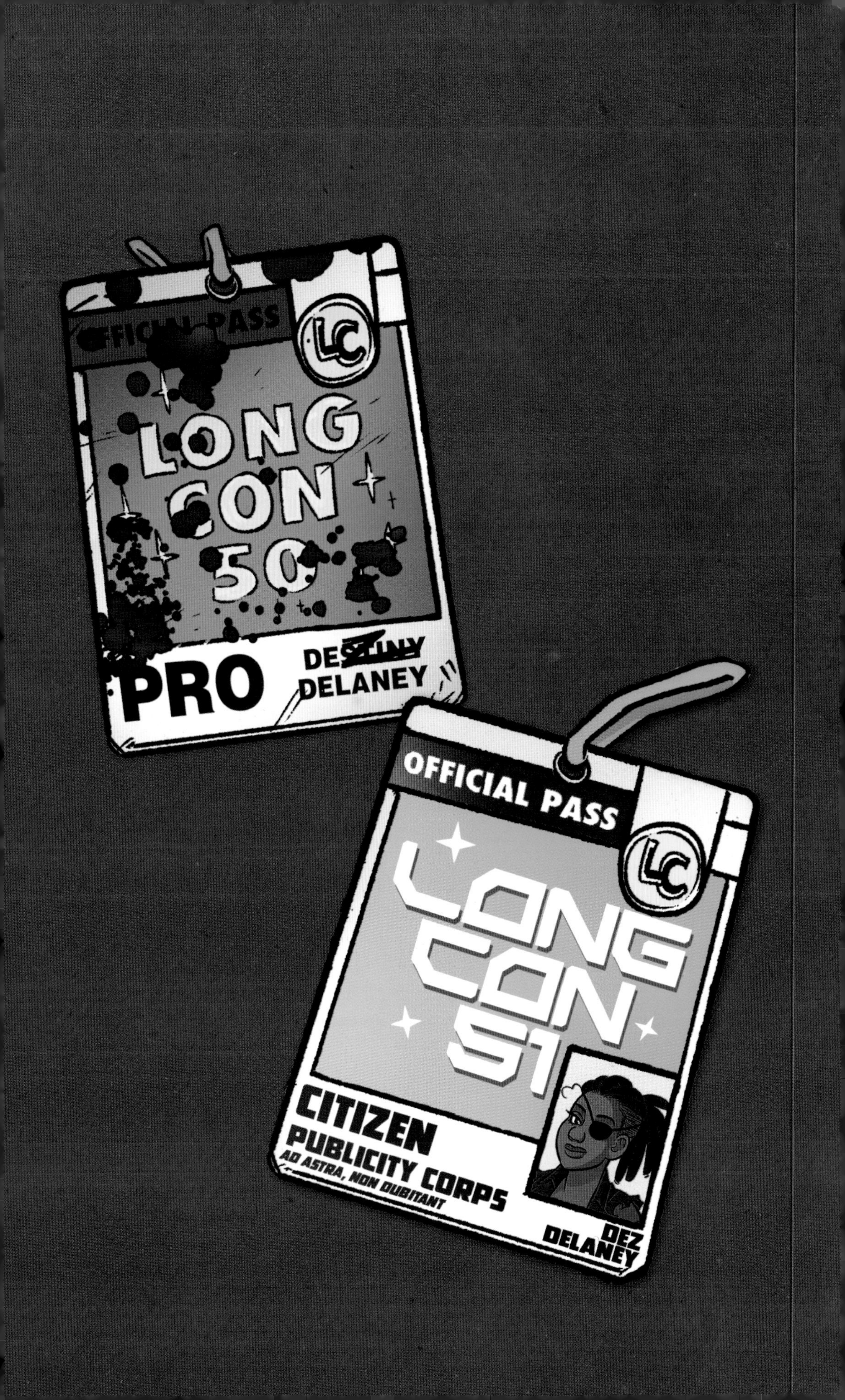
OFFICIAL PASS
LC
LONG CON 50
PRO
DESTINY DELANEY
OFFICIAL PASS
LC
LONG CON 51
CITIZEN
PUBLICITY CORPS
AD ASTRA, NON DUBITANT
DEZ DELANEY

THE LONG CON™

CREATOR CHECKLIST

DYLAN MECONIS

Dylan Meconis is an Eisner, Reuben, and Kim Yale-nominated cartoonist. She's the creator of graphic novels *Bite Me!*, *Family Man*, *Outfoxed*, and the forthcoming *Queen of the Sea* (Candlewick, 2019). She's a studio member of Helioscope in Portland, Oregon.

For all the comics pros, organizers, and fans who've helped me survive 15 years of conventions.

dylanmeconis.com
@dmeconis

BEN COLEMAN

Ben Coleman is a freelance writer and a film and culture critic for the *Portland Mercury*. He was an ensemble member and contributing writer to Atomic Arts, the innovative and nationally-recognized theater company that reimagined shows like *Star Trek* for live audiences.

Thanks this time to Kendra and Adam, and to the staff at Baby Doll Pizza Lounge, who kept us well-provisioned with pizza and whiskey throughout the writing of this book.

ohcoleman.com
@OhColeman

EA DENICH

FILE PHOTO

AM 3:46
APR. 19 1989

EA Denich is a cartoonist and illustrator. She lives in Southern California.

Thank you to everyone who made this book possible: my editors Ari and Robin, my wonderful writing team Dylan and Ben, and of course to the Long Con *fans! We couldn't have done it without you.*

ghostgreen.tumblr.com
@ghostgreeen

FRED C. STRESING

Fred C. Stresing is a comic book artist and colorist currently holed up in an underground bunker in Savannah, Georgia, waiting for the air to clear. He hopes to color and draw more comics once society is re-established.

Dedicated to my wife Meg. Thanks for wandering the wastelands with me.

artofstresing.com
@FredCStresing

ADITYA BIDIKAR

Aditya Bidikar is a comics letterer based in India. Apart from *The Long Con*, he is currently working on *Isola*, *These Savage Shores*, *Bloodborne*, and *Punks Not Dead*, among others.

To my cat Loki, who did his best to not let me work on this book.

adityab.net
@adityab

MORE GREAT BOOKS FROM ONI PRESS!

PAMELA RIBON ♥ CAT FARRIS
My Boyfriend IS A BEAR

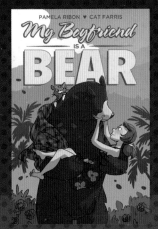

MY BOYFRIEND IS A BEAR
By Pamela Ribon & Cat Farris

PIZZASAURUS
REX
JUSTIN WAGNER
WARREN WUCINICH

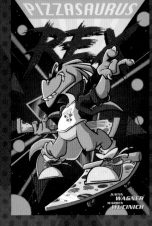

PIZZASAURUS REX
By Justin Wagner & Warren Wucinich

LUCKY PENNY
ANANTH HIRSH YUKO OTA

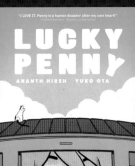

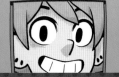

LUCKY PENNY
By Ananth Hirsh & Yuko Ota

"Stylish and sweet, Kim Reaper is sure to leave you in giggles!"
KIM REAPER
GRIM BEGINNINGS
BY SARAH GRALEY

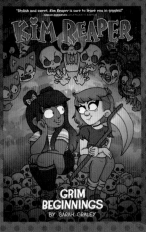

KIM REAPER, VOLUME 1: GRIM BEGINNINGS
By Sarah Graley

LETTER 44
VOLUME 1: ESCAPE VELOCITY

LETTER 44, VOLUME 1: ESCAPE VELOCITY
By Charles Soule, Alberto Jiménez Alburquerque, Guy Major, & Dan Jackson

THE BUNKER
JOSHUA HALE FIALKOV | JOE INFURNARI
VOLUME 1

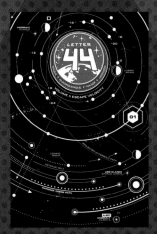

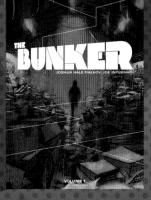

THE BUNKER, VOLUME 1
By Joshua Hale Fialkov & Joe Infurnari

ONI PRESS

For more information on these and other fine Oni Press comic books and graphic novels visit www.onipress.com.
To find a comic shop specialty store in your area visit www.comicshops.us.